Alban Fire

Published by Botanis Press, LLC
Mystic, CT, USA
www.botanispress.com

ISBN-13: 978-0692545447
ISBN-10: 0692545441

To my mother

Sarah Dane-Brown

And in memory of my father

Bert Brown

ALBAN FIRE

PART I

Chapter One

The veil between the worlds was thin that evening, so thin it was considered like to tear, and the gods only knew what would venture forth from the dark places of creation if that came to pass.

The several thousand Cornovi tribesfolk trekking through the moorlands upon the Sunpath Road were united not only in the white of their robes and the roots of their lineage, but in the unvoiced dread within their hearts, threatening to fulminate into unbridled terror. When they reached the terminus of their journey, the Spirit Hollow, they trusted they would learn something of events to come, but few doubted that terrible those events would be. For 'twas Mabon, and Sawhane, and a full moon besides, and twenty generations of memory couldn't summon an instance when all three had converged at once.

Mabon, Sawhane, and the full moon together. It was nearly unthinkable. Each occurrence was holy in its own sacred right: Mabon, when night and day were equal in length; Sawhane, archway to the Dark Half of the year, when spirits roamed and reigned over the world; the full of the moon, when Lady Lhore revealed herself completely. Any two arriving together was portentous, and a triumvirate could only foretell disaster. The nature of that disaster would be revealed in sight of the Godskull, at the end of the Sunpath Road, where the Ceremony of Light and Dark would soon be called to commence.

Where I'll be off to, thought Elyn, *if I can get this stupid candle going.*

Perhaps alone among the Cornovi pilgrims, Elyn did not dread the coming rites, partly because she had more immediate difficulties, and partly because she was nine years old. She was kneeling before the entrance to an ancient barrow, amid a field of such low, round turf-and-stone mounds, knowing she looked ridiculous and feeling the eyes of her mother upon her. Her slight frame was contorted at exotic angles as she spread her robe to deflect the wind, and at the same time tried to spread the flame of her lamp onto the wick of a devotional candle, a light to shine for the ancestors in their underworld gloom.

It was a fierce wind rising on the moors that evening, the kind that hammered waves against the anvil cliffs of the northern coast. As was common knowledge, the gale began as steam beaten by the oars of father-god Lugh's celestial ship, Wave Sweeper, a burning sky vessel also called the sun, as it sank into the Sabrina Sea to the northwest, boiling the surface with its approach. The gusts gathered over the waters and burst onto land atop sprays of foam, rushed along forest-bottomed valleys and whistled through hillside granite crags, caromed off the broad sparse teeth of the mountains a few miles distant, and swooped upon Elyn in the Barrowlands to snatch at her flame like a falcon at a field vole. It was a messenger wind, speaking omens with a savage insistence, in a language she could hear but not understand.

One wisp of air current snuck around her defenses, tricky as Gwidion, thief of gods' swine, and caused the lamp's fire to gutter and dwindle. Elyn feared for a heartbeat her flame would go out. She didn't know what would happen if her small lamp lost its battle against the gale, but she was certain it would be nothing good.

The consequences would surely include her mother's grimace of utter disappointment, renowned throughout the region even beyond the invisible walls of her clan-web, but Elyn could sense that look coming to her mother's face even now. Worse would be if such displeasure was shared by the powerful spirits dwelling within the barrows that loomed before her. The beings of the Otherworld were known to be as numerous in their forms as they were in their methods of torturing the faithless, especially nearing the twilight time of Twilight Day.

Failure to maintain the light could even cost Elyn the chance to see the Godskull, and that above all was a possibility she refused to contemplate. To go to the ceremony, to behold the avatar of the great god Cerunnos in the form he had taken eons ago, was the greatest ambition she'd known in her nine harvests of life. The answers to so many mysteries were almost within her reach, and after traveling so far she would not be denied. *Not now that the Skull is less than half a mile away, not by a candle and a few puffs of wind.*

The other Cornovii of good rank, the ones allowed among the barrows and only ones to halt in their travels, were offering their devotions in practiced fashion, and most had already moved on to rejoin the procession streaming toward the ceremony. Her mother was among those who remained, but only for Elyn's benefit. The candle she'd brought was glowing softly and steadily beside her, her mother's offerings and effigies impeccably arrayed before the entrance to one of the barrows. The earthen halls of heroes and half-breed gods had stood since before the oldest lines of Britain began, certainly since before the Cornovii had come south 20 generations before to rule in Dumnonia, carrying the Godskull before them. The timeless domes seemed to glower at her in the lessening light, and Elyn was embarrassed in the sight of relatives dead and living both. Whatever her efforts, the fluttering lamp flame twisted away from the wick, just as her youngest brother Uly had avoided the spoon at mealtime.

Toward the end.

There came a gust that wasn't followed by another, and as the lull continued, Elyn hurried to take advantage. At last her lamp flame was steady against the candle wick, and soon an infant fire was born on the spirit light. She placed a

11

bronze cylinder around the tallow sphere, bringing out the shadow play cut into its surface as the candle shone through – forms of stags and fish and warriors, a pictorial page from the endless chapters of unwritten Cornovi lore.

Elyn quickly went through the liturgy, trying (and failing) not to mumble, pulling the offerings from the pouch slung at her belt – herbs, an egg, a clay rendering of—

"Elyn…"

I'm hurrying, Mother, she thought, trying to keep in her mind which offering went with which god or ancestor and why, muttering such prayers as, "In remembrance of our well-named aunt Lady Aildaeth, tender-hearted, we give to you this skein of wool in request of a soft winter and abundance in our pastures," but too quickly and in about ten syllables.

"Elyn!"

A ripe pear and a string of Iberian beads were all left in the pouch. She couldn't think of what the beads were for, and the pear she wanted for after the ceremony, on the long journey back to the feasting ring when she was sure to want some food in advance. It was elective anyway – "a pear to Epona for love and long life," and Elyn could skip that.

Then she remembered her brother Uly. He had driven her mad, the way he wouldn't eat, the way he whined that high, long whine at every hour. She remembered stomping her feet at the toddler one night, crying "Stop that!" when she simply couldn't take another moan, and remembered the way he had curled up and tried to stifle his whimpering. Then one morning the house was silent. For a brief moment when she saw him lying peacefully for once, though with lips of blue, she was grateful to the gods that his soul had left him.

12

Elyn ran back to the barrow and knelt with the beads. "Please hear me, blessed Breneg, take these beads and tell Uly I'm sorry. Protect his shade from terrors and gloom. Great is your name, mighty Breneg, Lord Jackdaw, Just and Wise. Having paid, I abide." She got up and turned just as her mother was opening her mouth to call again. Giving the pear in her satchel one squeeze, Elyn hurried toward the road, the ceremony, the Godskull.

Viewed from afar it was a ribbon of glittering cloth, a swift river that resolved into rapids from a nearer remove, and from closest vantage one saw it was a flow composed of humanity. The procession of the Cornovii stretched before and behind Elyn for the better part of a mile. In their scores and hundreds, those who were able among the ruling tribe of Dumnonia made their way to the Spirit Hollow, candles before them and draped in white cloth. And Elyn was one of them.

My tribe, she thought, her world widening before her, *the Cornovii.*

There were more humans surrounding Elyn at that moment than the sum of all people she'd ever seen. At the port of Aberfawey, on her one visit to a settlement larger and further away than Eilwath, she'd beheld souls by the dozen, foreigners thick among them, men as tall as hedges and black as new-turned sod. The harbor had teemed with life. This procession was incalculably larger.

It resembled a flood of water in both look and sound, as a thousand murmuring voices mingled on the road. The talk was subdued in volume but not in intensity, as if spoken near a deathbed, though some phrases rose up clear above the low din and carried a hint of argument with them. Everything Elyn caught fell along one of several spokes on a revolving wheel of conversation: King Cunomor, the

13

Council meeting at Glevuna within the week, the confluence of Sawhane and Mabon that year, and how it was all connected.

"It's the influence of that Roman religion. That's what's turning Cunomor's head."

"It's the High Crown that turns all king's heads. And Cunomor's a king, ain't he?"

Elyn heard another pair chattering.

"The priests called Sawhane too early and they know it. They answer to you-know-who's ambition before the gods now."

"You think? So what good are they?"

"We'll see tonight."

And from yet another quarter:

"We shall see if he even stays for the entire ceremony. I'll lay you twelve to my one he's off on his chariot to Glevuna before the dance."

Elyn's attention to such talk waxed and waned. She had an age-appropriate interest in topics political, which is to say fairly little, and had already heard plenty of the same in her clan lands – never from her family, though, at least not when her father was in earshot, for Father was King Cunomor's Master of Mines.

It was not what she heard that had her nonplussed, but the sight of her fellow tribesfolk. Elyn was struck by how much better off she was than other young people. Her robe was brilliant white, edged with delicate embroidery of green and bronze lines, intersecting to form a design that looked as if miniscule bees had discovered art and formed their honeycombs along her cuffs and hemline. She only needed to look at the others, who were dressed little better than the slaves she'd seen at the port, to know that their everyday trek through life was harder than any she'd made on any day, this one included.

"Aye, Cunomor has his scars, and sure enough tonight he'll find the finest bard in Dumnonia to take to the Council... and sing about them until the other kings' ears fall off."

"That's how he plans to wrest the High Crown from the young cub, I'll wager."

The young cub could only be Aurelian, the Golden Prince. Elyn heard he and his court described many times, and none could decide whether the monarch or his palace at Glevuna was more beautiful. Once she'd dreamed of him, and the stirring she felt at his image, imagined though it was, defied her understanding. She spent a few moments revisiting the memory of the dream, and marveling that one could remember a night phantom so clearly when so much of waking life was lost forever to the past.

Elyn's brief reverie was lanced by a woman's voice nearby.

"The important thing will be the choosing. We may just be done for if the wrong girl gets the red."

Elyn looked up at her mother, who might have been her twin if twins could have birthdays separated by twenty years. Her mother had not spoken those words, and the stoic set to her face gave not the slightest suggestion she heard anything said around her. Elyn turned toward her just the same, for the only time the girl had heard similar talk before, her mother was the source.

15

It had been a week earlier, when Aunt Megga came by to dress her mother's hair, and the women believed themselves alone. Elyn had not meant to overhear them, had only been stalking a lizard and come near to catching it just outside the entrance to their dwelling, but she stayed to listen.

"I'm glad she won't be chosen," her mother had said.

"But it would be an honor," insisted Megga.

"You remember I had that honor once. It is enough for one family."

"Can you be sure she won't be chosen?"

"Nothing is sure, but it would greatly surprise me."

"Ah. You've taken steps, then – I could have guessed," Megga had said, with a laugh Elyn knew adults gave when discussing a secret. "Then I raise this cup of Gaulish red – may Elyn remain unchosen."

Reflecting back, Elyn couldn't understand. She had been chosen to go, as her mother would inform her the next day (the happiest of her life hitherto), and before her moonblood at that. She had prayed that the gods bring on her moonblood early, as only girls of age were allowed into the presence of the Godskull. Never did she expect to go to the ceremony until she'd seen her tenth summer, probably later, and whatever uncomfortable feelings the conversation produced were overwhelmed by joy at the news. Elyn was going to the Spirit Hollow, and was going to see the Godskull, and anything else was just talk.

As if signaled by a soundless herald, the chatter around Elyn dropped to a few scattered whispers. The topmost branches of an oak grove peeped above the nearest hillcrest beyond them, and she knew her quarry was almost within sight.

In the sudden silence she heard the wind's rush-and-rumble redoubled. Elyn tracked the path each gust wrought through grass and heather, watched a distant copse of elm as branches swayed and clattered together with each surge of air, as if invisible giants were shouldering them aside to march through the canopy.

North is where giants do come from, she thought, *if there really are any.*

Elyn turned her head, and there was the Godskull.

The skull must have belonged to the avatar of a god, exactly as her people claimed, for it was like no creature she had seen or heard described. It was enormous, even against the enormity of the titanic oak to which it was fastened, just as large as her most fantastical childhood imaginings had promised, and every bit as strange.

It resembled an immense horse or deer – a beast large enough that she could pass her fist into the black infinity of either eye socket – but it was the growths on its head that marked it as belonging to an alien realm. Where a deer might have antlers, the Godskull had what looked like two massive hands, each of which could cradle a grown man, grasping toward the congregants, spreading too many fingers, all spindly and curved and looking like bat wings composed of bone. In any case, she thought, they were nothing like what ought to be growing from something's head.

The skull was suspended in such a way as to appear floating in front of the enormous oak, hovering above a large cavity within the trunk, a passage to the Otherworld itself. The oak, sacred of Lugh the Thunderer, clan-father of gods, was the largest single thing she'd ever seen, so impressive and timeless that it took a while for Elyn to realize it was barely alive. Each single branch was the size of a mature tree, but more had broken off than remained, and those that did

17

were sparse of foliage. Most of the green on the tree was the inadvertent gift of the life-sapping vines that slithered up the trunk and wound around the branches like massive stalking serpents. The prize the creepers seemed consciously seeking was the Skull, but so far it had escaped their predations.

The artifact had been carried by her people from its tomb in their ancestral homelands all the way to the peninsula of Dumnonia twenty generations before. Her tribe claimed through the Godskull authority none other could, and the lineage of the powerful Cornovii chiefs was displayed in the fingerlike prongs of its antlers. From each spindle hung a ring of metal, solid or twisted, bronze or iron or gold, once worn around the neck of a bygone Cornovi leader. Those who commanded the respect of the clans in life found a place upon the Godskull in death. The torc of King Cunomor would jangle in the moorland wind someday, though Elyn noted that the skull was running out of prongs. Perhaps the Godskull sprang a new bony spire for every hero-king who passed into shadow.

Another kind of shadow fell across Elyn's excitement as she continued to regard the relic. It was important, could not but be important, but it was also not alive. She'd hoped to see something ecstatic or chastening in the look of the Godskull, but suspended from the great oak above the great circle, she saw something dead. It was like hoping to see a snake and only seeing its discarded skin.

Yes, Elyn was afraid, but not of the Godskull. She could not just then admit it fully to herself, but a realization had formed, and filled her with a deep roiling terror for which there was no name. It worked through her consciousness so that within a few moments of witnessing the Godskull, she knew what she would have to do. No matter what it cost, she would have to see what lay beyond. She would have to know.

"Joined is the battle of dark and light!" called the head priest. "Thin is the veil between the worlds."

Spontaneous calls, songs and chants now created cacophony within the amphitheater of the Hollow. Drums beat and fifes sounded, a din intended for the gods' ears, that could be heard by mortals for miles around.

Not all joined in, and her mother was among those standing stoically and waiting for the noise to subside. She petted the back of Elyn's head where her hair was smooth and unbraided, but she did not glance down. Elyn was tense, and confused, but it did not dimish her anticipation of when the tribe would greet Elyn's personal patroness, Lady Lhore, whenever the goddess emerged to give chase to Lugh and loose the hounds of mischief on the world.

Whatever her misgivings about the Godskull, Elyn did not doubt the moon's divinity. In any of her moods the Goddess of the Dark Half was a comforting presence to Elyn, who was convinced she'd seen the deity's face afraid, and tearful, and jolly too. When half-hidden, her look was young, revealing a coy smirk, innocent yet alluring. Fully uncloaked, her eyes were kind, though with brows knitted in mild concern, trying to smile through a secret pain. It was a familiar look to Elyn – she'd seen the same vexation on her mother's face, more often of late. She felt her mother's fingers worked along her scalp, and Elyn smiled.

An outbreak of gasps and wild pointing to the sky jerked her mother's hand away. The prayerful fell silent at the sight in the darkening sky, for even as the sun was half-way disappeared, the moon – full, close – was on the rise. A space of just two minutes separated the start of sunset and beginning of moonrise, and now the two deities faced each other in the twilight, each claiming its half of the sky.

19

The mood of Lady Lhore was instantly evident. When she rose her brows were knots of anger, her mouth a horror, her color the red of water used to treat a bleeding wound. The Cornovi trembled.

A jangling, clacking, snorting noise grew in volume, and the assembly turned to see the bulk of Lord Grundfyrdd appeared atop his enormous, glitteringly-adorned war stallion. Grundfyrdd rode to the top edge of the Hollow, but never did a hoof step into the sacred site itself.

"Continue, priest," he boomed down into the grand earthen bowl. "The king is nigh, and he will want to be greeted with some knowledge of the gods' will."

The priest continued, and the king soon arrived, resplendent and proud, carried on a chariot as chieftans had been for a millennium. A handsome man with a yellow, pointed beard, somewhere between youth and middle age, his most distinguishing feature was the long red scar that ran from above his left eyebrow to the back of his neck, forever commemorating the sword blow that sliced off his left earlobe. It was the leading disfigurement on a face that boasted others, including a nose bridge with a novel bent, but it meant that even if he were stripped naked, even if he were inspected by a blind man, his warrior prowess would be known. That at least partly explained the confident grin on his face.

Minutes later, though, as King Cunomor addressed the anxious congregants, some of the confidence ebbed from his face, as he faced a harangue from many among his subjects. Chief among their complaints was Aurelian, and Cunomor's alliance with the Golden Prince. They were Celts, they said, not Roman slaves. Cunomor called for calm.

"My good people, favorites of powerful Cerunnos, why do you speak of Rome when its grasp has not been felt for a century?"

"Aurelian is a tot playing Caesar!" came a shout.

"He is my kin, and a true friend of Dumnonia," replied the king, drawing jeers. "What cause have you to fear the Empire in its ruin, when we have a true and strong enemy preparing to flood western Britain with blood? I have fought this foe before and will fight them again – so must we all. You watch the sky for a dead eagle, when a living wolf prowls our lands!"

This brought cheers for the king from his allies, and one hollered, "My family prospers under Cunomor's trade, and my steel will prevail under his colors against the Saxon filth!" More emboldened voices joined. Cunomor waved for silence.

"I know the quality of your lives in my reign," said Cunomor. "I know the baubles you give your lovers, the wines you drink and the foods you eat, for under my rule I have brought things back to these shores not seen since the Romans removed their yoke. Yet do we owe tribute to any but our gods?"

"No!"

"Do we owe fealty to any other tribe or nation?"

"No!"

"Rejoice! We are fat when others starve, we work our fields when others bleed in theirs; never conquered by Romans or Saxons, we milk peace like a cow and slaughter our enemies like swine. Am I not your king and do I not speak true?"

"Wrarrr, yeah!" shouted Elyn with all the ferocity she could muster, eager to test her lungs against the throngs that screamed out honors to the king at the top of theirs. Cunomor seemed to grow taller with each shout of his name, while his opponents slouched into silence and averted their looks.

"The council means I must depart now, with haste," he said. That quieted the crowd quickly.

Someone behind Elyn whispered "Didn't I tell you? Can't be bothered."

"Chief Grundfyrdd will serve for the rite of the initiates, vested with all of my offices."

He had lost the crowd again, but not for long. "And of course, at the feast he will roast my two largest bulls, both of pure white, each enough to provide a hero's portion for a hundred warriors."

The largest cheer of the night rang out. The king was still being lauded when he remounted and rode out of sight, casting one more crisp, majestic wave.

That man knows how to be a king.

A few more sacrifices, more things Elyn had trouble following or seeing for its importance, but before boredom set in again, a row of horn players stepped up and unleashed a harmonic but commanding blast.

"Go now, Elyn, follow our kin to the feasting place."

The time had arrived when only full initiates could remain, and the moment of her daring and disobedience was upon her. Elyn took a long breath.

"Shall I go with Mudri Tamara? She and I haven't visited in some time." Her great-aunt Tamara was a dear woman, but also the least perceptive and most forgetful kinswoman Elyn knew, at least among those who'd made the journey to the Hollow.

"That is fine, child, but you must go - now," said her mother. Elyn knew something was wrong – her mother hadn't given her the probing stare that even a slight degree of suspicion would normally raise. She barely glanced down.

Elyn picked up the skirt of her robe and hurried over to Tamara, venturing one look back before joining the old woman. She saw only one person who had not attained their initiation age, a young girl very much like herself, down to the finely embroidered robe of pure white. She had a look of apprehension, despite the friendly manner of the priests who led her away from the circle.

That is what chosen means, what mother and Megga were talking about.

Elyn knew she'd chosen right. The veil between the worlds was thin, and she meant to see through to the other side.

She inched her way up the animal track with small creeping steps, wincing at every scrape of pebble beneath her sheepskin sandals, crouching every time she sensed she might be seen.

A burst of noise from the hollow below sent her ducking, and she had the slight urge to curse her Lady Lhore, now less bloody but still scowling, for being so bright above and creating so few places to hide. Elyn's robe, though fine, was too long by half an ankle-length and itched where it touched bare skin, two minor annoyances on the Sundown Road that became real impediments when sneaking around hillsides. White was also not ideal for sliding in dirt, and it was possible she would have to "accidentally" slip into a brook on her way back. She'd still get in trouble, but it was better than telling the truth.

Another blare of trumpets sounded below, and whatever mysteries were privy to the initiates alone, they were minutes from being revealed. Elyn needed a place to secret herself, and spied a spray of rock on a ridge higher up and further away by a dozen yards – reachable, but only by a dash across bright moonlight and up a bank of loose dirt and crackly bramble. She would have to time it well, but had no way to do so, not knowing the rhythms of the ritual.

Elyn took two steps, then three, and readied to run – then she saw him, and stopped dead.

A gaunt figure almost without form, so silent, so tall, moved past her on a nearby trail and was gone in one bat of her eyelashes. It was a man, but wasn't; more like liquid shadow, vapor amid vapor, dark against darkness.

What was that?

She instantly began to doubt her eyes – nighttime and imagination and Sawhane and Mabon... *No,* she thought. She would not allow herself to doubt, especially not on Twilight Day, not when she'd already seen a Godskull and a king, and felt the spirits moving over the earth. She knew who she'd seen.

The Willow Wizard.

Adults spoke of him in whispers, as if afraid he was forever lurking within earshot. Children told stories of him that began as hard to believe, and once each had piled his or her additions to the tales on top of the others', the Willow Wizard's legend grew to a mountain of impossibility. But what was impossible?

What was true? These were the questions that frightened her, and which she persisted in asking herself for exactly that reason.

She let her look linger on where the Wizard had been, then reluctantly turned back to the ceremony… and was shocked again. Only feet away from her stood a figure, a male. His arms were outstretched toward her, and he was approaching.

"Don't scream," he said.

Elyn screamed.

In between his words and her shriek, a belly-shaking blatt of horns assaulted the air, so her call of alarm was heard only by the stranger and herself. About to run, she stopped herself when she realized that though he was a male, he was small: as many as three years younger than she, he stood a head shorter, and almost as thin. *A little boy.* She giggled in relief, but was sick of surprises getting in her way of finding out the magic at the heart of the Cornovii's pride and power, its link with the Otherworld. Trying to look stern, Elyn demanded of the boy in a harsh half-whisper, "What are you doing here?"

"Watching," he replied, matching her tone and volume. "Same as you."

She took in his garb – he was wearing a green tunic and leather belt. Dumnonian…

"You're not Cornovi," she hissed, "so you're not supposed to be here."

"You're not either!"

"Yes I am, I'm a Cornovi tribeswoman of rank."

"You're just a girl, and if you're supposed to be here then why are you whispering and crouching down like me?"

She opened her mouth to retort, but without anything coming to mind and the ceremony underway, instead she said, "Okay, you can watch. But we need to get to that ridge up there." His eyes followed her pointing finger, and he nodded. "Come on, let's go now!"

The boy hesitated only a moment, and to her surprise, stayed on her heels the whole way up, even leaping to catch onto a bracket-like root only moments after she completed the same maneuver. Soon they were up, unseen, and trying not to breath hard as they looked down. They could see perfectly, and the ceremony was entering a new phase unlike anything Elyn could associate with what she knew of her religion.

The drums began to beat a marching tempo and the strange horns blared again, which they now saw were bizarre trumpets with bells that stood up vertically many feet in the air, fashioned like serpents and other long-necked beasts. A new dance had begun in the Hollow, a dance of war. The drumming was slower, but precise. Wrists and fingers that had been oscillating impossibly fast now pounded a steady beat against the painted stretched skins. The circle too seemed smaller, with so many who had filled the arena now gone. The last of the female initiates were dancing from the Spirit Hollow, in twisting skips and arching leaps that sent their robes billowing about them – all but three women, or rather two women and a girl. The trio stood in the center of the circle, the most richly illuminated figures, suffused within the light of all four braziers. *Three of them,* thought Elyn, and of markedly different ages as well. From within the tangle of Cornovi lore she knew, the answer arose.

"Virgin, Mother and Crone," she whispered.

"What?" the boy asked. Elyn ignored him.

The men were still there, mostly - warriors, each holding a staff atop which were mounted the antlers of a buck, and each wearing a cap skinned from the head of a doe. They pounded with their poles on the ground in time to the drums and blatting carynxes, shaking the hills around.

The ring of men parted at the end furthest from where Elyn and the boy crouched, and a wolf was led forward, walking on its hind legs.

The children shared a look, then turned back to the creature, which was shaking and emitting pitiful pleas to its captors, masked men who held fast the chains around its limbs and neck. "Please, oh great gods, please…" it whimpered as it sometimes limped forward, was sometimes yanked toward the circle of stones.

Its approach toward the light melted away the illusion, and the wolf resolved itself into a man – though he looked bestial enough. He'd been fitted with a wolf's hide as a cloak and cowl, but beneath the lupine covering was a broken, naked figure. A portly man of middle age, he'd been beaten, his beard stiff with his own blood and rusty streaks smearing his bared flesh. He tried to avoid walking on a badly swollen left ankle and mangled toes, freshly pulverized. Wide eyes shone out from the same holes its original owner had looked through, but instead of the intensity of a wolf tracking prey, his eyes blazed bright with terror.

Elyn had heard from one of her young cousins that someone from Clan Thyrowan was going to be punished at the ceremony, but she hadn't imagined anything like this.

"Who is he?"

"I don't know his name," whispered Elyn. "His clan isn't well thought of, my dad says."

Elyn's father had said a lot more about them when she wasn't supposed to be listening, and not delicately, but about this particular man his parents were oddly silent – pointedly silent.

"Why is he in a wolf skin?" the boy asked, forgetting to whisper.

"You can only stay if you stop talking! Just watch, okay?"

The beaten man was thrown to his knees before Grundfyrdd, who stood directly beneath the Godskull, so that looking up at either was to behold the terrible countenances of both.

"Lagonos, you are judged guilty of rape and kin-slaying by your king. Do you profess your innocence?"

The man tried to say something, but it didn't penetrate through his blubbering.

"Do you confess or protest this judgment?"

"I... Grundfyrdd, it wasn't like that... you weren't there, she was... she said..."

"Your own *niece,* Lagnos" hissed Grundfyrdd into the face of the accused.

"By marriage!" Lagnos yelped. The High Priest had heard enough, and stepped forward.

"He does not accept the judgment of man," said the wizened cleric. "The judgment of Cerrunos will determine his fate in this life and those to come. Cerrunos, be among us!"

The drumming abruptly stopped.

"Cerrunos, we call to you!" wailed the priest in half-song, his reedy voice still strong enough to carry. "We hail you, Lord of the Hunt! We hail you, Judge of Passage!"

"Hail Lord of the Hunt!" returned the tribesmen.

"Hail Cerunnos, we cry for the blessing of your presence!"

"Hail Judge of Passage!"

"Cerrunos, we beckon to you, come forth!"

From the back of the ring, behind the Passage Oak, stepped forward a tall and muscular buck, a proud spray of antlers adorning its head. To Elyn, though, it looked afraid. Two burly warriors urged it forward into the ring of men, which parted to let it thought and closed up again behind it.

"Cerrunos is among us! Hail!" cried the priest.

"Hail!"

Each warrior dipped his knee and bowed briefly, but so that not one of their antler-topped staves moved from its place in the wall of barbs. The stag began to charge around the human-formed enclosure, snorting and bellowing. It continually made as if to run at one of the warriors before balking each time, then settled into a tense trotting pattern at the end of the ring opposite from where Lagnos knelt.

The guards undid his shackles and took the chains away, which ratcheted up Lagnos's twitching and widened his eyes in fear. An acolyte priest carried a bowl over to him and calmly tipped a slimy, lumpy mixture onto the prisoner's head, which oozed down his face and the wolfskin hide.

"Agh!" shouted Lagnos. "It's – ugh, it's… dung!"

"And gizzard and blood, the wolf's very innards and excrement when it was slain." said the High Priest.

Lagnos, shocked into silence, looked up at the High Priest with an expression pregnant with many emotions, which sagged into a mask of profoundest despair. He burst into a keening wail punctuated by sobs.

"Get up!" a voice shouted from the crowd. "Get on your feet Lagnos."

The beaten man twisted himself toward the voice.

"Help me, brother!" Lagnos moaned.

"Face your fate," said his brother, a man who bore a close resemblance to Lagnos, though he was shorter than the prisoner, and lean muscle where his sibling had too much fat. "Rise to your feet, or none shall pray peace for your shade."

Lagnos took a moment, then found his way onto one knee, and finally into an uneasy stance. He was downcast and unmoving on his feet until he began to sense what was happening across the ring from him, and lifted his head to look.

The stag had begun to smell the blood and dung and wolf-stink emanating off the predator nearby, and showed signs of panic. It was on the run again, but flailing, crazed in its attempts to escape. The warriors were ready. It leapt, and the antler wall rose to meet it. It kicked its powerful hindquarters against the motile barrier, and the men still stood their ground, even those it injured. The creature made no progress.

Then it stopped, shook the arsenal adorning its head side to side, and seemed to focus. It had spotted Lagnos. Facing its opponent squarely, the buck lowered its head, stomped its forelegs, and charged.

Lagnos stared, paralyzed, at the oncoming animal, and sensed up barely in time to leap out of the way. The buck clattered its antlers against the warriors' staves at the edge of the ring, but quickly double backed. It charged again, and this time it did not miss. As Lagnos squeezed his eyes shut, antlers hooked into his side, spinning him a half turn in the air so that he narrowly avoided coming down directly on his head. He screamed as the beast tried to trample him, rolling aside just as the stag's hooves beat down, leaving craters in the ground where they impacted.

Lagnos crawled toward the edge of the ring, trailing blood, thinking only of getting away from the beast. He was met with a faceful of horns as the warriors jabbed him pitilessly, driving him back toward the center.

"Stand your ground!" shouted the brother.

"Pagos, help me, save me!"

Pagos strode forward and shoved his antler stave hard at Lagnos, one of the prongs entering a tear in his side.

"If you have no care for our pride," he said, grabbing Lagnos by the neck and drawing him near, "have a care for our souls." He forced Lagnos's head around to view the Godskull in its perch. "Our lord is watching. At least you can be credit to our clan in your death, brother, since you were not in life."

Pagos released his brother and returned to his place in the ring. As if entranced, perhaps finally realizing his fate was unchangeable, Lagnos slowly stood again. He was still looking at Pagos when the stag charged at full speed and caught him full in his gut, tossing him backward. Lagnos sat on his rear and looked into the opaque brown eyes of his divine judge, the living avatar of Cerrunos, as the animal bucked bony spines into his chest, sliced open a line across the bottom of his jaw, kicked forward deep into flesh and tramped bone into splinters. Only when Lagnos was completely still, no longer even holding his hands in front of him, did the stag disengage and trot back to the far end of the ring, exhausted, snorting with what seemed like satisfaction.

The priest approached the stag, his palms facing up and his eyes facing the ground. Placing one hand on the deer's neck to calm it, the priest dribbled oil on its head with the other, all the while whispering into a twitching ear. At some signal or understanding that Elyn saw no sign of, a portion of the ring parted, and the stag bounded off into the Mabon night.

Lagnos, forgotten while the High Priest communed with the god, resumed his groaning and rolled from his back onto his stomach.

"He's alive!" said the boy to Elyn, poking her arm. She thought of chastising him again, but she was suddenly very weary. "What does that mean? Is it over?" *He's relentless,* she thought.

"I don't think it's over," said Elyn, pointing to the stone circle.

The priest came forward again.

"Cerrunos has accepted a sacrifice of blood, but the sacrifice of life is spurned."
An uncharacteristic murmur among the armed men rose and fell quickly, and
even the priest sounded nervous. "We must peer deeper through the veil."

"I don't think that's good," said the boy. "So now what happens?"

Elyn had a sick feeling she knew, and did not want to voice it.

Lagnos had managed to get himself into a kneeling position, eyes shut in agony,
his silence more eerie than his caterwauling. Blood streamed off the tattered
flags of flesh hanging from his face, legs and torso. His head slumped forward
when the two acolyte priests came forth and hauled him upright, and the wolf's
hide Lagnos still wore now looked like it was attacking him, clawing at his back,
reanimated and claiming for itself the life the stag had so barely spared.

The under-priests dragged him backward toward the center stone of the circle.
From his place among the ring of warriors, Pagos's eyes reflected the firelight of
the braziers as anger and shame.

The three masked women portraying Virgin, Mother and Crone, who had been
as frozen as the monoliths in the circle throughout the ordeal, protected from the
stag's rages by the brazier fires, now took their places. The old woman prayed
over a rattle and mumbled incantations to herself, while the Mother led the
young girl forward. One of the lady's hands lay across the girl's eyes, another
across her mouth. *Nothing to protect her ears,* thought Elyn, to whom the
sounds were the most horrifying part of the experience.

The fight seemed gone from Lagnos as they dragged him to the center stone, and
it was hard to tell if he was still conscious. He was – at the sensation of the
granite against the back of his neck, Lagnos used the last of his strength to strain
against his captors, an insensate protest without plan or control. He grabbed at

the nearest officiant he could reach, the Mother, and hooked two fingers onto one eyehole of her mask. She recoiled in time to avoid being caught by Lagnos, but his grazing fingertips pulled her cloak and mask partway askew. The acolytes quickly subdued him, and the High Priest appeared behind Lagnos to pull back the convict's head, exposing his throat and chest.

"Oh great god Cerrunos, let your faithful see your will clear and true! Let your wisdom water our understanding that it may grow!"

It all happened within a few seconds - the slowest seconds of Elyn's life. The Mother turned in her direction, face partly uncovered and her hair spilling out, arranged in elaborate plaits and braids that Elyn herself had woven that very morning. The Mother was… *Mother.*

That was the moment Grundfyrdd stepped up briskly and plunged a long, thin dagger of gold into Lagnos between his neck and collarbone, driving the blade at an angle designed to puncture a lung and pierce his heart. Grundfyrdd withdrew the metal spike immediately, and a geyser of blood erupted from the opening. The Mother – *my mother* – quickly uncovered the Virgin's eyes, but not mouth. Elyn and the boy had a view of the girl's face, and all the screams that didn't escape her lips were there in her eyes. Mother used force to position the Virgin directly in front of Lagnos's spurting wound, which sprayed crimson against the girl's pristine white robe, dying it a design that grew redder and redder with each pulse.

When the eruptions diminished, the Priest filled a horn with Lagnos's blood. The Crone shambled forward to spread wide the Virgin's robe in front of her and peer at the stains, Mother holding the girl still and mute all the while. The Crone spoke to the priests who crowded around to hear her interpretations, while the girl stood in the midst of the stone circle, frozen. When the reading was finished, the acolytes removed the prophetic robe and left the Virgin naked before the Godskull and the assembly of the Horned Ones. A new robe, dyed red (presumably with berries), was draped over her nakedness. The old robe was tossed on the brazier, and the priests and Crone huddled in conference again.

At last they turned, and the High Priest raised his arms.

"Take care, all you clansmen, all you Cornovii – the veil is thin tonight and soon to be torn! Malicious spirits will feast and revel on the earth for an age! The old prophecy is the new – the prophecy that has never failed will not fail now.

"Fathers, strengthen your arms and shrink your bellies. Sons, put seed in your women and grain in your stores. Wives and mothers, prepare to weave the men their shrouds. We have been shown the seasons hence. They are seasons of storm. The gods have spoken. Take heed all who hear."

The carnyxes blared again, and the drums beat fresh, now a cadence for the congregants to leave the Hollow and attend the feast. Torches were lit, revealing more of the surrounding moorland (the children ducked down automatically), yet a great pall seemed to hover around the Cornovii as they returned to their kin. Elyn could almost hear their thoughts: how to tell the news, what do next… how to survive.

Elyn and the boy remained in silence for many minutes after the ceremony concluded. It was he who rose first, standing over the still-squatting Elyn, not knowing what to say, or if to speak at all. Finally he said, "What is the prophecy? The one that's never wrong?"

Elyn arose, but did not look at him. She was staring at the last remaining Cornovi man in the Spirit Hollow – Pagos. He picked up the wolf's skin torn from his brother's back. Even from that distance she could sense the violence emanating from the man.

"It says 'When the kings of Britain gather, the land is soon to bleed.'"

"Oh."

The boy started to walk off, while Elyn remained still. A few yards away he stopped.

"My name is Daweth," he said.

"Bye, Daweth."

Elyn turned away and began to walk in the other direction, not sure how to get to the feast without crossing into the firelight, only wanting to move, and be alone. She remembered her small bag and reached in, rediscovering its forgotten contents – the pear. Without conscious decision she turned on her heels and ran back to the boy, Daweth, as he shuffled in the opposite direction.

He turned when she ran up and smiled. She noticed he was missing an incisor. *So young.* They stood there for a moment, looking at each other. She didn't know what she was doing – but Elyn was glad she'd seen the ceremony with Daweth, and knew she hoped they would meet again, unlikely though it was.

When he looked like he was going to say something else, (*Something stupid probably*, she thought) she thrust the pear into his hand and wheeled around, running off into the night, not knowing or caring why she'd done it.

I'm not hungry anymore, she said to herself, hurrying along the paths that glowed silver whenever the moonlight tore through the passing cloud bands.

That wasn't true though – she was still hungry, though not for anything in her stomach. Despite its horror and mystery, Elyn wasn't satisfied with the Mabon night at all. There was more, much more, the real that lay under the ritual. She *knew* it. She looked up at Lady Lhore, Mother Moon, as she ran, seeing that face she'd studied so well.

That isn't her face, Elyn thought, with a mixture of bitterness and a new, burgeoning excitement. *That's her mask, is all. But there's something behind it.* She thought of her own mother, understanding so much more and less than she had that morning. *Yes, there's something behind it. And I'm going to find out what.*

Chapter Two

BANG.

He opened his eyes in the gloom and gasped. He wasn't drowning anymore, but there was something wrong, something just as dangerous.

BANG.

He erupted from his bed into a fighting stance, and readied for whatever had come to kill him. On his feet semi-steady, out of the dream but not awake, he struggled for clarity even as he tensed for attack.

He looked, and there was nothing. The room was empty except for gray darkness and his panting breath, and his bed, and the blanket his sleep-thrashing had sent to the floor, and a stool and a pitcher and basin…

BANG.

He turned toward the noise.

A gust of chill air shot through a partly-covered window, the one he'd fully shuttered before bed, and a backing breeze sucked the atmosphere out of the room and BANG went the broad wooden slat against the wall. *Ah.* He relaxed. *A mischievous wind and a free shutter, and I'm in a panic.* He smiled at his foolishness. He crossed the room, the bottoms of his feet protesting the coldness of the floor, and guided the board back through its brackets, sliding it closed across the window. He saw the latch was busted.

"Latch is busted," he murmured to himself, pulse slowing. *Latch is busted, latch is busted, latch is…* The words echoed in his head three or four times more.

That means something, the echo, he remembered, but he wasn't sure what. His alertness had been a fear response, and as alarm receded, his consciousness sagged. He staggered back toward his bed.

He had a vague notion of being asleep and dreaming. *It was THAT dream*, a voice within warned, but it was a gauze-shrouded thought, and weariness was the stronger sensation. With the window shut and the room warming, fatigue reclaimed the ground the momentary shock had seized. He slumped onto the mattress, and in only a few blinks his eyelids glued themselves together.

Water rushes all around, pushes stinging into his nose, balls him up and hurtles him forward, a plaything for the current. His existence is a torrent in his ears, his only reality the cold hands of the water contorting him at their will. He knows nothing except that he is about to drown.

He bolted awake and rose again, physically shaking the dream from his head. He did not want to remember, lest it suction him below the surface, a vicious whorl in the nightmare waters. The drowsiness lingered, grew insistent, but he was awake enough now to recognize the danger that sleep posed.

Focus.

He glanced around. The room was empty. Why? It shouldn't have been so bare. He tried to recall. There was something missing.

Something missing, something missing, something miss…

The echo did not stop or diminish. It only grew louder. Suddenly he was terrified, he was slipping, but still on his feet… *still on my feet… still on my feet… oh no I know what this is, oh no, it's happening… happen…*

His mind was all echoes now. Breaths came quickly to keep up with the frenzied heart convulsing anew in his torso. His chest felt like a chamber full of churning liquid one moment, the next a vessel drained to void. The dream loomed in his mind, a boulder tottering on a promontory, ready to crush the sanity below with one heave. He was on the bed, *must have sat... must have sat... Water rushes all around...*

The list, he thought suddenly, a lifeline in the storm. *Questions. Remember the questions.*

On the verge of oblivion, he clung to the words without comprehending their full import, like a shipwrecked sailor hugging whatever rock he drifted against. The questions were the only solution he'd ever found.

Begin. Where?

A room, it was his room, his room in... Dumnonia. Britain. Near Eilwath, a village.

Good. When?

Goodwhengoodwhen... He fought through the noise and tumult congesting his brain, forced himself to rise again, walk back toward the window. It stuck when he tried to open it, so he looked through the small aperture he'd created, leaning for strength against the wall. Outside his house only a dim remnant of the day rimmed the distant horizon, a hint of light.

Twilight.

There was another glow, in the distance – firelight – and a noise. *Drums.*

When?

He slipped again, and the dream was waiting. *Water rushes all around...*

WHEN? The still-lucid part of him slapped the face of the drowning man.

The fires, the drums. September. Mabon eve, an early one.

Who?

That was always the hard part. Who now, who here? It had been easier before, when there were fewer guises and not as many miles on the road. The identities rolled by in a loop, but the right one slipped through his grasp on each go-around. He tried to keep the rest of his brain blank, lest the echoes take over again. *Who?* Other people's names he remembered... Uleara... Ecbert... *Tonight is Mabon... don't slip again... something missing, something don't slip missing something missing something someth...*

"Kieran," he said aloud. "My name is Kieran."

And the storm ended.

Kieran exhaled, exhausted but grateful. The sound of his name was a soothing balm, and at hearing it spoken the echoes and anxiety fled from his mind as vermin from a light. Despite the darkness of his chamber, a gloom seemed lifted, the night now a visitor rather than invader. The room was again just a room.

Kieran was undoubtedly awake. He'd planned for more sleep, but it was equally well that he get moving. He gave one wistful glance toward the beckoning bed and instead assembled his garments, simple in that he was donning every stitch he still owned. Kieran paused by the mirror to check his...

"The mirror," said Kieran to the empty bedchamber, with a smile of relief. "That's the something that's missing."

It was missing because he'd sold it the day before, along with everything else except what he was taking on his journey. The mirror was one of the few luxuries he'd afforded himself these years, a large disc of polished bronze that was easily the most expensive item for miles, but which none but himself knew he owned. No one had ever been inside his house. The mirror was a vanity, though, temptation. He was vain enough to imagine it finding its way to the court of Emperor Anistasius in Constantinople, but that was as far as his wistfulness extended to something so shiny but so lifeless. *I shouldn't have had it at all.*

He knew what he would see in the mirror's face, anyway: a man approaching old age who had known about 45 winters start to end, tall and tending toward gaunt, still strong but beginning to feel the years bore into his joints. Eyes set deep above sharp cheeks, and a beard, dark brown and gray, on a lean, streamlined face that could still sometimes break into a smile. Some over the years had called that smile too broad, curved or too toothy in its fullness, but that was not why it was so seldom seen of late.

Kieran Daethryn, Kieran the Stranger, pulled on his wool cloak, tattered at the edges, a once-vivid blue that many seasons of wear had drained to gray. He slung on his satchel and left his fine house near Eilwath, never to pass its threshold again.

The walk up to the Cairn Mount was more difficult than he remembered. *Strange that a year should make such a difference*, he thought, trying not to take joy in this being his final excursion up the Three Hill Trail. With the full moon in a sky only partly troubled by clouds, and the Cornovii celebrating Sawhane so prematurely, he had to walk the long way, against the steep sides of the hills, to reach his spot without detection. The wisdom of the Old Kind taught that he was to "Dwell in the shadow to walk in the light," but on that night he was forced to seek the light by walking in shadow. It was the sort of thing the Cornovii expected on Sawhane, when they said the veil between the worlds was thin.

Maybe they're right.

Step by step he walked the three miles, almost without incident. Though he felt several times he was being trailed, he never spotted the possible stalking presence, and he was seen only once, while passing near enough to the Spirit Hollow to hear the frenzy within. He did not try to eavesdrop on their ritual, but it was plain that the celebrants were beyond anxious, stirred up by rumors of war and the convergence of their holy days. The air hinted that violence would be soon be done.

It was then he saw someone, a child, white-robed like the rest but well separated from them. She stopped, staring at him, no doubt agape as well, but Kieran did not hesitate in his stride. He found sheltering shadow within an instant and disappeared from her sight.

I would be the Willow Wizard to her, I suppose, he mused. *And why not? Every kid needs a Willow Wizard to tell of.* Kieran trusted children more than their elders, and as a class of person, liked them better as well. To that girl, he must have seemed otherworldly, wise and ancient.

Ancient at least, he thought, veering on to the rightward and steeper path. Forty-five years or thereabouts come and gone, making him on the cusp of old age. Climbing that hill, with the wind starting to chill him, he could feel it. Old age was dangerous.

Yet in three days I'll be dead or immortal, he thought, *so it's meaningless to dwell upon.*

Despite this sentiment, he was aware that the unease from his first waking hadn't fully left him, and it was very much the wrong day for distraction. He would need all his wits and every ounce of concentration, now that he was on the eve of setting the mechanism he had meticulously constructed into motion. Instead of perfect focus, though, he sensed long-thwarted fears, unaccustomed doubts stir with sudden life below his practiced calm. And his sins…

The only evil ignorance, the only sin turning away. Let yourself forget and let evil remember you.

Under the eyes of the Old Kind Kieran repeated those words for three years, until they were as his heartbeat.

We dwell in the shadow to walk in the light.

For his seven years near Eilwath he'd said the teachings as prayers, but for a time he had forgotten to inhabit them, forgotten what they meant even as they were on his lips. It was so easy to turn away and play at ignorance at the beginning, for the shadow was cold and solitary, and then a light that seemed so warm.

He could not bring himself to think on her, on them, as a regret, but neither could he deny there were many dimensions to the greatness of his sin.

Kieran reached a bend that revealed Uleara's small church house, nestled into a hillside across from Kieran's path and resting on a plateau that was part natural and part embellished by the abbot's efforts, though Kieran had helped. Uleara, the only man he could call friend, knew far more about Kieran than did all the

44

other inhabitants of Dumnonia combined – enough indeed that he sensed of how little of Kieran he actually knew. They shared a visit about every other day, and Kieran kept a small workshop at the periphery of the church grounds, which the abbot never entered from a mixture of good manners, respect, and fear.

The abbot would now be snoring away, likely in his cups. Only a single light glowed on the church grounds, a lantern slung on the bronze cross dominating the outside yard, an advertisement to any weary believer in need of shelter and a challenge to the pagan Cornovii within its view.

Until tomorrow, Kieran thought, rounding another curve that took the church once more from his sight.

He neared the place of his vigil, and thought of the ritual he was to perform. It was in stark contrast to the Cornovi spectacle taking place behind him, which Kieran could perceive as a glow from within the Spirit Hollow when he faced the direction he'd come, and which he was glad he could no longer hear. Their rite claimed the same ancestry as Kieran's, but was countless generations removed from its wellspring, warped and muddied by many bends. Kieran's knowledge was pure from the source.

Kieran sat still as the stone beneath him, a black figure in the pre-dawn dark. Icy blasts beat at his back and bit at his skin, causing the fringes of his cloak to flap like frenzied pennants on the battlements of his lean form as he stared eastward, anticipating the first foray of dawnlight.

The dark purple of the sky was mellowing above the land to the east, beyond the Brythonic Sea, the peninsula called The End of the Earth by those who lived on the vast continent of which it was the far-western appendage. Kieran had never set foot on any part of it, and now likely he never would. There was a time when he had done things he didn't think himself capable of, and had been willing to do more, in order to cross the channel and seek for answers in the capitals of the known world. It had all been futile. Not futile – misinformed.

As sunlight began to color the horizon, as the time for the Ritual of Being and Becoming drew close, part of Kieran wished he'd made it. The seven years of preparation, and before that his reconstruction in the hands of the Old Kind, and before that... He could not help wondering if it might have been different if he'd chosen another path, found his way somehow across to the far shore.

It could not have been different, though. Kieran knew that as well as he knew anything.

The rite was one of the oldest and most arcane known by the Old Kind, so potent that traditionally its secret was entrusted to only two people. Kieran made three. It was doubtful any in living memory had every performed it, so none knew precisely its outcome. It was performed at certain turns in the cycle of creation, and could subtly but definitely affect the great wheel's motion, yet always left the one who administered the rites permanently changed. Madness and enlightenment, the brave rendered cowards and the simple turned genius, these and more transformations were chronicled. What it would do to him was a question Kieran put out of his thoughts but kept at the periphery of his consciousness.

The wind's fury had mostly subsided, but it still sporadically sent raging gusts across the hilltop, making difficult his preparation of the rite. From his bag he meted a mixture of carefully prepared plant matter onto a tinder of dried moss and wood shavings, all within an iron brazier he forged specially for the occasion. The wind extracted its tithe from the concoction of roots and herbs as he poured it out, and caused all of the brazier's contents to jitter dangerously toward the rim. If he were using flint and steel to set the flame, a persistent breeze would cause the sparks to go every which way. That, however, was not how he intended to light the fire.

Kieran unstoppered a little vial of bone and put a glass rod no wider than a reed stalk into its mouth. He drew forth a tiny bead of a substance that smoked and glowed faintly at the tip, then positioned the rod above the cauldron and brought it down upon the tinder with a sharp stroke. A spike of white light erupted from the brazier, and instantly the contents were aflame.

Kieran carefully laid aside the glass and the bone vial, and took up a sort of bowl, a hollow bronze sphere with a quarter of its top cut away. Timing his motions to coincide with lulls in the wind, Kieran sprinkled water from the jar over the burning contents of the brazier, causing smoke-laced steam to arise from the fire. Each time he scattered water with his left hand, he collected the steam into the bowl with his right, trapping the vapor so it slid down the inside and returned to liquid. He did this until enough condensation was rippling in the bottom for a good-sized gulp.

The ceremony needed to be complete before the sun first emerged, and Kieran saw it was instants away from full daybreak. He took a large pinch of the fire's ashes and dropped it into the bowl, swishing the residue into the water. He closed his eyes and tilted back his head til his cloak crumpled down and his hair spilled across his shoulders, then drained the draught into his mouth, waiting for the water to collect in his throat to the last drop before sending it down in a single gulp.

At once, the floodgates of his mind flew open. What poured through was the dream.

47

Water rushes all around, pushes into his nose, balls him up and hurtles him forward, presses against him like the earth of a coffinless grave. The torrent strips away every sense but terror as it tosses him against rocks and sucks him under, only to eject his body to the surface an instant later.

He perceives his surroundings atop desperate gulps of air, seeing for mere seconds at a stretch. He is in the midst of a rushing river, filled with boulders and fallen branches, raging through a deep woods. These sights disappear as down again he goes, a plaything for the current, muscles useless against the rapids, fighting with every fiber not to inhale when a collision punches him under his ribcage. He feels his resistance fading, and knows he is about to drown

He does not realize he is gripping a thatch of submerged branches, noticing only that his progress has stopped. Awareness dawns, he remembers how to control his arms, and slowly he drags himself up, above the water, fighting the rush of the river while he pulls along the sodden tree, muscles screaming, each second wearing down, closer to being seduced by the promise of oblivion if he just lets go.

The roar fades, the torrent loses interest in him, his feet find purchase. He senses he will not drown after all, and lets himself collapse onto a dirt bank, the cold and shock too powerful for him to note the sharp stones cutting into his skin.

He flips onto his stomach, gripping at the mud, and vomits water. He coughs and gags, inhales with a profound "gwwohhh," and coughs again, to the limit of violence, feeling his lungs will invert themselves, every inch of his air tubes aflame. He retches until it is all expelled, until his next breath is not his only thought. He lays prone on the riverbank, exhausted.

48

Calm returns, until he closes his eyes. In darkness he is beset by sensations. Cracking lightning, whipping wind, screams. Many screams. The storm. He remembers the storm, but not...

A terrible thought forms, and he is asphyxiated anew. Its reality spreads through his comprehension like poison in his bloodstream. His eyes open wide in horror. He does not know anything but the storm. Before that, he is blank. I don't know my name. *His anguished cry rings through the forest.*

Chapter Three

How long he lay soaked and dazed by the riverbank he did not know, nor where he was, nor his identity, but when he heard voices through the woods, approaching, he knew enough to hide.

His left ankle was sprained – he thought broken – so it was with difficulty he hobbled over the dead branches and fungus-riddled logs that littered the forest floor, trying to scramble to a spot of concealment. More difficult was biting down on the scream that nearly leapt from his throat when he lost his footing and put his full weight on the injured ankle, feeling the joint slip and a jolt of pain race up his body to lodge behind his eyes. At last he found shelter in the hollow of a massive tree, hurtling himself into it just as the glimpse of a man appeared.

He remained motionless, curling himself into as small a mass as he could, while a group of men passed by on the other side of the tree from him, chatting amiably in a language he did not understand. He remained out of sight until they were well down the path, and fought back the marauding pain and paralyzing terror just long enough note which direction they were headed. When he finally ventured the most careful peek achievable, he saw only one detail of the last man to disappear out of view: the glint of his axe. Even at such a distance it was clear it was not intended to fell trees.

How do I know it's an ax? he thought. *How do I know language but not what it's called, and nothing about myself? How do I know "myself" is myself?* These were not leisurely musings, but rapit bolts, each thought horrifying singly, maddening taken together. *What is my* name?

His thoughts were scrambled, his memories incoherent or nonexistent. He had nearly drowned, that he knew. And before? The feel of an impossible wind, a face with no detail, the world breaking apart. A storm. That was all. Everything else was tumult or blankness, despite his best efforts of concentration. Each time he tried to reach for one of the wisps of memory that floated by in his mind, it only drifted further out of his grasp, as a dream one remembers less the more one tries to recall it. There was no sign of any who might have been with him before the disaster, and no wreckage to be found washed up near him. He knew little, but he knew he was alone.

He remained near his hiding place for the rest of the day, though no one else came by. For a long stretch he simply sat, staring at ancient, unfamiliar wilderness, wondering what his next steps could or should be, and if his heart would ever stop beating so. His first deliberate act was to make a splint for his ankle, using thin pliant vines to secure four straight sticks around his lower leg. He stopped wondering how he knew what to do, afraid to drive the knowledge away, hoping the more he forgot what he'd forgotten, the more he would remember. He tried focusing on small tasks to stave off the lurking insanity. Stranded and powerless in an unkown land, to survive he would have to focus on nothing but survival.

With sunset approaching, he set off in the direction he'd heard the men go, with the aid of a stray branch he used as a cane. He soon discovered a faint foot path that led through the forest to a recently cut clearing, which still smelled strongly of sap and wood chips and contained many stumps glowing under the high sun above. Crouching low in the midst of a clump of bushes and saplings, he peered out into the open space.

He saw a pair of mules harnessed to a rig, trudging forward as a man half-heartedly whipped their haunches. The man was dressed in a rough-knit gray tunic and loose trousers, and wore a pointed cap. He, like the mules, looked underfed and bored. The mules were harnessed to one of the massive stumps, which was gradually coming loose, spraying dirt as its roots groaned and snapped from the ground. Further on, he saw a cratered field where the land had already been denuded of stumps, and gazing further still, his attention was tugged skyward, to the oppressing sight at the far end of the clearing.

One entire side of the deforested space was bordered by a palisade forty feet high, composed of massive tree trunks (almost certainly the trees that had once stood in the clearing) sunk into ground and covered in planks. There was a defensive ditch dug around it that was lined on both sides with abatises – rows of sharp wooden stakes lashed together in an X-pattern. A primal impulse told him it was a place of danger for all but its masters. It was a fortress.

No sooner had he discerned the structure's purpose than he saw the men who manned it. They swarmed around the far side of the fort by the dozens, making final preparations for the night. They wielded pikes and axes, and many also carried dead fowl drooping over their shoulders or full sacks trickling flour. Some, he noticed, had fresh blood splattered on them, though whether it was animal or human could not be known. Higher up, along the top of the palisade, where the posts had been hacked into an irregular row of spikes, Kieran could see bullet-shaped helmets tracking back and forth as sentries walked the wall. All the warriors wore long beards, many of which were strung with beads or had lengths of bone braided into them, and most were armored in knee-length chainmail they wore above embroidered tunics and loose fitting pants.

He did not glean much from his brief watch in the thicket, but he did become certain that he must remain invisible for the moment, and make as little an impression as possible when the time came for him to reveal himself. He had no idea what dangers he would encounter as a stranger in this country, but from what little he'd seen, he guessed they were numerous and grave.

With sunset at hand, though, that concern was to wait.

He hastened to return to the tree hollow before it was too dark to see. By the time he reached it his ankle hurt badly, the pain a coil of carnivorous worms working steadily through his muscles and bone.

"Focus," he hissed to himself, which, said aloud, helped him beat back the agony.

He gathered some rocks, dead moss and small twigs, and set about making a fire. It occurred to him that the firelight could earn unwelcome attention from the fort, but being in the woods at night without one was the far less attractive option.

Not having any idea why it should work, only that either deep memory or inborn instinct told him it would, he rubbed and twirled a spindle of stick against a thick, dry branch, keeping on even though it was not producing results after half an hour. It was twilight before the acrid smoke smell started permeating the air around his tiny campsite, rising up from the branch, and though he felt his strength ebbing fast, he twirled and rubbed at a faster pace still, trying to outrace the coming of night. Around him emerged the sounds of woods enveloped in darkness, a forest that was not afraid of humans – the sounds of rustling, of padding steps, the loud, savage calls of animals that hunted each other within steps of where he lay… that might hunt him.

He'd watched for and imagined an ember coming to life from within the heap of dried moss and brittle twigs, and when it appeared at last he almost didn't believe it was real. It grew, though, along with the smoke, smelled not seen in the inky blackness of the forest. He could feel the shift in the pile before anything appeared to happen, and seconds later he smiled in relief and triumph when a *whoosh* announced the burst of orange and yellow light mushrooming from the small stack of fuel. The immediate vicinity became illuminated.

He and the animal recoiled at the same instant. It had been stalking him, but was startled by the light, and he saw it only in flashes: a pulse of muscular gray, a glint of white teeth and a pair of covetous yellow eyes, then the flick of a heavy fur tail as the wolf turned away, backing beyond the perimeter of the light. Kieran pressed his back against the tree, and looked for a weapon.

The next ten hours were the longest and most terrifying Kieran ever knew. In a sphere around the reach of the fire, which he worked conscientiously to keep alive, the forest was a black, blank mass, but one filled with eyes that flashed in the firelight as their owners watched him, feet from his shelter. The wolf appeared again in the early morning, circling around the fire's ring of light and working its way closer. It stopped and made as if to pounce, and Kieran knew he must act or die. He began to holler, and picked up a flaming stick from the fire. He shouted and waved the torch with abandon until the wolf retreated into the darkness, growling. Kieran retained the stick in his hand until the fire at its end turned it to charcoal, and when it was wholly consumed, he dug a rock from the nearby earth, and readied his grip in case the wolf returned. He remained tensed, prepared to hurl the stone at the wolf or any other threat in range, for over an hour.

He slept in snatches of minutes, awaking with a start each time and immediately reaching for the rock near his hand. He'd had to use it once as he awoke to a badger sniffing at his feet. After that he did not return to sleep.

In the misty light of dawn, Kieran finally felt safe enough to relax his locked muscles. Blinking with exhausted eyes at the sunrays that pierced the forest canopy, and looking at his pitiable encampment, he resolved that he would never again spend a night in the woods alone.

His joints cracked when he unbent from his crouch, while a cascade of burning needles tumbled down his legs as the blood began to circulate through them again. He was obliged to use the oak as a support while he relieved himself upon the fire pit and collected whatever of his faculties there were, then grasped his makeshift cane.

It occurred to him as he began his trek along the merchant road that he might be smarter to remain in the vicinity of where he had washed onto the riverbank. Even though that meant staying near the garrison of warriors as well, he had a suddenly strong impulse to keep watch for any of the others who might have come with him. However, the thought was concocted of as many parts fatigue as logic, and he decided against it when he realized that he probably would not recognize his former companions if he saw them, which would render the extreme risk of remaining in the area unnecessary. That left his only recourse to start moving.

He hobbled along the rutted path itself when he could, and ducked into the forest as quickly as possible when he heard human noises. Each time he tore for the security of the woods, crouching behind rocks and bushes to stay hidden from the travelers, he put more strain on his ankle, which was swollen and purple between the sticks of the splint. The pain was bearable, but just barely.

He spent the day walking, toward what he did not speculate. As late morning evolved into early afternoon, fatigue verged on delirium, and his ankle demanded attention he finally had to pay. The pain in his leg had overpowered

55

all thoughts for several miles, so when the highway crossed a narrow creek that disappeared into a stretch of piney woodland, out of view of the road, it came as a massive relief, the perfect spot to rest and recover.

He followed the creek upstream, intending to soak his leg and sit for a good long while, if not even brave a bit of sleep. He had trouble uphill on the narrow path that led toward a ridgeline, and he gritted his teeth as his ankle endured constant abuse and the wood of his ersatz cane cut into his hand, but the thought of even a few minutes' ease just ahead spurred him onward. He crested the rise that hid the rest of the woods from the road, quickening his pace in anticipation of reaching the place of respite.

As soon as he stepped atop the rise, though, and surveyed the scene before him, all thoughts of sleep at once disappeared.

The forest floor before him was a killing field. Scores of bodies lay slain in various poses of agony. Broken javelins, spear shafts and arrows stuck out of the ground and the corpses indiscriminately. One warrior had three iron bars sticking from his torso and one from his back, the handles of pyramid-bladed throwing darts like the one Kieran cut his foot stepping on. Shields were shattered with the impact of axes, and lay strewn about alongside the owners they had failed to protect keep alive. Many of the fallen still held as firmly to their armaments in death as they had in the last moments of their lives, and some weapons were gripped in hands that swords had orphaned from their wrists.

There were no useable weapons, though – anything of value the dead had possessed was now property of the battle's survivors.

None of the men had escaped mutilation before death, and many had been so badly bludgeoned or slashed their bodies were unrecognizable as anything but animal carcasses. The blood that once gushed, and still trickled, from these assorted injuries ran down a hill, creating a network of rivulets that looked like nothing so much as a system of arteries, and the viscous liquid made a soggy marsh of the forest floor where wine-colored pools collected.

He wandered stupefied among the corpses. He surveyed the faces of those who still had them, as if to plumb from their expressions some clue as to who they had been in life. Each had reacted differently at the realization that the end was upon him. Most had stared into the face of death with expressions of terror, anguish or hatred, but he found exceptions.

One of the men who had assumed a different posture toward oblivion was interesting for other reasons too. He had been a young man, his beard thin and the rest of his features smooth, who took his earthly departure with incomprehension, but also a sense of dignity, judging by the last look on his face. He had fallen across the creek, damming it up, and the stream water flowed over his body to create a transparent death mask, which shimmered over his surprised expression and staring but sightless eyes. A blue cloak, presumably his, lay nearby, which appropriated immediately.

Scanning the corpses, he saw that most of the dead men wore tunics of similar color, to each other and to the dead man in the creek, and had green sashes tied around their waists. A few, however, wore no sashes, and were dressed in brown and red, with loose trousers covering their legs and ruined chain mail atop their tunics. It dawned on him that these others were warriors of the fortress, perhaps some of the same men he'd spotted the day of his arrival. However, their representation among the dead was miniscule, only a handful, compared with the dozens of their nemeses who lay lifeless nearby.

It was a rout, he thought. *This battle really only had one side.*

57

He looked down again at the young man in the stream, and laying aside his revulsion, an idea came to him. He examined the lad and confirmed his suspicion that he differed from all the others, even his comrades, in a significant way that was quite apart from his naïve expression. The cool running water had preserved him from the putrefaction beginning to set in among the others, and the young warrior's tunic was not covered in drying blood or flecked with bits of bone and muscle as were his comrades'. The tunic was clean, and the right size, and a quick decision solved the first of his problems.

In negotiating the removal of the young man's dress, he found lying beneath the soldier a sword in good order, which the winning warriors had missed in their plunder. Its hilt was polished and it was sheathed in an elaborately carved leather scabbard.

That solves another problem, he thought.

He buried the clothes he'd previously worn, really scraps of material shredded in the storm, and with his new dripping wet attire and weapon, he immediately quitted the ghastly scene. Not back to the road, though. His leg still needed soaking, and more than before, he needed to sit down.

While he let the chill of the stream soothe his swollen ankle, he contemplated his situation, which was still little improved from where it stood in the morning. Despite his new acquisitions, he remained loath to be seen by any inhabitants of the land, especially as he knew there was a force of warriors nearby large enough to slay forty men and sustain almost no losses – and he was wearing the clothing of their enemy. *I must be sure to correctly guess which way the ones dressed like me live.* He now felt a tug of regret that he had not simply tried to clean the blood from one of the winning side's tunics, but every move was improvised, and the most important thing was to keep moving. *And I wouldn't have found the sword. I guess I'm just lucky.* That thought made him chuckle aloud.

His leg feeling better and his vigor part way restored by his rest, he returned to within sight of the road, hurrying past the grisly battle site, and resumed a place of concealment to watch the passing traffic. People came by sporadically, but none to suit his aim for some time. At length a caravan of ponies and carts passed, with what seemed to be a large family walking beside them, and no one visibly armed. His moment had come. He let them disappear from view, then emerged from his hiding spot and set off, slowly, after them.

Keeping pace with the little caravan was arduous. He had to keep limping along well into dusk, but at last, rounding a curve, he saw them stopped and making camp at the roadside, and at that he abruptly collapsed in exhaustion.

As night set in, he snuck close to the travelers and hid behind one of the wagons, while the family communed around the fire, cooking, singing songs and talking, unaware of his surveillance. By ones and pairs the travelers turned in, sleeping in small tents or cart beds, while he began to feel his jaw quaking with the intensifying cold of the night. He had sworn he would never spend another night as he'd spent the one before, but he restrained his eagerness and remained in his hiding place well after the last person had clambered into the cart. Only then did he dare to expose himself to sight to absorb the heat of the dying fire.

He let its warmth envelop him, and felt comfortable for the first time in two days. He caught himself beginning to nod a couple of times, and on the third flirtation with sleep he roused himself from the spot and chose a place to nod off, a patch well away from the tents but within the corona of the camp fire, which would ensure that the other creatures with whom they shared the forest would keep well away from him. He wrapped his entire body in the pilfered blue cloak, and welcomed the soft embrace of sleep within a minute of lying down. The final thing he heard was someone calling "Kieran, Kieran!" to one of her companions, and he thought, "That's a nice name." He needed something to call himself, and his last waking decision was to adopt the name as his own. *A temporary fix,* he mused, before beginning to snore.

When he awoke it was high morning, approaching noon. Kieran, as he was newly self-dubbed, developed a racing pulse within five blinks of opening his eyes, panicked by the lateness of the hour. He blearily beheld an abandoned road blazing with the brightness of day. The travelers were gone, along with most traces of their campsite. After checking his person with a sweep of his hands, Kieran found he was no more injured than he'd been, and was otherwise unmolested. In fact, inspecting the camp's extinct fire ring, he found a few hunks of good meat and an intact turnip, and got the impression they had been left deliberately.

Kieran built a fire, and put a thin flat rock on top of it to cook the meat. Meantime, he began munching on the turnip, which he eventually put on the fire as well. Fear had kept his hunger at bay for two days, but watching the turnip char and hearing the meat sizzle, it ballooned into voraciousness. The instant he deemed it sufficiently cooked, he snatched the strip of meat from the rock and tore into the flesh, heedless of the pain as it burned his mouth. The turnip was consumed rapidly in its turn, and when Kieran had cleared every particle from the cooking stone, he lounged against a boulder and smiled with contentment, his shrunken stomach pleasantly full. Even his ankle felt better, when left perfectly still. He let himself believe things were looking up.

Within the hour he was violently ill. Intense cramps cut into his abdomen like a hacking blade, and far before the food had been given a chance to restore his undernourished body, Kieran vomited all of it up in a string of wracking bursts that left him empty and weak. He began to shake, and he couldn't be certain if it was the malady or the terror of the malady that caused chills to shoot along his limbs.

He realized he didn't want to be on the road if he were to pass out, which became a real possibility as dizziness set in. Kieran tried to climb up an embankment and into the forest, using exposed roots as handholds, but his ankle and strength gave out simultaneously, and he slipped backward down the slope, landing hard on a rock that delivered a jarring blow to the base of his skull. Woozy before, he was now entirely without equilibrium, and as his head throbbed he realized his vision was severely impaired. Kieran felt himself being pulled toward unconsciousness. He fought to stay awake, but each time he closed his eyes they became harder to will back open. On his back, splayed halfway into the rutted path, he turned his head down the road, and, as if through gauze, saw a man coming toward him, pulling a cart. *How nice to go for a ride,* thought Kieran, as he closed his eyes and his consciousness winked out.

He awoke several times in the next few days, but briefly. On the first occasion, he opened his eyes to see the deep blue sky blazing through a canopy of trees. *The forest is moving,* he thought, and had only enough time to realize it was he moving, not the foliage, before he was out again.

Intermittent snatches of consciousness became indistinguishable from the confused but vivid nightmares that tormented his sleep. Here a field of dead warriors was rising to claim Kieran for their number, and here a woman's hands drew a dripping, cool cloth along his cheeks and forehead. Soft murmurs from unseen people at his bedside would give way to the yapping of wolves giving chase, while he tried to run with leaden feet from the monsters. He dreamt of his mother, whose face he could not see, and playing by a stream he knew as a child, which became a raging torrent that snatched him from the bank and continually dragged him under as it churned through gargantuan rapids. When he was finally deposited on the riverbank, Kieran jerked awake, his fever broken at last.

At first he felt nothing. He felt normal. Soon he became aware that his tunic and the blanket around him were drenched with his sweat, and, feeling for his injured leg, found a new splint and cloth bandages around his ankle. Though Kieran initially perceived only pitch dark around him, his eyes adjusted to recognize the purple pre-dawn light coming through loose slats in the walls and around the door of the enclosure where he lay. His fingers searched his bedside and found a ewer of water standing next to a bowl. He probed the bowl's interior, but at the touch of a substance cold and viscous, he withdrew his fingers, thinking he knew what he'd felt. Still, to be certain, he held his hand near his nose, and sniffed. Then he smiled, and licked his fingers. *Soup.*

Where he was, and under whose care, was entirely mysterious, though a few clues as to his general location were offered by the gathering light of morning. He was able to discern a saddle, bridles, brushes and a feed bin affixed to the wall opposite him, and he soon picked out whinnies and the stamp of hooves next to the tiny, squat building. Something else, which looked out of place among the other accoutrements, rested on iron pegs against one of the walls, far from his reach. It was his sword.

His adjusting ears soon picked up other vocalizations, these human, and they were coming nearer. Kieran was forced into a quick decision. Scrambling from under his blankets he crossed the room, walking upon the sprained ankle gingerly. Just as he heard the door begin to open, he grabbed the sword and wheeled around, pointing it at the doorway, without removing the scabbard from the blade. Though his weapon was ineffectual in its sheath, he readied himself to face whoever or whatever was entering his stall.

The door creaked wide, and there stood girl of about seven, skinny and braided, holding a wooden pail sloshing with milk. The girl and Kieran stared at each other for a moment. When she glimpsed the sword Kieran pointed harmlessly but menacingly before him, her eyes widened until they seemed to occupy her entire face. She dropped the pail, which spilled its contents across the dirt, and ran off hollering.

Kieran knew she would soon be back, with others in tow. *Do something*, he urged himself.

The voices and footfalls of a group of people, adults, approached from nearby. He could think of nothing to prevent the coming encounter, and realized the sword would scarcely improve his odds against numerous people, who could themselves be armed. This time when the door opened, his weapon lay at his feet, and he stood quaking.

The girl was first through the door, and immediately after her a press of people jammed their faces in the entryway to see inside. Kieran told himself to prepare for anything, but he would never have thought to prepare for what next occurred.

Their faces broke into smiles, and they greeted him effusively. A middle aged woman at the front of the pack, plump and large bosomed with a grin that made goose eggs of her red cheeks, rushed forward with arms wide and enveloped him in soft, pungent flesh. Kieran tottered under the weight of her embrace as she cooed alien words in his ear.

She released him at the prompting of a man who called out from the door. Kieran now saw the rest of the group – six of them all told, a family, from the balding and frail father who stood uneasily against the doorjamb, to the small girl who was still staring goggle-eyed at Kieran. There were two other children, a boy and a girl both about eleven who looked to be twins, and a well-built young man in his late teens, standing next to the father, as erect and proud as the aging man was bent and withdrawn. He alone regarded Kieran coldly.

The woman went to her elder son, slipping a hand around his waist and looking at him with supreme maternal devotion. He kissed her forehead, nodded assent at something she said, and turned his eyes back to Kieran. When the youth asked Kieran question, his tone was friendly but the glare was still present. The rest of the family turned their looks to Kieran, and six expectant faces his awaited his response.

Kieran was again paralyzed. There was nothing to say, as he had no idea what he was asked and could not have responded even if he did. These thoughts evidently appeared in his countenance, for the friendly faces before him gradually lost their look of familial concern and, as the silent seconds started to pile up, began to contort in bewilderment. The little girl asked something of her father, at which he turned to Kieran and repeated it. Confusion was giving way to suspicion, led by the elder son, whose whole demeanor was now overtly hostile.

Kieran seriously considered running, trying to barrel through the brood and sprinting out of there as fast as the injured ankle would allow. Then, in one last attempt to clarify his words, the father pulled at his own tunic and nodded to Kieran. Kieran looked down.

Like a blow to the head the realization came. Kieran at once grasped why this family had taken care of him. The design and color of his tunic, purple and green with a thistle motif, was repeated with a number of variations on the dress of the people before him. It seemed to be a mark of clan

They think I'm one of them.

This revelation brought about greater clarity in all of his thinking, and he was seized with the sort of idea that had thus far eluded him.

Kieran looked soulfully into each family member's face, summoned all of the true pain and confusion he'd felt since being marooned, and let out a long, loud, primal roar. He clutched the back of his head and began to utter random syllables that couldn't be interpreted as any sort of language, except that of unthinking anguish. He rolled his eyes in mad arcs and uttered sounds so disturbing he hadn't previously known he could produce them.

The family was terrified. Even the young man was startled, and each member of the clan, youngest to eldest, backed instinctively toward the door and huddled closer together. Kieran's moan gave way to babbling, which he consciously diminished in volume and pitch, so that none of the family outright panicked.

Kieran ceased his blather and groaned pitifully, staggering toward the bed, stumbling and knocking into objects on the wall. The father and mother immediately leapt forward to help him. The man steadied Kieran and directed him onto the pile of hay where he'd lain, while the mother secured blankets around him and called for the twins to bring the ewer of water. Kieran grasped its handles, shaking with feigned palsy, and tipped it to his mouth to slake his very real thirst. The father and mother both put their hands on Kieran to coax him into lying down, and he acquiesced, leaving the family's shocked faces to assume gazes of pity. Even the formerly suspicious elder son finally gave up his misgivings and joined his kin in sympathy.

Kieran leaned back and closed his eyes, feeling the smallest bit in control of his existence.

At midday, the family was gathered around Kieran's bed, but their focus was not on him. His act had evidently been convincing enough that, as with all people in the presence of someone they think inferior or damaged, they spoke only to one another and paid him little mind, except to spoon more stew into his mouth or ask him something he wasn't expected to answer.

While nobody was paying attention to Kieran, Kieran was paying great attention to them. The father was quietly telling a story, and Kieran could discern from the wistful way he wove the tale and the respectful silence in which the others listened that the man was recounting something from the past. Small flicks of his hand, muted cries of glory or agony and the wondrous expression on the twins' faces let Kieran know the aging man described a battle, and from the way the father ended his tale, his resigned tone and the downcast eyes of his clan when he was done, Kieran reasoned the man and his family were on the losing side.

The young man muttered "Saxoni," and spat on the ground.

The rest let out a grunt of acknowledgement. After a solemn silence had elapsed, the elder son began speaking again, almost as if to himself, his tone acid, his voice rising in vehemence and volume. The word appeared again, "Saxoni," along with others: "Anglis," and "Jutes" and "Freisii." Each time the youth spoke one of the names, which sounded like a curse on his tongue, the family winced.

If they hadn't been rapt in the young man's words and silent contemplation of their woe, they would have noticed Kieran sitting ever more upright, ears pricked forward and a small, happy smile working at the corners of his mouth. He finally knew where he was.

I am in Britain.

The plight of the Britons was well known. It had been three generations since the Western Roman Empire relinquished its province of Britannia, and took its legions with it, leaving the natives to the predations of their old enemies. The Romans had in their day erected two enormous walls and garrisoned thousands of men to contain the savage Picts and their brethren in the extreme north of the island, but with the barricades abandoned, the painted hordes poured south, putting entire towns to the spear.

Faced with annihilation, the kings of Britain sought an unlikely source of salvation. Though for hundreds of years Germanic tribes had sent raiders to plunder the coast of Britain, these Germanii were the most skilled and organized warriors to be found for hire. The High King of the Britons, Vortigern, sent envoys to the Germanic chiefs, offering them land in exchange for their services against the northern menace. The Germanics accepted.

They proved as good as their reputation. The mercenaries won stunning victories against the Picts and stemmed the invasion, driving the fearsome tribes back beyond the walls. Then, with their employers' thanks, the Angles, Saxons and Jutes settled into their new holdings in Britain.

It was not long before all-too-predictable troubles arose. Some Britons found that what they'd promised in a time of threat they were reluctant to part with in a time of peace, and attempted to renege on their offers to the Germanics.

Meantime, as more Saxons and Angles poured across the Channel, the lust for conquest endemic in their society was revived, and slight pretexts served for large increases in their lands, with swords held to Britonic necks. Blame belonged to both sides, but most victories belonged to only one.

The experience of Britain was common. All over the old Western Empire, relentless waves of Huns, Franks, Vandals and Goths had transformed Europe from the Pax Romana into a patchwork of kingdoms ruled by Germanic chiefs. It was as if waters that had been lapping against a jetty for centuries were suddenly whipped up by a storm into titanic breakers, which brutally beat at the resisting rock until, section by section, a once-impervious wall crumbled and was swept into the sea. Britain had fared comparatively well in the face of the Germanic invasions, but as had been the case in Gaul and Africa, Italia and Hispania, Britain was expected to be totally overrun, soon, and without much difficulty.

Kieran saw that he had truly been fortunate. It was equally possible an Angle or Saxon could have found him first, and, dressed in the manner he was, that would have meant nothing good.

My life for a clean tunic.

After hours of attention by Kieran's bedside, the family remembered their usual duties and, seeing that he was healthy in body if not mind, dispersed. As quickly as he had been surrounded, Kieran again found himself alone, now armed at least with a name for the land.

Kieran pulled off his blanket and examined his ankle. The mother had done an expert job replacing his splint, and the compound she'd rubbed on his leg, though foul-smelling and unpleasantly oily to the touch, had been restorative.

He unwrapped the bandage and pulled off the splints one by one, taking a significant amount of hair along with one of them, as they had been glued to his ankle for days. He gave his foot a tentative wiggle, and not finding it painful, described a full circle in the air with his toes. There was tightness in the movement, and an ache crept in at the conclusion of the maneuver, but the time had come to test his full weight standing.

Kieran positioned himself to rise from his bed. Slowly he eased himself forward onto his legs, making sure not to favor his healthy one. He stood up. Nothing happened.

He walked a few paces – tiny steps that barely lifted his feet from the ground. He paced the length of the stall and back. He hopped in place. He stood on the balls of his feet. There was discomfort, but nothing to prohibit him walking unaided, and almost no pain.

The joy of possibility rushed upon him, and Kieran began to contemplate his immediate departure. Several concerns, though, stemmed his exuberance and forced him to return to the bed, from which he contemplated his next moves.

His mind ranged over all his options and every contingency he could conceive, from remaining in the permanent care of the family as an adopted son to stealing their possessions at sword point and helping himself to a pony for good measure. Neither of those extremes would serve, for though he did not know who he was, he knew his own mind. The course he had chosen by morning fell somewhere in the middle, a path to freedom without real harm. When the moment came, Kieran rose from his bed and put his first true plan into effect.

Every noise was exaggerated in the still before dawn. The creaking of the stall door when he opened it sounded to him like a tree snapping in half, and each footstep on dew-kissed grass was the splash of a boulder hurled into a lake. The sword was worst of all. To Kieran, the jangle it made hitting against his hip was as loud as the clank of a prisoner's chains.

These sounds only made him increase his pace as he crossed the compound where the family lived. The stall was offset from the clutch of earth-and-plaster buildings the family occupied, on the other side of a fence of thin branches that surrounded the settlement. When he found and slithered through a break in the fencing, he made for what he guessed were storage huts, and once inside, by smell alone, knew he was where he needed to be. He had found the food.

By the time he was done, Kieran had made a noticeable dent in the family's supplies. He took only what three days would require, but soon he had half a sack full of cheese, cured meat and various hardy vegetables and tubers. He nimbly ran to the edge of the woods on his newly-mended leg, and turning, saw that none had witnessed his theft. He was free.

Yet he was not. Looking back from the edge of the compound, with dawn light almost strong enough to reveal him, Kieran saw for the first time the ring of tiny buildings that constituted the family's ramshackle settlement. He saw now the extreme poverty of his hosts, how precarious their existence in the world, little more secure than his own. It took strength to tend to a stranger while so much went untended in their own lives, and this Kieran could not repay so coldly.

He returned to the stall, unbelted his scabbard and laid his sword upon his bed. He laid it neatly and conspicuously, so as to render its meaning of gratitude inescapable. Though he knew he would come to regret his decision, as his belly would be forced to forego food the sword could have purchased, he was at peace when he crossed the yard once again at a near sprint, making the tree line just as the little girl and mother appeared at the door of their hut.

70

There ended the vision. Kieran snapped back to the hilltop above Eilwath, shaking and drained.

It was his dream from the night before, though not confounded by impossibilities as in dreams, for it was a memory. Nor was it just any memory. For a long time, it had been the earliest memory Kieran possessed.

That was WRONG, Kieran thought, closing his eyes again, now in disbelief, and no little anger. *That was no vision. So that's it, then? That mother of nightmares is my destiny? I am shown what I know and want most to forget?*

Forgetting the only sin, a voice within him sounded. It was then the vision came, the true vision of the ritual. Kieran saw before him the thing accomplished – saw the future in his mind's eye, no dream or plan, but a fact, a place laid out waiting for him, for them all to arrive. He saw every step, in succession and at once. He saw even the chance for it to fail, to be a glorious failure. He saw possibility disappear as events unfolded and created certainties. Kieran opened his eyes.

He was staring into the just-emerged sun. He averted his look and blinked away the spots before his sight, and a smile crept over him. From the start Kieran had known he would be tested, from without and within. This was his final test, to push forward without peace of mind, without assurance of success, yet perfect faith in it.

The vision had not come from celestial heaven or the powers of the earth, but from within. What he was forced to see was what haunted him, and now he would assert meaning over the mother of nightmares.

I was given a start not of my choosing, he thought, his breast warming with a sense of joy where clammy fear had been. *The finish I will make myself.*

The instrument and the arm to wield it.

The time for rumination was at an end. With a small groan Kieran lifted himself from his perch and gave his limbs a few stretches, then collected his implements and began down the trail.

The emerging day began to sketch in the familiar shapes of the village and its environs in the valley below. Soft tendrils of light crept over the hills, painting the landscape its proper colors but tinged with orange and pink. Daybreak outlined low huts and long barns, revealed the chessboard of hedgerows and stone walls and fences and fields stretching beyond sight, and picked out individual trees from small forest nearby. Birds began to chatter the trills and chirps that started off each dawn, as shaggy cattle shook awake and lowed, and fires appeared here and there, peeping through the veneer of morning fog like scattered embers through ash. Within minutes the farmsteads were all astir, and the shops in Eilwath came alive with belches of black smoke and the first tentative sounds of industry.

Yes, much to be done, thought Kieran.

The day had come at last.

Chapter Four

Kieran grunted as he lifted the sack from his shoulder and poured the last of the barley crop into his cart. It was the final few bunches from the section that was his to scythe and haul, a plot of growing land which was shorn east to west at season's end, a small sea of bristles.

Though it had been declared the Dark Half of the year by the priests of the Celts, and throughout the former and standing Empire *autumnus* had begun right on schedule, the sun that shone that day cared nothing for these calendars. Lugh's ship burned across the sky with all the intensity of midsummer. Brown blooms of perspiration adorned Kieran's chest and underarms, and he could feel a slick of sweat running down his spine to pool at the base of his back. Grain dust and grit adhered to his damp skin wherever it was exposed, and he sometimes flinched when the stalks rubbed against his forearm, the inside of which was a mass of red bumps from a season's worth of barley heads whipping his skin.

The pain was proof of his work, and for that it was welcome. Kieran felt good despite his brief sleep and long night, fatigued but invigorated, and decided to cede himself a few minutes leaning against the cart. He sighed and massaged a sore shoulder (*More signs of age*), and smiled when his old dray horse, Brecca, noisily shat behind him. He had wanted to finish the last of his acres before sunset, and the glow in the late September sky told him he'd beaten his goal by two hours or more. His muscles ached and his sweat was turning chill against his skin, but he remained leaning there a time, taking the occasion to be between doings for a change.

Kieran let his eyes range over the fields at the acres of the other harvesters, their wheat or barley in various stages of cutting, and his own acres of neatly hewn stalks, a testament to his industry in the last months. Further off were the gentle hills of heather and fern abutting the grain rows, and the deep, tall forest beyond, just coming into color. Birds flitted between the groves and the grain, patterned with expressive plumage: the magpie splashed with pure black and white as bold as its nature; a songbird with a happy yellow breast yet wearing a black hood to remember that death was always stalking; a slick falcon with wings dark silver on top and all mottled russet all underneath. He breathed the air to the base of his lungs. Another season was complete. His last.

He was reluctant to move from that spot, as if with enough will he could make the moment his eternity. The swish of the scythes and the whisper of the barley spines sweeping across each other, accompanied by the humming of a million invisible insects and the far off lowing of the cows, was the music he wanted to hear in the turbulence to come. When he closed his eyes, he wanted to always be able to conjure the shivers of green and gold the wind sent through the fields, and the broad-brimmed hats of the harvesters bobbing among the stalks. The feeling of peace when it had all been cut and carted was irreplaceable, and so Kieran lingered, and let it creep into his pores, savoring it as a man will when he knows he will never see a place again.

There was a sourness in the atmosphere, though, faint but pungent, and even the sight of the idyl before him was not sufficient distraction. The day was beautiful, all was in its place and functioned as best pleased nature and the gods, yet a tension pervaded the fields, the creation and bane of the harvesters that afternoon, as if all the uncertainty and fear and suspicion had been woven into an unseen blanket above that muffled and smothered and weighed down the workers in the grain acres. Kieran had heard enough of what happened at the Mabon ceremony, and this was undoubtedly the unspoken yet palpable aftermath. The prophecies of the sacrifice hovered in the fields like gray haze after a barn fire.

Much work lay ahead, so Kieran lifed the gate on his cart and prepared to get Brecca moving. He knew the moment had truly passed when a group of men walked with purpose toward the crossroads of the cart paths, two tugging a wagon, and the man leading them Pagos. He thanked creation for the seconds of serenity, then cast a blink-quick look over at the knot of Cornovii from beneath his hat brim, sighing at the sight of the inevitable come at last.

Now there's this business, he thought.

"Stay easy, big girl," he cooed softly to Brecca, patting her solid neck. He unhooked his scythe from his belt and laid it in his cart, casually but carefully within sight of all the harvesters, who came from a few different clans but were all now turning to watch what might unfold.

It was obvious even from here that Pagos and his band had broken the proscription against alcohol in the fields. There was sound logic to keeping drunkenness at a minimum among a people prone to grudges, and who toiled many hard hours for little return, while wielding sharp sickles and scythes.

Sound logic indeed.

It was possible from the look and odor of them that they hadn't slept the previous night either. He'd heard them throughout the day whenever he was within earshot, because rather than simply whisper about him as they did when they felt unfriendly, today there was no mistaking what they said.

"Fuckin' foreigner, kick his Saxon ass is what we should do. What any man'd do."

"Defy King Cunomor? The bugger's under his cloak, and don't forget it."

"I'll honor the king's law. But maybe that cloak won't always protect him."

Then Pagos spit in Kieran's direction, and the men moved off to a different part of their acres.

Blowing off steam, Kieran thought at the moment, but didn't quite believe it. What it indicated was that they knew he was planning to leave that day, probably from the sale of his household goods the day before. They knew their only time to act against him was right this moment.

Kieran went to get a drink an hour later at the cart, from a bucket he had brought for all to use, and as he did, Pagos and five of his clansmen stepped into the crossroads. Pagos climbed up the wheel of the cart to stand in its bed, causing water to slosh from Kieran's bucket.

"We have a problem," said Pagos, looking down at Kieran, but only by an inch.

"I hope we can fix it," said Kieran, noticing that half the men still held their cutting implements. Pagos, however, still had his at his side, in accordance with law.

"You keep putting your water bucket on our carts."

"I bring my bucket for everyone in my turn, as do all those who own fields. It is for everyone."

"No, it's for Cornovii, or maybe Dumnonii. But it's not for you. That's our water and our cart."

"Please accept the bucket as a gift."

"You can't give what already belongs to someone else. It's on our property, so it is ours by right."

"Then please accept my apologies."

"Those would be lies, probably, so I don't think I will."

Kieran nodded, and began leading Brecca away, anxious to move on through the dance. Stage two was beginning now.

The Cornovi phalanx shifted into his path and closed ranks. Their faces were emotionless, all except Pagos, who smiled with his lips but whose eyes seemed to pulse with loathing.

"How are you so learned but don't get this concept? Cornovi path is for Cornovii, foreign turd."

"I use it every day," said Kieran, wishing they could shift the discussion to Latin, and aware as he rarely was of his unmasterful Britonic and distinctive accent that he could not seem to lose.

"Everyday you trespass, and we've had enough. You bring misfortune on my clan and homeland, you defile it with your presence, you place yourself above the rightful masters of the Great Peninsula. We've known trouble upon trouble since you arrived, my kin more than most."

"It is the only path."

"To a powerful wizard? That can't be right. And it's not our concern. Go through the woods."

"The river is there."

"Ford it with your fine horse, or cross by some dark trick of magic. You will not step upon our path again."

Some of the reapers were pausing to watch the faceoff. *Even if we went through the woods they'd provoke a confrontation*, he thought. Kieran considered attitudes of the men fanned across the road in front of him. In faces rouged with drink and rage, hands gripping lethal tools ever more tightly, he read that they did not intend to let him leave at all. *At the river maybe, no witnesses, let the water do the work for them… finish the work it almost did once.*

He pondered his options, none good, all bent toward survival and escape at any cost. No way to avoid bloodshed. He looked at his horse and barley crop, the cart with his sickle and scythe, and started to make the old inhuman calculations about gain and efficiency, speed and violence.

Now I feel tired, he thought.

"I am under King Cunomor's protection," said Kieran, "his personal guest in the lands of his dominion." They would take his reminder as an acknowledgement of fear, but Kieran meant it for the ears of the reapers who were watching but not participating. He wanted to keep them that way. "You would risk your lands for me, when I am leaving them before another sun shines?"

"What would I risk, foreigner? I'm a law-following man, and don't ever act against another without being brought to it. Of course, every law from Dumnonia to Egypt says a man can defend himself from a threat."

If there were only three, or four… but six of them. His mind went to the sickle in the back of his cart, miles away since it wasn't within an armlength.

"I give my oath I will not try to harm you," said Kieran. He took his hand off Brecca's bridle. *One move, that's all I get...*

"Your oath is worthless, because I know you will try," Pagos said. "But let's test it."

Pagos hopped down from the cart, and the line of men behind him stepped forward as one. Kieran readied for the flash of metal, then the onslaught. *One move.* His footing was good, but he regretted his hat. Pagos reached to his side, and swung.

"My lord Kieran!"

The voice stopped the scene as if it were a friese. Attention turned toward the main road, from whence the voice boomed. A horse and rider approached, the former large enough to support the bulk of the latter – Grundfyrdd.

"My lord Kieran!" called Grundfyrdd. "A word if you please!"

He'd never been pleased to see the magistrate until that instant. Kieran noted that Pagos's sickle was still in his hand and paused in its downward arc toward Kieran. Seconds passed as they stared at each other before Pagos relented and hooked his blade back onto his belt.

I wouldn't have been fast enough, Kieran thought, with latent dread.

Grundfyrdd was the area tribute collector, ritual ceremony overseer and magistrate for King Cunomor. He looked every inch the role. He had the round belly, bald pate and heavy-browed, scowling face of a man who made old ladies pay their levy without a thought and settled disputes with the dispassion of a knife. Despite his demeanor and the remorseless way he dispatched his duties, though, he was a forthright man, and did not take advantage of opportunities for graft as most other magistrates did.

"I trust your harvest is finished?"

"It is," said Kieran.

"Then journey with me. We have things to discuss."

He turned and began walking his horse back toward the road, never looking at or saying a thing to Pagos and his followers. Kieran did not look back either as he led Brecca forward down the path, which had become unobstructed at Grundfyrdd's approach. When he got to the main crossroads, at the border of woods and fields, he took his sickle from the cart and buried it deep into the wood of a hitching post with a swift stroke. It would make a fine addition to a person's fortune, for the first who dared claim it.

At and down the main road, Kieran saw a large wagon with covered lading, and some men-at-arms in conference with Grundfyrdd. The sight of six trained warriors, who kept looking back toward Kieran, caused him to examine whether exchanging Pagos's crowd for this one had really been a favorable trade. However, a call and signal from Grundfyrdd as they approached sent the wagon and its guards moving down the road. Grundfyrdd slowed his pace.

Kieran looked at the man. The way King Cunomor's man in Eilwath exploited his position was by voicing his thoughts unfiltered on all occasions. He seemed to have one delight in life, which was to say everything as bluntly as possible, especially in situations that called for the most tact. Kieran remembered that when many of the farmers and villagers had been calling for him to be run off into the woods or worse, Grundfyrdd's voice had been one of the loudest for worse. But that, again, was part of a past he was journeying further away from with each turn of the cartwheel.

Looking down from his mount, a massive, ornamented warhorse, Grunfyrdd puffed his chest and said, "You're leaving."

Kieran nodded.

"When?"

"At first light"

"And you're taking that Uleara with you?"

Kieran nodded again.

"Good. I'll say I'm surprised it took this long. I'll also say, even if other folks won't, we'll all be glad to see you gone. It doesn't matter what you've done and who you've done it for, we all know there's something not right about you. People like you only mean trouble for people like us."

Grunfyrdd paused, still glowering at Kieran, then said, "I have a message from King Cunomor."

"Yes?"

"He sends his final thanks for your assistance with the mines. It was more lucrative than he'd imagined, and he says he is glad he spared your life and let you live among us. Though he reminds you that once you leave Dumnonia, all obligation – and protection – from him to you is ended. I don't think I need to explain what that means."

"No." They spent a silent minute, then Kieran asked, "And what of you?"

"What of me what?" barked Grundfyrdd.

"Why did you spare my life? It was quite the coincidence you should happen by, just as Pagos was… seeing me off."

Grundfyrdd glowered for a good space of seconds before answering. "I reckon my boy would've died without you, without what you did, what you gave him. I never said anything. Never thanked you. Now I have."

Grunfyrdd spurred his horse and began to ride away at a trot, visibly embarrassed that his last comment to Kieran was a friendly one. Some distance down the road, his nature overcame his good graces, and he turned his mount back toward Kieran.

"I wouldn't bother King Cunomor at court with your foolishness," he called. "War's broken out, and we all know there are bigger things afoot than whatever your matter before him is." He shook his reins and turned again, hurrying down the road, forcing a group of tradesmen to scramble out of his path. Kieran could only nod his head and smile, thinking how the world would be if more men were made in Grunfyrdd's mold.

Chapter Five

Kieran followed the deeply rutted cart path, leading Brecca and her burden for a
mile or so until they had almost reached the fortified earthen wall that ringed the
village of Eilwath. The emerald grass and moss carpeting the time-worn slopes
of the wall testified to the fact that it had not known an attacker in centuries.
Like every other structure or earthwork in the village – and many of the people –
it seemed to have borne the passing of eons with little concern and less desire to
change.

Change is coming, though, thought Kieran. *They know it now, and they're
scared.* Kieran needed no further confirmation than to see how busy the road
was – busy with carts laden with possessions heaped high, led by people making
their way for the ports. Britonia, the peninsula across the sea near the Frankish
kingdom, was being colonized, and after the previous night's ceremony was sure
to welcome a flood of colonizers fleeing the onslaught of war.

All this news was lost on the mill and granary that stood against the Eilwath
wall, which looked like it had erupted of its own accord from the riverbank. The
three-story oaken cylinder that housed the grain, capped with a conical roof of
cedar and built atop thick posts that kept it off the ground, had once stood erect
and pointing skyward, but the ages had sunk the supports and warped the wood
until the silo now listed and bent radically. It appeared to be a giant crooked
finger jutting from the soil. The mill house attached to the granary was afflicted
in a different manner: its peaked roof sagged in the middle, and the thatching,
which hadn't been replaced in ages, was disintegrating rapidly into greenish
brown muck. This was Kieran's first stop.

He gave a perfunctory knock on the door and let himself in. Navigating through
a cramped and cobwebbed living space, Kieran made his way to the milling

floor, where he found the grainer's wife, Lihane, feeding threshed wheat into the works. Her figure, silhouetted through the haze of grain dust, was small and stooped, but proud, traits both common and fitting among the villagers of Eilwath.

She smiled when she greeted him, but it was a thin smile. The way she batted the thick black hair from her eyes, and her halting gait down the steps to where he stood, spoke of a woman intensely strained. Part of it was always there in her, born of life with a perpetually empty womb and a husband who beat her daily for it. Part of it, Kieran recognized, was that she was alone with him.

She was prompt in retrieving his sum for the season: a large leather purse stuffed with high-value coins, as he had requested.

"Heavy, innit?" she said quietly and with a blink-fast smile as she handed it over, not meeting his eyes.

"To be lightened again all too soon," said Kieran.

She was still not looking in his direction, but something in her manner was different than usual, even if she knew, as apparently did everyone, that he was departing. Lihane did not have to stoop far to pick up a short stool, but stretched herself full height with visible pain to reach a cupboard above the counting table. She retrieved a pouch like the one she'd given him, only smaller, then carefully clambered back to the ground and shuffled forward. Lihane met his eyes for the first time.

"This is for our friend," she said in a near-whisper, though the mill was loud and they were alone. She seemed convinced in some inner place that her husband could hear and see her even when he shouldn't have been able to, which doubtless was how he intended her to feel. However, she managed a true smile when she said, now almost to herself, "For his faithful."

"I will give it to him," said Kieran, laying the jingling pouch in his satchel next to its larger sibling. Something changed in her then, or at least in her figure. Lihane seemed to straighten, and a decade came off her face.

"I was married before," she said. "He wasn't very handsome, but he was strong, and he knew how to make me smile. I loved him truly, and I know he loved me. We had a child, the boy's life thread was severed soon after his birth cord." A few years returned to her look. "It was early summer, and were hoping to fill our larders for three come harvest." She stopped, trying to keep her composure. "Before the harvest my husband was taken by a Saxon blade. They said he fought well. His comrades carried him home, and the sight... the sight of him..."

Lihane choked up, but no tears came.

"Devlyn has never gotten me with child. He says I am barren, that no man in his line has ever failed to plant seed. But it cannot be. I would have had a warren of little ones if not for the war. The war killed more than men, it killed futures, killed children before they were conceived. And now it will happen to more futures, leave more widows to be beaten, with husbands whose loins aren't fertile."

Lihane looked very deeply into Kieran's eyes then. "That should never happen to another. I don't know what you are doing at Glevuna, and I don't even know if you are a good or true man. But if there is power in you as they say, and a noble heart as well, then you will stop this war. Yes?"

It was taking all of her overtaxed strength to hold her composure.

"This story I know too well," said Kieran. "It is a bleak heart that wishes others to live a tale of that kind. I am not such a one."

Lihane ventured a very rare, very soft touch of his arm.

"Brighid favor your journey," she said, turning her dark brown, time-blackened eyes to meet his. Kieran saw they contained a tender look of sympathy he was certain took effort to project. It reassured him that people are not slaves to their personas; that they can always surprise, by choosing other than the routine. He to her from the doorway and ducked under the threshold, continuing his final day in Eilwath.

He rolled at a crawl through the village, riding behind his horse in the now unladen cart, passing the hamlet's low, circular buildings, which the folks of the village painted in white or red. He knew each one of the huts, barns, sheds and storage pits of Eilwath as intimately as if they'd been in his own yard, and as he rode by them all, winding through the handful of broadly curving dirt paths that comprised the streets of the settlement, he was overwhelmed with the associations he'd formed with them, good and ill, but in hindsight all ultimately to the good.

Then there were the villagers themselves, peeping out from windows and doorways, or pausing in their outdoor labors to watch him leave. He waved to everyone he saw, his neighbors and acquaintances of seven years, regardless of whether they waved back or simply stared: the family of men in the tinsmith's shop, the tanner and his apprentice, the weavers' daughters, and others, all of whom he knew, but not in the way they knew one another. None embraced him or showed him particular fondness – none even came up to his cart. It was as if he were leaving for the night rather than forever. Some exchanged good wishes with him, but it did not escape his notice that most of their farewells contained a hint of relief. However, Kieran was more understanding of their attitude than he was wounded by it. On the precipice of the undertaking ahead, he was in a mood to leave the ill will of the past, at least the recent past, behind him. However, there was one more confrontation left him – the one he dreaded most of all.

"Good day, my lord" said a group of mud-caked children he passed at a crossroads near the abbey. They were four members of a five-member gang: Two brothers, Eoin and Bannan, along with their cousin, a dull youth named Luvox, and a fourth boy, Aelfarn. Their reputation in the village was as the mischief makers, though none more deserved nor reveled in that distinction.

The brothers, Eoin and Bannan, were middle children of a family of low social standing. Their father made bad deals for their crops that left them nearly penniless, then he drunkenly offended a man from a neighboring tribe who was the son of a chieftain. The amount that was demanded in recompense was more than the family could pay, so it was taken in land. The father died suddenly thereafter and left a widow with five children, none of whom she could look after while she courted another husband.

They were beaming as they gathered around Kieran, for they knew interesting things were likeliest to happen in his presence. All the children of Eilwath treated Kieran with affectionate awe, as they had heard he was a wizard. If anything, the wonder with which the children beheld Kieran only fueled their parents' antipathy toward him, but given the choice between having the friendship of the adults or the regard of their children, Kieran's preference was clear.

"Have you been behaving?" he asked the eager upturned faces.

"Yes!" they cried in unison.

"Really?"

They looked at one another, until Bannan said, "Eoin stole Dunnach's clothes when he was swimming, but he was sorry later."

Eoin curled his lip at his younger brother and punched his arm.

"Have you seen the lady Boudicca today at her stall?" asked Kieran.

"I saw her there," said Bannan.

"Is she alone?"

Can I really do this? Kieran asked himself. *Must I?*

"She's…"

"Wait," said Eoin. "What'll you give us if you tell? Maybe we shouldn't."

Kieran smirked. "How does this sound?" he said. "I bet you I can hold three kings and three bears in my bag, and if I win, will you tell me?"

"THAT bag?" exclaimed Eoin, looking at his satchel. "No way."

"Then it's a bet?"

"Sure!" the brothers said, while Aelfarn stood by sullenly. *Speaking with him will be difficult too.*

Kieran made great theater of rummaging in the satchel before he pulled out three of the coins within. "See?" he said, handing one to each. "A king on one side, and a bear on the other."

"Hey, you tricked us!" squealed Bannan.

"Did I? I'm sorry. I suppose I'll be having those back then…"

As he reached for Eoin's coin, the lad pulled his hand back, and said, "Okay, you win. We saw Boudicca, she's been at the stall all day. The kids are there too."

"And her husband?"

Aelfarn snorted, disgusted. He was old enough to know why Kieran asked.

"Didn't see him," said Eoin. "Could be fishing."

Eoin was turning the little disk in his hands, entranced. Each coin was made of burnished bronze, stamped instead of molded to create smooth edges, and they shone brightly. They bore the profile of Aurelian on the obverse, his head crowned with a laurel in the Roman fashion.

"I won't be seeing you anymore," said Kieran, "so you boys be good to your mothers, and don't get in too many fights. Most things in life aren't worth it. Hear me?"

The brothers nodded automatically, though they barely heard, intent as they were on the treasures in their hands. Aelfarn paid no attention to his coin, and instead gave Kieran a defiant look.

"Alright then. Run along now. Except Aelfarn."

"Bye!" the brothers cried, running off to brag of their good fortune to the children in the village. Kieran knew it would give the parents another cause to

89

curse his name, but that was no concern now. Aelfarn did remain, but it was clear he wished to be anywhere else.

Aelfarn's family was estranged from its clan, and one of the poorest around. Kieran and the Abbot Uleara had taken him as a protégé of sorts, after he'd come to the Cairn Church begging on behalf of his parents. The boy made up for his lack of material wealth with immense academic talent and an abundance of curiosity. With no status at stake and no supervision at home, Aelfarn was free to spend time up at the abbey, helping with upkeep and chores in exchange for lessons in Latin, music and philosophy from the Abbot, and tutoring in herbs, compounds, mechanics, astronomy and other natural phenomena from Kieran. "I told you this was going to happen."

Aelfarn didn't respond, but instead picked up a stick and mindlessly poked it at the road.

"You and I will see each other again. Maybe soon."

"You can't promise that," came the boy's sullen reply.

At twelve years old, the skinny, shaggy-haired youth was at the exit of childhood, but not yet through the door. He averted his eyes and worked to hold back his emotions.

"I'm almost certain," Kieran said. "Meantime, you must continue your lessons. Wherever the abbot may be, seek him out."

"Mother says I can't spend with him anymore on account of I got to earn my keep. It's like she says. I can't earn my keep with the abbot."

Kieran wanted to contradict him, but there were more pressing concerns, and time was growing short. Anticipating Kieran's next question, Aelfarn withdrew a folded and sealed parchment from his tunic. "I did what you told me to." As if signing his own execution order, Aelfarn handed the message to Kieran.

"Does the abbot know about it?"

"No."

"Did you read what was in that envelope?" asked Kieran, though he could see for himself the wax was intact.

Aelfarn looked down, but when he raised his eyes again, there was fury in them. "No. But I did ask! I asked Abbot Uleara about 'a message' and he didn't know what I was talking about! That's how I know you don't want him to know about it – that you're hiding something."

Kieran ignored this momentarily, and cracked the seal. He read the short note within several times. *The die is cast.*

"What does it say?" asked Aelfarn.

Kieran considered his response, then handed the parchment to the boy. "Read it yourself."

Aelfarn did read it, becoming more and more consternated as he did.

"I don't understand – what does it mean? 'The beast will hunt before its moon?'"

"It means I need to go."

Aelfarn thought. "It means there will be war no matter what," he said, "and you're part of it."

Kieran sighed. "War is always inevitable, one just needs to wait long enough. But yes, nothing can stop the death that is going to come to our lands."

"So why do you need to go?"

"To see if it can mean something."

"I don't understand," said the boy hopelessly. Kieran put a hand on his shoulder.

"No matter what your mother says, I want you to promise you will keep up your studies," said Kieran. When Aelfarn did not respond, Kieran asked, "Do you remember what we talked about? The keepers of the light?"

"Yeah."

"You are one. You are a keeper of the light."

Aelfarn momentarily brightened, but said, "No. That's just a," he searched briefly, "metaphor."

"Sometimes it is," said Kieran, "but it can also mean something very real indeed. Have I ever lied to you?" Aelfarn considered briefly, but shook his head. "Then you must believe me now. It is important that you remain with Uleara, because you, Aelfarn, are important."

"It doesn't feel like I'm important," said Aelfarn.

"You may not for a while, but it's true." Kieran saw his protégé was revived in his spirits, and smiled. "Pain gets better. Things get easier. But we must endure the pain and suffer the hardship before that happens."

Aelfarn's face went through many expressions, but he said nothing. Kieran patted his shoulder.

"I will see you again, and until then I will keep you in my heart and mind. I... care about you, Aelfarn. I always will."

Kieran could do nothing more but begin walking back toward where Brecca was tied. Before he reached her, he felt skinny arms girdle his waist from behind as Aelfarn ran up to him and hugged him tightly. "I'll keep going to see the abbot," the boy whispered. "I promise, I'll do what you said." Aelfarn never saw how widely his mentor smiled in that moment, for Kieran kept going. He had to keep going.

Chapter Six

As the children had said, Boudicca was at her family's roadside produce stall - and alone.

If anyone but Kieran had been watching Boudicca's face when she turned to see him standing in front of the stall, it would have been instantly obvious what existed between them. Boudicca put down the bushel of small purple carrots she was carrying and advanced a bit toward Kieran, never taking her eyes off him. Kieran advanced toward her a ways too, and they stood without speaking for a long stretch of seconds, just looking at each other, endlessly communicating what could not have been voiced.

Kieran at last moved forward to close the gap between them, but Boudicca backed away, and with a sly smile adopted a businesslike demeanor and took her place at the stall facing the road.

"Good day, m'lord Kieran," she said in the sing-song lilt of a shopkeeper. "It's been a fair while since we've had the pleasure."

Kieran returned her smile, and took his place as customer. They had played the scene out many times before, and Boudicca had commenced the closing performance.

"That it has, dear lady," he said. "And a thousand pardons for it."

"Thought you might have forgotten us," she said, thrusting out her hip and giving a slight pout. Kieran's smile broadened.

"No, I didn't forget."

They stared at each other for a few silent seconds more, until Boudicca said, "So sir, what is your pleasure this fine day?"

"I believe I'll have the usual."

"Forgive me sir, it's been so long. Could you remind me again what your usual is?"

"Surely you remember my fondness for that delicious sloe pie of yours."

"Oh of course," she said. She moved her hand from her hip to her mouth, and gave an exaggerated "Hmm." "You know, I don't think we have any up here, m'lord," she said, locking eyes with Kieran again.

"You never did seem to remember to keep them stocked at the stall."

"I guess some things never change. Well and of course I haven't served that particular dish in quite some time, you know."

Boudicca dropped the rigidity of her shopkeeper role and walked from behind her stall in a slinky saunter, showing fully how good she still looked.

"I didn't know that," said Kieran.

"There may be some back in the store house. I'd be happy to go get some if you like."

"I don't want to trouble you."

"Oh no," she said, standing inches in front of him, close enough that he could see the discolored dot in her left iris, the imperfection that perfected the blue-green pool around it. He could feel her breath. "It's no trouble. Only, sometimes it takes me a while to find it, you see."

"Well it seems only right that I should help you find it. Since I'm putting you to the trouble."

"Like I told you," said Boudicca, taking Kieran's hand in hers and, with a thorough look around for the prying eyes of others, pulling him in the direction of the store house, "it's no trouble at all."

Boudicca kicked the shed door closed and grabbed Kieran in a mad embrace, fingers searching insatiably over his skin. He held her, held her tight, but when she pressed her lips into his, Kieran did not yield. He let her discover it, her kiss trailing off as she stepped back from him. She looked into his face with hurt, with longing thwarted. With a step forward he swept her back into his arms, and held her close again, smelling her hair, feeling the heat of her mingle with his. She clung on tight. Minutes passed as hours while Kieran and Boudicca shared the last act of their affair, chaste though it was. Neither one wanted to give it an ending.

Finally, they unlatched and sank to the floor, but kept each other close. "I really did think you were going to forget," said Boudicca, nestling into Kieran's shoulder and squeezing his fingers in hers.

"I wouldn't ever forget."

"I always knew you would leave. I didn't know when, but I knew it." She snuggled closer. "Have you seen Aelfarn yet?"

"Yes."

Kieran brushed a wave of strawberry blond hair from her large light eyes. Time and a half dozen offspring had not robbed those eyes of their childlike delight, though the hardness of life had imprinted crow's feet at their edges and dark crescents below them, which grew deeper by the year.

Perhaps because she had been reflecting thoughts much the same, Boudicca tugged at Kieran's beard and said, "There's more gray than there used to be."

"Is that a bad thing?"

She thought for a moment. "No. I think it makes you look like an elder, or a war chief." A pained expression came to her face, and she turned to him. "I don't care that I won't see you again. I mean, of course I care, but I wouldn't try to stop you leaving. I just don't want to have to worry about you. It's alright that you aren't here as long as you're somewhere, or... that doesn't make sense, but do you understand?"

Kieran pulled her to him more tightly.

"You don't ever need to worry about me."

She sighed, half contented, half anxious. "But I do."

There was a thud from just outside the barn door, which had swung back partially open, and both Kieran and Boudicca startled. They rose and went to look – the bottom half of the entryway was occupied by Daweth, Boudicca's second-youngest son, who was bent over searching on the ground. He stood and turned to look at them with a blank expression. He was holding a pear. His features betrayed no judgment of the scene, yet his eyes revealed that he knew something perhaps even the two embarrassed adults did not. Daweth was an observant but withdrawn child, and his quick wits were already apparent at the age of six, but only on those occasions when he elected to show them.

Unconsciously Boudicca adjusted her clothing.

"Were you trying to find me?"

"Da wants to know where you are and how are we supposed sell food with nobody here," said the boy, who continually shot flash-quick glances at Kieran.

"This is Kieran."

"Hello Daweth."

"Hi."

Boudicca beckoned the youth over and drew his head to her bosom, kissing the spot on top that his hair spiraled out from, and said, "Tell Da I'm just taking care of a customer and will be back shortly."

Daweth nodded at his mother, gave Kieran a long, searching stare, and ran off toward the stall by the road. Boudicca's look when she turned back to Kieran was too complex for him to penetrate.

"He's been playing with that pear all day," she said, not wanting to say anything real. "Lugh knows where he got it." She broke into a fragile, bittersweet smile.

"Boudicca…" Kieran began, but she stopped him with a shake of her head.

"Well sir," she said, her eyes shining with nascent tears, "it appears I'm being called away. Did you find everything to your satisfaction?" Her lower lip began to tremble as if straining under the weight of her smile, and all at once she broke down, burying her face in her hands and heaving with uncontrollable sobs. She collapsed into Kieran's chest, and he cradled the back of her head and stroked her between her shoulders. She soon recovered herself, sniffling sharply and rubbing the tears off her face.

"I don't want you to leave."

"Please don't make your last words to me a lie. You don't have to explain anything. Just kiss me. Allow me to let you go."

He did as she commanded, kissing her deeply, consumingly. Their lips strained to stay pressed together when at last Boudicca slowly pulled away, and stepped back.

"Goodbye, Kieran the mysterious stranger. May the gods and spirits and heroes of yore bless your purpose and journey."

Kieran stood mutely before her, searching for a suitable thing to say. When he gave up, he reached into the purse Lihane had given him and pulled out a stack of coins. He tried to press it into her hand, but she pulled it away.

"What is this?"

"It's for Daweth."

"I already told you, he isn't..."

"I know. So use it for all the children, use it for yourself... it doesn't matter. There's enough for all of you. Please take it."

They locked eyes again, and, as if in a hypnotic state, she slowly stretched out her arm and let Kieran fill her palm with silver and bronze.

"I'll have Uleara send word when he returns in spring," said Kieran. He saw the look this produced, and added, "It will be excellent news. I promise you."

They embraced again, exchanged their parting words, but it was unnecessary. They had made their farewell, and now it was simply a matter of Kieran leaving, which he did quickly and without a backward look.

Chapter Seven

As he dug in the garden, by the stone he'd left to mark the burial spot, Kieran allowed himself to admire his house, the fruit of his own craftsmanship. He had gotten help, to be sure – from villagers who thought it would either demonstrate good will or repay an obligation (to Cunomor, not to Kieran). It was known as a half-timbered house, built on a solid foundation of granite and cement, with thick oak beams at angles that reinforced one another, sandwiched between walls of clay and covered over with plaster. Common in other climes and times, it was unlike any house a Dumnonian would think or want to build – and that was much of the point. Kieran wanted no undue closeness to the villagers, for, as that morning had demonstrated, closeness of any kind could get him killed.

A man can feel lonely even if he courts it, thought Kieran, flashing on the last image of Boudicca he would behold.

The house would soon be occupied by Deargh, the firstborn son of a prominent family that controlled (on Cunomor's behalf) the tin mines nearby, and who was soon to marry a girl of equally prominent family that controlled the port at the mouth of the River Fawey. He was a charming lad, owing to his utter lack of physical appeal (lame-foot and large overbite), and terrified that his new bride would feel uncomfortable in so uncosmopolitain a place as Eilwath – her port town boasted nearly a thousand souls.

Deargh offered a tremendous sum for the house, greater than Kieran judged it worth. When Kieran refused let him buy it and instead presented the house as a wedding gift, Deargh summoned the strength in his stringy frame to lift Kieran off the ground with his embrace. *He treated me as if I were human*, thought Kieran. He looked up at the impressive structure again. *If I hadn't given it to Deargh I would have had to burn it to the ground.*

101

Kieran's fingers closed around what they sought in the dirt, a four-foot-long oblong box. He did not open it, knowing well what was inside. It contained an ancient pain and the hinge of the future. But it was not time to contemplate such things, so he simply ran his fingertips over the lacquered wood, wiping the soil of seven years off the wood's agate-like sking, then gently, slowly, he lifted the box and carried it to his cart. There he wrapped it in a layer of blanket and secured below the rest the supplies he was taking, filled in the hole in the garden, took one last look around his former home, and left it for good.

Up a path of rough stone steps, near the summit of Cairn Mount, was the church itself. It was simply a large, round house with a rectangular apse sticking from its side and a few neighboring outbuildings. A large tin cross above its door was all that advertised it as a church, but it provided ample room for the flock of nine believers (Kieran was included but not a true convert) who gathered Sunday evenings and at high noon on feast days to worship.

The namesake of Cairn Mount stood on a patch of even ground at the very summit of the peak. The *cairn* was a mound of rocks shaped like a man, and as tall as two. Monolithic legs of marble supported a body of stacked slate, on top of which were balanced the smooth, flat river stones that created the head. Nobody knew who had constructed it, or when. Local lore incorporated a range of speculations, but the most prevalent was that the cairn had once been a giant who made unwelcome advances on the earth goddess and was turned to stone as punishment. Cairn Mountain was seen as a place of ominous energies that should be generally avoided, which made it one of the few locations Abbot Uleara could build his church without invoking the villagers' ire.

Kieran pulled into the small courtyard of the abbey as dusk fell, and climbed down from the cart to tie up Brecca near the trough. The door of the abbey was closed against the gathering night wind, and Kieran knocked loudly.

"Who goes?" called the abbot from within.

"You know who it is."

"Eh?"

"Open up."

"Is that you, Muriel? Wait a few moments while I put on my clean breeches."

"It's damned cold out here."

"Is that any way for a lady to talk?"

"Uleara!"

The door swung open and there stood Abbot Uleara, howling with laughter. His cherubic face was ruddier than usual, and not simply from laughter; his eyes were bleary and his breath sharply sweet. Kieran got a sinking feeling that the day's trials were not yet behind him.

"How long have you been drinking?" Kieran asked in Latin.

"Me? Drinking? I couldn't conceive of the thought," the abbot answered back in the same tongue. "And I must say I've never seen you so lovely, Muriel."

The abbot laughed again, causing his chins to jiggle, and ushered Kieran inside. Uleara's manner was jolly as ever, befitting his boyish pink face and rotundity, but there was a briskness in his movement and a tension in his laugh that indicated he was forcing his jocularity. He handed Kieran a steaming goblet.

"Cider, hot and spiced."

"*Gratias tibi ago*," Kieran said as they locked arms for the first swig, an automatic and unbreakable custom.

"I'll tell you, my friend," said the abbot, wiping foam from his lips and rising from his seat, "of all your contributions to the life of Eilwath, and to my personal emolument, none outmatches your cache of cinnamon, and its use as a spice. I can't even remember now when it was used as a medicine, much less what it was used for when we could get it."

"It wasn't my discovery."

"Regardless. I thank you. And the town thanks you, even if you won't ever hear it from those ingrates."

"I might not act any differently in their situation. Some of my activities have been... hard to take."

"Gah!" said Uleara, bending to stoke the fire in the main hearth, beneath a spit that held two rabbits roasting. "Don't defend them. I've known these people my entire life. And you don't need to hide your feelings about them around me. I know how they are."

He laughed again, too loud, failing to conceal the tightness behind it.

"If only they knew the whole story," the abbot continued, "though of course I myself don't even know it entirely. I'll tell you though, Kieran," he said, becoming earnest, "it was none of your learning, talents, powers, what have you, that made them fear you. It's that you never used it in the way they would have. It's that you went and sowed and harvested grain every year for Lihane and that husband of hers when you could have bought every acre you tended and hired ten workers to take your place."

"I like to work the fields."

"See, that's the sort of talk that's earned you your reputation. Believe me, Kieran, it is no accident we are such fast friends. No one else will have us.

"Here I am," continued Uleara, looking up at Kieran while he distractedly worked the fire with a poker, "a Christian in a pagan land, an outsider in my own birthplace. I have been to Hibernia and Gaul and the lands of the Picts, and that sort of travel shows on a person, especially to people who have never been more than twenty miles from the boundary of their village. I know what it's like to be whispered about."

"At least you have the advantage of being related to half the village."

"Like it or not," snorted the abbot. "Not even the good half."

Kieran scanned the abbey, which was only one long room with a high, peaked ceiling, that dog-legged into an annex at the far end. Everything was in its usual place, from Kieran's books and charts to the abbot's five-stringed lyre to the positions of the pieces on the *latrunculi* board from their ongoing game.

"Blast this fire!" called out the abbot from across the room, frustrated by his inability to stoke the flame. "It never gets warm enough in here in the winter." He poked one of the rabbit carcasses. "Should do for the rabbits though."

"I told you, I should have fashioned you a hypocaust."

"Is that another one of your marvels?"

"No," laughed Kieran. "It's a system that creates hot air beneath the floor. I told you, the Romans used them for centuries. I have one in my own house. Of course," he continued, "no need to worry about that now. Nobody will be here to mind the cold."

The abbot sat down and reclined, drinking deeply from his cup and wiping at a grease spot on his tunic, but with a troubled look that had nothing to do with the stain.

Kieran rose to inspect his papers, keeping Uleara in the corner of his eye. He could tell the abbot had been going over his scrolls, trying as always to decipher the language and symbols he used. It was Uleara's curiosity that prompted Kieran to keep the sword and scabbard at his own house rather than the abbey, where he kept most everything else concerning his work.

"I saw Lihane today," said Kieran.

"Yes?" said the abbot, straightening. For all of the history, philosophy, poetry and natural studies he and Kieran would discuss far into the night, Lihane was indisputably the abbot's favorite subject. He kept his longing for her poorly hidden, though, which led to no end of sorrow for the grainer's wife. For every attention she received from the abbot, she received it tenfold from her husband in large-fisted blows.

"It was to collect my earnings, for the journey," said Kieran.

"Of course," said Uleara with an uncertain twinge. He quickly asked, "How is she?"

"Well, as always. She's a special woman. I see it now, why you feel as you do." Kieran savored a small moment of anticipation before he said, "And she gave me this for you." He handed Uleara the coin, who marveled at it much as the children had, though for a very different reason. "For your faithful, she said."

"Oh Kieran, I do believe some day the Lord will bring our paths to a more satisfying meeting, if it be His will. I do believe I would miss seeing her in the village if I went to Glevuna."

Uleara, falling deeper into his cups, didn't realize the way he had phrased the statement, but Kieran did.

Uleara suddenly brightened, and said, "Speaking of which, you should have heard Dierdre at the bakers' kilns yesterday. Naturally they have heard of your, our, trek, and she just let fly." Uleara raised his voice to a high, willowy pitch and quoted: "'You tell the Golden Prince that it's all fine and well for him to march against them invaders and the like, now that he's full king, and we're all behind our good Cunomor and trust his will be a wise voice at the council table, but you tell him, Aurelian that is, that out here on the Peninsula we'd no sooner have a meddling boy king from some arrogant Romanish tribe miles away than all the Saxon hordes you please."

"You have her perfectly," said Kieran, laughing.

While Kieran continued laughing, the troubled look returned to Uleara's face.

"I'd say Dierdre feels the way most of them do, though, don't you?" said Uleara. "In Eilwath I mean. And you'd probably hear the same talk among a lot of our kin on the Peninsula, and certainly the Catuvellauni and their allies."

"Yes, I expect you're right."

"About not wanting to be subjects to someone else's king."

Kieran nodded.

"He is scarce twenty years old and yet has the temerity to see himself made high king."

"His father was immensely respected, and to all reports did an admirable job preparing Aurelian to credit the family in his own reign," said Kieran.

"But Aurelian is not his father," Uleara rejoined. "It's remarkable, that one who was a child five years past would command every man of the Britons with a few nods at the council table. I'll grant, by kinship or treaty he has the allegiance of most of the chiefs on the island and leads an army of thousands. Yet he is untested. He is... unknown."

Kieran knew what Uleara was gathering the spine to suggest, but he said nothing.

"I was thinking," said the abbot, "how do we know Aurelian will receive us? He could just as easily have us hanged as Germanic spies. It isn't as if you've lost your accent. And your reputation... you *think* it will compel an audience, but aren't kings jealous in their power? Perhaps these perils haven't occurred to you, but..."

Kieran sat down beside Uleara and looked at him, but still held silent.

"Kieran, why don't we forget this business?" The abbot grasped his friend's arm. "I have an invitation to Riems from one of the friars there. We could go on pilgrimage. They are gathering a great many scholars and Christian ministers to the Frankish court, and I am certain you would be welcome."

The abbot pressed on when Kieran maintained his silence, but with an air of fading hope.

"Yes, it would be good to shake off the dust of Eilwath for a time. Not for a paltry prize like Glevuna, but a Continental court. And after, who knows?" Uleara grew louder, but not bolder. "We could keep going, take a pilgrimage to Rome… though those roads haven't been safe since the Sacking. To Constantinople? Anywhere you want."

Kieran could see the fear in his friend's eyes, and adopted an understanding tone.

"Even if I could, I wouldn't do it without you." said Kieran. "It's not so easy to find a Christian around here, much less one who can recite his Latin declensions forwards and backwards with enough cider in his head to fell an ox."

Abbot Uleara smiled despite himself, but it melted as snow on a hearthstone.

"They only say Aurelian's a believer," said the abbot. "He may have accepted baptism, but he still stocks his counsel with man of the heathen gods. He is an ambitious young king, and I wager you'll find a crown in his heart where Christ should be. Kieran," he said thickly, "whyd'n you stay here? You can be my rector. We'll build the Cairn Church into a congregation to rival St. Peter's."

"You'll have to convert me first."

"Blast you!" shouted the abbot, gaining his feet. Kieran was startled. He had only seen Uleara angry once or twice, and if he hadn't he would have thought the emotion impossible in his friend. Yet the abbot was suddenly burning, eyes alight with rage. "Ever since Aurelian rose to prominence the only things that seem to live in your mind are your blasted innovations and the blasted court at

Glevuncaster… and the blasted barley harvest! And when I dare press you on why it's so urgent you have an audience with the great Golden Prince, all I get in answer is, 'I have plans.' As if I don't have plans – as if we all don't have plans! My plans are to spread the word of Christ through the heathen reaches, but you have precious little regard for that. Instead you'd have me trail you like a spaniel to Aurelian's court without deigning to let me know why. It's outrageous."

Kieran stared without expression at his friend for an instant, then rose and walked over to the wall that held his books and scrolls. Carefully he began putting the scrolls in leather and wood cylinders and capping each one tightly.

"What are you doing?" asked Uleara, the anger sapped.

"If you won't accompany me I won't compel you. But I'm leaving at first light and I'd like to be prepared."

The abbot continued to watch Kieran, his temperature lowering with each second. Kieran did not look up, but instead conscientiously collected and packed seven years' worth of notes, sketches and diagrams in their cases.

"I will tell you, my lord, neither your plans nor mine count for so much as the flutter of a gnat's wings before the mind of God," Uleara said, though weakly. "He will make the plans, and we will follow them, whatever our own desires might be."

Uleara took a drink, but only a small one, and sat. His complexion had greened to where Kieran thought he'd be sick at any moment, and his mouth hung slack as he slumped over his bulging middle. But the abbot continued, after a long pause, "No, I tell you, I won't go. Find another Christian to offer up to his highness. Aelfarn and I will do very well without you."

Kieran continued packing.

"Just tell me this," the abbot said after a gulf of several silent minutes, all of the fight now gone from his voice, "are you doing this because it is what you believe is right, or is it merely vengeance?" He waited, then said: "How large does Freya loom in your designs?"

The name hit Kieran like a slung stone. He paused in his packing, and stared blankly, unseeing, at one of the scrolls before him. It took him some moments to reply.

He said faintly, "I can't remember what she looked like." He paused again, but added nothing.

Uleara seemed to regret his words. After years of friendship, Kieran still had only offered the abbot fragments of his past, amounting to no more than a tenth of his story, and very little of it cohesive. *To a purpose*, Kieran assured himself.

"Kieran," the abbot pressed, "stay here. This is folly driven by an old pain that you cannot or will not salve. A great friend you have been, and your powers, your learning – I admit it, I am in their thrall. But kings are no respecters of any power but their own. You approach this mission of yours with an assuredness that you cannot honestly come by, unless you now claim prophecy among your talents."

Kieran looked now at Uleara with the soft confidence that had compelled his friend to agree to many of his ideas – including his project to build a workshop next to the abbey's stable and stock it with a number of objects whose uses were still unknown to the abbot.

"I have something to show you," said Kieran.

111

The flame of the lantern was nearly carried away by the wind several times as Kieran and Uleara made the short but perilous trip to the workshop. It was set off from the abbey by a few dozen yards of uneven terrain, and a bridge of planks spanning a narrow cut in the mountainside. The workshop was small, little larger than a two-horse stable, and made more cramped still by the vast assortment of glass containers, metal instruments and objects of mysterious origin that filled narrow shelves and a work table in the center of the space. It was difficult enough for one person to operate in the workshop, but with two people there, especially when one was as spherical as the abbot, every movement had to be carefully calculated so as not to cause disaster.

Uleara positioned himself in a corner to keep from interfering with his friend, his girth and the cider working against him. Kieran lit another lamp, sparking to life dozens of little lights reflected in the many glass and metal articles around the room, and moved a crate of scrap metal from the lid of a chest in the opposite corner. He unlocked the clasp and lifted a small object, draped in velvet, from the trunk, gently as if it were a newborn child.

"Move that," said Kieran, indicating a rack of small jars on the work table. The abbot did as he was told, though nearly elbowed a portable lathe from its shelf in the process, and Kieran put the object in the center of the table.

"Come close," said Kieran.

The abbot inched sidelong to stand next to his friend, who gave him an impish smile, made ghastly by the dim lantern light, and yanked off the velvet covering. A soft glow of ultramarine filled the workshop, and the abbot's mouth fell open. Kieran could see an expression of almost religious awe grip Uleara as the shimmering light played on his face.

"My God."

"That is what I have for Aurelian."

The abbot continued to stare, agape, then suddenly stood straight up and hastened, as much as his corpulence made possible in the confined room, for the door.

"Where are you going?" asked Kieran.

"Dawn is only hours off," the abbot replied, grinning like a child, "and I have much to do before we leave."

PART II

Chapter Eight

Kieran was dancing as hard as he could, even while a pudgy eight-year-old boy poked a stick between his ankles to trip him up. The pantomime troupe, its members grotesquely masked or brightly painted, performed just a few steps to his left, but were upstaging him by a far sight. Kieran anxiously looked over as the gaggle performed in time to the musicians' playing, executing its mix of acrobatics and comedic gags without flaw.

He turned his eyes to the *thane*, or warrior chief, and the knot of troops and attendants surrounding him, for whose benefit the duel between his act and theirs was being staged. The thane was a large man in all features and dimensions, made larger by the layers of armor and boar's hide piled on his chest and shoulders, and though his warriors varied in size and appearance, all looked able and prepared to commit any act of violence imaginable. These men, and the men and women who served in their households, watched from the shade beneath a copse of trees.

Kieran noted with alarm that the pantomime performers were drawing more and more of the attention of the thane and his assembled coterie in the audience, and that meant Kieran's chance of winning the bushel of food the warrior chief would award to the more amusing act was growing slimmer.

That means I'll be growing even slimmer too, he thought.

The pantomimes completed a complex series of leapfrogs and tumbles that culminated in a fart gag. It had the thane's men howling in laughter. Few eyes now remained on Kieran, and he perceived boredom encroaching on the merry expression of the thane, which indicated that he was about to declare an end to

117

the contest. That was when Kieran leapt forward with what he hoped would prove to be his trump card.

"WARRIORS YES WARRIORS, HER-BA-HEE-DA-LA! WARRIORS GREAT WARRIORS, DAR DE GLUFF BAR HAR!"

Kieran sang badly out of tune intentionally and at the top of his lungs, and did such a vigorous dance to accompany it that he unwittingly kicked the stick back into the face of the bratty boy trying to trip him, who instantly burst into tears. The attention of the warrior chief's band again swung Kieran's way, and as he finished another round of his approximation of the song he'd heard the clans sing dozens of times, he ended his performance with a pratfall that genuinely hurt his ass. The thane and his men stomped their feet and roared with approval, while the pantomime troupe contemplated defeat for the first time. The thane waved his arms to signal the contest ended, and summoned Kieran and his competition toward him.

He drew out the tension of the moment, moving first as if to hand the bushel of food to Kieran, then to the pantomime troupe, then Kieran again. He held the basket aloft, and with a look of tremendous moment placed it in the outstretched hands of one of the pantomimes. The audience roared again, and Kieran hung his head.

After the thane congratulated the troupe, he motioned to Kieran. Looking into his face with a sincere expression, he spoke in a tone that Kieran took to be consoling, then held up a finger and reached behind his hide-covered seat. Kieran's spirits lifted, a hope began to glow that he might not walk away hungry after all. The thane motioined him closer.

Kieran approached, limping and slack-jawed in portrayal of his character, while the thane made a show of rummaging for and then finding something in a nearby chest. As Kieran broke into a grin, the thane abruptly whipped around and socked Kieran squarely in the jaw. Kieran went flying backward and landed in a sprawl, while the warriors howled in laughter. A few darted forward and gave Kieran a series of quick kicks and jabs, to the continued cheers of the throng.

Kieran, curled on the ground, looked through his fingers to see the thane's grin fade as his amusement diminished. Growing bored again, he ordered the assaulting warriors to cease their attacks on Kieran, and, looking to a decrepit slave woman, gave a perfunctory gesture toward Kieran with his head. The thane then seemed to forget about him altogether, and with a shout and a laugh led a choice selection of women off to drink in his tent.

The slave woman came forward with a bucket containing edible refuse, spare ends of vegetables and heaps of discarded offal, and tipped it toward him. Kieran hesitated when he saw and then smelled the bucket's contents, and the woman said something matter-of-factly, to the effect of "take it or leave it," which was identical to her expression. Kieran took it, stretching out his grime-caked hands to accept the vegetable bits and entrails the servant glopped into them. He bowed in an appreciative gesture even as she turned her back, and Kieran spent no extra time reatreating to the patch of road he'd staked out as his own. There he carefully stored the pile of refuse from which he would pick out his meals for the next day, and went off into the woods to tend to a tooth which the blow from the thane had knocked loose.

After he overcame the urge to faint, Kieran peered into the blood-dimmed puddle over which he had extracted the loose tooth with the aid of two pointed rocks, and had to convince himself that the face reflected back was his own.

Three months wandering in Britain had produced upon him the effect of years – hard years.

It wasn't that his features were now partly covered in the thick beard he would wear for the rest of his life, or that his face had thinned from lean to cadaverous. What caught Kieran's attention about his unfamiliar likeness was the eyes. In the rings and rays of his irises, Kieran saw signs of the most profound alterations he had undergone, which were visible only to himself. He saw two candlelights at the end of their wicks, dim and threatening to die.

Ah, but what I've done to live.

In the three months since he was marooned, Kieran had learned far more about himself and far less about his past than he wished to know.

While very clear, very traumatic memories from his recent past were mounting, his long term memory remained largely absent. A smattering of recollections from his life before had come drifting back, flotsam from a wrecked ship washing onto the shores of his battered mind, but most were only indistinct impressions, and the more concrete ones were truly unhelpful.

I know I played with a dog at some point. The puzzle's nearly solved, he thought ruefully.

There were other, more positive developments, however, tangibly beneficial to his survival. Weeks of wandering the lattice-like roads that hashmarked the island, passing notches of humanity carved from the grudging wilderness and trailing bands of travelers gave Kieran the beginnings of a mental map of Britain and its various peoples.

From his first interactions with others he knew he had to be very clever to continue his existence, as initially he knew nothing of the culture, language or customs of any of the tribes on the island. That meant the need for a ruse that would hold up under prolonged scrutiny. He remembered the feigned head trauma at the Britonic farm, and reasoned what worked once could work again, if modified. Kieran developed the character of a half-wit – a good natured simpleton with a prominent limp, competent enough to be useful, dimwitted enough to seem innocuous, and most important, not expected to possess any language skills.

It had served him well to date, insofar as rote survival was the standard, and the Germanics, he thought calling themselves "Angles," had taken it upon themselves to bestow a name upon his character. Each time he acted out the spastic hijinks that usually resulted in him getting food, the Angles would cry "Croepschen, Croepschen!" and clap. This happened with several Angle warrior contingents, so eventually Kieran began initiating the chant himself, calling "Ich Croepschen!" when he gained the attention of a potential donor. He ate better after that.

It also helped Kieran in another way. To give a name to the character he was compelled to inhabit most of his waking hours was a guard against his dual lifestyle becoming a congenital condition. Kieran never wanted to forget that the poor creature he became for the eyes of everyone else was not who he actually was. Kieran was Kieran, and Croepschen was a fiction, and not the other way around. He felt he would need to keep telling himself that as the weeks stretched to months, and possibly to years.

The natives and the invaders were mainly identical in how they treated Croepschen. Once his tunic had become too soiled and tattered for the Celtic pattern to be discerned, he endured endless kicks and curses from Britons and

Germanics alike in order to gain his meager sustenance. However, from his closer vantage, he was beginning to see the differences between the cultures.

At first the Germanics left Kieran terrified and disgusted, though they had better food and thus the better scraps, and Kieran argued with his stomach for days against approaching them and willingly putting himself within their reach. They were also enemy to the Britons, and he well knew he owed his life to the natives. After a time, though, he could not help feeling drawn toward the orderly yet dynamic society of the Saxons, Angles and Jutes, who had created a vibrant culture behind the violence and subjugation that was their most indelible hallmark.

They were literate, for one, or at least more literate than the Britons. Runic symbols covered religious icons and altars, and some of the wealthiest had collections of epic poems from which they read. There were bards among the caravans, attached to a household or wandering the roads like Kieran, but they were not held in the same awe as their Celtic counterparts. The Saxons and Angles were often not content listening to epic tales, but would freely participate, acting out the roles at their will. When poets were scarce the travelers remembered songs and stories as best they could, adding embellishment upon embellishment until contests developed. There was some religiosity in a Saxon at his lyre, but little sanctity.

Each night, sitting at the edge of a Germanic camp, appearing as a harmless, ratty beggar to any who thought to look over at him, Kieran was hard at work, listening to them. He would listen closely to the chants and songs and snatches of discussions that made their way to his ears, and found he was able to pick out certain words that sounded much like those he knew in a nameless tongue. Over many evenings he attempted to gather and parse the meaning of as many of these words as possible. It was slow work, and grueling, but night by night, campsite by campsite, he made progress.

Kieran looked up from the puddle to hear a commotion from where the caravan sat, followed by the rumble of hooves and whine of axles. The retinue of the tooth-loosening thane was moving on down the road. Kieran returned to the spot where he'd secreted his larder of nearly inedible scraps, to cook his poor meal and see what he could consume without gagging.

A bit later, Kieran was nudged from a shallow sleep by a quaking of the ground. He knew within moments that another war party was coming down the road toward him, and from the noise it was making, Kieran judged it to be massive.

This is no thane's caravan, thought Kieran. *This is the procession of an eorl.*

Kieran watched hidden as the vanguard of the procession came into view. First appeared the band and color guard, with men who beat clubs against giant drums of stretched hide, and others who blasted rams' horns and sent flights of birds erupting from the canopy. Beside them marched elaborately adorned members of the retinue in brightly polished armor and vivid particolored tunics and cloaks, supporting banners painted with grotesque pictograms of gods and animals that bounced with the marching rhythm of the drums. The designs on the banners were typical of the Angles, and the man they flanked, a fiery-haired man not far out of boyhood, was fully bedecked in the most luxurious metals and materials known to the north of Europe. He was no doubt an *eoldermann*, also called *eorl* – greater than a lord, lesser than a king.

That at least I know of these people.

Eleven men rode up next, resplendent in respectable jewels and furs, though tarnished by the gleam of the noblemen they trailed. These were the eorl's captains, each himself a thane in command of his own band of warriors, which could contain from several dozen to a few hundred men. The combined thousands they commanded were the men Kieran saw immediately after. At the front were the javelin experts, then the close-quarter combat champions, and following them the enlisted volunteers, farmers, potters and smiths who were paid good wages to kill and die for the glory of their preferred thane.

The size of the procession was such that it took a length of minutes for the warriors to pass, but the noise did not pass with them, for there followed the train. Wagons and coaches, elaborately painted and decorated, transported the households of the eorl and his thanes, while the families of the rank-and-file warriors that trailed them carried their loads on foot or upon mules. The remainder was a hodgepodge of carts: carts for provisions and auxiliary equipment, carts of tradesmen whose services were often required immediately before and after combat, carts of merchants, carts for performers, carts being followed by prostitutes, beggars, and madmen.

Kieran believed he could sustain his manner of living for a few months more, but he knew time was growing short for him to change his path or perish. It wasn't just a matter of his physical wellbeing, though that was on a steady trajectory downward. He could feel the effects his way of living was having on his mind as well, and those, for Kieran, were the more disturbing.

Kieran's perception of time had shifted, warped without a way to track the procession of the days. Fatigue sometimes conjured hallucinations, prismatic fire in the clouds, little elfin men peeping at him from trees at night. He sometimes fell into the grip of manias that would tempt him to take off running in the first direction he chose, or to simply surrender, lie in one spot until one of the myriad dangers succeeded in snuffing him out.

Survival doesn't matter if I lose my sanity, he would think in the wake of the manias. *My mind is the one thing I won't relinquish to stay alive.*

Kieran was transfixed as the last of the caravan disappeared from sight. He felt too physically weary to undertake any sort of adventure, but his strength of spirit all at once seemed as formidable as his body was weak. A voice from within told Kieran he might not get another chance at salvation if he let the eorl's procession slip by. So he didn't.

With the final hour of light fading, the procession finally stopped. When Kieran, exhausted, caught up to the multitude they were setting up their enormous camp at a crossroads. The first firelights had been lit, and the evening air was suddenly aroar as thousands fell into chatter and song. Kieran, from a distance, made the preparations to don his Croepschen character. *On with the show*, he thought, then hobbled into the Angles' midst.

Kieran had seen large towns since his arrival, but only from their outskirts, never daring to venture into any. The Germanic camp was what he imagined one of the more bustling of the towns must be like during a festival day. He was so thunderstruck by the assortment of sights and sounds around him that his Croepschen ruse kept slipping, and he continually reminded himself to hold his focus.

Up close, limping and dumbly smirking his way through the heart of the encampment, Kieran felt as if he were daring into a den of powerful predators, but watching them at play in the afterglow of a successful hunt. Everywhere the retinue celebrated their campaign, and the people paid him little mind in their revels. The few who interacted with him did so as part of their general merriment, commanding him to dance or feigning a few jabs in his direction, but in what passed for good nature. Kieran knew from brutal experience how to discern between smiles of amusement and smiles that forewarned violence. A couple of the men clapped him on the back and offered him their drinks, but none tried forcing him into drunkenness as previous warriors had (where followed laughter at his antics and a good-natured beating thereafter). These men were only diverting themselves briefly before going off to join an axe throwing contest or puke at the roadside.

Though he did not believe he had much to fear from this band of warriors, Kieran did not linger among them long. He instead made his way to the rear of the caravan, which fast work had transformed into a moveable merchant city.

This was the support side of the war party, as evidenced by the awnings beneath which food was being prepared by camp cooks and individual family's wives, elderly, spinster sisters and children. Tunics, shoes, dresses were all being mended or made by women, while craftsmen worked to repair weapons and other implements, or replace leather armor, scowling and cursing as they struggled to complete orders with the meager means they could manage by the roadside.

In most cases the reasons were apparent why the men at the back of the caravan were not up front with the warriors. Many wore the scars and depleted looks attesting to their soldierly youths, but their status was insufficient to merit one of the farms handed out to favored warriors upon retirement. Nonetheless they retained their handiness with tools and weapons, or had enough strength to remain otherwise employed.

Then there were the men who never had been warriors, nor could have. They were misshapen, feeble-minded, sickly, or what the Germanics called "gentle," but in all cases, physically or by temperament, they were ill-suited to a warrior's life. These men apprenticed or worked in gangs to complete menial, arduous assignments, and seemed perpetually misplaced, perpetually resigned to a twilight sort of life.

One smith, though, looked out of place among the other craftsmen. He had a quickness to his eye that told of a great reserve of intelligence and wisdom, and his large hands worked his iron implements as nimbly as a woman's fingers at a loom. More impressive was his physique. At several inches over six feet he was the tallest man in the civilian side of the camp, a title for which Kieran would have contended if he weren't purposely stooped. The smith's shoulders popped out in solid half-moons beside his trunk-like neck, and his arms were heaps of coiled muscle stacked one atop the other. He would have caused a great deal of damage on the battlefield if his hammer pounded skulls instead of steel.

Kieran kept the smith in his sight while he carted bundles of kindling from the edge of the woods to a pile near the fire, puzzling what his deformity might be. Kieran soon found out. A gigantic pine log that had been placed on the warriors' pyre was too green, and when its sap exploded in a series of bangs, everyone stopped mid-speech and action to turn and look – all but the smith, who continued to shape a red-glowing bar of iron on his anvil.

He's deaf, Kieran thought, unable to suppress a small smile. *Fate has a twisted way about it.*

The hulking man had a serenity about him that Kieran admired as much as his keenness and build. When Kieran noticed that the cooking fire under the smith's dinner cauldron was in danger of dying, Kieran, carrying a bundle of twigs, approached the man and extended his arms in offering of them.

127

The smith did not pause in his work as Kieran came toward him, but instead let the hammer continue to fall with unwavering regularity against the metal on the anvil. His face was almost as imposing as his body, jug ears and small eyes making the whole of it seem to billow out, while his wild beard and thick brows heightened the effect. However, as that fleshy soot-smeared face looked down at Kieran and arched an inquisitive eyebrow, there was no trace of malice in his undersized eyes.

Kieran motioned with the bundle toward the fire, and by a nod the smith signaled his acceptance. Kieran gave his "Croepschen grin" and fed twigs into the smoldering charcoal until the flame was revived. Kieran bowed when the smith nodded his head in gratitude, and went to fetch another bundle of wood.

Hours later, the camp seemed to yawn collectively and commenced the great winding down for the night. The family men whose broods were in tow returned to the embrace of their wives and children, leaving the others to lay out their bedrolls and tents, if they had them. Dark weather was hovering above the camp, and the feel of the air foretold coming rainfall.

Kieran knew he faced a wet night, and shivered in reflex. He vividly remembered each rainy night he had known in Britain for the misery it inflicted.

His mood sagged as he contemplated where to sleep beneath the stormy clouds, with only his hole-ridden cloak to keep off the rain. If it remained a drizzle Kieran could perhaps get some rest, but anything heavier would keep him awake and leave him fatigued for the full day's march ahead. He was suddenly thrust into a funk, made all the deeper for its proximity to the heights of his earlier joy.

With the chatter of the camp dying out as steadily as the fires, Kieran perceived a loud noise piercing the darkness – or rather, several loud noises. *Clank, clank,*

clank went the noise, thrice in succession, and then the sequence was repeated. Kieran looked about him for the source, and spotted the deaf smith, still pounding his iron. However, the man was not shaping a sword or horseshoe, but instead intentionally sending a signal, and Kieran realized it was meant for him. The smith confirmed this by waving Kieran over toward the cart that carried his anvil and tools. Kieran's spirits rose, and when he hobbled over he saw the smith had stretched an oilcloth tarp from one of the sides of his cart to the ground and secured it with stakes.

With a sweep of his large hand the craftsman invited Kieran beneath the tarp, where overlapping deerskin rugs had already been laid. Kieran looked at the man with as profound an expression of gratitude as he believed his simple character could convey, and shambled under the sheltering skins. He wrapped his cloak tightly around himself, feeling the soft bristles of the deerskin beneath him, and nodded off just as the first few drops of rain patted against the tarp. Though the storm produced a steady and at times heavy downpour, not a drop fell on Kieran's sleeping head.

For three more days Kieran traveled in the train of the warriors, and over the course of those days he became the smith's assistant, insomuch as he could with Croepschen's limited capabilities and Kieran's handicap of not understanding the majority of the Ænglisch tongue. Despite these constrictions, he met with approval from his new master, whose name he learned was Ecbehrt, and even from the thane for whom Ecbehrt served, who smiled at the cheerful refrain of "I am Croepschen, pleased to meet with you." He also insinuated himself with the noble families, the important wives and children in the train. Kieran may have grown tired of the repetitive games, performances and ritual exchanges in which he participated, but he never allowed Croepschen grow weary. His character was a grown child and must emulate children in their pursuits. His work was rewarded, though, as each night Kieran ate as well as he had since leaving the Britonic family, and each night slept sheltered beside Ecbehrt.

They made a strange pair: Ecbehrt towering and stolid, silently surveying his surroundings, while Croepschen, gaunt, bent and frenetic, babbled and danced along with the caravan. Some laughed and many more remarked at the two of them and their sudden friendship, but none interfered. Croepschen was worshipful of Ecbehrt, but infinitely supplicating to others, as Kieran had invented him, while Kieran's true calculations ever continued. Remaining in the smith's good graces was his only viable means of making his position permanent, which had become Kieran's sole object, so Croepschen's affection and cheerfulness never flagged.

Among those who took note of the odd alliance was a man in his mid-twenties, who Kieran had seen among the core elite at the eorl's bench – likely a cousin or nephew from the familial way in which the other war chiefs treated him. The man had the deep red hair of the eorl, and his ruddy round cheeks and blond eyebrows guaranteed he would retain a boyish look until old age, should he attain it.

Kieran did not draw any particular conclusions from the looks the young noble sent his way when at the back of the procession, though he would in hindsight attach a great deal of importance to them. Kieran was exclusively focused on the looming date of the caravan's end.

At dusk the next day, the procession came to a four-way crossroads, and from an outbreak of farewells among the women Kieran knew the moment of the caravan's dissolution had arrived. He told himself not to have a heavy heart, to shake off his sentimental melancholy and coldly assess his best prospects for continued survival, as he had so far succeeded in doing.

This time, though, Kieran found it harder to set aside his emotions than at any previous point since his first few days in Britain. He had not only come to rely on the sustenance these people provided, but on their company as well – especially in the case of Ecbehrt, with whom Kieran was developing a genuine rapport. Kieran found it hard that night to maintain the vacant, blithe character of Croepschen, ever eager to offer a jig or a few sticks for the fire, while his every thought turned toward the choice the daybreak would force: which route to follow away from the crossroads, a question of both literal and metaphorical significance.

As the night progressed, Kieran noticed a few sets of eyes periodically following him. One belonged to the young noble with the ruddy face and hair, whose stare appeared to vacillate between amused, nearly fraternal, and demonic. Kieran did his best to make sure Croepschen didn't register any understanding that something might be amiss, and in fact waved at the young noble with a good-natured smile, which was returned with a smile that held some menace.

The other set of eyes belonged to one of the elite women with whom the ruddy noble often interacted. Her eyes contained no familial warmth – only the intensity of a raptor tracking its next meal. For these and other reasons, Kieran stuck close to Ecbehrt as the priests slaughtered a ram in offering and the final night's revels began.

A few hours later the final event of the procession commenced: the distribution of war spoils. The eorl himself handed out rewards to his best fighters, advisors and other favorites, and the thanes and elite fighters gave gifts among themselves and to the camp at large. It was an event everyone in the caravan crowded around the warriors' pyre to witness, and drinking continued at a staggering clip throughout. The free flow of alcohol led to an ever rowdier and more participatory crowd, and ever livelier exchanges among the nobles and fighting men. One by one, the thanes and war leaders stood to lead toasts, songs, and blessings to a variety of gods. The spectacle lasted over two hours, reaching a climax as the same time as the inebriation, when gifts and tributes were given as easily as the drink.

Kieran at length allowed himself to relax into the convivial atmosphere, not knowing when he would be allowed near such festivities with as much ease again. All too quickly after finding it, though, Kieran's peace was shattered. A chant was building among the Angles, which first rose from the core nobles near the bonfire, but soon spread through the ranks to the outside of the circle, where Kieran and Ecbehrt stood. When he heard what they chanted he at first refused to believe he understood correctly. As the chant grew louder, it became unmistakable.

They were chanting "Croepschen."

All heads turned his way, and even Ecbehrt looked down on Kieran with a surprised expression. Kieran looked from face to face for a sign of what it meant, but before he could glean any answer, he felt many pairs of hands urging him forward, toward where the nobles sat.

As he drew near, the calls of "Croepschen!" emerged anew, now from the innermost elite of the eorl's court. Through great effort on Kieran's part, Croepschen bore a bewildered and mildly cautious demeanor, while in reality he was almost out of his mind with terror. He saw every man among the Anglic elite was in an advanced state of intoxication. The ruddy young noble now had a face the hue of a ripe radish, with eyes bloodshot to match. He was one of the few standing, but he did so only with the assistance of one of his warriors.

A noble came forward and laid a hand on Kieran's shoulder, making him flinch. Turning to look, Kieran realized with a shock that the noble was not simply one of the eorl's retinue, but the eorl himself. The eorl laughed in reaction to Kieran's expression, and spoke to the crowd in a voice that was authoritative but playful, and noticeably slurred. Some of his address was to the ruddy young noble alone, who seemed pleased but bashful, and received periodic chucks on the shoulder from the comrades at his side. Some questions were posed to the throng, who in all cases roared approval. The entire affair seemed rigidly scripted yet somewhat like a self-parody. Kieran noted nothing yet had been required of him, which made him especially nervous.

At last, Croepschen's part was cued. The eorl turned to Kieran and in a good-natured tone asked a series of questions. In his scattered state Kieran could not comprehend any of the eorl's words, even those seemingly familiar to him, and thus the puzzled expression on Croepschen's was entirely authentic. Finally, one word emerged from the eorl's questions that Kieran was certain he understood: "weorc," or "work."

"Work?" Croepschen repeated back at the man. The crowd burst into wild applause at Croepschen's first word before them.

"Ja, work," said the eorl.

"Ich work – yeu?" or "I work, you?"

"No," he said. "for he," pointing to the ruddy faced noble, who gave Kieran a drunken salute.

Kieran turned to Ecberht, watching from the outskirts of the circle of the spectators, and gave him a questioning look. The smith seemed to be conflicted, but after a few moments' consideration he definitively nodded his large head.

Kieran smiled at the eorl, at the young noble and his entourage, and at the crowd around him. He threw back his head, did his signature jig, and burst forth with, "Croepschen work!" A wall of approving shouts instantly rebounded from the ring of spectators.

The throng quieted as a man stepped forward from the shadows. He was covered in a white robe that began as a broad hood and ended at the soles of his feet, and held a bone goblet decorated with gold. Kieran recognized him as a priest from the ram sacrifice earlier, and the expectant hush over the camp indicated no parody was being partken of now. The priest came within arm's reach of Kieran as the eorl stepped aside. He began to intone a solemn chant, describing patterns with the goblet in the air. Then he stopped, and made a motion for Kieran to put his right hand over his left shoulder. The priest did the same, and, looking square into Kieran's eyes, he pronounced a long recitation, which Kieran guessed was an oath. When the priest stopped and Kieran didn't say anything, the priest repeated the last line, following it with a question that ended in a leading, "Ja?"

Kieran looked again to Ecberht, who again nodded. Swallowing hard, Kieran turned back to the priest, and nodding, said, "Ja." The priest handed him the goblet, and Kieran drank, letting a generous quantity of liquid spill from the corners of his mouth. He handed the emptied cup back to the priest, who turned to the ruddy noble and, raising his arms, shouted a sentence that had an air of finality. Indeed, when he was finished, the crowd again applauded, and many hands reached out to clap Kieran's back.

Ecberht now emerged from the crowd and led Kieran to the young noble. Through the swimming eyes of alcohol there was approval in the scarlet face, though Kieran felt a chill at its edges. The noble made a sign in front of Kieran, and then with a wave of his hand dismissed him.

Years later, Kieran would come to discover the meaning of the words in the oath the priest recited. Had he known them at the time, he still would have responded affirmatively to the priest's question, but would have taken a few more seconds of deliberation before doing so.

The oath was:

"I, Croepschen, a stranger among the People and marked as a creature of Loki, today acknowledge my betters here assembled, and the gods assembled in halls beyond our sight. Every Angle knows today's king may become a slave, and a slave may win fame and a throne for himself tomorrow. But today I am a slave, by my own word and heart's hunger, and am the tool of my master even unto my own demise. While in the jaws of my bond, I wish that my name should never be sung, for lips would be better used to sing my master's song. Let no man remember me, that my master's memory will occupy more of their hearts. Until such day as I pass to other realms or am released of my bond by the laws of the Angles, my life is my master's, and his every want is all I hold dear. Before my betters and the gods, these words I take as my own words, and these thoughts as my own thoughts, by the sign I do here give."

To this, Kieran said "Ja," and in his first moments as a slave he felt only relief.

Chapter Nine

"You've been quiet," said Uleara. "I mean, even more than usual."

It had been miles since Uleara and Kieran last spoke. For several hours, the only sounds they shared were hoofs thwopping against dirt, the roaring gusts of the coastal winds, the squawking of gulls, and the fugue of the cart's creaking axles.

"I was thinking," said Kieran.

"That's dangerous. What about?"

"The clouds."

"Ah, of course."

"We shouldn't stop to eat before Glevuncaster. The weather isn't going to hold."

Dark, full clouds had been gathering above since they'd branched off from the ancient Fosse Way and taken the coast road northward, a storm blowing in from beyond the Sabrina Sea.

"You really think so?" asked Uleara with disappointment. "It's not me, you understand, but the horse. Agalyn gets cranky when she's hungry."

"She'll be crankier if we have to travel the last few miles in the mud," he said. "So will I."

"Who could tell?" Uleara chuckled, wattle shaking. "You haven't said ten words since we left the baths."

Kieran looked at Uleara without expression.

"I'm glad I could at least persuade you to stop at the Aquae Sulis."

"Yes, that was a good idea," Kieran said.

"It's fallen on hard times since I visited as a youth, mind you, but they've maintained the caldarium and the frigidarium nicely. Hot and cold – and what more do you need?" He puzzled for a moment. "How do they keep that water so warm this time of year?"

"It has a hypocaust."

"Oh! That's what that is." Uleara frowned. "I somewhat regret turning down your offer."

They trod forward in silence for another minute.

Uleara cleared his throat, and said, "I was thinking too." He looked to Kieran, whose eyes remained fixed on the road ahead. After a long pause Kieran finally returned Uleara's gaze, his brows raised in pique.

"And?"

"And it was about what those drovers said last night," said Uleara. "Do you remember?"

The cattle drovers were rough characters, who bore the marks of inbreeding and a life that knew nothing but poverty and ignorance from birth to burial. However, they had let Kieran and Uleara camp on one of their pastures, away from the road, and share some of the cider from the small keg they had with them. Also, being situated as they were by a well-traveled thoroughfare and a day's ride from Glevuna, political news had filtered down to them, which they shared as freely as their drink. It had not been to Uleara's liking – the news, not the drink

"I remember they could hold neither their wine nor their water," said Kieran, "and I suspect they have a fondness for their livestock that goes beyond husbandry." The abbot laughed at the last part, and Kieran even bore a faint smile. It was a funny thought, likely true.

"But they did talk quite a bit about other things, didn't they?" said Uleara.

"Yes, even as you do now," said Kieran. "Perhaps this once, abbot, you could get to the heart of the matter without first nibbling around its edges."

"Forgive me, my lord," said Uleara, bowing as grandly as he could on horseback, affecting a clowning demeanor to mask the sting he felt. "I beseech your pardon."

"Go on, your holiness."

"It seems that even a rumor of King Tyndarios withdrawing the support of the Demetae means Aurelian's position is not as secure as we thought. Isn't that so?" When Kieran didn't answer, he continued, "Demetae men and the strength of their king's lands could tip the balance in a struggle for power, or the tribe could bargain for a separate peace with the Saxons, as the Belgae have. Things were different before war loomed, but now all is far more… visceral. There is a real possibility that, in one manner or other, Aurelian and his court end up slaves or food for beetles. I am not certain that's a court we want to be in."

Kieran took a long time to answer, as if thoroughly chewing his words before he ejected them.

"It will be I, not we," said Kieran. "You are returning after the winter, and in the interim I assure you neither usurpers nor Germanics will have occasion to sever that fretting pate from your neck. Nothing happens before spring." After a pause, "I thought we were past this."

"I am here, in case it escaped your notice," Uleara said. "Yet my conscience will not be at peace should something terrible occur, when I may have prevented it by giving voice to my misgivings."

"Noted."

"And immediately ignored."

"I thought I'd made a believer of you with that demonstration in the shed," said Kieran.

"As Thomas, removed from Christ's divine presence, began to question the power of the Lord, so perhaps am I afflicted. And by the way," Uleara said with a worried glance back at the cart, "are you sure that... thing is secure? You said we would not want it loosed from its mooring, and I fear the road has been unkind to our materials in the journey."

"It is fine," said Kieran. "As you have rightly and persistently pointed out, if there is danger for us it lies down the road, not behind the dray horse."

"But you said there isn't any danger at all."

"Because there isn't."

They lapsed into silence again, but the air between them was charged. Uleara was well aware that the clouds had little to do with Kieran's mood, which had blackened like the sky, minutely but steadily, as they approached Glevuna. He

139

knew the change had something to do with what one of the drovers told Kieran, beyond Uleara's hearing. It might as well have something to do with the oblong box in the back of Kieran's cart, the one he'd covered up when he caught Uleara looking. Uleara wanted to ask about it, but the abbot was not convinced the answer was worth inciting Kieran further.

Yet as they trekked their last few miles to the court of Aurelian, Uleara was himself growing impatient and irritated. The germ of suspicion that Kieran was hiding something important from him had taken root in Uleara's brain even before they left, and with each passing day small clues had fed it until it now attained the stature of certainty. He let his uncertainty loose.

"I still don't understand what it is."

"What?"

"The… material you showed me. It looks impressive, but what is its purpose? For that matter, what is ours?"

"There will be time for that."

"So you say. But there's more you don't say. Such as regarding that box of yours." He let the prompt linger and waited for Kieran's answer, which did not come. "I said, such as…"

"Uleara, would you like to know what's in the box?"

"I would, yes."

"By all means, have a look."

Uleara had not been expecting this response, and said, with more pout than he intended, "I may yet. We need not stop now, though, with the rain coming. God forbid you get cranky."

The abbot looked over at the ever-impassive face of Kieran, neither smiling nor afrown. *He hides well those wheels turning behind that benign expression and lips that seldom move*, thought Uleara, who felt a deep chill thinking that perhaps these years of friendship had all been to position Kieran for some unknown end. Perhaps Uleara and Aelfarn, and even Aurelian, were simply pieces on a latrunculi board that Kieran moved at his will.

However, looking again, past his own ire, Uleara saw mostly sadness in his friend's face, which had softened from its stony set of minutes prior. Kieran was not gazing down the road, but into memory, fixing a stare on the horizon that Uleara had seen often in the seven years of their acquaintance.

Then the most unexpected thing happened.

"I'm sorry," said Kieran.

At first Uleara thought it had been a trick of the wind. The surprise was plain enough in the abbot's expression that Kieran said it again. "I'm sorry, Uleara."

Uleara said, "About what?"

"You have been an honest and steadfast friend, and I have ungenerously expected you to maintain your loyalty even when I did not return it by giving you knowledge of my plans."

"Kieran, you are forgiven," said Uleara with a happy sigh. (*And perhaps you ARE a wizard as well*, he added internally.) "I am honored to join you on any

141

quest." He reached out his arm, and they clasped wrists, gripping as tightly as their bond. "So," said Uleara, "you'll be informing me of everything that we are doing now?"

"No," said Kieran. Uleara jerked back his arm.

"Then what was the apology about?"

"I thought I should say I'm sorry at least." Kieran saw his friend pained, and added, "I have reason for you not to know, and it is as much for your sake as mine – rather, more. At any rate, if all goes to plan you'll have everything answered tonight."

"I suspect not," huffed Uleara, who then said, "Well, there isn't much I can do about it now."

"No, there isn't," said Kieran, pointing to the grand city that had just become visible through the trees. "We're here."

Chapter Ten

There were few sights in Europe to match Glevuna as it hosted the High Council.

Once known as Glevumensis and Glevuum, the city was the former Roman capital of western Britannia, and in its time was as celebrated a hub of commerce, administration, industry and art as its sister city on the Themesa River, Londinium, which now lay in near-ruins. Where most of Romanized Britain had devolved, rotting into a depressed, mutated form of its pre-conquest condition, Glevuna was a shining exception.

The residents were descended at one point or another from the retired Roman soldiers who settled there hundreds of years earlier, and at some point from native Britons thereafter. Many of these Roman-British families became prominent merchants or wealthy landowners, and built elaborate villas both within and without the walls of the city, which was also home to marble-ensconced basilicas, theaters to seat a thousand, a hippodrome and a grand forum. Aurelian's father had taken pains to restore it to its former glory, and the Golden Prince, five years into his reign, continued the project with elan.

Even at the top of the hill from which Kieran and Uleara first glimpsed it, one could see Glevuna to be a thriving city of several thousand people, the only true city in Britain. Stacks of building materials and trellises of scaffolding rose from all sections, promising even greater grandeur for the *urbs* yet to come.

Wondrous though Glevuna was in an average week, as the High Council drew nigh it was nothing short of majestic. The population had doubled as the gathering of rulers and their retinues attracted merchants, craftsmen, mercenaries, prostitutes, thieves, and every other manner of person from the whole of native-held Britain. As they approached, Uleara and Kieran joined dozens of others who were still streaming in from every direction, pulling their livelihoods up the road, and pushing them on any prospective customer in earshot. Smoke poured skyward from every quarter of the former *colonia*, carrying odors that reawakened Uleara's hunger, and the strains of music and laughter could be heard above the patter of the rain from half a mile distant.

The road leading into the city's southern gate was lined with junipers, trimmed to the shape of spearheads. Aurelian had ordered terra cotta planters in the shape of upturned half bells to be placed at regular intervals along the Roman wall that encompassed Glevuna, and from a closer remove, Kieran and Uleara saw each one was overflowing with bright flowers that burst forth in every conceivable color. Mirroring the vivid hues of the floral accents, banners and streamers festooned the tops of the newly-plastered walls, snapping and twisting in the storm winds. On that gray day Glevuna was a collection of tethered rainbows.

"It is magnificent," Uleara said as they neared the city gate.

"Aurelian is using his city to make the case for his crown," said Kieran.

"Well, he presents a strong argument," Uleara returned.

The judging panel of Aurelian's preparations, great lords and kings culled from every corner of unconquered Britain, were in residence around Glevuna in a U-shaped second city made of many hundreds of tents. Grand pentagonal tents of the kings, and the simpler tents of their retainers, dyed in every color man could produce and sporting pennants adorned with animal and deity figures, filled a vast field on the side of the Sabrina River where Glevuna lay, and the slope of a broad hill on the other. It was as if Glevuna were under a very congenial siege, which was not as far from the truth as Aurelian would have liked. Unfurled, the

144

full splendor of the kings of Briton and their courtiers was magnificent, and adorned the Glevunish countryside as heather covers the moors of Dumnonia.

Just outside the gate, a line of stablemen and grooms waited to see to the animals of those who could pay for their services. Kieran flagged down a lad of about fourteen, who rushed up with scrawny limbs jangling in fatigue from a long week of work, and paid the boy for both himself and Uleara. Kieran included a gratuity that was princely even during the Council of Kings.

Before Kieran allowed the lad to take Brecca's reins, he stroked her neck and spoke into her ear. The horse whinnied and nuzzled against Kieran's head. Uleara looked to Agalyn, whose reins he relinquished without any ceremony, and the expression on her face confirmed that they had nothing to say to one another.

The boy began leading the horses to the public stables, and Uleara turned to Kieran.

"You tell your horse secrets you can't share with me?" said the abbot, with some seriousness.

"I've known her longer." Kieran smiled. Uleara did not return his grin.

"Do we know our cargo will be left undisturbed?" asked Uleara.

"We just fed that boy's family for a week. He will give us as good care as there is to be had."

"He still might peek into the cart."

"I've taken precautions. He will find nothing, this I guarantee."

Uleara bristled at the haughtiness he perceived in Kieran's tone, but nonetheless kept at his side while they walked through the arched Roman gate into the city.

They were immediately beset by a crush of people, a mingling of tribes and classes inconceivable elsewhere but Glevuna, and any time except the Council. Uleara was muscled aside by a Demetian warrior, one of four carrying the palanquin of a noble who jangled by flashing precious metal with every movement. For every litter floating above the crowds there was a score of blank-eyed paupers barely managing their ways through them. These were not beggars, but those who believed their only salvation for whatever had laid them low could be found at the feet of the island's great men.

"There are multitudes of them," said Uleara in pity. "Do you think many will be heard?"

"Hardly any," said Kieran, who was paying little attention to Uleara and instead trying to see above the crowd, which was propelling them along toward the central square of the city. When they stood at the intersection where West Gate Street became East Gate Street and North Gate became South, Kieran stopped and began looking about in each direction.

"What now?" said Uleara, who had to shout over the din.

"I meet the contact. He is supposed to be waiting at the One Eye Dog Tavern."

"Oh, wonderful," said Uleara with relief. "I may finally get something to eat. I wonder if they sell…" He paused abruptly. "Wait. What do you mean 'you' meet the contact?"

"I have to go alone."

146

Uleara looked at Kieran, aghast.

"I'm sorry my friend," said Kieran, "but it is a condition of getting to see him at all, and it is vital this meeting take place."

"To what end?" demanded Uleara. "Why is it so vital?"

Kieran, however, was once again not paying attention, instead scanning the streets around. Without warning he tore off toward North Gate Street, at a rate Uleara would never have guessed he could achieve, and Uleara, with a thought to his meager purse and a look at the chaos around him, saw no choice but to follow.

Buffeted by pedestrians and encumbered by his size, Uleara was hard pressed to keep Kieran in his sights as the leaner man wove deftly among people and barriers jamming the roadway. He at last caught up to Kieran beside the door to small storefront, above which hung a shingle with a black-and-white dog painted in profile, only one eye showing.

"You made it," said Kieran, as the panting abbot joined him. "I must within, alone"

"Kieran…"

"Stand watch – if it gets too miserable out here you can wait in the tavern across the street." Uleara had to concede the spot he indicated, open to the street but protected by an awning and warmed by braziers, looked inviting. "I will return shortly, don't worry."

"But…"

"Oh, of course," said Kieran, turning back after he was already making for the entryway. He pulled some coins from his purse and handed them to Uleara. "My apologies." Kieran turned again toward the tavern.

"Kieran!"

Kieran spun around and looked and Uleara with a perfect mask of amiability, beneath which there was turmoil, as only a person who sees another more days than not for seven years can. Myriad things Uleara wanted to say rose to his mind, but none rose from his throat, and with no more spoken between them, Kieran turned again and disappeared within the One Eye Dog.

Uleara, with naught else to do, bunched his cloak around his neck, ducked under a shoe merchant's awning, and settled in to wait.

An hour passed, and no Kieran. Even when Uleara ventured a glance within the confines of the One Eye Dog he did not spot his friend. The weather remained as chilly and wet as before, and if anything worsened.

A gust of wind tore through the street, sending the merchants scrambling to secure their wares, and making Uleara hug his cloak even tighter around him. The rain Uleara had assiduously tried to avoid now drummed down on his tonsured head and collected in the folds of his cloak. His thoughts matched the cold, ugly weather completely.

Where by thunder is Kieran? He felt like a string wound tightly around a spool, ready to snap and unravel at a moment. *I am not some page. Kieran gives me the orders one gives to a child, or a dog: come along, wait there, stay silent. I am a man of God, by God, not a stooge for a lunatic with a glowing glass jar.*

Uleara's nose picked up the bouquet of the food carried on the wind from several streets over. With olfactory senses heightened by hunger he could discern vegetables stewing, and crackling fresh bread rising in the ovens, and a hog being roasted over a pit fire. His rekindled hunger also fanned his ire, as he remembered how he had been deprived of his opportunity to eat once again.

Alright Kieran, you're on your own, thought Uleara, and strode toward the tavern Kieran had pointed out. No sooner had he reached the door, however, than a rush of people out of it pushed the abbot back into the street. Behind the wave of panic Uleara saw uncontrolled flames filling the small space. The people watched passively in the street as the fire consumed the interior of the structure. Uleara's hopes for dry climes and a meal crumbled with the burned-out building.

Uleara looked again to the entrance of the One Eye Dog, and once again saw no sign of Kieran. A cry from nearby drew the abbot's attention to another tavern just within sight, across an intersection and down another street. A boy was calling out: "Drinks, drinks of the gods! Heat for the body, balm for the spirit! Specials today for exchange of fowl or grain – but coin is always welcome! Get dry and wet in the same spot! Drinks of the gods, inside!"

He was tempted to go in, but a sense of duty to his extraordinary friend and his utter uncertainty about anything he was doing in Glevuna (*How did that man talk me out of talking him out of this, whatever this is?*) pulled Uleara back. He did venture a long look at the establishment, and to his moral dismay saw well-attired men and women so jocular he could hear above the noisy street the peals of laughter they propelled into it, while they festively fed and imbibed inside, under a roof. They looked every bit as dry, warm and sated as Uleara was damp, chilled and famished. A last glance toward the One Eye Dog confirmed the change in Uleara's mood from anxious to angry, and he abandoned his post in favor of his stomach, his gullet, and his dignity. None, however, were fated to be served well.

Uleara's butt was no sooner ensconced in his barstool than his look was drawn to a woman leaning against the long stone counter, a woman whose attire gave him little choice but to look. He could clearly discern her nipples poking from her low cut dress, which was stretched around taut, full breasts, and hair done up in the towering fashion of Roman grandees revealed an elegant neck and highly pretty profile. His gaze lasted longer than he thought, perhaps. She turned and met his stare.

Uleara turned away in embarrassment, but when he hesitatingly looked back toward her she was smiling, and making her way toward him. The man in Uleara felt his pulse quicken, but the priest reminded him of his celibacy until marriage. Then his senses got into the mix, and made him think about her smile, her walk, and her clothing. It was then Uleara realized his mistake.

"Magdalen," he intoned softly, eyes madly seeking any sight but her approaching face, and cleavage. As she sidled up to him and ran her hand down his biceps, Uleara swallowed against a dry throat, and prepared for what would only be the latest indignity in what was becoming a very long line that afternoon.

"I've got a few minutes if you've got a few coppers," breathed the woman into his ear.

"I'm terribly sorry, but I don't indulge," said Uleara, trying to avoid her eyes, but noticing that she was very pretty, and young enough that her profession hadn't taken any physical toll. He added, "Lovely as you are."

The abbot gave an imploring look to the beefy used shoe merchant who had abandoned his awning shortly after Uleara did. The man merely shrugged.

"Oh come on," said the woman with a giggle. "And you're a Christian priest? I've had a few of you lot. You ain't bashful once the robes are off. But you are a sweetie," she said, pressing against him. "I'd give you a deal."

"That's… very generous," said Uleara, "but I must refuse."

Imploring green eyes and a full form beneath the clinging dress, had, if but briefly, caused Uleara to consider her proposal, but it was out of his head just as soon. Though many of his fellow men of the cloth might not have had such qualms in his situation, Uleara did. He instead thought of Lihane, and of his solemn vow before God, on consecrated ground, that he would never stray from the righteous path – but if the Lord could include Lihane at some point upon that path, he would be grateful.

"What's the matter? I've seen you. You've been lurking around here all day. Whatever you're waiting for, I bet I can make time go by a little quicker." She pressed closer, palming a hand around one of his butt cheeks and squeezing. "Warm you up a little."

At the goosing, Uleara broke the embrace and backed off from the woman. All of his good cheer soured.

"I said no thank you, my child, and I meant it."

"I ain't your child, fatty," she said, pushing the hem of her dress back down to her knees and whipping her head around. "Just try and see if you can get any jelly in this city now! There isn't a girl who'll touch you. We all talk, you know. You're hexed with all the girls, dough ball, I'll make sure of that!" She gave him a rude gesture over her shoulder as she stormed off. Uleara stared after her, but instantly forgot the incident when she passed in front of the One Eye Dog just as Kieran was rushing out the tavern door. Before he could call to him, Kieran bustled down the street and disappeared into an alley. Uleara elbowed past the tavern customers into the street and began running toward where he had last seen his friend, but realized it was a futile effort.

And clearly he does not care enough about my fate to bother letting me know his destination, thought Uleara, as irate as he could remember ever being.

"Curse it!" he said aloud. He squared his shoulders and marched back into the tavern as if into a wrestling ring.

Minutes later, Uleara tore into the largest and most aromatic pasty to be bought in Glevuna. The golden pastry shell and its contents of mutton, onion and peas, were piping hot. That alone aided Uleara's return to a semblance of serenity. He noted the steam escaping from the top of the half-moon crust, now half-consumed, and put his face over it to feel the heat on his skin.

Uleara checked how much more money he had of what Kieran had given him, and ordered a honey and spice liquor, *hedromel*, that they served from a heated cauldron.

"You a petitioner?" asked the server who delivered his drink, a grubby and thin youth with stringy hair that kept his face mostly hidden. "That's smart, the Christian garb. Aurelian's particular to them, you know. Are you the real thing or just trying to get in good with one of the priests at court?"

Uleara puffed and straightened. "I am the abbot of Cairn Eilwath, actually."

"That's Ænglisch to me, friend," he said to Uleara with a smile, which he quickly dropped, muttering, "Genuine article, then."

Uleara silently sipped the hedromel, studying the street scene before him. *If Kieran won't deign to divulge anything,* he thought, *perhaps I can do my own reconnaissance.* "Tell me," he asked the server, "have you heard much of what transpires at the Council?"

"I hear some things," said the youth, with an inflection of interest. His fingers moved minutely against the bar, in a gathering motion. Uleara watched this without comprehension, then made the connection.

"Oh! Money, yes?"

The server rolled his eyes and blew a lock of hair from his face. "Right the first try. Four coppers, and you'll get everything I know."

"That sounds reasonable," said Uleara, but with an uncertain look.

"Hold right there, I'll be back," said the server, who darted off into the back of the tavern. Uleara undid his own small purse and looked within. Four coppers was the entirety of what remained. *Perhaps we can agree to three coppers, for most of what he knows,* Uleara thought.

Before he could put it to the youth, however, shrieks of alarm and loud calls for assistance rang out in the street, and the flow of humanity on the boulevard slowed. Everyone watched a cluster of soldiers in what closely resembled Roman battle wear part the crowd, heading from North Gate toward the tavern in which Uleara sat. Alarm spread on the faces and into the voices of those who saw them at close range, and as they approached Uleara could tell why.

153

They were six in number, splattered in red from their sandals to their helmets, for those who still had theirs. Bruises and lacerations marred each face, and worse wounds were field dressed to shockingly little effect. However, they were not the worst off. Behind them they dragged a seventh, and his appearance made people turn away when he passed through the crowd. Some began to cry.

The soldiers stopped when they came to a two-story building just doors down from Uleara's tavern, and one called up, "We ask for a Caolfhin." There was no reply, so the soldier said, "In the name of Guddad we seek Caolfhin."

The head of a plain but pleasant looking brunette of fifteen popped out from the window, and the girl shrieked. Moments later she flew from the downstairs door and into the street, and threw herself onto the mangled soldier. The passersby who could see the scene were nearly silent, and the girl's wrenching sobs of "Guddad" seemed to echo throughout the city. Uleara edged closer in time to see the dying soldier spit his last blood and succumb.

"It's an omen," a boy said.

"Them's from the Legio Nova Augusta, the new Legion," said an old man quietly to no one in particular. "Them's Aurelian's boys."

"Fuck me," someone else replied.

The traffic began to resume its usual pace and the volume of the street wound back up to its former height. Uleara remained staring at the girl who lay across the body of her young man, back heaving with grief. He pivoted to move, and a form came up beside him.

"I know of what you discussed in the tavern," he said in Latin. Uleara turned to see a man of medium height and handsomely proportioned features, only marred

154

by a deep scar running from just above his ear to just above his Adam's apple. "I heard your conversation, with the barkeep."

"I beg your pardon?" said Uleara. "You were listening?"

"We might be able to exchange information."

"Exchange? You don't even know…"

"The Bishop of Eboracum gives a lecture on bearing false witness today, near the old forum, at three turns past noon," said the stranger. "You should be there. You might hear something interesting."

"I don't…"

The stranger was away, quickly shuffling into the crowd, gone. It was more than Uleara could process, so he didn't, just then.

"There's trouble coming, that's as sure as the tides," said a hawk-faced woman to a friend as they walked off. "Looks like I'll have something to tell the girls back home after all."

Chapter Eleven

Kieran returned to the One Eye Dog engaged in conversation with a short, hunched man wearing a cloak that covered him head to foot and obscured his face. The man was whispering to Kieran with animated gestures as Kieran bent forward to hear him, and darted the direction of his look like a frightened sparrow.

I'm not worldly compared with some, Uleara thought, *but that is the most conspicuous inconspicuous person I've ever seen.*

Kieran spotted the abbot and waved him over. When Uleara joined them, the stranger turned deliberately toward the abbot and cast a blank, shaded look from beneath his hood, then turned away quickly and began his fidgeting again.

"Where have you been?" asked Kieran.

Uleara felt on the verge of eruption, but in deference to his unfamiliar surroundings he restrained his anger, and said in Latin, "Where have I been? I was saving myself from starvation and a case of the chills, which left up to you would have both befallen me. Where were you?"

"Things took longer than I expected. There were complications."

"Oh, there were?" said Uleara with deep sarcasm. "Well tell me all about them."

"Listen friends," interjected the stranger in his native Silurian dialect, his eyes glittering in the shadowed cave of his hood, "I don't care what language you want to talk in, but can we do it out of the street?"

"Of course," said Kieran.

156

"My house will be best. Follow me."

The stranger led them along the bustling West Gate Street toward the river, with Kieran at his side and Uleara at the rear. Many lamps and torches were lit along the way even though it was the middle of the afternoon, as the coal-black clouds above and the wind-driven rain diminished visibility at any range. The flames illuminated elaborate frescoes and tile work accenting every edifice, memorials to the day of Roman rule and a tribute to the respect Glevun held for the old Empire. In the torch glow the lifelike images on the frescoes danced to life, while peddlers and pedestrians took on a fearsome aspect as shadows befell the hollows of their faces.

The further they progressed along West Gate Street, the greater the degree of dilapidation they passed. Soon the cityscape gave way to ruins and there wasn't a street at all, only a path of dirt and broken paving. In some cases, the buildings had been purposely torn down, each of the valuable Roman blocks taken to be used in improvements elsewhere. In other cases, the Earth reclaimed for herself the building materials fashioned from her clay. Many roofs had caved in, and more than one building, including a grand basilica with a curved colonnade and crowned with a dome, was slowly being pulled down by vines and mosses, which spread along the facade like the fingers of a great hand, gradually crushing the edifice in its grip. Often only the foundations were visible, surrounded by lots repurposed as pasture land, or wild spaces for saplings and shrubs to take root.

Even a valuable *villa urbana* that had once served a Roman-British magnate was falling victim to the depredations of ecology and elements. Its entire streetward side had collapsed, giving Uleara a cutaway view of the interior of the grand house, and treating him to sights of its former splendor. In what had been the entertaining room were the intricately painted the scene of a nymph's grotto and

157

a couch built to resemble a dolphin, both of which were in the final stages of being annihilated by nature, as if she were demonstrating her contempt for humanity's amateurish imitations of her genius.

Still intact, though, were highly detailed portraits of the former owners, painted in fresco on another set of walls within the villa. In the gloom of the storm they seemed to Uleara like reproachful spirits of the dead, their eyes appearing to stare into his soul. He was reminded of a passage from the Hebrew Bible, Job 34:14. *If He should set his intention to it, and withdraw to Himself his spirit and his breath, all flesh would perish together, and mankind return to dust.* Uleara made the sign of the cross to himself.

After traveling past these scenes of urban disintegration, when they were close enough to the river to hear the splash of the fish and the knocking of the boats in their berths, the Silurian led them off the main thoroughfare into a narrow street that was filled with refuse, fish innards in particular, and alive with rats. It proved to be the portal into a network of cramped avenues that teemed with people and echoed with shouts and music. It had been nearly invisible from the deserted far end of West Gate Road, yet seemed to claim nearly as many inhabitants as the center of the city.

Uleara realized they had passed into the famous Bower district, the Silurian ghetto, and it made him anxious. Longtime neighbors of Aurelian's tribe, the Dubonni, that ruled Glevuna, the Silures had set up a colony of sorts within city, which was not as unusual as it might have seemed to one unfamiliar with Silurian custom. Silures went where they pleased if it could be reached by water, and claimed title to all navigable passages. They tolerated others on "their" river or sea as a guest, and it was a dangerous gambit to challenge a Silure in a maritime setting.

The balance the Silures struck with the other tribes was that they eschewed dry land for the most part, and lived in cramped, makeshift villages beside their harbors when settlement was necessary. Most times their boats were their homes, as their land-based dwellings reflected. Extended families of a dozen or more would live in an apartment designed for five people, and whether it was before dawn or after midnight, yet more Silures seemed to be constantly coming or going from each one of them. They maintained their comfort in these confines by way of the ingenious but mad-looking storage devices they built, and the pulley-rigged ropes that supported awnings, hammocks and window screens. They were the only tribe in Britain that cared about economizing space.

They were also the most drunken, pugnacious, cursing, dishonest, sentimental and unpredictable people on the island. The Silures were famous for their perplexing system of gods and the weekly feasts they held for their pantheon, debauches of brawling and sex, the only times strangers were invited into Silurian society for reasons other than business. They were renowned as one of the most intermarried tribes, essentially one clan. It was a saying Uleara had heard, and repeated, that "a Silurian wedding does not unite families, but reunites them."

"Are you certain about this," Uleara whispered to Kieran in Latin.

"As certain as I can be. What reason have you not to trust?"

"Latin again, eh?" said the man in the common Britonic. "So you don't trust Laghal. Okay. But be careful with that high talk in these parts. Words put a mark on a man as much as his dress – and don't you know, we Silures just can't be trusted." Laghal smiled at Uleara, but his eyes, from what could be discerned under his hood, showed nothing amiable in them. Uleara glared back, but said no more and continued walking.

Lord forgive me, I will admit it. I have a distaste for the entirety of the Silurian kind. Help me to forgive as you forgave, Uleara prayed within, even as he cast an inimical glance toward Laghal. Moments later, the Silure held up his hand, a gesture for them to halt.

They were in front of a door at the back of a two-story building, in an alleyway so tight the door could not open without scraping the building opposite it. Piled beside this entrance were several amphorae, barrels and chests, stacked together under an oilskin tarp. The inside of the house was as cramped and chaotic as the street on which it lay, the rooms dominated by nautical equipment, stored but looking strewn in the claustrophobic environs, and a multitude of religious idols, each illuminated by a pool of burning oil, casting monstrous shadows every which way.

The other adornments on the walls included the large image of a man with an exaggerated phallus carved into a beam near the entrance, and equally lewd graffiti on the walls and doors of the small rooms that branched off of a narrow corridor.

"Was this a brothel?" Uleara blurted.

The man turned slowly.

"Who says it still ain't, mate?" he said. There was a frozen pause, then the man began convulsing with laughter. "Nah, I'm tugging your line. It's just me and my family, and my wife's family, or two of her brothers' relatives any rate, and a few relatives in from Caerleon, and of course some Brigantine boys I used to crew around with when we sailed the Euwerddon Sea. But nobody else. Don't fret, they won't bother us. Have a seat if you like."

Kieran and Uleara both sat, on a bench that had once been part of a boat and was still surrounded by fishing nets and tackle. They silently absorbed their surroundings, and listened as an intense conversation took place in one of the adjoining chambers.

Soon Laghal returned with two bottles, the contents of one clear and the other red, and three short sipping cups, the whole kit of which he did not carry so much as suspend from his fingertips, and all of which he plunked down in one dexterous motion.

"Trick my Da taught me," he said as he whipped back his hood, revealing an unpleasant but not malevolent face. His features were small and pointed, and his complexion was darker than even his Silurian heritage would suggest. Laghal's hair was wooly and black, but brought out the gleam of the dark, bright eyes beneath his mop. He smiled at his two guests, and with a furtive glance back toward the other rooms, hung his cloak on a peg by the door.

"Drink up, there's plenty there," said Laghal, untopping one of the bottles and taking a seat at the table with them. "I can get the wife to put on some cider to steam if you'd like."

Uleara would have liked nothing better, but could not bring himself to ask even that small favor of the Silurian. *I'll end up with a cup full of piss or poison.* The Silurian was oblivious to Uleara's attitude, or ignored it if he was not. Kieran, however, regarded Uleara with an expression that straddled reproach and concern.

Kieran acted first, and poured himself a shot of the clear liquid. He sniffed it and took a short pull, smacking his lips and smiling at the Silurian in appreciation.

"That's excellent *chouchen*. Really excellent."

161

"Ought to be," said the Silurian, downing his cup, "it's from the stock of the Hebudians, over in the Nameless Isles, between Caledonia and the Endless Ocean. It's the only way they keep from freezing in the winter, poor bastards."

The Silurian passed a cup to the abbot, who took it reluctantly, but drank as the other two had. It did warm up Uleara considerably, and calmed his agitation. Seeing how quickly he had dispatched the first, the Silurian refilled his cup. When Uleara hesitated, the Silurian said, "No need to be shy, Christian, plenty more of it to be had."

Uleara drained the second cup and relaxed in his seat, and his eyes began to unfocus as he watched the firelight flicker beneath an idol of a woman holding a snake. He noted the house's proximity to the river, visible through a window on the opposite side of the main room from the door. The swaying lanterns on the bows of the boats were the only other source of light in the apartments, besides the fire in the idols.

"I'd appreciate it if you would fill my friend in on what is happening," said Kieran. "Tell him what you've been telling me."

"With respect, are you certain that you want to share this? He's trustworthy, I mean?"

Uleara bridled inside. *Question my trustworthiness?*

"I deem him the most trustworthy man I know, Laghal," said Kieran, "and given what I know of your dealings I find it hard to believe you would anoint yourself a judge of who should be trusted and who should not."

A flash of resentment came to the dark eyes of the Silurian and he set his jaw, but the emotion passed from his face, and he only gave a nod of acknowledgement in reply.

"Well then, here it is," Laghal began to Uleara. "The Golden Prince, who was nearly assured of the Crown of Crowns yesterday, is today watching his chances slip from his hands, and there are those who believe that come tomorrow he will no longer even be king of Dubonni."

"Wait, what? Are you certain?" Uleara asked.

"Nothing is certain until it is certain. Yet it's well known there are those even among his own tribe who have secretly despised Aurelian since before his father's passing, but who have never believed they had a real chance to undermine him. Now they see their chance."

"Is this true?" asked Kieran.

"It had better be true," said the Silurian, "it cost me a lot of money to find out what you keep interrupting – which means it cost you a whole lot more, druid."

Druid? Uleara thought.

A noise caused all three to turn their heads in alarm, but they saw it was only a little girl peering from the doorway.

"Gwenna!" shouted Laghal, at which the girl's face went wide in fear and she disappeared. Laghal got up to bawl out his daughter.

"Druid?" whispered Uleara to Kieran. Kieran only gave him a shake of the head. Druids had inhabited the island even before the arrival of the Britonic Celts a thousand years before. The Romans drove all but a few to extinction, and since

163

then, whether they had died out or fled the island, the Old Kind had not been seen in Britain for hundreds of years.

"No peace in my own home," said Laghal, taking his seat. "To resume: that is how things stood until this afternoon. Aurelian and the Dubonni could still rely on the support of the Deceangli and Demetae to put Aurelian on the throne, though barely, and they are pushing for King Cunomor of Dumnonia to endorse the Golden Prince for high king. He is, after all, Cunomor's cousin, and the Cornovii stand to gain considerably from Aurelian."

"Why could Cunomor not seek the high kingship himself?" Uleara asked.

"His scars are five parts dueling and sport to every one part battle," said Laghal. "He fought the Saxons, sure, but kings of Dumnonia pick and choose their wars. They are good when they show up, but when that is doesn't have much to do with when it's needed."

Uleara made motion to speak again, but Kieran stopped him with a hard look. The three drinks of the hour almost led Uleara to give vent to his frustrations then and there, but again he restrained himself, sighing loudly in passive protest and slouching in his seat.

"Of course, on the other side, the Catevullani lead the opposition, with the Brigantes and Parisii joining their cause. They claim that with King Drystan's Catevullani bearing the brunt of the fighting in the south against gods-rot-him King Ceradic and his Saxons, and the Brigantes holding off both Angles and Picts in the north, their coalition has the right of selecting the king."

"That leaves undecided the Dumnonii, the Durotriges – and the Silurians," said Uleara, with emphasis on the final name. He gave Laghal a stern look, but the

Silurian pressed on with his briefing, lowering his voice to just above a whisper and leaning further across the table.

"That was a few hours ago. Since then Bograg has come down to get his bucket." That was one of those oblique references only a from-the-cradle Silurian could decipher. Uleara took it to mean, "All Hell broke loose."

"Were you in the city before, when the war party returned?" Laghal asked Uleara.

"The Legio Nova?" asked Uleara. "I was."

"It wasn't the entire legion, but it was Aurelian's elite corps, hand picked. They were massacred. We only saw what was left after Ceradic and his men were done with them."

"What were they doing near the Saxon lines?" asked Kieran. "The truce is still in effect."

"Truce," snorted Laghal. "A truce is supposed to be honored by both parties, not maintained by one while the other continues raiding at will, as the Saxons and Angles do. But no matter. It is being said Aurelian's warriors were sent there on a special mission, but none know what it was, except Aurelian and the Dubonni court. Fewer than half returned, and those only because they were able to cross a river swollen from the rain that the Germanics did not want to brave. At least as many of the New Legion died in the crossing as in the fighting."

It is as the boy near the tavern judged it, an omen. Uleara crossed himself.

"With the situation as it is," continued Laghal, "I have information that the Demetae are considering withdrawing their support, and King Cunomor has

165

been silent on whether he will decide in Aurelian's favor. The Golden Prince suddenly finds his position very much in doubt."

At that instant a furious gust of wind knocked open the shutters, and as the gale blew through the apartments it carried off everything it could, including most of the illumination. Other family members, the men shirtless and sporting ratty culottes, the women thin and with hair severely pulled back and covered, came back in to relight the idols, saying blessings under their breath as they did. They fled the room as quickly as they'd entered.

"Well, it seems as if Fahelane is confirming the omens," said Laghal, "What were we talking about? Ah, right. Aurelian stands virtually alone. The Deceangli are remaining steadfast for the moment, but they are the only tribe the Dubonni can count upon at the High Council, when the vote will be held."

Laghal sounded as if he was going to continue, but before he did he looked to Kieran, who gave the slightest of nods. The Silurian returned the nod and leaned in very close to Uleara. In a voice even Uleara barely heard, he said, "There has been talk all over the city – among those whose talk you can trust, I mean – that some may not wait for the vote, or even the morning, to decide the matter."

Uleara felt a chill. "Decide how?" he asked.

"Remove the question."

Uleara looked back and forth between the other two, before saying, "You mean, do something to Aurelian

"He faces many false friends and open enemies, all of whom would love the chance to stick a *gladius* between his ribs. Gods man, why am I explaining this to you? With your purposes…"

Laghal stopped short, mouth open, knowing he'd just spoken a few words too many. The Silurian withered under Kieran's gaze of deep displeasure.

Let's get some answers, thought Uleara. He smiled, without mirth. "So Kieran has filled you in on our intentions here, has he?"

Laghal's eyes told of how many mental calculations were being made behind them. After waiting fruitlessly for Kieran to speak, he finally said, "Not too much. Not much at all, really. And anyway, I make it my business never to make other people's business my business, catch me? Secure as Lugo's chest," he said, tapping his forehead.

"But the basics?"

"Well, I…"

"Laghal."

Kieran said it slowly, deeply, with subtle but profound menace. A look of clarity came to Laghal. He calmly said to Uleara, "Your purposes are unknown to me, and I will say as much to any who ask, regardless of how they ask it."

Uleara's eyes were like lighted coals. He took his breath in gulps for a moment, then pivoted toward Kieran, lips working over his teeth.

"It's good to have people you can trust," he said.

Uleara whipped back to Laghal. "And where do the Silurians stand? Would they be part of the Dubonni coalition, or perhaps among those looking to 'eliminate the question.' Eh? Are we here for treachery? For murder? That would be my guess if there's a Silurian involved."

Laghal jumped up.

"You, a Dumnonian, is going to talk to me that way?" yelled Laghal. "Look mate, I know you've had a burr up your ass about me since the street. It's no concern to me what your opinion of me is, honestly, though normally I don't let a dressed egg like you speak to me like that. And out of respect for Kieran I won't beat your teeth into the back of your skull for insulting my tribe and my family in my own home. But you need to bear in mind that we Silurians, who you think of as so dirty and beneath you, have been your betters in all ways for hundreds of years. The Romans didn't even bother to try to conquer Dumnonia, that's how terrific you people are."

Laghal came around the table, and Uleara jumped back defensively in his chair.

Pointing a finger at Uleara and coming so close to the abbot that their breaths crossed paths, Laghal hissed, "We and the Ordovicians are the only ones who stood up to the Romans during the invasion, when everyone else was bending over to make it easier for them to have their way. The Ordovicians don't exist anymore because of it. We were the ones making it so all Britons got their fair cut of Roman trade during the occupation. And if it weren't for us 'murderous' Silurians patrolling the eastern shores and chasing off the Germanics, the war would have been lost twenty years ago and every Briton would be speaking Ænglisch!"

From behind Laghal a man came charging out of the archway that led to the stairs. He was of stocky build and taller than Laghal, but had the same sharp features and curly, dark hair, as well as particular carriage that suggested both seamanship and paranoia. This man was also extremely angry, and his face was of a burgundy hue similar to his brother's.

"What's the ruckus, Laggy?" shouted the man. "There trouble here?"

A teenage girl holding an infant appeared behind the man. Six more heads emerged from behind the arras leading to the catacombed hallway, one of them Gwinna's and the rest belonging to Laghal's wife and other children. Looking to the window, Uleara saw yet another half dozen men observing the events with neutral faces.

Utterly surrounded.

Laghal's brother strode into the center of the room.

"What's your business here?" he demanded.

Kieran looked to Laghal, who, as if commanded, forced a grin and said, "It was a stupid argument. These men are my clients. We were just discussing terms and it got heated. You know me, eh?"

The bigger man was entirely unconvinced.

"Business is one thing, brother, and if these men are here under your banner as you said, they are your care in dealings. But when I hear some rat bastard landsider putting down my clan and race within paces of my fists, it becomes a matter for all proud Silures. We have to stand on Teulseth's Rock each one of us." He turned to Kieran and Uleara. "So which one of you *culcopons* do I have to put right about what's what?"

Though he and Kieran were standing next to each other, Uleara felt the innumerable pairs of unfriendly eyes surrounding them focused on him alone. With a glance to his side, Uleara saw that Kieran was, as usual, the most serene person in the room. Uleara had no doubt he would be able to smooth the ruffled

169

feathers of Laghal's brood with only a few words and that ineffable way of his. In fact, Uleara could tell this was what Kieran was moments from doing.

He will weave his spell and get us out of the saucepan, soon to be moving again, thought Uleara. *And if I knew to what purpose we were working, or were once consulted, I might not be doing this.*

Uleara stepped forward. "I said it."

The room fell silent. Laghal's brother looked murderous. Even Kieran was now, for the first time, surprised.

"Uleara, please," Kieran said. The imploring look on his face had two depths, one concerning the immediate situation and the other conveying a more profound appeal. The genuine, plaintive expression was almost enough to stop Uleara's words, but not quite.

"No. I will no longer suffer insults, commands or company I am not happy among."

"You're in rough waters, fat man," said a woman holding a toddler.

"Quiet, woman," shot Laghal.

"You be quiet," she returned, but ushered the children from the doorway nonetheless.

"I'd consider your next sounds carefully, Christian," Laghal's brother leveled at Uleara.

"I always consider my words carefully," said Uleara. "I consider the words of others carefully as well. And all I'm hearing is conspiracy. I don't know what the aim is and I don't know what the stakes are, but I know I don't care to know."

To Kieran, he said:

"You represented yourself as my friend. You were supposed to be the person above all others I could count on. And now you relegate me to your hunting hound, telling me to fetch or stay or be quiet, serving your sport through my obedience. Whether it is a ghost of your memory, a past you have kept hidden, or some other force entirely, something has transformed you, I fear – though my greater fear is that you have not changed, but only been revealed. Curse your glowing thingy and curse your quest, I'll have no more of it."

And here he addressed the room: "There is something here, now, in this city, that is certainly so important that men are speaking murder about it. It is called worldly gain. But as it seems none tire of pointing out, I am a Christian, and the throne I serve cannot be found in this kingdom or any other on Earth." He looked to Laghal's brother, who was considerably less sure of the situation than he had been at the outset.

"If you want to follow me into the street and claim the blood your clannish pride obviously demands, so be it. But I will not spend another second in this place. Farewell."

Uleara, who had edged toward the door during his harangue, now placed his hand upon it and pushed to make his exit. The door flew open with far more force than his fingers had generated, and as Uleara stepped through the threshold, his progress was arrested by a solid wall of humanity. From very close range Uleara beheld the bear and dragon emblem of Aurelian stamped on a bronze breastplate, which Uleara, looking up, saw to be worn by an enormous soldier.

Uleara backed off as the soldier continued through the door, followed by three of his cohort, who were of similar magnitude, official bearing and elaborate armor. The lead soldier surveyed the room, and said directly to Uleara, "We are looking for a tall man with a skunk's beard, and a fat Christian priest." With a smirk he asked, "You haven't seen them anywhere, have you?"

Uleara looked behind him, and found the room utterly empty of people, except for Kieran. All the other Silurians had disappeared the moment Aurelian's soldiers showed themselves. *Credit where it is due*, thought Uleara, quietly stepping to Kieran's side.

The soldier didn't wait for a response to his query, but continued, "King Aurelian has been looking for you. He has made his want of your presence known. You will come with us."

Uleara felt in his heart the passion of discord gone, replaced only by apprehension. Yet it seemed to the abbot that Kieran and God were evidently in league, at least as far as forcing Uleara to remain on the adventure. Uleara sighed, looked to Kieran and held out his hand in a gesture that said "after you." Flanked by their escort, they marched out the door.

Chapter Twelve

I was resigned to my fate, thought Kieran, *but it wasn't my fate after all.*

Until the previous winter, Kieran's life as a slave was one he had come to accept. It was a difficult life, to be sure, but Kieran knew too well how things might have been. He never forgot the vast improvement a dry place to rest each night and a meal every morning constituted compared with his original circumstances. Without memories of his life before the riverbank, it was possible he was in the best circumstances he'd known. This was a fact he kept close by, to employ whenever discontentment began to overtake him.

By way of his disabled Croepschen character, Kieran was absolved of the most grueling tasks, though this was a double-edged proposition. Kieran never fully got over his guilt at watching the others toil to the point of collapse, while he, fully capable of giving them aid, did nothing to lift the burden. Though Kieran knew well enough why he could not spring forward and grab part of a line while boats were being hauled onto the beach, the physical impulse often arose and had to be forcibly restrained. To reveal himself in even the slightest degree under the wrong circumstances could mean death, and that knowledge was enough to keep him unambitious.

Yet there was Ecbehrt. So much of what had made Roscinham tolerable was due to the giant deaf metalworker, who proved to have permanently adopted Croepschen once the caravan reached the village. The other slaves and freedmen laborers varied in their treatment of the "Loki-spawn" new slave, and the household proper was indifferent to him, but Ecbehrt made sure that no one would seriously consider doing him harm. Croepschen was his ward.

While the smith had gladly shown Croepschen every bit of kindness and conscientiousness, he had unwittingly shown Kieran his craft. As the twisted slave he toted and tottered about the shop uncomprehending, but the unimpaired Kieran underneath was watching the forge, hovering near the work bench, Ecbehrt plying his craft, Kieran his secret apprentice. For this too he was grateful.

The best memory Kieran had was of the *Litha*, and it was because of Ecbehrt. Litha celebrated the pause in goddess Sunna's yearly wanderings across the sky at *Midsummor*. The people of all Germanic settlements offered a great bonfire with many sacrifices set ablaze, to nourish Sunna in her travels and prepare her for *Ragnarok*, the Final Destiny of the Gods, when she would die by the teeth of a demon wolf and bear a child on the same day. It was one of the holiest yet merriest days of the year. For the people of the village, it was an event that was the focus of eager anticipation and extensive preparation for months.

Kieran had been awakened on his first Litha Morn by Ecbehrt standing above him, wearing a grin and sporting glittering eyes to befit a child on his birthday. Awaking and getting up in character was always the most difficult part of the Croepschen role for Kieran, but that day it was not a concern. Seconds after Kieran opened his eyes, Ecbehrt, who was usually gentle to a fault in his handling of others, almost pulled Kieran's arm from its socket as the titanic smith yanked him to a standing position.

Kieran quickly discovered why his hulking friend transformed into a tot on the Litha. It was Ecbehrt's day to be the man he might have been, but for a case of the measles as a youth. From the time after the first offering at the Midsummor festival until the last fire was extinguished, Ecbehrt was the best Angle in Roscinham.

At the axe and javelin throwing grounds, Ecbehrt was the equal of the most celebrated warriors in the horde. At wrestling, he was, through a number of rounds, their betters. Ecbehrt spent his day proving his mettle, to the general aplomb (though occasional chagrin) of the thane's men, each one of whom considered himself the most ferocious Germanic to ever don a boar skin, until he met Ecbehrt in the wrestling circle.

Ecbehrt also found time to join Croepschen in playing with the women and children. Kieran thought it one of the most endearing images he'd seen when a group of girls wove field flowers into strands of Ecbehrt's hair and beard – especially when a warrior who dared taunt him for his floral adornments found out what it felt like to be trounced by a deaf man wearing a crown of daisies.

The male children played a game like tag, except a person became "it" when he was tackled to the ground, tied up and blindfolded by the person who had been "it." The game introduced Anglic youth to a chaotic and dangerous world, and its direct applications were many. Above all, it was a prelude for warriors, the start of their training to kill foes even with sweat running into their eyes amid the confusion of the battle's gyre.

Ecbehrt wasn't deaf from birth, Kieran thought, *and must have once played the game as an equal once.* Likely he would have been marked early as a fine prospect for the field of war. Then, after his illness… The realization heightened Kieran's respect for the way Ecbehrt bore his lot in life.

Kieran had a feeling that Ecbehrt's intoxication later on might have been spurred by similar thoughts watching the children's game. He was not a devoted drinker, but that night Ecbehrt demonstrated he did not need much practice to turn in a great performance. He put away an entire cask of barley *beor* and several short draws of *hedromel* before the children went to sleep, and by the time the adults were ready to retire as well, Ecbehrt had long disappeared in the company of a serving girl who was in the household of one of the thane's captains, and neither were seen again until morning.

Kieran had witnessed all of it, and it made the Litha one of the best days he knew at Roscinham.

He'd begun to feel increasingly remorseful that his relationship with smith was founded on a lie. One of Kieran's most fervent wishes had been to someday reveal himself to Ecbehrt, drop the ruse and show his true self to the man who was his only personal connection on Earth.

The chance never came.

Kieran and all the others who dwelt on the peninsula were under the dominion of Thane Agelrot, the ruddy young noble to whom Kieran sold himself on the last night of the caravan. Roscinham had been given to Agelrot by his uncle the eorl, on the very night Kieran too became his property, in celebration of Agelrot's coming of age and success in assaulting the Britons. These details and many others Kieran learned from his increasing comprehension of the Germanic tongue, which the speakers called *Ænglisch*.

The village, home to around two hundred souls, was built atop a finger of flat land that extended half a mile into the sea, and whose plateau at its highest elevation sat fifty yards above the waves. The north side of the finger was a sheer cliff, and the south was formed of sandy soil that sloped gently into the water. The curve of land south of the finger created a natural harbor, and on any given day, accounting for trading schedules and naval actions, one could usually find a dozen or more sleek longboats beached along the shore. The largest were capable of delivering six dozen frenzied warriors into the heart of a coastal village, or a barrage of flaming missiles that could raze it to the ground. Each ended in a curved bow, carved as a dragon, eagle, wolf or god, striving to stop an enemy's heart at its sight.

Strength was the ultimate virtue in Roscinham, as in all Germanic villages and towns, and Agelrot did his best to make sure that each thing associated with him conveyed vigor to the greatest degree possible. This ethos was evident in everything, from the dozen deadly longboats in their moorings, to the great hall at the center of the village, forty yards long and twelve high, to the gigantic rams in Agelrot's personal pens, each sporting thick shaggy coats and not one but two sets of curling, sharp horns.

Strength primarily came through his fighting men, and Agelrot kept them on display as well. Most of his troops lived permanently outside Roscinham, within a mile or two of the village, on their own farms. However, Agelrot's most cherished fighters were his household troops, thirty in number, whose thirst for riches in peacetime and hunger for conquest during war kept them fiercely loyal to him and always present at the village core. Many of these had grown up alongside Agelrot, who was twenty-three but still acted as a person half that age, finding no end of encouragement from this inner guard, and they were treated with all the privileges lifelong friendship demanded.

Lady Lorelei, the most beautiful and feared woman in the village, was also to be included among Agelrot's treasures. She was his wife. After his enslavement Kieran quickly realized that Lorelei was the same woman who had leered at him during the caravan two years earlier, and subsequently he did his best to avoid her.

One morning in the bleakest part of winter, when the village stores were dangerously bare and the whipping winds seemed to find no end of cracks and holes through which to torment Kieran in his shack, he awoke to hear moaning nearby. Kieran rose from the bundled rags that were his bed and tracked the source of the low wails. They were coming from the annex to the smith shop, in which Ecbehrt made his home, and Kieran opened the door to discover the smith thrashing about in his own bed insensate.

Ecbehrt had been forced to work night and day for a rare winter campaign Agelrot was planning, and the combination of little food and miserable conditions had produced a cough in Ecbehrt's chest that worsened for a week. The smoldering sickness had finally erupted.

As Ecbehrt shivered and moaned before him, Kieran could tell he was critically ill. His normally well-colored face was ghostly, and when Kieran examined him he discovered a feverish forehead and pounding pulse. Kieran could not assist Ecbehrt alone.

He almost forgot to transform into Croepschen as he tore out of the annex and sped through the pathways that led to the village apothecary. The low-gated compound where the Priest of Remedies and his acolytes operated was deserted, and Kieran cursed aloud when he remembered they had gone into the woods to replenish the medicinal stores before the warriors departed for the campaign.

The crone who lived in a cave near the cliff side of the Roscinham peninsula was Kieran's next hope. She kept away from the village for the most part, but was renowned for her skills with the occult, reinforced by her costumes of feather and lizard skin, and a dwelling as crammed with mystical implements as it was hard to find. Kieran had observed her twice, and knew her successes had more to do with a good grasp of human nature than any alliance with supernatural forces. Even so, she was knowledgeable enough about physiology that she was his next best chance of saving Ecbehrt.

178

She proved another dead end. Kieran stood outside the entrance to her cavern shouting for ten minutes before taking the initiative to enter. Much to his dismay he found the crone in her sleeping chamber, dead drunk, rolling augur bones on the floor over and over again and reacting to each toss with either a smile, a grunt or a "bah!" Kieran tried for five minutes to explain the situation to her, even going so far as to completely drop his disguise for the first time since he had adopted it, but it was to no avail. She still sat swigging from a pig's bladder of beor and rolling the bones as Kieran sprinted away.

As a final recourse he went to the great hall of Thane Agelrot himself, and came upon him eating with his court. Among assorted cousins, visitors and favored warriors, members of the pre-campaign hunting party Agelrot had assembled, Lady Lorelei was also in attendance. She gave Kieran a sly smile upon his entrance.

The notables, Lorelei excepted, barely looked up from their breakfast as Kieran, portraying Croepschen, hobbled into the area before them as they dined. Croepschen could not address the nobility without first being recognized, and an agonizing span of minutes passed before at last one of the lesser in the coterie glanced at Kieran and said, "Are you lurking here for a reason, retard?"

Kieran immediately burst forth, as articulately as he could in the guise of Croepschen.

"Ecbehrt sick. Bad sick. Need help, bad. No time, need help."

Others in the throng looked up now, but not Agelrot, whose magma-colored head was still bent over his victuals. Those who now paid Kieran attention did so with blank faces, as far from concerned or urgent as he could imagine.

179

He repeated again: "Ecbehrt sick. Bad bad bad. Bad sick. Need come, need help."

"Go bother the apothecary."

"He gone. No time!"

"Wretch!" burst Agelrot, his face red to match his hair as he finally lifted his head from his plate and fired darts at Kieran with his eyes. "Do I look like a priest, or that crone in the cave? Ecbehrt is the strongest man outside of this room, and will recover, I am sure. Do what your feeble brain can for him or find someone else to alleviate the problem, but leave me to my meal or by my oath I will flay every shred of skin from your back."

At that statement, the hunting party bowed their heads again and resumed their feeding. Kieran, stunned, stood in the hall a few seconds more, searching for something he could say that would compel help to come from these men. He backed out of the grand room and into the village square without finding it.

Later that afternoon, Kieran was the sole person there with Ecbehrt when the end came. Kieran kept giving him water and comfort to the extent he could, but at last the large man went limp against his bed and closed his eyes forever. Kieran stayed by the corpse, weeping, keeping vigil, waiting for someone else to arrive and initiate the rites of the dead.

The first to come by was one of the very men who had sat stone faced before Kieran's pleas in the hall of Agelrot earlier that day. He let the spurs he had brought for repair fall from his hand when he saw the still body of Ecbehrt and Kieran crying beside him.

He immediately ran off for aid, and a group including a pagan priest, one of the apothecary's assistants and Agelrot himself arrived shortly thereafter. The learned men declared Ecbehrt to be deceased in their expert eyes, and Agelrot ordered preparations made for his cremation. He then delivered his only other comment on Ecbehrt and his passing, words the thane forgot the moment they left his lips, but which would stay with Kieran long after.

"It is a tremendous shame we have lost such a skilled smith," said Agelrot. "It will be difficult to replace his craftsmanship. Find me someone who can handle the smith shop tomorrow while we arrange for a permanent substitute."

After that, it was impossible for Kieran to remain in Roscinham one second longer than necessary for him to effect his escape.

Months had passed, but now Litha had come again.

Kieran's eyes were intent on the horizon. The very smallest arc of the solar circle appeared behind the murky gray landforms on the other side of the Channel, and the sun cast its light upon the waters. Little bits of illumination floated and undulated across the vast plain of sea separating the island of Britain from Europe, and soon Roscinham, his place of confinement and his entire world for eight seasons, was illuminated before Kieran by the first rays of sun. Despite the obvious drawbacks, Roscinham was a place whose unique geography and natural beauty lent itself to contemplation. Kieran released a long sigh, and cracked his neck.

Kieran looked out at the water, across the flat expanse of sea toward the dull clump of land on the eastern shore, anticipating the dawn. It was what he had done every daybreak for the past two years.

Earliest morning was the only time of day that was truly his – his only chance to simply exist as Kieran, not Croepschen, until after everyone else in the village of Roscinham had retired to their beds. He had nights as well to pull off his mask and occupy his own skin, but those were taken up almost entirely by Kieran's clandestine activities, which consumed all of his concentration and left him with only a scant few hours of sleep.

Kieran rubbed the small of his back and winced. It was now constantly sore from both the hunched posture he affected, and also the all-too-true rigors of life as a slave, which consisted of little more than taking things from where they were and moving them to where he was ordered to put them.

If only they knew what their idiot does while they sleep, thought Kieran, looking down upon Roscinham from his regular pre-dawn perch.

It was with satisfaction Kieran peered across the Channel to the dimly-formed land mass on the other side, and watched the eastern sky to see the day begin. It would be his last as a slave.

Whether I am alive or dead, by nightfall I will be free, he thought.

From the perspective of any uninterested observer – and the Angles were not as a rule interested in their slaves – Kieran had completed his routine as usual that day, though it was Litha and he was granted an extra hour of sleep. He arose, trekked to the thane's hall to clean and restock supplies, and returned to the smith's shop at his appointed times. He was at his rock the minute he could normally be found there, were anyone ever to look, and departed from it punctually too. Where he went from there, however, was well out of the ordinary, even for the Litha.

182

The germ of his escape plan was planted by a persistent cough in a slave who kept the flock. The man, Tredan, was roughly Kieran's height and build, and from the back they had been mistaken for one another more than once. As the shepherd's health weakened, an idea within Kieran grew strong, and when he was buried, Kieran took action.

The first and least worrisome of his labors was the tailoring. If discovered while sewing a duplicate of his usual attire, Kieran could rip it up or pretend to have found it, and he was free to work on the outfit at any hour he could.

The digging was a different matter. For two nights he'd quietly, slowly filled sacks with dirt from atop the burial spot and then put the sacks into the pit, covering them with dirt so that the grave looked undisturbed. On the third night he revealed Tredan's shoulder, and then put the sacks and dirt back and waited until Litha Eve.

Last and least forgettable of his preparations was the exhumation, undressing, redressing and storage of the corpse, which had occurred hours before Kieran was to be found sitting on his rock on Litha Morn. The close call near-discoveries, the feel of deceased skin, the physical work to get Tredan's body in place was not an ordeal to repeat, but it was done. Now all that needed doing was the rest.

It was just before the noon ceremony, and Kieran limped through the Litha festivities passing groups of merrymakers around banquet tables that completely filled the southern slope of the peninsula, all the way down to the harbor. He surveyed the faces around, and saw no suspicion or even note of his presence on any. Success demanded their obliviousness remain intact while he retrieved a wheelbarrow and three barrels from Thane Agelrot's reserve cellar, and wheeled them in the direction of the water, as he was soon to do.

Most of the revelers were working on a good head of beor already, and the ceremony was soon to start, when the entire village would be gathered well away from the northern cliffs, where Croepschen was about to have a fatal accident. Yards away from the cellar doors, Kieran let himself rejoice.

"Croepschen!" The voice came from behind him, but some distance away. Kieran pretended not to hear and continued apace. *A few more feet...*

"Croepschen!"

Now Kieran knew he had to halt, and silently cursed as he looked to see an acolyte of Baldur, assistant to the Master of Revels, approaching him with a quick step.

"Croepschen my creature," said the man, "fifty of Brechteld's men just arrived and we need three more casks each of beor and hedromel, from the main storehouse. Do you understand, six total? Three of each?" he asked, holding up the corresponding number of fingers on both hands. Kieran nodded.

"Good. We will need them before the ceremony, so hurry."

The man raced off, his stride telling of the thousand other pressing matters to which his mind was bent. Kieran hesitated, and thinking on it briefly decided to continue on his course to the closer cellar. *An honest mistake.*

"The other cellar, Croepschen." Kieran faced the assistant, and could tell that the man was going to watch until Croepschen obeyed correctly. Almost involuntarily, he altered his steps to take him toward the thane's primary cellar, on the other end of Roscinham.

What Kieran did not see as he changed his course was the pair of beautiful green eyes tracking his movements. Minutes later, out of sight or earshot of the village, Kieran was in the storehouse stooping to lift a cask of beor when he the door opened behind him.

"Ah, here you are."

Kieran was compelled to turn, and tried to keep the fear from his face as Lorelei, at her most stunning, climbed over the threshold and closed the door behind her, bringing the light in the room to the level of late evening. She stood there for a moment, her splendor incongruous with the space around her, boring into him with her gaze. The storehouse seemed suddenly quiet, and very cold.

"Am I interrupting important business?" she said, stepping nearer. Kieran registered the fuchsia dye on her lips, the ringlets of honey-red hair spilling down her cheek, the gown of scarlet and indigo that accentuated her hourglass curves and left half of each breast uncovered. She smelled of springtime and sexuality and walked like a dream. However, in her eyes was a rapacious gleam.

"We haven't spoken very much," she said, and gave a short laugh. "Of course not. Who speaks with a simpleton?" She laughed again, a series of short bursts which were, like her voice, subtly tinged with rancor. "Unless that person isn't really a simpleton at all."

Kieran felt his heart leap, and his mouth became dry. He cowered slightly, and looked for the exits. There were two – a stack of crates blocked one, and the thane's wife blocked the other. Kieran was trapped. Lorelei saw the fear in his face, and her smile spread.

She strode toward him, walking in and out of sunbeams streaming through small gaps in the doorway and wall. Each time her face moved from shadow to light, Kieran could see a look of impending victory.

"I have been watching you, ever since you came to us," said Lorelei. "You put on a good performance, I'll grant, but sometimes you let yourself show. Good is good enough for most of the oafs around here. But not me, Croepschen. I smell a hidden ingredient in what you're serving."

She began to circle him, as a cat circles a small creature that wanders into the open. Kieran concentrated very hard on maintaining a look of incomprehension, rather than guilt and terror, which is what his breathing and heartbeat would indicate if Lorelei came closer.

He attempted a vacant smile, and said, "I dance? I work?"

She laughed again. "Maybe."

Lorelei circled closer, lowering her voice to a purr.

"When that deaf smith was dying I started to really see it. A half-wit who suddenly learns how to speak? Starts to stand upright, starts looking defiant? I don't think so." She paused, and made sure her next words hit home. "You let yourself slip, dear Croepschen."

Kieran was livid at his former lassitude and petrified of the present moment. It must have shown.

"Nervous?" she asked. Lorelei was close enough that when she said the word Kieran felt the jet of air that carried it against his cheek.

He allowed some of his inner fright to creep into Croepschen, and stammered, "I... I go?"

"You aren't going anywhere."

She was now almost touching him. Kieran as Croepschen let out a cry and backed away. "No, I good!" he yelled, flailing his arms and moving gracelessly toward the wall. "No hurt!"

"You know I'm not going to hurt you. I just want to end this game. Let me see you as a man." She moved to close the distance Kieran had created, with such ease it was almost imperceptible. Kieran's pulse thundered. He knew he could run, and Croepschen could plausibly claim he hadn't understood what she was saying, that he was frightened (that, at least, would be no deception).

Except Kieran was forced to recognize that part of him wanted to be unmasked. He had spent two years living a life of servitude and subsistence, made worse by the constant lie he had to tell with his every action and utterance. He had wished for some way he could be released from his double prison, and here, in front of him, was his opportunity. The fact that the opportunity assumed the form of a woman of remarkable allure had to be considered as well, for Kieran was fully a man indeed, and one who had not in his memory known a woman.

No, it's not that easy, thought Kieran, shaking off Lorelei's spell. As Croepschen he said, "I no know what you want. I work? You no hurt?"

"Oh by Thor, please stop it," said Lorelei, frustrated. "For two years I've watched you, and for two years I have thought something was off about you... about you not being off. And now we're here."

187

She backed him against a wall of flour sacks. As Kieran tensed, Lorelei leaned close, pressing her palm against the stack of grain and easing her body against Kieran's. He held his breath as she ran a hand down his chest.

"My Croepschen," she cooed, tightening her embrace, "or whatever your true name be, I know you have longed to let your secret be known, and to know a woman's touch. Don't you want it?"

She shifted her hips, and her pelvis fell into alignment with his in such a way that it sent a thrill of pleasure through both of their bodies. He inhaled her scent and felt her warmth, and gloried in the glow of desire radiating from her. His fear began to give way to her nearness and her enticements, his awareness of her womanness. She felt him begin to yield, but so did he, and he said, "This bad. I scared"

"No no no," she breathed. Her hand moved along his back, and she deepened and protracted her rhythmic grinding against him. "This natural. This what you want."

She worked her lips against his, coaxing open his mouth and pushing inside with her tongue, her arms and legs enfolding him in a firmer embrace. Her hand moved over his crotch, and Kieran could do nothing to prevent the reaction her fingers would soon perceive. He had no way to flee and no way to fight what his most basic biology dictated came next.

He relented, pushing into her kiss, her hand, her breasts, her body, seizing her, taking control. He was exposed.

After a few brief seconds of fumbling in the furor of lust, she pushed at him, hard, sending him back against the flour. Kieran saw her look instantly turn from enticement to domination, and the grin on her fuchsia mouth spoke not seduction, but savagery.

Shit.

"Ha! I knew it!" she said, clapping her hands together. "By the gods, I knew I'd draw you out. Well, speak! Let me hear what the Loki-spawn of Roscinham has to say for himself."

Kieran could do nothing but stand up straight and answer. "Your language – I do not know it good."

"Huh, well, that's better than before at least," she said, still delighting in her triumph. "Tell me you have at least some vague spark of intelligence behind that blank stare. Are you considered quick of mind?"

Kieran thought for a moment and shook his head "no." She smiled.

"Ah, so there are brains in there. Very clever, Croepschen. The wise man plays the fool to the end." She began to circle again.

"I am sure you haven't yet realized the source of my interest, but a smart man like you could see I find intelligence an attractive quality in a man." She laughed and tossed her hair in parody of an ingénue, but quickly resumed her previous mien. "I wager you're also quick enough to see that your life no longer belongs to my husband, who lacks that quality, but to me. One word to Lord Agelrot, one hint about your deception, and you die. If you dare defy me, the few minutes longer you live will feel like years under the torment my husband can inflict, when he's motivated, and I will ensure he is at the top of his form. Tell me you understand."

189

Kieran nodded, feeling no more powerful or capable than his Croepschen character.

"We need to have that understanding between us," she said, "because you and I are going to be extremely well acquainted." She was kittenish again, her eyes once more half-lidded and full of desire. "My husband, you see, is not terribly up to his most important duty, which is to produce an heir. I know not if he prefers the intimate company of his men – he spends enough time with them – or if he's simply as profligate in his lovemaking as in his other responsibilities. It is not a concern of mine. I have my entertainments."

There was a savoring twist of her lips, and it produced an unpleasant effect coupled with the hard set to her eyes and other features. Kieran sensed a well of fury within her, and it splashed into her words as she said, "I will be the mother of a great warrior, a great leader of Angles. I will not let this family be overtaken in its favor or position, and I will not be relegated to a shack, to begging through my old age because my husband is not the man his father promised. Sunna is my guide, and my place is beneath her glow."

Kieran understood why Lorelei had cornered him in the shed, why she had been eyeing him all along. She could get herself with child by no other man in the village, for any might tell the tale of its conception. Any but Croepschen, who was also disposable. Kieran knew from instinct, terrifying in its clarity, that when Lorelei was finished with him to her satisfaction, she would have him killed. The last of his libido disappeared.

Lorelei looked ready to take her privilege with him then and there (*to harvest my seed and discard the chaff*), but before she pounced they both perceived the swelling crowd noise in the village, which signaled the approach of the noon ceremony.

"Tonight we shall begin, after moonrise, in the copse by the beach," she said, moving close again. She kissed him aggressively, cupping his private reaches once more, and rasped, "It is an auspicious night to conceive the next king of the Angles, and I think you will find the process more than just bearable."

Lorelei laughed and went for the door. Before leaving she turned and sternly declared, "All is as before. You are still a wretched simpleton and shall remain so. Wait a while after I leave before you come out of here. And one more thing." The savage smile was back, mingled with madness. "I'll be watching you, closely, and so will others. Day and night. We wouldn't want our Croepschen to wander off by himself." She closed the door, and Kieran followed, eventually, even remembering to deliver the casks of beor.

The ceremony was the same as it had been the year before, and as in the year before, Kieran wanted to turn away and shut up his ears at its climax. Dozens of cages containing chicks, lambs and rabbits were set ablaze and consumed at the crest of noon, amid a cacophony of screeches and screams. Kieran believed he knew how each of them felt, a caged beast being sacrificed to ends that it cannot understand.

I resolved I would end this day a free man, regardless of whether alive or dead, thought Kieran, *and I will keep my word.*

Kieran had nothing, though, with which to fulfill his promise. Under close scrutiny there was no way to move Tredan, which he would have to do regardless of escape, and before the rotting smell advertised the corpse's whereabouts. His learning of smithy was no help, much less his servile skills. All Kieran really had was the secret of his hidden identity.

He caught sight of Bogmel, and hope reached a toe back into his heart.

Might that be enough?

Bogmel, the man chosen to replace Ecbehrt as smith, was of good build but small spirit, whose sad, jowly countenance and bald head Kieran had come to know well. Bogmel did a passable job handling the forge and anvil, but no companionship emerged between he and Kieran. He treated Croepschen much as did everyone else – as if the slave were only sometimes visible.

The new smith was sitting by himself, munching on a haunch of hare at the outskirts of the festival, and Kieran casually moved his way. Careful not to seem it, Kieran remained focused on Bogmel as he ate his solitary meal. Bogmel was in all ways downtrodden, and as nothing was wrong with his mind, senses or anatomy, it seemed he'd been kept out of the longboats and battle formations of his brethren only because no one much liked him. He didn't seem to much like himself either. To Kieran he looked like a man who would agree to just about anything to improve his place in the village, as long as he did not have to do much to achieve it.

I think I have the perfect solution, thought Kieran. *For both of us.*

Kieran stayed near Bogmel for the remainder of the afternoon, waiting for a time when he could approach him with privacy. The opportunity came when, filled with beor and mutton, the smith chose not to use the overcrowded refuse pits, and instead walked the long way to relieve his bowels near the copse of trees Lorelei had chosen for the late night rendezvous. *Fitting.*

Kieran followed him and secreted himself in a clump of bushes behind the smith. Bogmel hiked up his tunic and went onto his haunches, and Kieran chose the moment to speak.

"If you shout or run you will not make your dreams real."

Kieran's words literally scared the smith into defecating, though he was already bent and bare-bottomed. Not knowing what to do, the smith remained in position and looked around with the expression of a man whose shit was interrupted by a voice of the faerie folk.

"You have can knowing and power, to make Agelrot and warriors they like you," continued Kieran, in a timbre that he hoped bespoke power. "Quiet be, and must you stay without fear." It was the most eloquent Kieran could be in Ænglisch, but Bogmel's fear smoothed out deficiencies of grammar.

"Wh…who are you?" stuttered the smith.

Kieran stepped out of the bushes, fully erect, sporting the muscled physique two years of labor.

"Croepschen!" he cried. "By what miracle or enchantment are you transformed?"

Perfect.

"It was a witch who made me free of being a crippled," said Kieran, "and now I give you free to choose: take riches or be turned into what I am before."

Bogmel cowered.

"No, no, I want riches! Do not harm me!"

"No harm I do to you. I have things not known to tell to you that will put you where kings sit."

Terror, disbelief and joy wrestled for control of Bogmel's face. "What must I do?"

"I will tell you, Bogmel, I will tell you all. And then you will rush to do what I say, because we do not have time." Kieran looked at Bogmel's compromised position and added, "But first clean yourself off."

The sun had set, the revels were burning out as quickly as the pyres, and the moon was halfway risen on the horizon. A group of men stood around a brazier in the midst of the copse of trees by the harbor. One wore bronze and steel that gleamed in the flame, his vivid red hair matching coals at the fire's edge. Three others, a smith, a leatherworker, and a slave, wore the best they could. The last man wore the white of a priest, and it was he who was speaking.

"...and as it was made before the gods, before the gods it will be unmade." He turned to Agelrot. "Is this arrangement well met by his lordship?"

"It is," said Agelrot, a little drunk, a little bored. The smith Bogmel had presented nonsense when asked why he would suddenly want to free a crippled slave, but he offered good money, and that made Agelrot less curious. Croepschen had been an asset toward general morale, worth a few laughs and a little bit of labor, but Agelrot preferred cash in hand to a crippled slave.

"And do you have both the slave and the payment?" asked the priest of Bogmel and his companion, a young fletcher serving as *aedwas*, or witness, who seemed more than a little drunk.

"We do," said Bogmel.

"Then let the exchange take place."

The money was handed over in a small oak trunk, which Bogmel's young friend watched depart with eyes that wanted to sprout arms and grab it back. "Take heart," whispered Bogmel to his pale and tottering aedwas, "you know we shall

194

have that tenfold soon enough." He smiled toward Kieran, the one who'd been healed by the magic that would make Bogmel rich, or transform him into a half-wit if he disobeyed.

"All are satisfied?" asked the priest.

"Yes," said everyone in unison.

The priest turned to Kieran. "Repeat the oath Odin gives for you to recite."

Kieran recited every word faithfully, doing his best with the ones he did not know. As he neared the end, Kieran spotted a form moving through the trees. It was a woman, a beautiful woman, approaching rapidly.

"And do swear faithful allegiance to all the lords of the Angles, and do swear to rise in service when called," said Kieran just as Lorelei, in a short-hemmed gown of midnight blue, came into view. He stepped up his tempo. "Now I declare my freedom, before all men and the gods. Let my name once more be sung if worthy it be of praise."

It's done.

Lorelei was now within hearing of the ceremony, and began to sprint toward the men in the circle. "No! No!" she shouted, but too late.

The priest tapped Kieran's head with an amulet, and Croepschen was no more. Only Kieran, a free man invested with the sacred rights and privileges of an Angle freedman, remained. He assumed his full height, relaxed his face, and cast a contented look at the startled Angles. Agelrot in particular was amazed by the transformation that took less than a second to complete.

When Lorelei ran into the circle she further surprised her fellow Germanics, and Agelrot, still processing the change in Croepschen, was doubly shocked by the sudden appearance of his wife.

"Lorelei! What by the Thunderer…?"

"It cannot be! Is he free?" she screamed. "Did you free this bastard?!"

"Lorelei, what business is it of yours? What do you care?"

She wildly scanned the confused faces of the other men, then came to Kieran, whose countenance was the picture of placid.

"You sneaky, rotten ass!" she cried. "You beetle! You will never be allowed to leave here, do you hear me? Never!"

"Calm yourself, you crazy wench!" hollered Agelrot, so ferociously that all was at once still. "I have no idea what you are talking about, but I tell you that this man is free, and unless you accuse him of a crime and have an *aedwas* to support you, he may leave if he pleases!"

Lorelei, panting, her hair as wild as her eyes, stood there for a moment pulsing with barely-repressed frenzy, as Agelrot glowered. A sound began in her throat as a growl, rising in pitch and volume until it became a primal wail. She began to cry, though not sob – her tears were those of rage when it finds no other outlet.

"You bastard," said Lorelei as Kieran eased toward the road that led from Roscinham. "You think you're smarter than me? You're nothing. You'll always be a dog, a mongrel dog, a clown on a leash."

"Lorelei, are you mad? Who is this man to you?" shouted Agelrot.

Kieran took a step toward Lorelei. "All Germanics know that a king may yet be a slave, and a slave may win a throne for himself tomorrow. But today I am free, by my own will and strength, before all men and the gods." He paused, then told her, just loud enough to hear, "And that is more than I can say for you."

She froze, silenced. The hate departed from her glare, so that only her profound sadness remained in her eyes. She slumped, head hung low, and that is how he left her.

Chapter Thirteen

Uleara didn't notice he was rapidly bouncing his leg up and down until he saw the look from Kieran, who was seated at the opposite end of the bench. Uleara ceased the motion, and turned away from his onetime friend with a scowl.

The abbot had pinioned back and forth across a range of emotions while he and Kieran sat in the antechamber of King Aurelian, awaiting their audience, but at the moment he settled at anger. He hoped Kieran could feel him fuming in his seat, a few feet down from him. There seemed to be miles separating the two men on the immaculately carved stone bench, of the same vein pattern and egg shell whiteness as the rest of the gilded marble antechamber, one of two dozen equally opulent rooms in the palace of the Golden Prince.

And can I enjoy it? No.

He was all the angrier with his Kieran because now, as they sat together in the grand waiting room, amidst torchieres that illuminated Roman finery so abundant it led one to imagine the Western Empire alive instead of decades dead, Uleara was as nervous as his bouncing leg indicated, and could have done with reassurance.

From a friend, thought Uleara, looking at Kieran. The abbot then caught the attention of one of the ceremonially armored men standing guard and asked, "Do you have any word as to when we might expect an audience? We have been waiting for over an hour."

"No," said the guard. "As I told you every single time you have asked, I do not. You will meet with the king when he wills it, not a moment sooner or later."

Uleara humphed and turned again in his seat. He and Kieran were waiting to be admitted behind an arras of heavy fabric that led into another room in the king's palace, a restored Roman villa atop the tallest hill around the Glevuna Vale.

Kieran might know what to expect to find beyond the threshold of the king's chamber, but I do not. I wonder if it would not be better to simply dart for the exit and take my chances.

He immediately dismissed the thought, but its desperate character reflected the height his anxiety had reached. He had never been put under guard, never been summoned before a monarch, and never been the object of betrayal by a close associate. Now, with all three circumstances converging, it created a maelstrom of nervousness in the abbot's soul, and its manifestations were as strange as they were plentiful.

I just need to get passage back to Eilwath. I will wait for the king to give me the chance to explain, and I will get out of here and never leave home again. Kieran can fend for himself, as he always does, but he gets not a mote more help from me. I'll tell the king that. He'll let me leave.

"The king will receive the petitioners!" shouted a herald who emerged from behind the tapestry. Uleara was on his feet at the first sound, while Kieran waited a moment after the herald's announcement before easing himself from the bench.

"Thank you," said Kieran.

The herald turned on his heels, held aside the arras, and allowed the striding Kieran and the fidgeting Uleara within Aurelian's sanctuary.

Aurelian's villa was so brightly lit that on a clear night one could see its lights from the roof of the Aquae Sulis, 30 miles south. The chamber Kieran and Uleara now entered seemed to contain the sun itself, so dazzling was the light of the flames from the abundant lamps and braziers, so many the reflections in gold, silver and polished gems.

The brightness was most effective in highlighting Aurelian, the young man at the center of the room, upon whom the lights all seemed to converge. His name could not have been more apt. He was extremely fair under a late summer tan, his hair like bleached straw made supple. Arched blond eyebrows, a sly mouth and a pert nose splashed with freckles formed a countenance made to be both playful and demanding.

Though much of the mystique surrounding Aurelian related to his youth, Uleara was entirely unprepared for how young the Golden Prince actually looked. Standing in the company of his war council, poring over maps on a table overflowing with charts and books, he seemed a boy listening in on a meeting of men. His frame was more adult than his face, as it showed signs of broadening into manhood, with gangliness giving way to solidity, but the fullness of maturity yet eluded his physique. Though there was no hint of timid youth in his gaze, his features were still soft with the vestiges of childhood, and his cheeks were clean shaven not because he preferred the Roman style (though it was easy to tell that patrician blood flowed in his Celtic veins) but because his blond beard was still sparse, and if allowed to sprout would create the opposite impression from manliness.

He's so young, thought Uleara, *yet these men listen to him as if he were his father. I have never seen its like.*

One thing that would have been obvious to most observers, and assuredly to the nobles gathered at Glevuna, was that Aurelian had never seen battle but from afar. Uleara, who was himself quite unfamiliar with military affairs, could nonetheless tell at an instant that the boy's hands were clean of blood. That is why he and so many others found it amazing that Aurelian had managed to hold his father's coalition together, and even expand it, without any accomplishments in war. The truce between the Germanics and the Britons had been in force since the Prince was ten years old, which put his age at twenty, but this fact did nothing to mitigate how stunning it was that battle-scarred old kings would show fealty to someone well described as a "lad," especially on the eve of conflict that would engulf the whole of Britain.

With a gesture from the king, Aurelian's aides gathered maps from the table and replaced books along the shelves, which contained the most precious of the chamber's many invaluable objects. There were so many volumes, in folios, bound books and scrolls, that Uleara momentarily forgot his nervousness and was entirely consumed in cataloging them.

The young king approached the pair, hands clasped behind his back and a golden eyebrow arched in curiosity.

"I hear you both speak Latin admirably, and I am expert," said Aurelian, in the Roman language. "I trust you will have no objection if we converse in the tongue of my imperial ancestors?"

"No, your highness," came two replies.

"Good. None of my enemies have acquired an ear for it, and it will keep our confidences from eavesdroppers. Have you been admiring my collection?" Aurelian asked, indicating the shelves.

"Yes, your highness," said Kieran.

"It's splendid, your highness," said Uleara.

"Much of the work was done by my late father, who, God rest him, was fierce about building his strength in every way, and was adamant that I get an education to flex the 'muscles of my mind.' That was his phrase. Are you an advocate of general education, Abbot Uleara?"

"Yes, highness," said Uleara.

It's the voice, thought Uleara. *That's how he's managed to keep these elders and warriors in his thrall. There's something as deep as a mountain's roots about it.* It was a sonorous voice, stronger and wiser than Aurelian's measurements suggested.

Uleara felt himself calming not just under Aurelian's tone but his entire manner. He marveled at the young man's seemingly instinctual way of putting people at their ease yet asserting his superiority at the same time. Uleara thought it a good trait in a king.

"And you – Kieran, is it? I hear you are also a man of learning. That you have a great aptitude for things mechanical."

"It is said, your highness."

"And did you acquire this knowledge during your time among our enemies the Angles and Saxons?"

"Some," said Kieran.

The king gave a smirk of appreciation at Kieran's unfazed candor. "You can understand, I hear things," Aurelian continued pacing. "Little around here, or indeed in all of Britain, transpires of which I am ignorant. I have an extensive network of people who would rather die than leave me without a controlling knowledge of what happens in my domain." Aurelian paused. "And that is how I know you two have been looking for me."

The king let his words sink in, then walked a few paces and dropped himself onto a divan covered in gilt fabric, without indicating that the supplicants before him could do so as well. It was a Britonic king's privilege to sit while others kept their feet.

"The reason I have taken precious minutes from tonight's preparations, and dismissed the council tasked with readying our forces for the fight of our lifetime, is that I cannot piece together why you are here." The king looked into each of the petitioner's faces. "A mystic who speaks with a Germanic accent, gifted in craft, and a Christian priest, of whom not much else is said."

Uleara humphed, but only in his mind.

"It seems strange to me that this pair, odd enough company for any circumstance, should travel all the way from Dumnonia to Glevuna, on the eve of the first High Council in a decade, and spread around sums of money that could not possibly escape notice. Coinage, I add, meant ostensibly to gain access to this very chamber, yet not once did either of you, nor any agent on your behalf, approach my heralds to seek an audience. I have seen a line of petitioners outside my door for a week, but I am told you never once joined it."

"Your high…" Uleara began, but Aurelian jumped to his feet, fair face furious.

"Did I ask you a question? Did I indicate you could speak? I did not. You will hold your tongue, or by God my guard will hold it for you."

Uleara was stunned into stillness, not daring even to breathe noticeably, nor let his gaze waver from Aurelian's hot stare. The young king relaxed, and sat back down.

"You will admit that what I have been told is odd, and as the rumors regarding my safety have doubtless not escaped your inquiries, I wanted to see for myself this mysterious duo and hear what they have to say." He paused again, waiting, before he added, "Now you may speak."

Uleara retained none of his bravado of the antechamber, and in light of the king's outburst, which served as a forceful reminder of their respective stations and powers, addressing the king was the least of the abbot's wishes.

Kieran stepped forward.

"Your highness, forgive us not approaching your court directly. As you sagely said, there is much happening, and we did not think it advisable to present our petition without first apprising ourselves of the situation. I trust you understand our position, but I own, it was a mistake."

"Yes, it was."

"However, your majesty, we have something of the most vital importance to show you. It may yet tip the balance of tonight's council in your favor."

Aurelian's expression of woe brought to mind the teenager he'd recently been. He sighed. "Has every set of ears in the city heard these rumors of conspiracy and dissolution?" he asked himself. "King Drystan and his coalition have made a strong stand, I grant them, and I have heard the self-serving omens the Celtic priests began to proffer minutes after they heard of the... misstep at the Saxon lines." Now he turned again to his guests. "But I assure you, I will not need some pair of Dumnonian commoners to secure my crown. Speak, though: what will you employ to rescue my reign from disaster? What do you want King Aurelian to buy?"

"It is an object that can be of considerable use to you – knowledge that could make you the greatest king on Earth," said Kieran.

"Well, what is it?"

"Pardon me, my lord," Kieran implored, "but it is simply better if you see it."

"This interview is all the time I have for you," said Aurelian, looking to an enormous hourglass in a gold brace, "and the sands say it is almost finished."

"King Aurelian, you are a man of great power and many capacities, and I am entirely confident that you will emerge triumphant from tonight's council," said Kieran. "However, should circumstances prove to transpire differently than they by rights should, whatever the cause, I would never forgive myself if I could have turned the course by insisting that you see the nature of the aid we offer."

"'Insisting?'" asked Aurelian

"I do not do so lightly, your highness."

Aurelian registered interest, then consideration. A few moments went by when it seemed Aurelian, as Uleara had seen all others do, would relent to Kieran's request.

205

"No, I think not. I thank you both, but I am equal to tonight's activities as it stands."

Uleara turned to face Kieran, and saw something he perhaps never once had before: uncertainty. Kieran had no ready-made response to the refusal, and Uleara could see him attempting to calculate a solution. However, as Aurelian said, "That will be all, I believe," Uleara was moved by the helplessness in Kieran's expression. It did not seem to be the sort of countenance one would expect from a spy or assassin. Uleara sighed.

One last chance I give. One more leap of faith I take, though I fear I will end up falling. But, he thought firmly, *I am going to get to the bottom of this all myself, and if I find that Kieran has deceived me again, there will be no stopping what I must do next.*

"Your highness, if I may," Uleara said, surprising both the king and Kieran. Uleara inwardly smiled that he had twice within a minute evoked such responses in Kieran, when the whole seven years he'd known him had produced as many.

Aurelian nodded for Uleara to continue.

"I am a Christian priest, bound by an oath before Almighty God and Jesus Christ the Son that I shall not bear false witness. If the full truth be known, I am a somewhat reluctant fellow on my friend's travels, and I cannot attest to all his methods or motivations. But in seven years of close acquaintance, I have never known him to tell a lie, and he does not do so now." Uleara braved a direct look in the king's eyes, and said. "He speaks the truth, your highness. You must see what we bring."

Aurelian was impressed, and again considered the situation. He folded his hands behind his back and began to pace, stealing glances at the hourglass all the while.

"I am certain you are aware that I have accepted Christ and profess the Christian faith," said Aurelian, with an air that his main audience was himself. "It is my honor, and I believe a condition of my reign under God's blessing, to bring the truth to regions that have never received the Good News, and turn heathen hearts to Christ. I will do as my forebears have, ever since the father of my grandfather's great-grandfather received baptism at Pons Milvius alongside great Constantine."

He wheeled toward Uleara. "Would you now take advantage of that sacred covenant to achieve your goal?"

"Never, your highness. These lips of mine have kissed the ring of the Archbishop of Riems, and would never despoil his reputation or that of his episcopal see by conveying a lie to a monarch, a Christian, and the defender of the Britons in the same breath."

"How many converts have you acquired?"

"Nine, your highness," he said, looking to Kieran, who did not contradict him by pointing out his refusal to take communion.

"A decent number in Dumnonia, and I now see it owes in large part to your oratory," Aurelian said smiling.

"I use the gifts God gave me when in service to just causes, such as preaching his glory, or in this case, attesting what my friend speaks as the truth. King Aurelian, you must see what we have brought. It is unlike anything I have witnessed on this earth, and my travels have been many. I would call it miraculous if I had the authority, and I believe my friend when he tells you that he can apply his knowledge to your benefit."

Aurelian had ceased pacing, and now stood, chin in hand, staring off at the wall.

"It has been a strange day indeed, full of many portents without clarity of meaning. I have been deemed unlucky on this day by the wagging tongues." He gave an appraising look to Uleara and Kieran. "All right, I will grant you a second audience, this one briefer than the first. You shall wait for my orders until after the council, at which time I will summon you."

"Your highness, time is of the essence and it would be…"

"After the council," said Aurelian, shooting Uleara a glare that froze him to the core. "All will go well, so it will not be necessary in any event. However, you have gained my attention, which in itself is a feat. I caution you not to make me rue that I consented to your petition."

Aurelian waved his hand and turned his back, and by this they understood that their time with the king was done.

Chapter Fourteen

The moment they were outside the glittering villa and back on the road down the hill to *urbs* Glevuna, Uleara spoke.

"I need money."

"For what?"

Uleara gave a humorless chortle. "I'm afraid the price of my performance in there was privacy."

"There seems to be a rashness in your manner, is all I suggest," said Kieran. "I am simply trying to discover the use to which my funds will be applied."

"I'm hungry then, if it satisfies you!" burst Uleara. "I will have twenty silvers now if you please."

Kieran considered for a moment, then withdrew his purse and counted out the requested coins. Uleara took them, returned Kieran's perplexity with a glower, and set off determinedly down the road. Kieran kept pace for a short while, then dropped back.

"Where are you off to, your holiness?" called Kieran. Uleara neither turned nor paused. "I shall await you in the tent, then."

You will await, but perhaps in vain, thought the abbot, entering the city gate. *That is a decision I will make, and I alone.*

It was raining again, the water streaming from tiles atop the colonnade that ringed the old forum. Uleara did not see anyone who looked like a bishop, and the only groups gathered were warming themselves around braziers. Even the peddlers were closed up, mostly, having left their carts and tables secure and gone off elsewhere. For such a day, the market square at Glevuna's center was eerily empty.

The area was not completely abandoned, though. Uleara paid attention to the faces he saw traversing the streets and alleys nearby, trying to match each man with the face he'd briefly seen. As before, though, he was seen first.

"You missed it," said a voice at his side, the same voice as earlier. Uleara turned, and the face matched. "The bishop was tedious at parts, but the people dressed like you seemed to enjoy it."

"He spoke on the sin of bearing false witness?" said Uleara, pleasantries an automatic response for him.

"He did. He was against it."

One block up North Gate Street a booming voice called "Four turns afternoon!" The cry was echoed by several other *nuntii* placed throughout the city. The scarred man looked at Uleara.

"I had an appointment," said the abbot.

The scarred man nodded. "Come," he said, "I have someone you should meet."

"Wait on moment," said Uleara. "I don't even know who you are."

"My name is Craddoc," he said. "I work for King Cunomor."

Uleara's jaw clamped shut. The man had nothing sly about him, despite the clandestine way he conversed. Uleara appraised his dress – not showy, but well made, and very clean.

"We can be of use to each other, Abbot Uleara," he said. "If you will accompany me, I know a place where we can speak plainly."

Speak plainly, Uleara thought. *What a novelty.*

"Lead the way."

The parlor was set off from South Gate Street by two perpendicular alleys with no outlets. It was a low-ceilinged, heavily cushioned room with no windows, lit by hanging lamps. There was a sort of bar, but the man behind it seemed like no kind of servant, and the two other men sitting along it were silent. The place seemed to have no purpose but playing host to meetings of a secret and perilous sort.

The scarred man, Craddoc, sat down in a pillowy lounge seat, and gestured for Uleara to do the same in one next to it. The barkeep instantly brought two drams of hedromel and set them on the table between two. Uleara looked at his, but left it alone. He was not in a drinking mood, or a mood for anything but to solve the puzzle before him and do what God would wish thereafter.

"The change in Aurelian's fortune is not all due to that disaster at the Germanic lines. There is a man, many suspect it is that beanpole wizard you were with, who has been moving many coins into diverse hands to make certain that Aurelian's coronation remains in doubt."

"Impossible," said Uleara. It was a reflex, for the abbot was no longer sure what was possible and not.

"Impossible? I think not. You see Glevuna, you hear the fear and doubt. Everyone sees danger and opportunity, which makes for dangerous opportunists."

"I can't believe it in him. I've known him a long time."

"Perhaps he has deceived you as to your purposes here." Craddoc read Uleara's face. "Perhaps he has not told you at all."

"Nonsense."

"I'm sure you're right. You're a priest after all, not a puppy. You would not simply follow someone, someone as, shall we say, opaque as your companion, without a concrete idea of why."

Uleara pinkened. "You are quite opaque to match. It is true what you say, I have observed Glevuna to be awash in cheats… swimming with swindlers. That could well include you. How do I know you're not lying?"

"He doesn't lie."

The voice came from a man Uleara hadn't seen before, wrapped in a cloak, who set a drink down at a corner table, and then sat himself.

"What did you say?'

"I said, that wizard you're trucking with, I know him. He's a Saxon dog." The man lifted his hood, revealing a comely face that burned with hateful eyes. "Have a seat."

"And who are you?"

"The name is Pagos. I know about you, Uleara, you and that man who calls himself Kieran. We were… acquanitances, near Eilwath. Sit down."

Reluctantly, Uleara sat.

The man started, "My grandfather was educated at a Roman school. He talked of an ancient war that was supposed to be the most famous in the world, between Greeks and some others."

"Trojans."

"Aye, that's them. That's right, because if you know the story, you know how the Greeks won, eh? With that wooden horse, a grand gift with a belly full of treacherous death. Maybe you're that Greek horse."

Uleara took a hard swallow of his hydromel. Pagos continued, sidling closer, "How did the Foreigner say you were going to be helping Aurelian?"

Uleara started to sweat. He took another sip. Kieran had shown him that miraculous substance in the workshop, and implied it would be a help to the Christian king. But what did he actually say?

Pagos gave a brief, unfriendly laugh, and took a sip himself. "You don't know why either of you are here, do you? That's a laugh, a priest of the Christ god duped by a Saxon wizard."

Come to your senses, thought Uleara, who said, "Not to be unkind, but whatever you presented to our King Cunomor, he must not have found it compelling."

"It was compelling enough to earn my attention," said Craddoc. "I was assigned by our king to investigate, and you now see me about my task."

"I know what the lad told me was the truth, and he was in the company of that outlander bastard enough to have the measure of his business," said Pagos.

"What lad? What was his name?"

"Aelfarn, think it was. Said he'd seen a letter or message for the 'Willow Wizard,' delivered it personally – and had a peek at it. I convinced him to give up the secret, and he did all right. You were all duped but me, but I have proof."

"What letter? What did it say?"

"That's no mind. What counts is it came from behind Saxon lines, and the boy said it was written in code. Sounds like a spy's work to me."

"I know this is confusing, and upsetting," said Craddoc. "Think, though, Uleara. If you care for the Britons, consider what's at stake if you've been deceived. I'd have a word with your friend – if you can find him."

Pagos was on the second hedromel put before him, though certainly not only his second of the day. He slurred, "Me and the boys could've done with the whole mess right there in the fields…"

"We don't ask that you do anything drastic, anything risky," said Craddoc. "Simply keep an eye out, an objective eye, when dealing with Kieran. And ask yourself honestly," he said, compelling Uleara to meet his gaze. "How much do you really know about him?"

Chapter Fifteen

It was noon on a late spring day when Kieran saw the foot that changed his life.

He had stopped into a Saxon market town to conduct some business, and had a few hours' wait before it could be completed. It was a mild day in *Dreimilche monath*, or the Month of Three Milkings (Maius, as the Romans called it), augmented by a sea breeze that took the sting from the sunlight and warm air redolent of floral scents from the many gardens the townspeople nurtured. Kieran was feeling cheery for a multitude of reasons, and with a pristine day to enhance his mood and a lunch of sausage and biscuit to digest, he resolved to take a stroll through the settlement.

Kieran had a special interest in the town, as it was among one of the last he planned to see before leaving the Britain behind forever. Only two days before, he had received word that his arrangements with a Jutish merchant were fixed, and in a month's time he would be sailing from Dovrus, the main port of the Jutes in their southeastern colony of Caent, to permanently make the Continent his home.

Kieran nodded as a group of young women passed by, and he heard them giggling together in his wake. He smiled, entirely accustomed to the treatment. Kieran – or "Ulstan," as he now styled himself, to sound more Germanic – received constant attention from not only women of marrying age, but also older women and, in a far different manner (usually), from the menfolk as well. In each village he visited, people of all stations paid him every courtesy and showed him every kindness. If a day went by when Kieran was not inundated by various offers from men and women alike, it was probably a day he saw no one.

215

There was no mystery as to what elicited the attentions. Everything about Kieran's appearance proclaimed him a very rich man, from the filigreed gemstone buttons of his quilted blue vest, to the red velvet tunic he wore beneath it, to the stately Friesian stallion with a coat of pure jet and plume-like mane that served as his steed. The simple act of riding into town atop his spectacular mount, bedecked in advanced fashions and wearing the singular expression of the securely moneyed, announced him as a man to be courted, catered to, and to act carefully around.

He hoped the effect would continue once he reached mainland Europe, as the people he was so greatly impressing thus far had nothing that he wanted. He had heard that there were those in the East, men of learning in Constantinople and elsewhere in the still-standing half of the Roman Empire, who still retained volumes of ancient wisdom. Kieran believed he might receive assistance in recovering his memory from such scholars, and perhaps recover still more as well.

At any rate, I'm not going to accomplish anything by staying around here, he thought.

In the time since his emancipation, Kieran had traveled the roads, first putting his theoretical smithing knowledge into practice, then mastering it, and finally transcending what he'd been taught and pushing past what the most learned could do. The items his workshops turned out were not what Germanics, the most sophisticated workers in gold and iron the world could claim, were used to, yet Kieran's works from steel swords to silver accessories fetched admiration and premium prices wherever he showed them. Still no memories from before the river had come back, except in twisted dreams that yielded nothing precise, yet it was clear his hands knew things his mind had forgotten where matters of metalcraft were concerned.

216

Eventually he put down the hammer and tongs and sold his secrets outright. Kieran made a fortune. His buyers included whomever he deemed trustworthy enough to keep the information to himself, and whoever was wealthy enough to pay for it. That second stipulation generally excluded the Britons, or *weals* in Ænglisch, from his clientele.

However, Kieran did take a few natives into the fold during his travels, both out of gratitude to the anonymous family of Britons who saved his life years before, and also from a sense of fairness. The weapons being produced with his knowhow were stronger and lighter than anything the island had ever seen, and he could not offer the Germanics that kind of advantage. He had borne witness to what they could do with the old technology, and was loath to contemplate the destruction they could wreak if left solely in control of the new.

Yet as much as part of him found it distasteful, uncomfortable and even somewhat humiliating, given his secret past, the allure of Germanic society remained strong.

A trio of young brides strolled past, and each in her turn gave Kieran an appraising and then approving glance. Kieran smiled after them in his wake, and acknowledged that perhaps the majority of the pull Kieran still felt from the culture of the Anglo-Saxons owed to the women.

It wasn't simply in the fact that the Saxon ladies were lovely, though they were: from the lowliest cherol woman to the noblest dame (though excluding slaves), the women were stately, elegantly attired and poised. Each took care with her appearance, keeping the folds of her gown carefully arranged and her flowing hair, usually a shade of red or blonde, combed smooth and tucked beneath a cap, or plaited into an intricate design and accented with flowers.

Underlying their outward splendor, though, was an inner grace, a sense of charm and delight that alleviated the often repressive atmosphere of the settlements, most of which were founded on a war footing. Undoubtedly a good part of the reason the women worked so hard to bestow upon themselves and their domiciles a persistent beauty was to offset the ugliness of war, which was never far from their doorsteps.

However, Kieran thought it probably also owed to one of the most appealing aspects of Saxon society, which was the comprehensive, logical and fair law code by which they lived. Under Saxon law, women were in almost all ways the equal of men, and in the writs for marriage were, in some ways, given more legal protections than their husbands, especially in matters of divorce.

There is just something about a woman who holds her head high, Kieran thought, involuntarily thinking of Lorelei. In retrospect, Kieran realized that Agelrot's wife simply represented the most extreme extent of a trait in Germanic women Kieran found otherwise appealing.

Yet another group of young women were gathered where Kieran passed, and he nodded to them as well. It was not unusual to see teenage girls at market towns on the busy days when, brought by their relatives or riding along with neighbors, they congregated there to meet up with one another and survey the selection of men. Their comments about the potential suitors they saw flowed freely, and often were spoken loud enough to be heard at a distance. Kieran was happy to note the stray comments about himself that wafted his way were almost always favorable, as in the case of these girls, who commented on his clothes and confident gait as he walked by.

He normally did not take much note of the clusters of bachelorettes in the villages. Though Kieran's riches, coupled with his enigmatic air and good looks, ensured that he never knew a lack of willing partners in the bedchamber, he was keenly aware that dalliances could lead to permanent life choices he had no desire to make. When temptation grew too strong he would visit professionals he chose selectively, and though he had been persuaded to join a maiden or two for a bit of intimacy, the occasions were rare and knew no sequels with any one woman. Attachments of that sort would be the end of his plans for escape from the island, the desire for which burned as strongly now as it had in Roscinham. The only thing he believed could lead to such an attachment was an error of judgment driven by lust.

Kieran, wearying of his walk, departed from the main street to seek a place to sit. He came to a cul-de-sac where, among other tradesmen and vendors who catered to the upper ranks, an importer of fine clothing kept a shop.

A woman who either owned the store or had been hired to act as its public face was demonstrating a selection of fabrics to a clutch of women who, from the way they were attired and the carefree way they speculated about the purchases, Kieran could tell belonged to the uppermost echelons of Saxon society. He bought a cluster of strawberries from a vendor and took a seat on a short bench outside one of the shops to watch her presentation.

"We just received this in last week," said the woman, whose only major flaw seemed to be an overreliance on makeup and hair accessories. "It is direct from the court of Clovis, of the Franks, and was specially made for the Countess of Orleans, his cousin. Look girls, look at this stitching. This is something your servants aren't going to make themselves – and you aren't going to look like this."

She clapped her hands, and a girl of around thirteen emerged, attired in a gown that was made of two different fabrics that intersected at the waist. The cut was

219

only marginally different from the standard most Saxon ladies wore, at least as far as Kieran could tell, but a wave of excitement pulsed through the gaggle of young women.

He glanced down at their feet as they stood or sat upon benches to see the presentation, and noticed that out of nine pairs of legs, only eight were turned toward the woman at the clothier's. The other pair, belonging to a girl he could not see but could tell was sitting at the back of the group, was pointed sideways. The legs were white, gently curved and elegantly proportioned, which made it all the more frustrating for Kieran, who could more or less see all of the girls' faces except that of the owner of the legs.

As Kieran watched, one of the unseen girl's legs extend, pointing the most perfect toe on the most perfect foot he'd ever seen into the dirt, and began to trace patterns in the dust.

What is she working on? There was no randomness to her movements – it was clear she was following a design. He stood to see from a better vantage, and then a surge of delight hit him when he realized what she had rendered.

Runes! he exclaimed within. He could now clearly see the shapes of the Germanic alphabet, the rune symbols, where her toe had traced their forms. He had familiarity with the runes, as some contracts into which he entered were of such value they had to be rendered in runes on vellum, written in *Wodensblot* - "Odin's blood," or ink, so named because the Germanics believed writing was first derived of the blood that dripped from the king of the gods when he sacrificed himself to gain the wisdom of the universe.

I have to see what she looks like, Kieran thought, trying without success to read what she rendered in the dirt.

His wealth excused a great degree of boldness, so he began walking confidently toward the girls to satisfy his curiosity. However, his way was blocked by a messenger who intercepted him in his course. The messenger had come at the behest of the goldsmith Kieran was in town to treat with.

"My master is ready to complete your transaction, my lord," said the panting messenger. Kieran was hesitant to leave before getting to glimpse the learned young woman with the lovely legs. However, he opted for the prudent course, and left with the messenger to close the transaction, which increased his overall assets by a third.

That night Kieran was invited to join some local merchants at one of their halls, and ended up drinking far in excess of his usually abstemious portion. He bedded down in the guest area of the hall and woke with a throbbing head.

"Stay," said his host, himself afflicted by the morning light. "One day's business isn't worth the hell of riding these roads hung over."

Kieran agreed, and delayed his departure from the town.

When he deemed it time, Kieran rose from his berth and went to the well on the village green to fill his leather bladder and let the air soothe his raging headache. As he took water directly from the bucket rather than the dipper tied to it, leaving the front of his under-tunic drenched, Kieran spotted a beacon of white flashing regularly against the grass.

She was lying beneath a hawthorn tree in full bloom, with white blossoms waving on its branches, like a snowfall that never reached the ground. The girl, or rather young woman, was lying prone on her stomach with her chin atop her hands, staring intently at something on the ground in front of her. Perhaps unconsciously, she was periodically bending one of her legs behind her until her

221

shin stuck straight up, causing the hem of her gown and the shift underneath to billow out and then settle gently down as she let her leg fall to the grass. It was a beautiful, dancing effect the motion created, but what caught Kieran's attention most was the leg and foot itself.

I think that's her.

He moved closer to her, but as he did she turned abruptly on her side and looked in his direction, as if she'd sensed he was coming. He froze, and not only because he did not know what to say if she approached. It was also that her appearance had stunned him into stillness.

Her eyes were aquamarine, and her hair auburn. She had berry red lips, and a long neck that sprang from an elegant clavicle and terminated at a sharp chin and soft cheek. Her body was trim but curvaceous, and her gown was modest but flattering. She was among the most attractive women Kieran had seen.

It was none of these physical attributes that had him paralyzed, though. It was rather an undefined and perhaps indefinable quality that pervaded even that momentary impression, and elevated her into a class Kieran had to invent simply for her. He felt as if he were looking at an entirely different kind of being.

She smiled and waved, and Kieran reeled in anticipation. However, looking behind him he saw another girl coming close, waving as well. The object of his infatuation stood, brushed blades of grass from her gown, and quickly ran off with the newcomer.

Kieran cursed aloud as she departed, and silently vowed that if he had another opportunity to speak to her, no matter what the circumstances, he would cut off his own foot before letting the moment pass without making an attempt to meet her. He was going toward the dairy stalls when he saw her walking away from them, carrying a large bushel laden with cheese. Beads of sweat dotted her face, which bore a grimace of physical struggle, and mud lined the hem of her gown.

This may be her at her least appealing, thought Kieran, filled with joy by the idea, as even in the state before him she still looked every bit as attractive as she had before. Kieran went over to her, nearly at a run.

"Would you like me to carry that for you?"

"I am perfectly capable, thank you," she said without looking over. Kieran was undaunted.

"I only asked if you wanted me to. I can see you're capable. Do you not have a servant or slave?"

"Our servants are busy in the fields, making sure we have crops enough to live on and sell." She now looked over with a guarded expression. "Where are yours? You look like you employ an army of them."

"I did not grow rich having others do my work for me."

She gave a snort of disbelief, but her lips bowed into a smile, and she stopped in her course. When she looked at him, actually seeing him for the first time, her smile broadened and her demeanor shifted.

That's more like it, thought Kieran to himself, reading her new attitude in her eyes, which he could now see were of such luminous blue they seemed painted.

"That is a novel viewpoint," she said to him, still smiling, which made him feel victorious somehow, "but then you look like a novel individual." They stood smiling at each other for an instant, then she continued, "I'm sorry, I'm not usually so abrupt with complete strangers."

223

"Well then, let us get acquainted, so you may be as abrupt with me as you want."

She laughed openly now, an enchanting laugh, sonorous and unabashed, neither harsh nor heavy.

It's perfect, he thought. It was a word that would occur to him quite frequently in her presence.

"I'm Ulstan," he said.

"Freya," she replied. It sounded so beautiful coming from her lips, Kieran had to try it himself, and repeated her name. She smiled.

"You can carry my bushel if you want."

"How kind of you to offer," said Kieran, and they laughed.

Kieran was proud as he walked beside her – proud to have her interest, and proud to remain somewhat suave while balancing an armful of cheese and paying attention to her monologue all at once.

"Men don't have to put up with this," Freya was saying. "You probably don't notice, but when a girl gets to a certain age, everyone suddenly has an opinion on what she can and can't and should and shouldn't do – oh, and of course not to leave out with whom."

She had been looking off, speaking to herself as much as Kieran, and when she looked back she smiled at the strain of effort that clearly showed beneath his debonair veneer.

"Well that's probably more than you wanted to hear about that," she said, walking closer beside him. "So what's your story, stranger?"

Kieran said, "What would you like to know?"

"Why not start simple - Where are you from?"

There's nothing less simple.

"Oh, no place you've heard of," he said.

"I believe it. You don't look like any Germanic or Briton I've ever seen."

"No?" said Kieran, betraying some consternation. "Well, you are right. I am not from the island, originally…"

"Oh, that's fine!" said Freya brightly. "I love foreign things. Have you been to Paris?"

"No. Why?"

"I have a cousin who fought alongside the Franks, and he told me of Paris. From the way he spoke of it, he made it seem the equal of Rome at the height of its plunder."

"I don't doubt it. I have not seen it though, I'm sorry."

"That's alright. You've still seen more than anyone else around here, I'm certain. The men like to brag about traveling across the North Sea when winter is in its rages. For what? They have the same lodges, the same farms, the same damp weather and the same boring Saxons in Germania that they do here."

Kieran had a mad impulse to ask her to leave with him, right then. Instead he asked her where they were going, and she replied they were headed toward the house where she lived with her family. As they eased along the path, at a rate Kieran tried to keep at a turtle's pace to prolong their talk, he became more engrossed with every word, every look and gesture from Freya, who so captivated his attention that he kept running into people or barely avoiding objects in their way as they walked.

"That age I was telling you about?" she said, branching off from another topic entirely, as Kieran knocked into a chicken coop. "I reached it six years ago, closer to seven. Of course my father isn't pushing for me to get married. I'm the only daughter of five children remaining, and he's left no doubt that I am welcome to stay under the family roof as his little girl as long as I please."

"Is that what you want?"

"I am a Saxon woman, and of good blood for what it counts. I don't believe that a woman's only choices upon coming of age are marriage or perpetual childhood."

"So what is the problem?"

Freya closed her eyes and sighed.

"My mother. She does not share my opinion…at all, and has no problem letting me know it. In fact, it is my opinion that if I have to hear her opinion on the subject one more time, I might actually kill her. She believes she is giving me enough choice by allowing me to select a husband from the men she and Hildegard the *fricwebba* keep shoving in front of me, which happens to be the strangest and least appealing collection of men to have ever stood beneath Odin."

226

"Hmm, that is a thorny problem. Looks like you really do only have one choice."

"Oh by the gods, you can't possibly be siding with my mother."

"No," he said. "I think your only choice is to foil all their plans."

"How so?"

"By running off with a mysterious stranger."

Kieran meant it to come across as another of his jokes, a charming flirtation, but she discerned the earnest feeling that lay beneath his glib tone. She stepped forward, and slid her fingers between his. He closed his hand to mesh them together, and Kieran felt as if hand had never been complete before that instant.

"I'm keeping my options open," she smiled up into his face. "But you know what, mysterious stranger?"

"What?"

"I think you should stick around here for a while."

Kieran thought she looked like she wanted to be kissed, and wasted no time in testing his hypothesis. It was a sweet kiss, not frenzied, not sultry, not even particularly protracted. It was simply the most important kiss he would ever know.

"I want to tell you," she said when it ended, "I don't go around giving kisses away."

"And I should tell you," said Kieran, "I don't go around stealing them."

The very atmosphere was changed around them. Kieran at least had no doubt that he would be staying in town. *I can afford to remain a day or two*, he thought, even then knowing deeper down that he was probably giving himself an inaccurate estimate.

Kieran left Freya where she requested, at the end of the side road that led to her home, and went to complete the last of his business. The thought of her, however, never left him.

He arranged to be around her as much as they could meet, and each visit only increased his ardor. While they were together, it felt to Kieran like an eternity; when they parted, the time seemed to have gone by in a wink. He began to notice details of the world around that had eluded him ever since he emerged from the river years before, and saw for the first time how he could appreciate his existence for the moment, and from within it. Kieran began to believe that he did not have to derive all his satisfaction from preparations for a distant date of deliverance that might never arrive.

As he half-expected, Kieran exceeded his timeframe, and contrived to find new business-related excuses to remain near the town, when not engaged in rendezvous with Freya. The only restriction on their time together was that she was adamant he not see her house, and that her parents not discover their trysts.

"It isn't that they would disapprove," Freya told him. "It's the opposite I fear. My mother already floated you as a possible suitor without even having met you, and if she knew we were..." She looked to Kieran for a fitting word, but only got a raised eyebrow from him that made her giggle. "Exactly. If she knew about us then I wouldn't hear a single word about anything else but marrying you. And I'm afraid that would just put me off you entirely."

She kissed him, and Kieran said, "If that's how it is then I'll make sure they never, ever find out."

Freya laughed. "You don't have to go that far. But I do want to wait until the moment is right."

As a consequence, Kieran kept most of his activities outside the town itself. He was foolish the way all the infatuated are, but wise enough to realize it, and knew his daily presence in the village coupled with the abandon new lovers are wont to display would surely lead to their discovery.

The clandestine nature of the affair only heightened his and Freya's ardor, and one night she surprised him by taking him to the loft of a rarely-used barn that belonged to her friend Felitrica's father, where they would be free of interference. It was an evident invitation to continue their physical relationship to its furthest extreme. Kieran spoke as little to her during their journey to the barn as he ever had, a result of excitement and nervousness, and as a precaution against inadvertently saying something that might make Freya revoke her invite.

All proceeded along the course Kieran had envisioned, and in the darkness and solitude, with the vibrant late spring night pressing around them, they tangled passionately for minutes upon end. Then it changed. At the apex of their passion, as Freya was on the verge of accepting Kieran into her, she suddenly turned away and became still and sullen.

"What is the matter? Do you not want this?" he asked after a few silent moments.

"Oh, by the Vanir I do. I do so badly. I did not promise Felitrica the use of my best dressing slave on the Harvest Day so we could sit up here and talk."

229

He smiled in spite of the deep pain etched in her expression.

"Did I do something wrong?"

"Oh, no, no Ulstan," she said. "It is nothing you did. It is something I did – something shameful on my part that you will soon enough know."

"What? What is it?"

Freya rolled her back to him and lay on her side such that the barn wall heard her words before Kieran. "You have such a different kind of way of looking at things from any man I've ever known. But I am afraid that even you have your limits of understanding, and that this will test them."

She turned toward him again, and her eyes contained a plea. Kieran braced for terrible news, but resolved that he would say "yes" to whatever she asked, if it were in his power to do so. Churning with apprehension but placid of exterior, he waited silently for her to continue.

She stared at him, stammered, and finally expelled, "I have been with another man!" She seemed to collapse from the effort of uttering her words. She gave a hopeless sigh and turned back toward the wall, curling her body up.

"What, recently?

"No. Before you."

Kieran was cautiously relieved, but also surprised. The plaintive look that had been there in her eyes, so foreign to the assured expression she usually wore, and her girlish posture as she lay waiting for his reply revealed a vulnerability she had never before exposed. Instead of diminishing his desire, however, it only deepened his affection for Freya.

"And so…?" Kieran said, simply to make certain that nothing else lay in wait, fighting to suppress a smile or laugh.

"Don't you comprehend?" she cried, turning toward him again. "I am no longer in my maidenhood! Another has taken me! And if that makes you want to discontinue our friendship and not see me again, I will accept it and know I was a fool to believe you would behave otherwise. I have yet to understand the pride that makes men do what they do, but I will take it as inevitable and return to holding my nose at the fricwebba's suitors."

Tears had worked their way into her eyes, and she seemed on the verge of letting them loose. Kieran knew he had but one recourse. He lifted her chin with his fingers so that he gazed into her frightened and despairing eyes, drew her close, and let his kiss be all the comfort she needed.

"Whatever you think of your past," he said, "it need never make you ashamed of who you are now," he said. "Not with me. Not ever."

He kissed her again, and when he drew away this time, he saw Freya's tears spill without reserve down her cheeks.

"I know where you're from," said Freya, her voice a thick whisper. "You think you're clever, but I know your secret. You are not from a different country at all." She squeezed his hand. "You were dispatched from Fensalir by my namesake Freya, for she knows my mind and saw that my only happiness would be secured by you."

That night they made love.

Kieran extended his visit by days, then weeks. He remained committed to continue his journey to the Continent; he simply did not know how to do so

231

without breaking his own heart. He corresponded with the Jutish merchant and secured the man's promise to put off his voyage, in exchange for a vast sum that Kieran offered to compensate his losses from the delay.

Still he had not told Freya he was planning to leave the village, let alone Britain, and did not have a clear picture of how to reconcile his competing desires when the time came. Kieran had tried without success to muster the courage to let her know his plans. Each time he resolved to confess, something in her laugh, her manner, her words, her very glance would stay his tongue and convince him to put off the revelation of another hour or day. He never did tell her.

After a number of weeks, the inevitable occurred when Kieran and Freya were caught kissing in a glen of the nearby woods by someone who informed her parents. Kieran was awakened at his lodgings, an inn down the road from the village itself, by the keeper of the house, who delivered a message from the thane. "Ulstan the stranger is commanded into Thane Eadweard's presence on matters the day cannot leave without seeing done," said the innkeeper, attempting to get the words right.

The innkeeper remained uncertainly in the hallway as Kieran made his ablutions and dressed in the finest pieces he owned. At Kieran's word the nervous man sent for the messenger to inform Eadweard that "the stranger" would present himself within the hour.

Kieran's perceptiveness did not fail when he guessed that Freya was involved in the thane's message. However, it was not until Kieran was directed to the "thane hall path" by townsfolk tripping over themselves to be helpful to him, and arrived at the very road to which he often accompanied Freya, that the reason for the secrecy she had maintained became clear.

She never told me she was the thane's daughter, said Kieran to himself. He was slightly annoyed with her for leaving him unprepared for the eventuality of this meeting, but more upset at himself for not having made the connection sooner.

A slave let him into the house and showed him to the threshold of Eadweard's chamber. While the slave announced him, Kieran saw a pale face crowned with red hair appear from another doorway. At first glimpse he thought it was Freya, but in a moment he saw that the woman was middle-aged, and while still attractive, she was years past the prime of her beauty. She gave him a smile of approval and what he also took to be encouragement.

That's Freya's mother, thought Kieran, as a gruff voice said, "Come in" from behind the door to the thane's chamber. Kieran entered.

The thane was seated on a low stool, cinching up the straps of a leather guard secured to his left forearm, one of the last things he needed to complete the hunting outfit he sported in every other detail. Eadweard had an almost spherical head, large and solid-looking atop an oxlike. His moustache was still black, though his beard and hair were gray, and his body was mainly trim, with only a small rim of fat at his belly and too much flesh on his upper arms betraying his fading physique.

It was the shocking blue of his eyes, just as blazing as his daughter's, which announced Eadweard as a man who was perhaps more keen of wit at his current time of life than he was at a younger age.

"I hear you've been seeing my daughter," he said, his voice like the grinding of boulders.

"Your daughter and I find each other interesting."

"I also hear you are kept busy at all hours in various dealings with both the Saxons and the tribes of the Weals. Being as you are a man whose time is in such demand, I thought I'd take it upon myself to arrange our introduction. I feared your commerce might indefinitely prevent you from taking the step yourself."

It had been two years since Kieran was freed from bondage, and on the day of his emancipation he made a vow to foreswear timidity and subjugation before anyone, man or woman, king or slave. However, Eadweard's words, without containing any overt threat, produced a prick of fear in his breast that he'd not felt for some time. Kieran knew the thane had little power to deprive him of his liberty or life, but suddenly, standing before Eadweard's intense glare, Kieran realized his fear in the man's presence was not due to any lordly power, but the power of a father over his only daughter. It was power to deprive Kieran of that he desired most.

"My lord, I was in error, and apologize for any disrespect you may have perceived," said Kieran. "We… I thought it better to clarify our own intentions between each other before I presented myself."

Eadweard overturned one of his boots and slapped the sole, which sent a spider dropping to the floor and skittering for a dark corner. Eadweard pulled on the boot and said, "What you were doing was staying clear of my wife's lust for Freya's matrimony, and it speaks to your wisdom."

He stood, the leather of his hunting outfit creaking as it stretched, and drew himself up to a height that the blockishness of his frame had belied. He and Kieran stood nearly eye-to-eye.

"Are you ready to go?"

"Am I to accompany you hunting?" asked Kieran. "I am not dressed for it."

"All the better. I am not interested in the material your clothes are made of. I want to see what you are made of. You don't mind getting your seams tugged a little?"

Kieran grinned. "As long as I don't come back in pieces."

Eadweard laughed. "I make no promises." He then said, seriously, "I want this to be clear: I do not care for your fortune and I do not care for your reputation. I have both of enough for myself, and when I die my daughter will inherit part of one and all of the other. What I care about is that you are the sort of man who can make Freya happy and be worthy of the honor. Her change in the past weeks indicates you can delight her during the first blush of affection, and I'll own I never saw her so girlish even when she was a girl. But lifetimes are not made of lovers' trysts."

Eadweard, at the door, turned to see Kieran somewhat overcome with what he'd said. He did not so much smile as let his brow unknit and his mouth relax, and said, "Come, man, don't let my words deter you. Freya values my opinion but relies only on her own, and you have all day to get me on your side." He motioned. "Shall we go?"

For several hours they traipsed through the woods, joined only by one of the thane's slaves, hunting for songbirds and small game. Eadweard was an expert shot with his yew bow, easily felling two birds and a badger within the first hour of their excursion. Kieran managed to badly frighten a squirrel, but that was all the luck he had. Instead he spent his time listening to the thane tell of his glory days on the fields of battle in Europe and Britain. Whenever the arrows

Eadweard or he fired went astray, and his always did, Kieran conscientiously collected them from where they hit.

The thane commented on this practice once or twice, but he was far more interested in other information from Kieran, and never ran out of questions to ask of him, inquiries that ranged from his opinions of minor political gossip to the family lineage of his mother. Kieran did his best to answer, though clear replies were elusive when it came to things most distant in his past. As the day progressed and their rapport did not, Kieran unhappily concluded he was not making himself understood to Eadweard's satisfaction.

At their midday break, while they spoke of various topics, Eadweard noticed Kieran examining the arrows he'd collected, then working on them delicately with the tip of his derkin and a thick filament of steel. After minutes watching him, Eadweard at last said, "What has you so concerned over dead arrows?"

"Oh, it is merely an interest of mine."

"You are an archer, then?"

"No, my lord."

"Have you ever taken part in battle?"

"No, never."

"Yet your wealth is staggering. You must have been a party to plunder or some other action of force to claim such riches."

"I avow I am unknown to war, except to see its effects on the slow and unlucky. However, I do like to make things - and make them better." Kieran stood, took up his bow, nocked one of his manipulated arrows against the string, drew, and fired. The arrow hissed through the air before thwacking into an oval-shaped knot in an oak tree thirty yards distant. "Better," said Kieran with satisfaction.

"Ah," said Eadweard slowly, nodding to himself and chuckling. Kieran turned with a quizzical expression, and Eadweard, for only the second time since their meeting, smiled. "Now I see why she favors you," said the thane. "She learns."

At the close of the day, while they traveled back along the road toward town, Eadweard asked the question Kieran had dreaded since his first moments in the thane's presence.

"What are your plans? Will you stay?"

Kieran had asked himself the same question for weeks, and still could not decide. Eadweard saw his hesitation.

"You, Ulstan, have the look of a wanderer. I have seen many in my day, and do not mistake me, many of them are good men. They are rootless, though, unable to find purchase in any one soil. Some meet a pretty girl, as you have, and convince themselves that they can give up their ways. But though their hearts may belong to the hearth, their spirits will always belong to the road, and in that contest the spirit will always win. They are fated, Ulstan," said Eadweard with gravity, making sure Kieran's eyes met his, "fated to never know a home that remains theirs for good."

They were nearly within sight of the thane's hall, where the road branched off back toward town.

"This is where we part ways," said Eadweard, who handed Kieran two of the shot fowl. "You were a novel hunting companion."

"I thank you greatly for the honor of your invitation, and for the excursion," said Kieran. Eadweard was turning his horse away when Kieran abruptly called, "My lord!" The thane stopped and looked back with great curiosity.

"I do not know if I will stay here, Thane, and you may be correct about my nature. Yet I tell you this: I have never before in my wanderings spent as much time hoping you are wrong as I have since I met your daughter."

Eadweard looked at Kieran for a moment, and said, "Farewell, Ulstan. If you do decide to hang up your riding cloak, I'll tell you that you won't find a better place than here. Nor, may I add," he smiled, "a woman more apt to make you want to stay home than my Freya."

When Kieran returned to the inn, he found a courier from the Jutish merchant of Caent waiting for him. The message was a simple ultimatum – Kieran had a week to get to the port at Dovrum or the merchant ship would sail without him, and no sum would delay the voyage any longer.

"That leaves me one, two days at most to leave! How does he expect me to wrap up my affairs here in so short a time? He knows that things here are complicated."

"I have delivered the message, my lord, and will await your reply."

Kieran grew pensive. "You will have to wait a while, as I have no answer yet. In fact, you may not have an answer until tomorrow. Tell the innkeeper to find you lodgings, and he will get his payment from me."

"At once, m'lord," said the messenger.

Kieran called for his horse and rode all the rest of the evening, hoping it would crystallize his thinking. The Friesian's hooves flew over the ground as quickly as Kieran's thoughts raced through his mind, but no destination was reached by either, and Kieran returned to the inn equally confused as when he'd left. That night he knew no sleep, as he vacillated between the two opposite poles that constituted his choices, his apprehension mounting as the day approached. When dawn was breaking, and all else had failed, Kieran took advantage of the clarity that fatigue sometimes renders and performed an experiment of thought. He mustered all the powers of his intellect and imagination, and projected his life forward ten years, using every bit of information he had at his disposal.

First he thought of Europe. He took his time, a long stretch of minutes, as he shut his eyes and imagined the splendors of Paris, the history of Rome, the knowledge of Alexandria and the pinnacle of them all, that shining citadel of civilization centered at Constantinople, where the Roman Empire still remained intact. His fortune would secure him audiences with the pope and any number of potentates he would care to meet. He would be among the learned and the sage, and perhaps he would at last unravel the secrets of his own former life and gain a future more like his past. For minutes on end he imagined the glories of the Continental life, as he had since the death of his friend Ecbehrt.

Then he imagined Freya, and the sort of life he might have with her if he remained in Britain.

His eyes shot open and he leapt from his mattress. He barely bothered to put on his tunic and shoes before running out the door of his room, hollering for his horse. Kieran was mounted and about to put spur to flesh before he remembered the courier who still awaited his word. He summoned the man, delivered the reply message, and then spurred his horse to hie toward town.

239

He met Freya on the road there, as she was traveling toward the inn to see him. Both read the gravity of the conversation to come in the other's face, and they branched off the road to dismount and speak in private.

"I heard there is a messenger in town who comes from Caent," she began without preliminary. "I have been told this messenger represents a Jutish merchant, and that this merchant is under the impression you are sailing to the Continent with him, never to return here. Is this true?"

"Most of it, yes."

Freya turned down her face as if it had just become a leaden weight, and she said flatly, "You never made any claim on me, and I never received any assurances from you. I know why you didn't tell me, and I want you to know that I will not ask you to remain."

"You will not, or do not want to?"

Freya did not look up, and several moments preceded her reply. "I don't want anything from you that you aren't willing to give." She paused, then asked, "What did you mean by 'mostly' true?"

"What I meant was that you were incorrect in a small detail."

"Which?"

"The messenger was here – but he is no longer. I have sent him back."

"With your message?"

"Yes, with my message, and also with a tremendous amount of gold."

"What for?"

"To serve as an apology for having needlessly delayed the merchant these past months, when it turns out I will not be sailing with him after all."

Freya looked up, joy filling her eyes and a massive smile spreading across her face. She seemed ready to literally leap from happiness, but restrained herself, and said instead, "Oh, that's good."

"I'd say so!" said Kieran, beaming, spreading his arms wide. Freya again restrained herself.

"It is good news to learn you aren't that sort of man."

"What sort of man?"

"The sort of man who would abandon his unborn child and its mother."

Kieran felt as if he'd been struck. Freya saw his look and smiled with the corner of her mouth, simultaneously biting her lip and nodding. "Before you ask – yes, I am sure. My moonblood is weeks late, so I went to see the midwife. She took one look at me when I walked into her hut and said, 'Congratulations.'"

Kieran's expression went through a rapid series of transformations, each a permutation of joy, disbelief or terror, but no words came. Finally, Freya burst out, "Well, say something!" So Kieran said the only thing he could think of.

"I love you."

Freya gave a small coo, and smiling said, "Do I hear a question in there? A proposal, perhaps?"

Kieran gulped. "I don't know what the formal... on these occasions..."

"Yes or no?" she demanded.

"I think that's something I'm supposed to say."

"Never mind that. What's your answer?"

"Yes."

"Good!"

They collided into each other's arms, kissing madly. When they struggled apart, Freya said, "Oh, my mother is going to be so happy."
"Your mother? You're joking."

"Not at all," said Freya. "She wanted me to have a traditional marriage, and we're getting wed because you secretly put me with child." Freya beamed. "What's more traditional than that?"

Chapter Sixteen

It cannot be so, thought Uleara, dodging past pedestrians in the packed avenue as raindrops drummed on his tonsured head. *Of all the things I might have suspected, that he would be actively moving against the Golden Prince... be a Saxon saboteur?*

Yet so much about their short time in Glevuna had been strange, and so much about Kieran's mood different, that Uleara was prone to believe almost anything. Kieran clearly had designs he thought Uleara would either disapprove or divulge, but that miraculous object he'd been shown, that shimmering jar of wonder, should have been immediately put on display as a present to Aurelian if it were of such great import, far from being kept secret.

Uleara abruptly changed his course, and he doubled his pace.

I hope I am wrong, thought Uleara as he arrived at the public stables, sweating and out of breath, but no less intense of bearing. Customers cleared Uleara's path of their own accord as he barreled through the crowd of people waiting for their horses and found the gangly boy to whom Kieran had entrusted Agalyn, Brecca, the cart, and, of supreme importance, what was inside it.

"Where are our horses and load?" Uleara demanded of the boy.

"You were with the skunk-bearded giant, right?"

"Where are they?" stressed Uleara.

"Follow me."

The boy led the way through the barns, guiding Uleara among the doors, passages, horses and people that they crossed in the crowded public stables. The boy at last stopped, opened a stall door and revealed Brecca. The cart was stored behind her.

"Leave me," he commanded, and as the boy shut the stall. Uleara ripped the tarp from the cart bed and began tearing through its contents, while Brecca stamped and whinnied.

"Oh be quiet," he told the horse. Uleara opened every chest, every trunk, looked in every corner. There was no jar, no substance, no glow.

Impossible, thought Uleara. *But I saw…*

Like a lightning shock he was struck by the truth. Uleara never saw Kieran load the jar, and now, in his gut, he knew it had not come with them.

That doesn't make any sense, he said, checking around in the stall, and finally in the saddlebags and Kieran's pack, which, as he now knew it would, yielded no jar. *If not to show him the substance, then why would Kieran need an audience alone with the king?*

It was almost in answer to his unspoken question, the oblong box in Kieran's pack beckoned. *He told me to look.* Even so, Uleara felt a pang of guilt at removing it, and even more so at lifting the lid, not knowing if a corpse or just soiled clothing were to be found within. The guilt disappeared immediately, as the sight before him was all the proof he needed that he had been utterly betrayed.

The only thing I need to know is what the demon I've brought into my midst will say when I show him the proof of his treachery.

Uleara did not want to waste one extraneous second before he found out. Box in his hands, he shoved his way out of the stables and, though he now felt fatigue strongly taking hold from all his many exertions that day, adopted his fastest pace yet.

When Uleara entered he saw Kieran seated on a plush cushion, in a spacious and elegantly decorated war tent Aurelian set aside for their use. He was looking over a scroll, and his pacific demeanor in light of what Uleara had just learned pushed to abbot to apoplexy.

"Where did you get that?" Uleara demanded, referring to the parchment in Kieran's hands.

"One of the priests lent it to me. Have you read Augustine of Hippo?"

"What is this?" Uleara removed the lid of the box and dumped its contents onto the table: a long sword in an ornate scabbard that shook the table with its impact. Kieran's face was neutral.

"It is a sword, Uleara."

"It is your sword, Kieran. It is the sword you packed and did not tell me about, while the luminous material that formed my entire basis for accompanying you is absent. Would you care to explain that? Stand up!"

Kieran did as he was told, and set aside the scroll.

"I will not tell you what I am going to do," said the abbot, cold fire in his voice, "but I will tell you it will end all of your secret plans once and for all, unless I hear a very good reason for all of this. I want to save you, Kieran, but you have very little time before I no longer can."

245

"My friend," said Kieran, moving to approach but pausing when Uleara took a defensive posture. "I know this has been difficult, and that it has been unfair, meandering through the dark while I have a torch before my eyes. You must trust me, though. You must rely on our seven years as friends to outweigh what you have seen in these last days and hours, for it will all turn out better than you can hope, I assure you."

"The time for vague assurances, for your endless requests that I have faith and patience, are past," shot Uleara. "Will you tell me what your intentions are, or will you force my hand?"

Kieran was silent and still.

"I give you this one last opportunity, because of our friendship, because of your wisdom and knowledge, and because I do not believe God would lead me along this path only to greet me with a cliff. Explain away my anxiety or suffer the result of your obstinacy."

Uleara waited, breathing hard, for Kieran to answer. It did not come right away, and when Kieran did answer, it was in a slow, soft voice, one past hope of accomplishing any change in his friend's heart.

"I cannot tell you more than I have. I wish I could let you into my confidence in this matter, but I cannot. I can only ask that you remain the steadfast friend you have been, and do not let from your grasp whatever scraps of faith you have left in me."

Uleara stared hard at his friend, then set his shoulders, gripped the scabbard of Kieran's sword tightly, and made for the door.

"You bring this on yourself. I will not be made to feel a traitor."

Uleara bent to leave and turned to Kieran, in one final instant of hope, praying Kieran would not necessitate Uleara's next steps. Kieran opened his mouth, and momentarily Uleara's expectations rose.

"Do what you must," said Kieran, who then returned to reading his scroll.

Uleara felt as if he was going to either burst out crying or pull the tent down with his bare hands, but he maintained his composure entirely as he departed, clambered back up the hill, and presented himself to Aurelian's household guard.

"I have something to tell the king," he said to the soldier.

"Go away, preacher. Don't you realize the council is about to start?"

"I do," said Uleara. "And that is why if you would like to avoid the wrath of the Golden Prince, you will make sure I get to see him before it does."

Chapter Seventeen

"Nobody would believe we're a happy couple," said Kieran, watching as his wife paced madly through their family hall, throwing orders at servants she usually treated as close cousins and every so often shooting him a glance of annoyance. "Not today." The smiling dog to whom Kieran spoke looked sympathetic but too happy to commiserate, and he soon trotted away. "Smart boy. I wouldn't want to get in the middle of it either."

Whenever their only child Andweard was beset with coughing, malaise or fever, it never failed to leave Freya unnerved. On this occasion, however, Freya was frantic, and that had Kieran more concerned than their boy's sickness. Andweard was running a temperature and had sniffles, but to no greater a degree than usual, which is why Kieran knew there was something else to blame for his wife's frenzied state. It didn't even seem to be related to the fact that Kieran was scheduled to leave the village within the hour, and stay gone for a week (*though that doesn't help*).

"Where is Hegda?" Freya demanded of no one specific, rummaging through the trunk that contained the most precious herbs and compounds they owned.

"Why do you want her?" asked Kieran. "You haven't started believing in elf magic all of the sudden?"

He tried to keep his tone light, but she gave him an utterly humorless look, and slamming the trunk lid said, "Nothing has worked: not the doctors, not the Greek medical texts, and not your odd notions, wherever you dreamed them up. Now it's time for the ancient wisdom."

"Freya..."

"Nothing is working!" she yelled. "Why do you insist on treating our sickly child as if he has nothing wrong with him? Will you finally understand how serious this is when we lay him on his pyre?"

"He isn't sickly," said Kieran, running a hand along his son's head, feeling the sweat trapped under the strands of his hair. "He's just... prone to sickness."

"I fail to see the difference," said Freya, mouth tight.

I see the difference.

It was true what Freya said, though. Since he was a year old, Andweard had been unable to go more than two months without catching some condition or other. Kieran had tried everything he could, consulted medical authorities both Saxon and Briton, and even followed the ideas that sprang to his mind from the depths where his still unrevealed memories lay. However, no solution was to be had.

Still, the boy recovered quickly from his maladies, numerous though they were, and when not laid up with some illness or other he was one of the fittest and most active boys around. *That's not sickly, that's just unlucky*, he thought.

Again, Kieran remembered, Freya was not angry at him regarding Andweard – nor, in truth, angry at him at all.

"Would you rather I not go?" he asked. "There is still time to send a proxy if you'd like."

"Oh don't talk nonsense, of course you have to go. The head of this household has sat in the assembly for fifty years, and that's just in Briton. It's four hundred in Germania."

"I know."

249

"Then why do you ask!"

Kieran had not seriously considered sending a representative to the *Witanagemot*, the annual assembly of elected freedmen and nobles who gathered to decide matters of law and justice in Saxon society. He was simply trying to find a way to soothe Freya's raw nerves, which were rubbing his raw too.

It's so strange, Kieran thought.

For seven years, very little had disturbed the profound happiness that pervaded their marriage, though the inevitable sorrows that visit all families came to their door as well. Both Freya's parents were taken by the plague of five years earlier, but that had not been the greatest sorrow of that pestilential season, though. The disease also carried away their second son, dead before his umbilical cord had entirely disappeared. Freya had spent the entire spring inconsolable.

The old women were adamant that it was a lucky thing the child was taken so young, before there were too many hopes and memories to burn up with his young body on the cremation fires. Their words did little to lessen the wound, but Andweard's survival was an important comfort, and Kieran's elevation to thane upon Eadweard's death provided a host of welcome distractions.

When misfortune did not mar their happiness, family life for Freya and Kieran was most days as sweet and passionate as from the first, and the two competed to heap attention on their darling and thus far only child. There were many wonderful days, and most of them involved nothing more than pursuits dreamed up on idle afternoons by Freya, Kieran, Andweard and their household staff, who were treated more as family friends than indentured servants.

"The carriage is spotted and nigh, my lord Ulstan," declared Brecht, one of the old personal attenders. Brecht had served the hall of Thane Eadweard since

250

Freya was still at the tit of her wet nurse, who while she lived had also been Brecht's wife.

"Thank you, Brecht. Alert those who will join me."

Brecht gave a short bow and strode away. Kieran turned back to Freya, who had ceased her panicked pacing and sat on a cushioned bench with a haunted expression.

"I had a horrible dream," said Freya, staring off. Kieran sat next to his wife, looping an arm around her shoulder and pulling her in for a kiss on her head.

"It's okay."

"No Ulstan, listen. It was not an ordinary dream, not even an ordinary nightmare. I do not put much store by omens, but this one... it scared me."

He hugged her to his chest, stroking her hair.

"Tell me."

"It was horrible. I saw you and Andweard..." She winced in remembrance. "It doesn't matter what I saw. It was the feeling, the sense that something terrible is about to happen." She looked up into his face. "Were you planning to take any sort of a stand at the Witanagemot?"

"What do you mean?"

She looked at him as if she had a dozen things to say of equal importance. Her eyes were searching as she said, "I don't like this new crop of war chiefs. They are not warriors, they're murderers. If my father and his battle brothers were

251

alive, they would put a stop to their schemes. But this new house – Ceradic and his men – their influence grows with the king's weakening health."

"It sounds like there's something you want me to do."

She gave him that strange expression again. "You are my husband and my love, and more important, a worthy man to sit in my father's chair as thane. I trust you to do what is right for us. I would only say… I can say, I know well the seasons of the Witanagemot, and this is a season where courage and controversy can provoke many dangers, even those unseen."

Kieran laughed and squeezed Freya again.

"Me, controversial? You know I have no use for politics. What do I care for that casual betrayal and constant falsehood in pursuit of position? I vote my conscience, and I speak up when the topic turns to, I don't know, damming a stream, or settling a contract dispute between merchants. That sort of thing."

Freya pressed her fingers to her temples and squeezed her eyes closed. When she opened them, their fathomless blue was like the sea after a storm, and she was calm again. She smiled.

"You knew I was a challenge when you met me," she said.

"I'll still carry your cheese any day, my lady."

She laughed, and they kissed, just as a carriage rolled up outside their hall.

"It sounds like the retinue is here," Kieran said, while simultaneously Brecht announced the same from outside. "Will you not greet your brothers?"

Kieran was traveling to the assembly with two of Freya's brothers who ruled lands adjoining his. Ahewan, the eldest of all the clan, had two years earlier been chosen eorl for all their lands, and would sit only a few places from the king at the Witanagemot. He and Cadman, the second-youngest son and one of the quietest men in Saxondom, were waiting for Kieran outside.

"No," she said. "Not now. When you and my brothers return, you will find a feast to greet you, plus a healthy child and a wife restored to her senses." She smiled.

Kieran took Freya's hand and lifted her to her feet, and they walked with arms around each other's waists to where Andweard lay. His fever had broken and his spirits had returned, and when Kieran approached his son's bed, the boy leapt up and enfolded his arms around Kieran's neck, pulling him into a hug with a force that foretold a physically powerful man to come, if the boy could stay healthy.

"Good journey, father!" said Andweard.

"You look after your mother now," said Kieran

"Then who will she get to look after?" said Andweard, causing a fit of laughter to run through his parents.

"I'll return in a week's time," said Kieran to his wife and son. "Then we will prepare for the Yeol."

Andweard smiled and clapped in excitement. Kieran leaned close to Freya. "I will miss you."

She sighed, but smiled. "I will miss you. But you will return soon, and then all will be well."

They kissed.

"It will," said Kieran.

As it had each year for a generation, the Witanagemot culled hundreds of Saxons from all over southeastern Briton, who traveled scores of miles after the harvest to meet, drink, and govern. Some, like Freya and her brothers, were hereditary nobles, though they were far rarer as yet in newly settled Briton; many were men elevated by their battlefield heroics and rewarded with holdings of land and livestock; and still others were elected representatives of their local *folkmots*, the councils by which freedmen of the Saxon lands pressed their issues and secured for themselves their rights and liberties. The *folkmot* tradition had lived among the Northern Germanics for centuries, but as the Angles, Saxons and Jutes moved to make Britain the permanent seat of their kingdoms, and the great-grandchildren of the original conquerors consolidated power and wealth, the Witanengemot emerged to reflect the new power of the nobility.

Whatever alterations had occurred in the composition of the Saxon assembly, its location remained the same. One of the first acts of the first Saxons to settle in Briton was to excavate the earthen amphitheater, the *thingstead*, in which Kieran and his fellow *Witanen*, or "wise men," held their ceremony. However, this too had undergone changes in the decades since it was first dug, as it transformed from a pit in a stand of woods into a more Roman construction, widened and deepened to accommodate the growing legislative body, and inlaid with stone steps and tiers of benches for the Witanen to sit comfortably during sometimes interminable deliberations. There were now even stands ringing the amphitheater from which the retinues of the assembly members might watch the speeches and debates, and stalls to provide refreshments.

However, most of the true work of the assembly was not done at the thing itself, but in any of the dozen inns, taverns and bawdy houses that appeared overnight before each Witanagemot, where humble farm houses, barns and storage sheds had stood only days earlier. The locals around the thingstead knew well the wisdom of inconveniencing themselves for a single week a year when the Witanagemot was called. They made the Witanen as comfortable as possible while the men hashed out deals among one another and settled differences in private with a few trusted aides, or *drengars*, to avoid the sorts of scenes before the full assembly that could escalate into longstanding feuds.

The meeting was scheduled to last four days, and the first three passed as Kieran had predicted. On those few occasions when he rose to speak, standing without the customary puffing of his chest and in a voice that sounded ulike the ursine baying of his fellow Witanen, it was only to address a matter that had a simple, apolitical solution. He never spoke when the topic was war, as he wanted to be accused of neither cowardice nor hypocrisy. On most questions his only action was his vote.

If a matter required the participation of the House of Wearding, to which his family belonged, his brother-in-law Ahewan was an eorl, and the others knew the ruling families and speakers of the folkmots from birth.

It was not difficult to perceive who had, or believed he had, far greater rights to be heard before the Saxon council than Kieran. Day upon day they stood and pontificated, voices booming until they were all hoarse by the end of the week, bedecked in shimmering furs and jangling jewelry and some arrayed in their finest battle gear. They cajoled and intimidated, bribed and flattered their fellow Saxon nobles into making their proposals law. More often than not they played as much to the crowds in the stands as to the Witanen, as, true to tradition, the throng cast an unofficial but weighty vote.

255

However, during his address, each man made certain to give due acknowledgment and deference to the King of the Saxons, the ancient King Ællis, seated at the apex of the ovoid arena. Despite his long flow of pure white hair, resting against the only high-backed chair in the thingstead, most in attendance still saw beneath the decrepit exterior to the man who had risen to become the overlord of the South Saxons, the greatest ruler the Germanics knew. Far from displaying resentment, the kings and chiefs to a man were happy to entrust their fortunes to such a successful chief.

Kieran was firm in his commitment to remain silent throughout the fourth day if he could, for the final time of gathering was reserved for discussions of war, and that was one area where Kieran had expressly forbidden himself from uttering a word.

There was one reason why, after only five years of being a minor thane, every one at the assembly knew who Kieran, or rather Ulstan, was. From the start of his reign, Thane Ulstan famously refused to commit his warriors to battles of conquest.

This not surprisingly earned the ire of almost everyone: the other eorls and thanes, the warriors under his command, and even the cherols in the town and three villages within his dominion. He released his men to defend Saxon holdings under attack by the forces of the Britons and for mercenary duty on the Continent, but never led any himself, and never authorized them to seize native lands without provocation. Complaints, threats and mass defections plagued the first two years of his rule, and even Freya, who stood by him throughout, began to question the wisdom of his policy after a while.

Though opposition persisted from without, inside the bounds of his thanedom things gradually started to change. Those warriors still under his command, and the freemen who had remained on his lands, soon began to congratulate themselves on their decision to stay. While surprisingly strong Britonic resistance led to a series of setbacks on the battlefield and stymied the Saxons' drive for conquest, Kieran applied his knowledge and knack for engineering to help his thanedom prosper. The crop yield from the fields increased each season, and with foundries and forges far advanced of anything the other Saxon chiefs possessed, his domain became the main producer of fine gold and bronze pieces, which enriched all of his subjects. Freemen moved to be near his town and its outlying villages, and warriors returned to his service, each offering contrition and receiving from Kieran absolution.

What kept him from real trouble was that in the long term Kieran fulfilled the Saxon lord's basic responsibility. Though it was unorthodox for a thane to enrich his domain without slaughtering civilians and sacking their settlements, his people nonetheless prospered, and that was the sole mark of success for a chief. It may have been an alien way for Saxons to live, but those under Thane Ulstan quickly noticed the significantly lower death rate and higher living standard they enjoyed through his leadership than other lords could provide.

Thus it was in full view of the other nobles and without a trace of shame that, on the night before the last day of the *mot*, Kieran stood in one of the mead halls of the lesser nobility, drinking his third horn of hedromel and speaking with his brothers-in-law about some of the very farming techniques that had earned him the admired part of his reputation. The hall was packed with nobles and folkmot representatives, and the thick air, redolent of alcohol, wood smoke, charred meat and sweat, carried their chatter, the mixture of speculation and gossip to be found at any political gathering.

While he spoke of irrigation and planting schedules, though, Kieran's mind was on the topic that had not been far from his thoughts the entire time: the source of

Freya's consternation. He had not yet felt the time right to broach the subject with his brothers-in-law, but neither did he want to return home without finding out what insights they had to share.

"And you say seashells?" asked Ahewan, eorl and eldest of the four brothers.

"Seashells, yes," said Kieran. "Finely ground and applied in the correct proportion, you will find your soil receives its crops far more readily, especially in fields you haven't rotated for a few years."

"So that is how you avoided the famine year," nodded Badewin, the youngest of the brothers and last to join them at the thingstead.

"Fortunately, yes," said Kieran with a humble smile.

"To my brother by bond, Ulstan, the smartest bugger I know," said Dagberd, second-eldest and the only one of Freya's siblings who had not entirely warmed to Kieran. Dagberd raised his horn, and his brothers followed suit.

"To Ulstan!" the others toasted, and Kieran raised his horn half-way in acknowledgement. They all swigged their drinks, but as Dagberd put his horn to his lips, he muttered, "though not smart enough." He had not intended to be heard, but the others looked up from drinking, including Kieran.

Dagberd, drunk, did not realize the import of what he'd said, but when he saw Kieran and his brothers staring at him, he said, "What's the matter?"

Cadman shook his head in reproach at Dagberd.

"What did you mean by that?" asked Kieran with eerie calm. Each of the men avoided his eyes. "What am I missing, brothers?" he asked. "This has to do with Freya, doesn't it?"

The brothers looked one to another, then all turned to Ahewan. The eorl cleared his throat and said, "Our sister is once again with child."

Kieran was shocked to the core by the news, which he saw from their faces was true. He could not imagine why Freya would keep such a thing from him, after all the tears she'd shed at the long fruitless attempts to increase their family.

"I only heard the day before we departed," said Badewin. "And I don't think I was meant to know, either."

"Why would she keep that to herself?" asked Kieran.

"Well, the *mot*, of course," said Ahewan. Kieran's uncomprehending expression did not change, so he continued, shaking his head, "I sometimes forget, you still don't know all of our ways. Freya would no more burden your mind with domestic concerns on the eve of the *Witanagemot* than she would order the swine pens left open overnight. Our women know the power they have over their husbands and lovers, and seek to limit their influence when the *mot* is nigh. The lords and cherol assemblymen must speak for all free Saxons within their domains, not just the Saxons within their households – and particularly not just those within their bedchamber."

Kieran was frozen for a moment as a thousand feelings ran through him. He took a long pull of hedromel. "I'm going to be a father again," he said.

The power of hearing those words spoken galvanized his thinking, and suddenly, from the tumult of his psyche, one single and singular emotion shot out like a beam of pure light. It was joy. His face broke into a grin that seemed to split it in half. "I'm going to be a father!" he shouted to the crowd, who roared back and raised their horns.

"You're going to bear us another nephew!" said Badewin.

"Gods grant a nephew, for any daughter born of you and my sister would have all menfolk under her feet."

Everyone laughed, and there was a round of toasts, increasingly exuberant and involving a widening circle of Saxon lords, some of whom were only acquaintances or near strangers. The gaiety attained such a zenith that none of the celebrants noticed that a pall had descended on the rest of the room until, one by one, the outer circle of well-wishers fell silent and turned, followed by those closer to Kieran, and finally his brothers-in-law as well ceased their happy chatter and cast their eyes in the direction the others' were pointing.

The huddle of noblemen parted and formed a corridor as a man strode forward. He wore an elaborately woven green tunic that poked out from his armor of oiled leather and glittering steel rings. The leather cuirass protecting his torso was crowned at its center with a brass breastplate in the shape of a wolf's head. The most striking part of his attire, though, was the black leather eye patch over his left eye, which had a silver silhouette of a wolf in full run at its center.

"Wulfric," whispered Badewin to Kieran. Ahewan said to the man, "Hail, Dragnar Wulfric!"

"Hail, Eorl Ahewan," said Wulfric, while looking at Kieran. "Celebrating good news?"

"Terrific news!" piped up Dagberd, not sensing the taut mood that had the others silent. "This proud cock just got my sister with child again!"

"Shut up, Dagberd," said Cadman. His brothers looked at him.

"That is good news," said Wulfric. "Congratulations."

Kieran nodded.

"I'm glad I can speak to you on this happy occasion, as I have more happy news to share. Eorl Ceradic of the West Saxons is growing a bloc to vote against the Britonic peace proposal and finally effect our full mastery of Briton. Tomorrow we shall have a glorious vote in favor of war, and on behalf of Ceradic, I am pleased to tell you that you may be among the first to announce your support."

Nothing in Wulfric's tone or words suggested the smallest scrap of happiness. In fact, one listening to the way he spoke, rather than the words themselves, would have believed he had presented a challenge rather than an offer.

"We have not decided these matters yet, Wulfric," said Ahewan.

"With respect, eorl, I was addressing your sister's husband," shot Wulfric. "Each Witan casts his own vote, and at this moment, Ceradic is interested in hearing how Ulstan will vote."

Kieran let the silence continue as Wulfric turned to him and awaited an answer. When Kieran did speak, it was with utter calm.

"I have not yet decided my vote," said Kieran, "and you may tell Ceradic that I thank him for his offer, and will have word whether or not I may have the privilege of accepting upon the morrow."

Wulfric snorted, and said, "I think you can see that it would be best for everyone if we could get this cleared up tonight, as men of good will, before bringing it to the thingstead.

"Let me explain," he continued. "Not everyone has your genius with crops and animals. Some of us rely on what we can win for ourselves, what we take by the right of being able to wrest it from another's grasp. A peace would be very unproductive for us and those who depend on us. Do I make myself clear?"

"You do."

"So will you answer 'yes,' then?" In his first overt sign of pique, he added, "I would think you would leap at the chance to prove your worth and mettle, with your reputation."

A sudden and perfect stillness fell upon the room.

"Wulfric…" said one of the men at his side. Wulfric brushed him away.

"We will have a yes or a no."

"It is something I have yet to decide," said Kieran. "And I'm afraid that is all the answer I have to give."

The crowd, including the brothers of the House of Wearding, was hushed and expectant. All looked between Wulfric and Kieran, who stared hard at each other. Wulfric after some time broke the look, and began to casually adjust his forearm covers.

"You have used a few Anglic expressions," said Wulfric to Kieran in an offhanded way. "Have you ever lived among the Angles?"

"I have traveled extensively, and spent a great deal of time among them. On trade missions."

"Of course. Then during these trade missions, you may have heard a curious story they tell around the southern shores of Anglia, especially in the area of Roscinham." Wulfric paused, looking intently at Kieran, who had guessed from the first what was to come and prepared his look of neutrality in advance.

"Perhaps," said Kieran.

"It is a strange story indeed. I'm certain you would recall if you'd heard it. It happens that about eight or nine years ago there was this slave who was kept by the Eorl Agelrot, may he taste Valhalla's delights, as the smith's apprentice. He was a half-wit, feeble of mind, and bent of form as well. A real prize."

Wulfric laughed, and some others joined in.

"Well it seems there was more to this little cripple than anyone realized, because one day, all of the sudden, he starts to speak. Why, he stands up straight and starts talking, and it turns out his mind isn't just restored – he's the rival of Ulysses."

"Curious."

"Very curious. One wonders how such a thing could take place. Now the man himself said it was a witch transformed him, or at least that's what he told the stupid cur who agreed to free him from slavery. It's of course nonsense, the idea of magic in this instance, though in a particular way he was telling the truth. There was a witch involved, but she was no sorceress of the Old Kind." Wulfric aimed his words like a dart when he asked, "Have you ever heard of a woman named Lorelei?"

Kieran had not heard her name pronounced in close to a decade. It sent a shiver through him, which remained imperceptible to the five dozen men watching him, but seemed to be picked up by Wulfric.

"No," said Kieran.

"Well even if you had, you wouldn't know this one anymore," Wulfric said with a cold chuckle. "At one time she was the very wife of Lord Agelrot himself. She was the one who brought the crippled slave out of his wretchedness, but not through the elfin magic. It was instead a more common restorative power -the magic of the great piece of *cunne*." General laughter ensued, and when it hushed again, Wulfric said, "He had a good act, I'll grant, but at day's end he was just a beggar who could keep a straight face – until Lorelei seized hold of his prick."

"Could such a thing happen?" asked one of Wulfric's men who was hearing the story fresh. "That a man could pose as a half-wit undetected for so long?"

"It would seem there are such vermin in the world," said Wulfric, turning back to Kieran. "But you have not heard the tale?"

Kieran shook his head.

"Agelrot did the decent thing by allowing this man to be freed, but about a year later, more to the story came out which might have made him think twice about putting such a man on the road. He came to find out that the transformation of the slave had in fact been provoked by Lorelei's pursuit of the supposed cripple. She, with the cunning of wicked women, had guessed he was a fraud, and was arranging a time and place where she could compel him to reveal himself even further, if you catch the meaning. Her secret would have remained safe, except she tried exactly the same thing on a hapless young hog tender not three seasons later, and even related the entire story to the bewildered lad!"

264

Many in the crowd howled at this bit, but those standing closest to Kieran and Wulfric knew that no mirth was contained in the proceedings.

"We only know this because of the boy's willing confession, and the unwilling tale that emerged from Lorelei's lips once Agelrot caught her trying to escape. It was tremendously unpleasant for her."

Kieran felt ashamed at the wry thoughts that sprang to his mind with the news, though they were mingled with pity as well.

Wulfric concluded, "The most fascinating part of the story, I feel, is that nobody knows where this slave ended up. There are a lot of theories, but not much evidence. He could have gone anywhere. What do you think happened to him?"

"Like I said, I hadn't heard the story."

"Oh you haven't?" said Wulfric, abruptly ferocious. Ahewan stepped between Kieran and the Saxon general.

"Is there something you're trying to say?" asked Ahewan, as his brothers closed ranks by his side.

Kieran and Wulfric glared at each other for a long moment. Wulfric's shoulders were bunched and his fists clenched, as if he were moments from springing forward. Kieran stood erect and unwavering. After it became clear no violence would ensue, though without removing the sneer from his face, Wulfric untensed his muscles and straightened up.

"You think about that vote," he said, and quickly walked off. Everyone in the vicinity watched he and his men leave, then exhaled at roughly the same moment.

The next day, as the sun was setting and the year's Witanagemot was about to be called to a close, all eyes at the assembly were turned toward where Kieran and his brothers-in-law stood. The nobles, crowd and king were awaiting their answer.

"They've done this on purpose," muttered Dagberd. None of the others spoke, but all knew it was true.

The proceeding was held in such a way that only those of the House of Wearding and the elected representatives from their lands, who usually took their cue from the ennobled brothers, had yet to vote. It had also been so arranged that those votes would be the deciding factor in whether or not the treaty of truce presented by the Britons would be accepted.

"Remember," said Ahewan to Kieran, "as we discussed last night."

Kieran nodded, and Ahewan rose before the assembly.

"Your highness, my fellow Witanen," he said, "by mutual agreement, my brother-by-bond Ulstan will speak for the House of Wearding on this matter."

"Then let him rise," said the king. Wulfric nearly jumped up, but Ceradic restrained him, and the drengar's one gimleted eye was left to speak his raging thoughts.

Kieran took a moment to collect himself, concentrating on what he and Freya's brothers had discussed the previous night after the encounter. He needed to be sure to get the particular parts of the phrasing correctly, or the entire effect could be ruined. *It must all remain in the language of law*, Badewin said. *It must adhere to code*.

Kieran looked to Freya's brothers, whose bodies showed minute signs of worry, but whose faces were firm in solidarity. He turned to the crowd pressing in all around and above him, silent and pitched forward in anticipation. Then Kieran spoke, his words echoing through the canyon of the thingstead.

"Your highness, my lords and free Saxons, I speak for my brothers-by-bond, our kin and freedmen under our banner, when I say that each man here today, each of you worthy Witanen, has presented his argument with force, clarity and intelligence, and I seek to be worthy of your example as I rise before you on this most serious matter.

"I have come among you as a stranger, and found kinship in the greatness of Saxon society. In might, the Saxon is unmatched, and in the matters of administration, his genius finds parity only when held against the Roman beast. I am honored to be in this company."

Kieran bowed, and the king nodded.

"There is only one thing that can decrease our prosperity right now, and that is failing to foster it. We have seen our lands bringing forth food that will, in time, fill stores to withstand any lean season. We have the opportunity to raise our sons and daughters to surpass us in any place, from the field of contest to the seas to the grazing lands. But we must seize this chance.

"There is something else that should give us pause," said Kieran, now looking toward, though not at, Wulfric. "Until now, we have not faced a united force of Britons, and our superior training, organization, and above all cohesiveness has won great triumphs. However, they are being pushed toward desperation, and nothing so unites feuding men as the shared threat of annihilation. In a twist that Loki might appreciate," and now he looked squarely at Wulfric, who returned a murderous glare, "our overwhelming strength might, at this moment, be our greatest weakness.

"Ask any man here, your highness, any except my brothers by bond who know me as if my true brothers, and he will tell you he has his suspicions about me. I am whispered about as a coward, as a traitor, as an interloper and an upstart. However, no man has ever called me a fool, and none can doubt that my slaves eat as well as many another lord's cherols. In peace, I can share this knowledge, and Saxons all over Briton can enjoy a time of increase without decrease. In war, I cannot."

"Then would you have us lay down our arms for good?" asked the king.

"No, highness," said Kieran. "It is the fate and the pleasure of the Saxon kind to ever increase their holdings. I say, though, that we may add the whole of Britain to our lands by combining stealth, cunning and ferocity. Let our people prosper, while building alliances with certain of the tribes of Britons who will accept subjugation over slaughter when the time comes. For those tribes opposing us, they will taste Saxon steel and fall as trees in a cutting wood. Then with Britain secured, there is no fruit of plunder in all the known world too far away to be plucked by Saxon ships.

"I am a stranger, yes, and perhaps I will never be viewed as an equal here. But I am too the husband of a Saxon noblewoman, and father to a Saxon boy who will as a man sit in this Witanagemot and cast his voice and vote among this gathering. When that day comes, I want him to be able to stand tall and say, 'Neither under my father nor under me have our cherols known a grumbling belly, our women a pauperish husband or our warriors defeat on the field, for each year without fail our riches are increased.' That is my vision for my son, and all of our sons." Kieran looked about the rapt audience, then returned his gaze to the king and said, "I, and by proxy the House of Wearding vote 'yes' to the proposal of peace."

All eyes turned to Ceradic and Wulfric, who both rose to address the assembly at the same instant. Before either could speak, though, King Ællis bade them sit by a gesture of his shaking hand. The eorl and his dragnar hesitated, but resumed their seats on the bench.

"The stranger speaks like a true Saxon today," wheezed the old king. His voice was weakened by age, but its timbre still recalled the battle commander who once slayed by his own hand fifty men in an afternoon. His words snuffed out the chatter as a strong wind kills a flame, and the hall turned its attention to the bent and palsied figure on the throne.

"In the full roar of battle we are wolves. We kill what stands before us, we consume what we wish. None can match Saxon bravery or skill." The king turned to where Ceradic and his apoplectic dragnar sat, and directed his words to them. "The wolf, though, like the great Saxon, knows when to hunt, when to tend his den. This is our season for tending to our new and great kingdom. There is always opportunity for war, when the season turns again."

"And when, great leader, do you expect this season to turn again?" asked Ceradic in his laconic voice, bearing a demeanor as restrained as Wulfric's was smoldering.

"In ten years' time," rasped the Saxon king. A murmur at once arose from the crowd, but Ællis motioned for silence.

"The body of the Witanen has advised me to my satisfaction, and been heard to theirs. I now render my ruling on behalf of all the Saxon people." The king raised his voice, with effort conjuring the virility of his youth. "Peace shall reign between us and the Britons for 121 *monaths*."

There was a stir from all around the *stead*, but silence returned when the king held up his jittery hand. "And," he continued, "so that our will shall persist in force even after I leave this realm and join my ancestors, I affix by word and Wodensblot the Seal of Saxneat, my direct progenitor and founder of our proud race. As it is written, a new crown must bow to an old, and by this seal, the treaty of truce is the word and will of great Saxneat as much as this assembly today called. There shall be peace for half a generation's time. That is the law."

Now it was no murmur but a roar that filled the *stead*, as arguments broke out within the noble ranks, and an imbroglio brewed among rival factions of spectators. Some rushed to prevent the Law Speaker from repeating the king's words and affixing the seal, as before these acts were complete the decree had not yet the force of law. Those who sought to restrain the Law Speaker were themselves restrained, and the treaty was made. Ceradic immediately went forward to protest to the king.

"We should not dither in returning home," suggested Ahewan, scanning rows of angry faces in the section of the amphitheater where Ceradic's men had sat, and were now rising.

"Where is Wulfric?" asked Badewin, as a din emerged near the path of their exit.

"There," said Cadman.

The effort of four large men was barely sufficient to hold back Wulfric, who surged toward Kieran, clawing at the air before him and trying to wrest himself free from the grasps of the men.

"Ulstan you bitch's whelp! You cost me ten years of plunder. Ten years! I will make you pay back every day of it, Ulstan. You hear me? You and the House Wearding. I will make you pay me back for every hour!"

"Let's go," said Badewin, ushering Kieran through the crowd.

"Promise me one thing, brothers," said Kieran. "You will choose carefully how you tell Freya of what transpired here."

"You need fear nothing from us," said Ahewan. "But hurry, or we may not get back at all."

Kieran said nothing as he saw his wife at the door to their family hall. He rushed forward, embracing her with one arm, and with the hand of the other cupping her belly, right above her womb.

"They told you," she said, blushing. Kieran smiled and kissed his wife deeply.

"I can't believe you didn't."

"I couldn't influence you."

"I know."

"You weren't heroic or controversial, were you?" she said in jest, though her smile faded when she saw the anxiousness in Kieran's eyes behind the warmth of love that also there glowed. The coaches of her brothers pulled up behind them while Kieran searched for the right words to say. Freya knew there was something deeply amiss, and looked on the verge of interrogating her husband, but thought better of it. With a blink she dismissed all worry from her countenance, and rose up on her toes to give Kieran another kiss. She slipped her hand into his and said, "It doesn't matter. You're home safe." She drew him into the doorway, and to her brothers, called, "Come inside! There's an early snow due to fall."

Chapter Eighteen

The guard was right - it almost was too late. Uleara was ushered along at a near run by the soldiers escorting him to Aurelian's chamber, and through the colonnade that lined the exterior corridor of the villa, Uleara saw the scene on the hillsides below, and knew the council was about to be called.

On every patch of open grass up and down the slopes around Glevuna, the various tribes held their religious rites for a successful meeting, the last necessary step before the kings could assemble. Rivers of torchlight streamed around the tribes' campsites as the people danced out the patterns handed down through the generations. Staccato drums, blaring trumpets, frenzied strings and a swarm of voices in song and prayer rose on the evening air, as the pagans of Britain made supplications to Lugh, Cerunnos, the Culcullati, and, among the unconverted in Aurelian's domain, Hebuna the Cup Bearer, who they believed to be Aurelian's adoptive mother and guardian of the Glevuna Vale. Whatever gods they beseeched through song, whatever side in the fight for the crown they favored, all Britons that night were united in prayer that the council would produce a leader to save them from the Germanic menace, once and for all.

The guards spared the preliminaries as they burst into Aurelian's chamber, Uleara behind them, and brought the conference between Aurelian and his advisors to a sudden stop.

"This man has something to share," said a guard, and stepped aside to let Uleara take the floor.

He told them all he knew, and repeated the parts King Aurelian and his advisors asked for again. Immediately men were sent to arrest Kieran, who was found in his tent reading a copy of *Confessions,* Book XI. King Cunomor, ruler of

Dumnonia, was notified as a courtesy that one of his subjects was being detained – the reply was supportive of the arrest.

The weapon Uleara brought with him, Kieran's weapon, was thoroughly examined, and a strange discovery was made: The sword and its scabbard were fused together.

"Whatever the villain was planning with this," said one of Aurelian's military aides, who had tried in vain to pry the blade from its sheath, "he wasn't going to be able to carry it out anyway. This thing is rusted completely."

"And you say you had no knowledge of this? Not even suspicions?" demanded Aurelian for a third time, trying to hide how deeply Uleara's revelation had jarred him.

"I had my suspicions, highness," said Uleara, "but Kieran's guile and seven years of friendship blinded me to the truth."

Aurelian scanned his advisors, who themselves looked one to another – all except one in clerical vestments, who stood next to Aurelian and gazed levelly at Uleara. The abbot recognized him as Theonus, Archbishop of Londinium. He was squatter than Uleara had imagined, with squinty eyes and frizzled white hair on his face and head. He was well known in the Christian community, mostly for his narrow escape from the Saxons who beheaded his predecessor and forced the bishopric seat into exile.

However, despite his unfriendly stare at Uleara, the bishop did not speak, and finally another councilor, an older man with a gray beard that reached his navel, said softly, "Perhaps it would be better to try to postpone the council."

"No!" bellowed Aurelian, rounding on his advisors. Vehemence now took hold of the king's manner, where indecision had once reigned. "That is preposterous. Once the rites have been sung, the ceremony proceeds. It has always been thus and I will not be the first to break with tradition, on tonight of all nights."

"There may be precedent…"

"I do not care. I have advanced my candidacy for the Crown of Crowns on a platform of restoring Roman order and the systematic defeat of the Germanic hordes. How like the bewildered babe they think me if I were to call off the council now, and due to such circumstances! Would you have me look like a nursling in front of the tribal lords of all Britain?"

Aurelian's intensity had been apparent to Uleara from their first meeting, but the passion that infused his voice and bearing were so strong that even Aurelian's councilors, who had known the young man since his mother bore him, looked at the monarch as if he were a stranger. Despite his fulminations, never during his harangue did Aurelain come close to losing control, and never once did the look of cunning and keen instinct leave his eyes. The realization hit all in the room at once that they were watching Aurelian emerge as a leader, very different from a mere king.

The effect was cemented when, as his fury passed, a new expression came to Aurelian's face, and his eyes lit up with inspiration. A wry smile bent his impish mouth at the corner, and he looked to his advisors.

"We are fools! We have been looking at his situation standing on our heads. How lucky we are to have this conspiracy exposed tonight! How God must favor our cause to send us these good tidings!"

"Highness, what can you mean?" asked the long-bearded advisor, his expression questioning of his sovereign's sanity.

"What I mean," said Aurelian, his feline smile spreading as he faced Uleara, "is that your friend, in trying to prevent my coronation, may have just guaranteed it."

Before he could elaborate, the attention of he and all the others was drawn to the outdoors, where the noise of the rituals had dropped off significantly. After the first sets of drums, trumpets and chanters fell silent, the rest of the clamor ceased almost all at once – within half a minute all the music had died out, tribe by tribe, and now silence pervaded throughout and around the city.

"It is now time for my prayers," said Aurelian. "Go situate yourselves in the hall – I will join you once the Almighty has done with me," he told his aides. "Except for you."

Uleara turned to see the king looking at him with a solicitous expression. The abbot was uncertain how to take this order, especially when Aurelian turned to the squat and squinty-eyed man at his right, Archbishop Theonus, and said, "You may leave as well."

"Your highness," the man began, aghast, but by habit maintaining his flattering tone, "on such an occasion as this, it would be wiser to have an officiate of the Chair of St. Peter to guide your prayers, no? A recognized one, that is."

Aurelian gave him a sidelong look.

"I need no conduit to the Lord at all," said Aurelian, "and a king no less than any man may choose with whom he communes in fellowship with Christ. Get to the hall, or remove your vestments here and now and walk back down the hill a layman, as when my father found you."

"But really, sire – him? This cabbage from the nether parts of Dumnonia, where he probably preaches the Celtic Rite and the heresies of Pelagius?"

The bishop had directed his invective at Uleara, but now looking to seeing Aurelian's face, he realized he had miscalculated.

"This cabbage from Dumnonia," said Aurelian, "is as of now taking your seat at the council. Be gone from my chamber."

The bishop was flabbergasted for a moment, too indignant to speak or move, but made haste for the exit as soon as he saw two guards begin to advance. Theonus collided with a gaggle of advisors eavesdropping at the door as he hurried from the room, and the aides rushed off after the bishop so as not to endure a similar fate.

"I ask that you pray with me," said the king to Uleara once they were alone.

"I, highness?" said Uleara. "Truly, as the bishop said, would not a representative of the Holy See be better suited to the occasion?"

"If I believed that I would not have dismissed the pompous cock," Aurelian said. "It is not an accident of chance, but providence that has brought you to me on the eve of this council. I know that you are truly a man of God, for I sense the divine presence in all that has transpired this day. Now at this moment of decision, you are the man I must have beside me, to help shepherd me on the path to victory, in His name. Will you join me?"

Aurelian, though young, had already mastered the ability to shape his speech so that it assumed the form of a question and a command at the same time. The abbot hesitated only briefly before he knelt upon the pillow next to the king. Both men clasped their hands before them, closed their eyes and let their heads drop.

"Heavenly Father," intoned Uleara, "we beseech, send down Your guidance to walk in the righteous path, to let our actions each be a stroke for Your glory." Uleara used the rhythm and melody that he reserved for sermons, which was largely absent his normal speech. "Lord Christ, who sits at the right hand of the Father, who lifts us up when we stumble and revives our strength when our spirits flag, help us to endure as you endured, to spread light and wisdom as did the Apostles for Your glory."

Uleara paused following the initial invocation. When he resumed he had not lost the sermonic rhythm to his words, but the timbre of his voice was changed. When it spoke again, it was from within his heart.

"Heavenly Father, no man knows his place in Your ineffable plan. We may only act by what you let us see and grant us to know. Dear God, light the path of goodness, which is so often shadowed by doubt, and let us see your light even when our eyes are dimmed by Earthly intrusions.

"We remember there is only one lawgiver and judge, Lord. You have brought down kings from their thrones and lifted up the lowly. You have set the humble on high and cast the haughty into the eternal flames of perdition. With his pride does a man dig the grave of his own soul, and only in humility may we know the blessings of the Lord. Heavenly Father, forgive us our sins and heal this land. Guide King Aurelian in your grace, and let him remember, this day and all to follow, that 'he who rules in righteousness, fearing of God, is like the light of sunrise on a cloudless morning, like the brightness after rain that brings the grass from the earth.' Let it be so in the reign of Aurelian, dear Lord we pray. Amen."

"Amen," said Aurelian, rising. "Thank you, Abbot Uleara. Now let us see if the Lord has heard us."

"He always hears us, your highness," said Uleara, who took some time to gain his feet. "What we have yet to know is how He will answer."

When Aurelian and Uleara entered the hall, nine other kings were already arrayed around the wheel-shaped oaken table, with the seat of the absent Belgic king conspicuously unoccupied. Each was adorned in the baroque splendor that marked the style of Britonic chiefs, displaying finely wrought ornaments of gold and silver, and wearing robes embroidered so intricately with patterns and scenes they looked drawn rather than sewn. Their garments stood in stark contrast to what Aurelian wore – an ankle-length tunic of eggshell white bordered with stripes of red, and cinched with a sash of purple.

Their manner of dress was not the only contrast between the Dubonnian ruler and the others, however. The youngest of the nine kings was at least ten years Aurelian's senior, and while the Golden Prince had a smooth chin and unblemished visage, his peers at the table seemed to compete for the longest beard and most scar-ridden face.

The kings nodded to Aurelian as he entered, but Uleara took note of how they leaned toward one another to whisper, and that their assessing stares regarded the host king closely. Their advisors behind them too whispered and stared, especially the women, who Uleara knew to be either priestesses of pagan cults or fierce and experienced warriors. Uleara focused on trying to maintain his composure as the momentousness of where he was caused his pulse to race, and sweat to appear under his arms and across his torso. In his anxiety he took the wrong seat, drawing more unfriendly looks.

When all were in their chairs, the doors slammed shut, blocking the sight of the multitudes outside. Hundreds of spectators had gathered around the hall to glimpse what they could of the royal assembly, which would likely be the only one they would see in their lifetimes. Once called, the High Council was barred to all but eighty-one souls: the ten kings, the seven councilors each was permitted to have sit with him, and the Supreme Magistrate, who presided over the council.

It was this man who now stepped forward, into a wedge-shaped notch in the table where the High King would sit, and stretched wide his arms.

"We hail you, the gods above and below, in the water and sky, and in the realms beyond our knowing. We hail you, the fairy folk, the giants, gnomes and sprites at the margins of our sight. We hail you, the Christian god, who claims dominion as grandfather to the world, most mysterious and terrible of the deities."

It is a long process away from paganism, Uleara thought, beholding in the flesh a vestige of what kings were when barbarians were truly barbaric.

"We hail you, all gods, spirits and forces around, in sacred Britain and the lands beyond, and to our ancestors, who live in the hills and in our hearts, to guide us now, and let us like the river find through winding courses the bosom of the sea."

"Hail," rose up eighty voices as one.

"Let the High Council then convene."

King Fyrthnal of the Deceangli was quick in rising to put forward Aurelian's name for High King. The Golden Prince thanked him and rose to present his own case. He produced detailed charts of the landscape along the treaty line and optimal places for defense and attack. Uleara, who did not understand much of the technical aspects of the presentation, was nonetheless impressed by Aurelian's breadth of knowledge, as the young king made allusions and comparisons to analogous military campaigns throughout history, naming generals and senators over a span of centuries.

When he finished, Aurelian gave a nod of his head all around, handed his final chart to an aide and resumed his seat. There was stillness.

The answer was quick in coming, as one of the kings on the opposite end of the table stood to address the gathering. Uleara knew from the armored woman by his side, a descendent of the famed Queen Cartimandua, that the man was Catalacus, the ruler of the Brigantes, and a foe of Aurelian.

"My fellow chiefs, we have heard one of our number's position and know his head seeks the crown. I put forth another, who I believe to be worthier of receiving it. King Drystan, of the Catuvellauni."

Drystan rose and nodded in acceptance of the supportive cries and thumps on the table from his allies.

"Anyone who has been in battle knows," he said, "a war plan is only as good as the general who will carry it out. I'll grant, King Aurelian's presentation was very impressive. I certainly couldn't keep track of all those same-sounding Roman names, Gaius, Gnaeus, us's and ums up their arses."

Drystan looked to see if Aurelian took the bait, but amid the mocking laughter the Golden Prince managed a passable smile.

"But I will take his highness's word that they were great generals all. The problem with the presentation is that these generals did not achieve their greatness with their noses buried in books, but on the field of contest."

Aurelian now crimsoned and did not smile. But with a ferocious light in his eyes, he yet maintained his composure, and sat back against his chair.

"I could have prepared a nice show for you, my lords," Drystan said, "but it would not speak half as well to why I should bear the burden of the Crown of Crowns on my head as the stacks of Saxon and Angle bodies I have left piled in the fields. My people, the Catuvellauni, along with our great and true allies the Brigantes and Parisii, know too well how to conduct this campaign, for we have never stopped from the last one."

"That's right," said Catalacus, the Brigantine, softly but poignantly.

"The Germanics raid our frontiers at their will. While we are implored to be patient from those on the other side of Britain, to honor the truce, Ceradic and his hordes kill our men and take our livestock.

"So there is your choice, my lords. You can have experience and proven skill in war, or you can have the more academic approach." Drystan looked at Aurelian, giving a wry smile when he said, "I am unhappy to tell you, the latter leads to scenes such as we saw this afternoon, just down the road from where we now convene. No matter how gifted a boy may be at his studies, when inexperience leads, good men get killed for nothing."

Aurelian was on his feet at once, his advisors rising with him, Uleara last. Every bit of tension in the hall showed on Uleara's features as he unsteadily stood by the king and his council, as all people within the chamber smelled a brawl.

"You say it is a choice between competence and inexperience?" said Aurelian. "Well I say it is a contest between honor and treachery!"

Aurelian did not shout his words, but they had an equal impact. At once the entire gathering was on its feet, while recriminations and challenges flew around the table. The Supreme Magistrate banged his staff and waved his arms until the room quieted.

"An insult has been thrown at the High Council, and thus a challenge made," said the presider. Facing Aurelian, he said, "How will you speak to make your accusation?"

"I need do very little of the speaking myself, for we may put the questions directly to the chief accomplice in these conspiracies. Call forth the prisoner!" shouted Aurelian to a guard by the door.

The hall was again amurmur. King Drystan rose and said, "My fellow lords, I welcome Aurelian's proposal. I know not who he plans to produce, but this mysterious witness can only cement my good name… and expose my opponent to be the rash upstart he is!"

Uleara now understood Aurelian's words, why the king believed Kieran would secure him the Crown of Crowns. He was going to put Kieran on display, a prop for Aurelian's wit and cunning, and a way to shame King Drystan from his claim.

The hall turned expectantly as a door opened, and the erect and placid figure of Uleara's erstwhile companion was escorted into the room.

"My lords," said Aurelian, "this is Kieran of the Dumnonii, and he will help us clear everything up."

Kieran's was the calmest face in the room, as the kings and their councilors each reacted to his entrance. Drystan's coalition wore expressions of skepticism or outrage, while allies of Aurelian were turgid in anticipation of what was to come. In those without a definite loyalty, expressions of confusion reigned.

Even the Supreme Magistrate betrayed uncertainty and misgiving on his face, as he said to Aurelian, "You have leave to address the prisoner."

"From where have you come?" asked Aurelian.

"From the village of Eilwath, in the southwest peninsula."

"That is the land of Dumnonia, is it not?"

"It is."

Aurelian turned to King Cunomor, and said, "Will you speak for this man?"

Cunomor took his feet.

"My lords, I know of this man through my magistrate Grundfyrdd. He came into my lands seven years ago, and since then he has never ceased to be a source of consternation and fear. He is tolerated because his wealth is large and his participation in the affairs of the village few, but he is no Dumnonian."

It's a lie, thought Uleara, looking uncertainly at his king. *Kieran secured you half your fortune at your mines.*

"Where did he come from, then?"

"I do not know for certain, royal cousin," said Cunomor, "but it is said he came from the Saxon lands."

There was a stir in the hall, and all eyes immediately turned back to Kieran. Aurelian smiled, while the prisoner's face betrayed nothing.

"From the Saxon lands?"

"It is said."

Cunomor reclaimed his seat, as Drystan rose again.

"I fail to see how any of this concerns my claim, or that of the Golden Prince," said the king of the Catuvellauni. "What is it my affair if King Cunomor chooses to keep a wolf amongst his flock?"

"You will see shortly," said Aurelian. "If King Cunomor cannot illuminate the identity and purposes of this would-be assassin, then I have brought someone who can." He turned to Uleara, who suddenly became aware that the wealth and power of Britannia personified was focused on him. "This is the Abbot Uleara, a learned man from the village where the prisoner resides. Is Uleara known to you, King Cunomor?"

The king stood again.

"Uleara is of an ancient Dumnonian family. Though his beliefs and habits are certainly unusual, he is regarded as forthright."

"Then he is an honest man?"

"He has that reputation."

Aurelian turned to Uleara and put a hand on the abbot's shoulder.

"It will be well," he said. "Simply tell them what you told us."

Uleara stepped forward, his eyes darting to and fro rapidly across the bejeweled assembly, only alighting on Kieran for a fraction of an instant each time they involuntarily found him. He drew a breath, trembling as he exhaled it, and once more recounted what he had to tell. He told them of his friendship with Kieran, the circumstances of the journey, Kieran's odd behavior and the beginning of Uleara's suspicions, his encounters with Laghal and Craddoc, and his discovery in Kieran's cart. The only information he omitted was the bit that still confounded him: the glowing substance in the glass jar. All else he put forth faithfully.

 "Again," said Drystan with irritation, "I see not what this man is supposed to be to me."

"Oh no?" cried Aurelian. "When you stand opposed to my candidacy, attempt to conspire with my clan and kin, openly incite your factions, and now a man comes to my city – my own city, the gates of which I've flung wide in friendship – with a secret agenda and a sword? It certainly sounds like the Brigantine way to me."

The hall rang with a bout of crossfire insults.

"I do not know this man nor have had any dealings with him!" shouted Drystan. "Why do you not ask him yourself why he has come?"

Aurelian feigned a smile and said, "Certainly, though we know what sort of reply to expect. We shall put it to the villain himself."

Aurelian approached Kieran, pacing before him.

"What is your purpose here?" asked Aurelian.

"My lord," said Kieran, "it is to see you crowned High King."

Laughter erupted from several quarters throughout the room, but not from any of the principals involved in the drama. Aurelian gave Kieran a piercing stare.

"You lie, villain."

"Respectfully, highness, I do not. It is as I told you before – I am an ally."

"You are an ally who skulks about my city, taking clandestine meetings with spies and concealing your intent from the only man on Earth who calls you friend?" asked Aurelian. "If that is an ally then I prefer enemies." Now the king led the laughter that followed.

"Yet I speak true."

"Well Kieran," said Aurelian, "why should we take a sneaking Saxon at his word? What possible business could you have here that would be for our benefit?"

Aurelian awaited a reply, but none was forthcoming. He turned to his fellow kings.

"My lords, I am sorry I captured the fiend. He disappoints! After weaving such a delicate web of lies, he cannot produce this one last one to save his life." To Kieran he said, "Tell us that isn't the case."

Aurelian smiled in victory, taking Kieran's silence for owning up to guilt, but a terrible sensation overcame Uleara when he saw his former friend's face. *Merciful God, he isn't lying.* All at once Uleara was gripped by the feeling that he had made the gravest error of his life.

Chapter Nineteen

It was *Modranicht*, "Mother Night," hours after all the festivities ended and the guests had gone home. The servants were asleep in their huts or their berths within the hall, and only the noble family, Kieran, Freya and Andweard, were left awake to see out the final hours of Mother Night – the last night of the year, and the holiest.

This year's Modranicht, the culmination of the winter festival of *Yeol*, had been particularly special. It was in itself a good omen that Freya was with child, always lucky on the night that celebrated the winter solstice and its place in the yearly cycle of rebirth. However, this year's Modranicht fell on the *Freidag* of the week, the day that honored Freya's namesake goddess. Accordingly, the gifts, food and good wishes had been doubly lavished on Freya and her family from villages and towns well beyond the borders of the thanedom, arriving throughout the day so that now an entire corner of the hall was stacked with tribute of different sorts.

Of all the gifts given, though, none matched in the eyes of the guests those that Freya and Kieran exchanged between each other. Days before had been the celebration of *Midvintersblot*, the midpoint of the twelve days of Yeol festivities and a day sacred to Odin, who Kieran had chosen as patron god of his domains. (Any god but Loki, after Roscinham.) That day, too, gifts had been heaped upon Kieran. When no one believed Badewin's present to him, a large pot of precious Wodensblot so Kieran could practice rune writing, could be outshone. Freya proved them wrong.

With the permission of her brothers, who were guests in their hall when she made the gift, Freya presented her husband with the finest sword her father had owned, the bejeweled and golden-hilted weapon he carried in battle against the

289

Celts of the Continent to secure the Burgundii a homeland in Gaul. Among the East Saxons it was a legendary weapon, and the cheers that followed when it was conferred upon Kieran showed how far he had advanced in the esteem of his subjects and adoptive kin.

Kieran's gift to his wife had been equally spectacular. He tracked down the sire of his great Friesian, which Freya had admired since Kieran first rode into her town, and on Modranicht morning the results were delivered to a pen he had specially made for the animal. The mare was by reputation the best ever produced from the horse trader's husbandry, and she had been already trained under saddle. From the first moment Freya mounted her, it was as if the two were sisters only separated by their species. Freya named the horse Brecca.

Now, though, the Yeol was almost finished, and bedtime was approaching them all. Outside the world was hushed as flurries of white snow fell silently in the dark, while within the great hall the sound that pervaded was the roar of the Yeol Log, an enormous cylinder of beech that the servants fed day by day into the massive hearth throughout the holiday season. It kept the interior of the hall heated and lit at all hours. It was, far more than the gift giving and feasts, the greatest part of the Yeol for Kieran, who never forgot his first experiences in Britain and could thus never know a place too brightly lit or warm for his liking.

"Shall you have one last story before you go to sleep?" Freya asked Andweard, whose increasingly frequent yawns and periodically closing eyes marked him as at the threshold of sleep. Freya, who cradled Andweard in her arms even as she nestled beneath Kieran's embrace, smiled down softly on her son and unconsciously rubbed her belly, where another child grew.

"How about the 'Story of the Toe?'" she asked.

Andweard groaned. "Not that *again*."

"But it's my favorite story," she said.

"Mine too," said Kieran.

The "Story of the Toe" was Freya's name for the tale of how she and Kieran met. She had regaled their guests that Modranicht with the anecdote, ending it with, "So were it not for this one toe and my boredom at the clothier's, none of us would be here tonight – and especially not you," hugging Andweard to her.

It was another sign of her return to gay spirits after the Witanagemot.

She heard her husband and brothers' account of the Witanengemot with patience and understanding. She scolded him earnestly for it, but what she did thereafter, directly at the conclusion of his tale, reaffirmed for Kieran that he married the best woman in Britain.

Freya stood there eying him in that way she had which instantly stripped him of any self-importance, but then laid her fingertips on his chest and sighed through her nose.

"I told you when we were married that I didn't want what the other girls called a hero, some man cut of the boldest cloth, thinking always of honor even when his home cries for his attention. And I didn't think that's who I got when I married you. But you know, it turns out that I was wrong after all."

Freya grabbed him by his coat and pulled him to her, kissing him for a span of seconds. She then released him, leaving Kieran with a stupid expression, and she smiled.

"Lucky me," she said.

They had been happy again every day since.

"Tell me of the Wild Hunt," said Andweard, rubbing his eyes with small fists and yawning broadly.

Kieran and Freya looked at each other, and she rolled her eyes.

"Did you not hear enough of it the other night?" she asked. At *Midvintersblot*, the feast day on which the blood sacrifice to honor Odin took place three nights earlier, the tale of the Wild Hunt had been given in every variant of detail. "I think every man and women at the feast had a turn telling it," said Freya.

"I want you to tell it again," said her son. "I want to try to be there along with them when I go into the night realm."

Freya looked to Kieran for an excuse, but he instead asked her wryly, "How can the Queen of the Hunt deny such a request on this night?"

"Fine, but you tell it then," she said.

"Alright," said Kieran, turning to Andweard. "Well as you know, the king of the gods is Odin, who is the husband of the queen, Freya."

"That's you!" said Andweard to his mother.

"That's only my name," she smiled, but her son clearly did not believe her.

"Odin is a wanderer, a spirit compelled by his soul to search the lands of men for greater learning and magic. He is restless, and many times he breaks Freya's heart by leaving her alone in his quests.

"Sometimes, a strong gale will pass by Valhalla traveling between the Nine Worlds, and when Odin feels this wind it calls to his searching spirit. In such times his soul will be actually swept away by these winds, and his body has no choice to follow. When this happens, he must find quarry to pursue, or his soul will wander forever and never again return to Valhalla.

"The dead host of warriors know this too. When they feel the wind and see Odin depart, his armies become frenzied with the joy of the coming hunt. Freya does not like it when her husband goes on the Wild Hunt, but knows that she must join him or he may never return. She calls for the servants to harness their gigantic goats to their chariots to speed the chase.

"With Freya alongside, Odin's riders call more and more of the dead and living alike to join, as the gods too don their hunting gear and spur their monstrous horses and mount their fleet chariots. Then the skies rage, as the armies of the dead ride across it, whipping their steeds, with gigantic night-black hounds barking and snarling before them. Any hunter who is able to hear the call of the horns may join the host, but if anyone jeers at them or gets in their way – BAM! They're trampled under the Wild Army."

Andweard jumped, startled.

"Ulstan, we should stop," said Freya. "It's frightening him."

"No, don't stop!" whined Andweard. "I just thought there was a noise."

Kieran looked at his boy, who was clearly more frightened the story would cease than he was of a few jolts. Kieran patted his head, and continued.

"Across the sky they ride, Odin and Freya side-by-side, driving their chariots forward, with all the great warriors of the past and present close behind, the

293

hoofs of their mounts causing rain to break from the clouds and sending sparks that we call lightning."

"Who do they pursue on the hunt?" asked Andweard.

"It is different each time," said Kieran. "Sometimes it is a prize stag or horse. Sometimes it is a fugitive of the gods' justice, sometimes a mortal who has sinned against his fellow men or Nature, and sometimes it is just an unlucky person marked by fate as the quarry of the host. However, one thing is always the same: The huntsmen never fail to catch their prey."

There was a noise that sounded like a muffled cry from somewhere near the hall.

"There it is again!" said Andweard.

"I heard it too," said Freya. Kieran nodded.

"I told you," Andweard said.

The family sat motionless, their ears straining, trying to pick up some second sound from outside. A minute passed without it repeating, and Kieran relaxed.

"I suppose…"

Suddenly there was a loud, urgent banging at the door. Now all three jumped in their seats, and Kieran rose and hurried to the door, to see who would be standing outside his hall on Modranicht in the midst of a snow storm.

He pulled away the oak and iron bar that kept the door closed to the wind and flung it open. Brecht, the old servant, stood there, framed by the pitch black of the night around, wearing one of the strangest expressions Kieran had ever seen on a man's face.

"Brecht, what are you doing here?"

The old man did not reply, but only looked at Kieran with the odd twist to his face, as his mouth worked itself open and closed. In the air outside, Kieran could now hear the night was filled with unusual noises. He could not tell precisely from where they arose, but now he could tell what they were. They were screams.

"King Ællis is dead," said Brecht, his voice weak and as strange as his look. "And they are here."

"Who, Brecht?"

The servant tried to speak, but could not form the words. He staggered forward, his movements showing he had been sapped of all strength. He looked at Kieran as he began to collapse, his features contorted in pain and dread. "I'm sorry," Brecht whispered, as his eyes rolled back in his head and he fell forward. There was a terrible sound as he collided with the floor and there remained, motionless. The shafts of two arrows stuck out from his back.

Freya screamed, and, as if her shriek was the cue, the night around the hall was suddenly blanched as dozens of torches were lit at once. In the torchlight, Kieran could discern familiar faces among the invaders, all of whom were clad in black. One countenance particularly caught Kieran's attention, and made his blood turn to ice: Wulfric.

He slammed the door shut and moved the bar into place, as the servants, roused from their sleep, rushed forth to heap obstacles in front of the entrance.

"Get the other one!" ordered Kieran, pointing to the door at the opposite end of the hall. Two of the servants leapt to his command, but no sooner had he spoken the words than a deep, powerful thudding against the second door shook the timbers of the hall. The servants tried to erect a barricade with the chests and benches nearby, but the planks of the door began to bend inward and crack with each successive blow, and at last the wood shattered as the steel head of a battering ram thrust through it.

Warriors poured into the hall. The servants were felled almost instantly in a flurry of arrows and axes, while several of the marauders rushed forward to grab Freya and Andweard from the place where they huddled and pull them toward the middle of the chamber.

Kieran dashed for the sword of Eadweard and grabbed it from its rest. He readied himself for the first battle of his life, believing that only death could stop him from trying to cut his way through to his family, yet the sword dropped from his hand even before he could draw it from its scabbard. Kieran looked at his left arm to see an arrow sticking out of either side.

"No no no," said a voice. "You had your chance to fight."

Kieran raised his head to see Wulfric stride into the center of the hall, surrounded by a semicircle of his men, and, beside him, the struggling form of Freya and his son, catatonic with fear, in the grip of three warriors.

"I told you, *waylander*, you would regret your vote at the Witanagemot."

A troop of warriors ran forward, and though he landed many blows, Kieran was subdued when one of the men wrenched the arrow in his arm and he dropped to the floor, howling in pain. They dragged him in front of Wulfric. Looking up from his knees, Kieran's eyes blazed silent hatred toward the Saxon chief, who laughed at his expression.

"What, no soliloquies now, Lord Ulstan? No fine speeches? Perhaps if your brothers-by-bond were here you would be bolder, but that would be difficult. We paid our respects to them before coming to see you."

Freya gave a cry, and her knees briefly gave out. Though he felt he had strength enough to snap Wulfric's head clean off his neck if given the chance, he did not have the strength to face Freya after learning his actions had gotten her brothers killed.

"Nobody is coming to help you, Ulstan. The fool Ællis is dead this *Tewesdag* last, and our great leader Ceradic is now lord of all Saxons. You will be happy to know, I am sure, that the Law Speakers refuse to lift the Seal of Saxneat from where the Wodinsblot stains your truce." He turned his face toward Freya, who recoiled. "Your husband is so noble, is he not? Does it not make you proud?"

Wulfric rounded again toward Kieran, snakelike, his one good eye deadly cold. "Every last man among your domains who ever lifted an axe or sword has joined his ancestors already, or will die before this night is out. Their blood turns the snow crimson throughout your lands. This is how you repay me for the plunder you cost me and my people."

Wulfric motioned for Andweard to be brought forward. Kieran hoped his boy was as uncomprehending as his blank expression indicated. When the one-eyed war chief touched Andweard's head, it sent a shock through Kieran and he renewed his struggles, trying to break the grip that held him. It was in vain. His effort only caused Wulfric to smile and continue stroking the unresponsive Andweard's hair.

"See now, Ulstan, how maddening it is when someone decides to destroy what you hold dear? Perhaps not. Perhaps you are still ignorant. What I have done tonight thus far has only been to compensate me for my losses." He leered at Kieran. "This is so you learn the lesson."

Wulfric produced a dagger from behind his back, and even before Kieran could cry out, he drew the blade across the boy's throat. Andweard's eyes opened wide in shock, and instead of a scream a series of gurgles emerged from his throat along with a cascade of blood. Andweard's eyes were still open but lifeless when Wulfric let his corpse drop to the floor. Freya burst into wild sobs.

"I'll kill you!" Kieran bellowed in rage, thrashing so violently he nearly succeeded in slipping the hold of his captors.

"You will, eh? Will that be before or after this?" said Wulfric.

At his word, the warriors holding Freya dragged her screaming across the hall and bent her over a bench. They began groping her, pulling up her gown and tearing at her bodice as she kicked and thrashed, cursing them and attempting to sink her teeth into their flesh. Kieran watched in mute horror, until he remembered the only appeal there was.

"She is with child!" he shouted.

The air changed instantly. The men, some of whom had already undone their trousers, stopped in the midst of their ravishing, though still held Freya down. Wulfric's face was at first disbelieving, then sour. Glowering, he marched over to where his men had Freya pinned. He pulled them off her, flipped her over onto her back with a powerful motion and yanked her dress up over her abdomen. There, for all the men to see, was the taut mound of her belly protruding from her lean frame, which at one glance proved the truth of Kieran's words. The men looked about them uncertainly, then to their chief, who stared hard at Kieran.

298

"You are quite lucky, the both of you," said Wulfric, with the look and tone of one robbed of perfect victory. "My men are superstitious. They will not allow her to be defiled."

Wulfric looked down at Freya and exhaled in regret. He nodded to himself, accepting the situation, and made as if to walk away. Then, turning, in a blink-fast motion he drew his sword and drove it deep into Freya's stomach.

Kieran's next moments lasted eons. Helplessly from his knees he watched Wulfric thrust the blade with both hands into his wife's abdomen, stopping only when it reached the hilt, then twist the sword sideways. Freya jerked and twitched, but after an initial scream she did not utter a sound. She looked at Kieran, those eyes of endless blue meeting his for the last time, then her head lolled sideways and she slackened as she released her final breath. Kieran thought he could see Freya's life leave her body with her last exhalation.

He stared mutely ahead, seeing nothing, his only thought a profound wish for Wulfric to send him to his death as well. Wulfric looked down at Kieran and said, "Anyway, I wouldn't want to be in any *cunne* that would bear your bastard."

Finish it, thought Kieran. *Give me the blade and let it be done.*

His silent imploration went unheeded. Wulfric, instead of plunging his sword into Kieran after he drew it from Freya's body, only wiped her blood onto one of the wall hangings, and returned the blade to its scabbard.

Kieran did not need to be any longer restrained. He made no motion to rise when Wulfric's men released him, nor even when they began setting torches to the hangings and furniture in the hall. While flames licked higher up the walls and

299

across the ceiling, Wulfric dropped into a crouch and held a velvet bag of coins in front of Kieran.

"Look at me, waylander," said Wulfric, repeating it several times until Kieran finally raised his eyes. "I told you, you will never be a true Saxon. Today is proof. But it's fortunate that I am a true Saxon, and will honor the law."

Wulfric dropped the bag in front of Kieran, and gold trickled from its mouth.

"That is the *wergild* I owe you for slaughtering your brood. You may count it if you like, it is correct to the grain – every fraction of an ounce I am required by our laws to pay you for the life of your bitch wife and your bastard son. This is what it means to be civilized, Ulstan: settling your debts."

Wulfric rose, while Kieran remained on his knees. The crackle of the fire consuming the hall had built to a roar, and as smoke filled the chamber, the support timbers groaned.

"The only thing I did not include was the *wergild* for the whelp in your wife's womb," said Wulfric, walking over to where the sword of Eadweard lay. He picked it up, turned and walked back to where Kieran still knelt, motionless. Wulfric dropped the sword in front of him.

"Come collect it."

The structure was weakening rapidly from the inferno, and Wulfric's men, clustered at the door, called out for him to leave. As the war chief joined them, one pointed to Kieran and asked, "Aren't you going to kill him?"

Wulfric looked at the kneeling figure in the middle of the burning hall and said, "We did."

Kieran did not notice them men depart. He absorbed all the Saxon chief had said as one comprehends the conversation of strangers, understanding without attachment. He could not respond nor even move, nor would have if he were capable. The entire House of Wearding, which stood for fifty years in Briton and four hundred in Germania and included every person on Earth important to Kieran, was exterminated by Wulfric in one night. In under a minute Wulfric ripped away everything Kieran had gained, had loved, had won for himself over the course of ten years, and left Kieran with less than he had when he was first stranded – for then at least he had the will to live.

He had no comprehension of how long he remained kneeling on the floor of his burning hall, but when the roof began to fall and the walls bend and shake, Kieran, choking from the smoke, automatically and without valuation picked up the bag of gold and the sword and walked from the building, avoiding the sight of his butchered wife and son. He heard the hall collapse behind him some minutes later, as he sludged through the snowy landscape, surveying the carnage Wulfric's band left in its wake. Each body lying dead in the snow was a friend or neighbor, and there were many. Wulfric had not stopped with people, but put horses, asses, pigs and sheep to the blade. Kieran believed himself the last living thing for miles around.

Then a miracle: He heard whinnying from across a field. At first he thought it was an illusion, but then remembered that night-black Brecca, the horse he'd given Freya that very day, was in a pen separate from the other horses, hidden by the dark of the night. The firelight reflected in the snow lit his path to the far field, where he found Brecca charging around her enclosure, wild with fear. However, when she saw him walk up, she seemed to slow in her gallop. Brecca became less and less agitated, slowing to a canter, then a trot, then, as Kieran watched, the Friesian approached the spot where Kieran stood against the railing. She snorted and shook her head as Kieran patted her neck.

"We must go," he said.

They tore through the night, heedless of pace or direction. Clinging to her mane and leaning into her gallop, Kieran's mind spun. He felt as if his brain was ripping apart, as if the maelstrom of emotions in his heart would cause it to explode from his chest. Before it consumed him wholly, he recognized it for what it was – the onset of madness. Then he recognized nothing. If it weren't for the sensation of the wind tearing through his hair, the feel of Brecca's sweat-slicked coat under his hands and the anguish that made lead of his heart, he would have doubted he was real at all.

Days and nights were devoid of importance, and Kieran kept no track as they passed. He registered that he and Brecca were headed north, toward fiercer winter, savage tribes and the purported fairy lands, but he did not care, in fact welcomed whatever might arise to take him to oblivion. They came across travelers, but the wild look in Kieran's eyes and his disjointed ranting compelled the people to give them a wide berth and move on quickly. Brecca stopped when she needed. Kieran did not perceive hunger nor thirst, nor fatigue, and if Brecca had not been in possession of that telepathy known to good horses well loved, Kieran would have several times wandered into the endless forests never to be retrieved.

The snows deepened and the temperatures dropped as they headed northward. Brecca's complaints became more frequent, but Kieran, deranged when not delirious, paid them no heed. Days passed when Kieran did not see a soul. He was deteriorating rapidly in both mind and body, and his sanity only returned under the direst of need, such as when he at last noticed the beginning signs of frostbite in his fingers and worked to keep them warmer.

There is no telling how long he would have pressed on if they had not at last come to where the road ran out and no others joined it. The terminus of the path was a promontory overlooking a rocky and desolate coastline that stretched interminably – black rocks, white surf, gray water, a sky that combined their colors. Kieran, undeterred by the lack of road, pressed on, tracking along the deserted stony shores, trying to find exposed grasses for Brecca to graze.

Many were the times Kieran, staring out toward the Endless Sea, was seized with the urge to hurl the sword and gold into the waves and himself directly after them, but each time he balked. He could not yet sever himself from his former life, even if all that remained was the pain. He could not die without knowing what had come before the river, without seeing what happened further down it. Sometimes, though – many times – he felt they just weren't worth having to relive the memories he did have.

When they had traveled the coast for two days, and Kieran felt his strength waning to such a degree that he knew the elements would soon accomplish what he himself could not, Brecca brought him to a strange structure. It was a stone portal, decorated with carvings and symbols Kieran had never before seen, which led down some steps to a boat slip. He thought it was another function of his madness when he noticed that the masonry on the moorings looked new, and that the area seemed swept and maintained, even though he had not run across another human being for a week. He was certain he was insane when, after resting by the spot a few hours, he caught sight of a boat gliding through the mist toward where he and Brecca sat. Only after watching for a span of minutes could Kieran convince himself it was no illusion.

There was a man on the boat. He was not an old man, but had the look of one. He was dressed like a man of the wild – pelts strung together with heavy stitching formed his wardrobe from his tasseled cap to his shoes, and a necklace of bones with an owl skull at its center hung around his neck. In one hand he held a lantern, and in the other he held the handle of the oar. He docked and moored the boat and stepped lightly onto the shore.

"Who are you?" he asked solemnly. His dialect was Britonic, but radically different from any Kieran had ever heard used. He understood the man more from intuition than true comprehension. Kieran gave an honest answer.

"I do not know," he said.

The man peered at Kieran for a few more moments, then said, "You are a stranger to these shores, with great and terrible secrets. I wonder if you yourself understand them."

The man took Brecca's reins from Kieran's hand and tied her to a post, smoothing her mane and whispering words into her ear. He turned back to Kieran.

"You are a man of destiny. We have not seen one like you in a long time. You will come with me."

Kieran did not protest as the man helped him onto the boat, nor even asked what would become of Brecca, for she was even calmer than he, and did not herself seem concerned about her fate. The man untied the barca and pushed off from the slip. As the shore disappeared behind a curtain of mist, Kieran had the sensation he was passing into another realm, another world. Kieran was a willing traveler, now, crossing the water on the stranger's boat, feeling madness and sorrow slip away from him, even as his grip tightened around the sword he still carried. He was peaceful at last, his mind and heart receiving a respite from their agonies, and neither hate nor sadness troubled him as he stared out on the black sea and gray clouds, and watched a large shadow on the horizon solidify into an island.

Chapter Twenty

"My lord Kieran?" Aurelian repeated.

Kieran's eyes refocused, and he found himself again staring into the face of the Golden Prince, surrounded by the other kings of Britain.

He had lapsed. Years of training, of preparation, all to bring him to the crucial moment and drive the hammer true, to be the instrument and the arm that wields it.

To not lapse.

He did not reprimand himself, though. It no longer mattered. He was restored now, and the moment had almost arrived.

Dead or immortal.

"I apologize, your highness," said Kieran. "I must not have understood."

"I was saying, Saxon, that you must think us naïve to believe that you, who lived a decade among the Germanic menace, who concealed your designs from your sole friend and who attempted to manipulate these proceedings, are not working as a Germanic saboteur."

"I do not deny the facts you claim, but tell you I am not a Saxon agent."

"So then what are you?"

"I," said Kieran, looking around deliberately, "am the only man on Earth who can help you save Britain from destruction at Germanic hands."

Kieran maintained his steady expression as the assembly hooted and jeered. Aurelian opened his arms and cast his look around the hall, as if to say, "Is he not mad or a fool?"

"And I suppose it is the habit of every champion to smuggle his sword into a king's court?" asked Aurelian. "Nothing marks your guilt more clearly than the weapon you tried but ultimately failed to conceal from your friend. Do you deny that you had such a weapon?"

"To know it is mine," said Kieran, who snuck a quick glance to where Uleara stood, "I would need to see it."

"But of course. Produce the weapon!" Aurelian called.

A door to the antechamber was opened, and one of Aurelian's men walked in, bearing a sword in his outstretched hands. The men and women of the assembly rose partway from their chairs and craned their necks to catch a look at the implement in question. A hush fell upon them.

The sword bearer approached Aurelian, who gestured for him to take it near Kieran.

"It is mine," Kieran said upon a brief scan with his eyes.

"Then you admit it!" cried Aurelian. "Come for Saxon deeds with Saxon steel."

"The make is Saxon, I own," said Kieran, "and some of the finest work they have ever produced. But this sword was not among any Germanics when it acquired the properties that will interest you, my lord." Kieran paused, savoring the silence. "That was the work of the Old Kind."

The room erupted.

"Impossible!" shouted one of the kings.

"Everyone knows the Old Kind left for the hills with the fairy folk centuries ago," hollered another. "This man speaks nonsense!"

"I tell you, my lords," said Kieran, "the Old Kind yet dwelt in realms of men, for I lived among them myself. I learned their secrets, their ancient rites and teachings, and that is how I have come to know the destiny of this weapon."

Aurelian let the jeers die down before approaching Kieran anew.

"It is nonsense," said the king. "This sword's only destiny is as scrap for a smith. It is rusted completely. My strongest aide could not pry it from its scabbard."

"And with good reason, highness," said Kieran. He turned to face fully the arrayed elite of Celtic Britain, and said, his voice clear and resonant, "This sword can only be drawn by the King of the Britons."

Kieran's statement was so unexpected that it produced an utter lack of reaction in any of the assembled dignitaries, who merely blinked and looked.

"It is rusted, I tell you," said the war chief of Aurelian's who had examined the sword. "That is no enchantment, but everyday poor upkeep."

"May I see it?" asked Kieran. The various warriors snorted in contempt and the guards took a step toward Kieran, but the prisoner and the king remained still, eyes locked.

"I sense a trick here," said one of Aurelian's advisors. King Cunomor, one seat removed from Aurelian, said, "Do not trust the demon. He has a reputation for craft." Craddoc whispered to him, while Pagos stood by, delighting in Kieran's approaching doom. "And he received a coded message from the Saxons."

All faces turned to Kieran.

"It is true, I did."

"Aha!" said Drystan. "And what was your mission? Assassination? Sabotage?"

"The message was from a friend, from... family. It said Cerdic's men will march on free Britain before the frosts."

The warriors were again abuzz, and even Uleara knew why. A fall campaign starting so late was risky, almost never done. It would be a full season in advance of the truce's sunset.

"Why did you not reveal this during our audience?" said Aurelian.

"I wanted confirmation, and, I admit, I wanted to control the information as long as possible."

"Your own boon companion no longer trusts you," said Drystan, off Uleara's countenance. "Such loyalty he displayed, while you huddled with infomers and led him into peril."

"And for that I am sorry," said Kieran, turning full to Uleara. "I betrayed your confidence by not giving you mine, my dear friend. I felt it necessary, but it was wrong. I apologize."

"What do you think, abbot? You know him best. Will I be in any danger?"

For the first time since Kieran was brought forth, Uleara met his eyes. Kieran was almost always able to tell what Uleara was thinking from his open and earnest face, but this was not such an occasion. Kieran could not guess how Uleara would decide the matter. And more, he saw something he'd never once seen from his friend. He saw the capacity to do hurt.

I'm sorry my friend. I hope I have not pushed you past your edge.

Uleara turned to Aurelian.

"Your highness," he said, "it broke my heart to find out this day that my friend of seven years was a liar. However, it would crush my soul to discover in him the sort of man who would, in this sacred assembly, make an attempt on your life out of vengeance or frenzy. I have faith my soul will not be crushed this day, or ever in life." He paused, gave one last look to Kieran, and said, "I sense no danger in him."

Aurelian nodded, and said, "I concur. Besides," said the king to his chief warrior, "you would see to it that he would be cut down within a heartbeat of even motioning to pull his weapon."

"Of course, highness."

"Then let him have it."

From the bearer's arms Kieran took the sword: his sword, Freya's gift to him from her family. He ran his hands over it, letting his fingers feel the carvings of the gilded hilt and find the grooves of the leatherwork on the scabbard. Kieran bent in brief prayer, then held it out in front of him, as if in offering, and faced the kings.

"There is no defect with this weapon, and its stubbornness owes only to the fact that it is not yet in the hands of he alone worthy to wield it." Kieran's voice was strange to Uleara, full of moment, full of power. "I challenge any man here to withdraw the blade. But I tell you truly, no man shall draw forth this sword who is not meant to wear the Crown of Crowns."

The advisors to the kings scoffed, but the rulers themselves did not. The kings looked wolfish as they eyed the sword, and at the competition in the unexpected contest: all the other ten kings. Each king, too, was now a contender. The kings pulled their aides in close to whisper, and the guards and warriors of each retinue heightened their alert.

At last one man, Catalacus of the Brigantes, strode forth to take up the challenge. King Drystan hissed, "What are you doing?" at him, but the Brigantine chief did not respond. Instead he took the sword from Kieran, put his hand on the hilt of the scabbard, and faced his fellow rulers.

"I as much as any king here have a right to take this challenge," he said, and attempted to pull the sword from the sheath. He yanked at it several times without success, and continued the struggle well past the point when it was apparent his efforts were futile. Finally, in disgust, he threw the sword to the floor, causing the entire assembly to flinch.

Kieran merely picked it up in calmness once again, and said, "Would any other of my lords care to try his hand?" None responded, though Aurelian would have if Kieran had not stopped him with an intense glare and minute shake of the head. Kieran waited for another to speak, then proceeded:

"I have come to Glevuna, to the High Council here called, not in order to play petty politics, nor to stage a contest of strength, nor to spy for the Saxon menace,

311

nor to waste any time, for if there is one thing no man among us need be reminded, our very existence owes to our swift action against the Anglo-Saxon threat.

"I have come to Glevuna, my lords, bearing this sword of destiny, touched by a greater power than you can comprehend, only to present it to the man who will wear the Crown of Crowns as King of the Britons."

Kieran turned slowly, letting the moment extend. He came to meet Aurelian's eyes, and there was a look upon the young ruler's face that Kieran knew few others had ever borne. His features were the same, but were no longer redolent of childhood or impishness. In the set of his mouth and the twinkling of his eyes, Aurelian radiated with the look of a person who knew he was about to become more than a human being, more than a king. Kieran knew that Aurelian sensed the sad and beautiful truth that a myth may not also be a man, and embraced the sacrifice for the incomparable possibilities.

Kieran knelt to one knee before Aurelian, holding the sword before him, hilt first.

"To you, Aurelian, I present this sword, a symbol of your right to rule as High King, and a staff to guide you on the road that fate has laid before you."

"NO!"

A man leapt forward, and Kieran had just enough time to recognize him as Pagos before a dagger slashed him across the arm. Pagos raised the dagger again and brought it down into Kieran's side. The sword fell from Kieran's grip and clattered to the floor.

"Kill the wizard, the traitor!"

The room was stunned. Kieran was the first to move: picking up the sword in its scabbard, he again offering the hilt to Aurelian, life dribbling from his stabbed belly. As guards dragged Pagos to a corner and gagged him, Aurelian crouched at Kieran's side.

"Why did you not act?" asked Aurelian. "You did not use the sword."

"It is… as I said," said Kieran. "The sword is only for he who is meant to wield it – only meant for you, m… my king."

Aurelian peered into Kieran's eyes, then wrapped his fingers around the hilt and readied his muscles. Kieran's thumb moved imperceptibly against a catch in the scabbard, and he said to Aurelian so that none but they heard, "I am going to make you the greatest king Britain will ever know. But first you must draw this sword clean and hold it aloft. And Aurelian," he said, making certain that the king heard him, though his words almost died in his throat, "whatever else happens, do not let go."

For a moment, not a sound was heard in the hall, not a movement made, even by Pagos. The second remained suspended like a filament pulled to its tautest. Then it snapped.

Aurelian gritted his teeth and pulled. The blade made a *shink* as it slid from its scabbard, and all among the assembly let in a collective gasp. Aurelian, as directed, raised the blade above his shoulder, pointing its tip to the heavens. The stillness in the room lingered, the kings and their coteries frozen by the sight of the sword unsheathed. After a few moments with nothing else, Kieran saw some resume their expressions of skepticism. King Drystan was among the first to recover from his surprise, and stood to speak. Kieran smiled to himself.

Five, four, three…

"Oh come now, my lords, can't you see…" started Drystan, but his next words were drowned out by a dozen screams and the sounds of chairs scraping the wood as they were pushed back by their owners' surprise.

Emanating from the surface of the sword blade was smoke, growing bolder. Strands of vapor slinked up the length of the blade, and flying up from the tip spread along the ceiling, soon filling the room with a layer of haze.

As the assembly marveled, Aurelian, moving as if compelled by a force from without, waved the sword in an arc through the air as the smoke billowed forth. The young king was just as awestruck by the sight of the sword as the rest of the assembly, but Kieran noticed with appreciation that he was trying not to look at it. Just as Aurelian brought up his other hand to grip the haft and center the sword to point above his head, Kieran whispered to him, "Keep hold!"

At that instant the hall was filled with a blazing white light. Every man and woman within cried out, and shielded their eyes from the glare, which had an intensity no fire from wood could match. The blade seemed to itself be composed of a sparking, spitting, writhing, living fire of incandescent whiteness that made the candles and braziers within the hall seem like dim stars before the light of the sun. Yet still Aurelian held on.

Many kings were crouched below or behind the table, and many of their advisors were beating at the doors of the hall trying to gain exit. Shrieks of terror continued throughout, until Kieran's booming call silenced them.

"Who here deems himself a worthy Briton, yet cowers and flees at the moment of Britain's greatest glory? Turn, and look upon your salvation."

Kieran called out his command several more times until every person within the room was staring in awe and wonder at Aurelian and his sword.

"Today," said Kieran, "from many squabbling tribes and petty peoples, we forge a nation, an example to history that shall live for all of recorded time. Today is the dawn of a new era, of legend and splendor. Today is the first day of Britain."

Uleara was on his knees, crossing himself and moving his lips in prayer, then snatching glances at the sword.

"Destiny has marked this man to lead the Britons against the Saxon threat, so all may know that loyalty to Aurelian is loyalty to all Britain. Now kneel – kneel before your king."

One by one, their eyes perhaps grateful for a respite from the fire of the sword, they fell to their knees and bowed their heads, until only Kieran, Aurelian and the Magistrate still stood. Kieran looked to the elderly man, and entranced, the Magistrate placed the Crown of Crowns with trembling hands on Aurelian's head.

"All hail Artros Ambrosius Aurelianus," intoned Kieran, with his remaining strength, "son of Utros Ambrosius Draconem, Prefect of the Glevuum civitas, Lord of the Dubonni, King of the Britons."

The call came back instantly, from every throat, with zeal, reverence, and pride.

"All hail Artros, King of the Britons."

Chapter Twenty-One

The council hall doors were flung wide, and with the sword still blazing, Aurelian stepped outside, holding the blade before him.

A throng of the curious had been gathered outside the council hall throughout the proceedings, eavesdropping and peeping through gaps in boards or bare patches of thatching. When the sword burst forth its flame, as brilliant beams of light suddenly shot out from a thousand cracks in the walls of the building, they knew something momentous had occurred, and when they saw what emerged from within the Council Hall no one needed command the throng to its knees – each man, woman and child knew his place was prostrated before Aurelian, bent before his sword of fire.

The newly-crowned King of the Britons walked up the hill to the summit. Kieran, heavily bandaged but still on his feet, was by his side at each step, the only person other than Aurelian who was not in the grip of awe. Uleara, following close, observed Kieran whispering to the king until they reached the top of the hill. Kieran remained in consultation with Aurelian until, at the very summit, the High King once again lifted the blade above his head. Thousands in the Glevuum Vale turned their collective gaze toward the hilltop, and marveled at the needle of light that pierced the darkness. Across the valley it looked as if he'd brought Venus down from the heavens. Messengers spread the word among the crowds, and the Dubonni roared in celebration when they heard who wielded it. Bells, drums and horns burst forth their sounds throughout Glevuna.

Around the hill, before the fire at last sputtered out, another noise rose up from all who could speak, thousands together calling toward the hill, shouting the name of their king, his Britonic name, an ancient appellation chanted for minutes on end.

Artros.

The name became a motto, an incantation, a war cry, as the happenings at the Council reverberated throughout the isles. Celebration mingled with preparation, for while the Britons had their high king, they also had a fight on their hands, and scant weeks to prepare.

All around Glevuna, warriors and workmen, clan fathers and carpenters assembled into the Britonic Army. Within Glevuna, celebrations were unending. Uleara had spent two whole days drunk and not spent a single coin. He remembered most of the bacchanal, and what he didn't remember he reasoned it was better to forget. He gave penance for all sins during those 40 hours, and received enthusiastic absolution from the star struck priest who delivered it. After several days, though, Uleara was weary, but the citizens were not weary of mobbing him in the street. Kieran spent that part of the week confined to bed, letting his wounds heal.

"One look at you and I'm glad I stayed in here."

"I never thought I'd be the subject of idolatry," said Uleara, who had just braved the world outside their adjoining apartments in Aurelian's palace, and slumped exhausted into a settee. Kieran tossed Uleara a pear from one of the fruit bowls that lay about the cavernous living area. Uleara bobbled it but made the catch, yet frowned when he looked at it.

"Are there bites out of all of them?"

"For our safety," said Kieran, swallowing a bit of plum. "We only need to be unpopular with one resourceful person to end up like Pagos, I have it from a centurion."

"Perhaps it is not professional of me, but Pagos put himself on the pyre."

"I can't argue," said Kieran. "So, what will the topic be today?"

Uleara smiled. The abbot hadn't stopped soliciting information from Kieran since sobered up from the revelries, and did not plan to. Already Uleara knew more about Kierans past than he'd ever gleaned – about Roscinham, and Freya. Not about the Old Kind, though – not yet.

"Well," said Uleara, folding his hands across his bulbous midsection and crossing his legs, "let's see what we've covered. The glowing substance was a compound of the Old Kind…"

"Not a compound, technically, but yes."

"And you coated the blade with it before we left, thinking I would never look," said Uleara, with his sore feelings on the mend but a pointedness remaining.

Kieran smiled. "You are a trusting soul."

"And may I…?"

"You may not have some. We need everything for the war effort, and there isn't any now."

"Blast."

Uleara rose and poured himself a glass of wine from a particolored glass decanter, vintage Roman. "And how, again, did your plan work? How could you ensure all the human pieces moved according to your strategy?"

Kieran laughed. "Oh, my dear abbot, would that not have been a holiday?"

"But they did. We did. Your game worked out perfectly."

"It was only what we call odds, Uleara. I had no guarantees, so I had contingencies, redundancies. For the handful of informers you met, there were a dozen more in roles that did never became vital. If you had not brought the sword to Aurelian, I had other avenues, though the one we took was the firmest."

Uleara looked displeased, but Kieran hadn't noticed, happy, it seemed, to be able to speak at liberty about his hitherto solitary pursuit.

"A latrunculi player doesn't know where his opponent's tile will land," Kieran explained. "He can make a good wager, but not a certain bet. Success is founded on improving position, on expanding options, on a solid understanding of the board and the tactics that will shape the game to ensure victory, regardless of the opponent's moves."

He is not denying he treated us as game pieces, thought Uleara. He stifled the resentment, though, asking "And who was the opponent in your contest?"

Kieran blinked. "Failure."

Uleara pondered this, sipping the wine. "So if the sword had not shown up, it would have been a plucked partridge, is that it?" Uleara was chuckling, but his friend's face had dropped.

"The sword had to get there. That was the one move that needed to be made."

"I still don't understand, why Aurelian? You have acted like it truly was his destiny to be chosen High King."

319

"I believe it was," said Kieran, all mirth gone. "A great deal depended on that one council."

"You seem quite convinced," said Uleara.

"I had faith."

Uleara gave a full laugh. "Oh, you are an odd one, Kieran. Hard to figure, through and through. But I believe I'll make a believer of you yet."

"That's where you're confused, dear abbot," said Kieran, "for I have been a believer all along."

Uleara was all at once rapt. He set down his glass and leaned toward Kieran. "You speak of the Old Kind. Yes, tell me. What are their ways?"

Kieran retreaded back, physically and on his face. "Not yet. Not yet. There will be time for that, but that time is not now."

Uleara was again disappointed, which Kieran clearly saw, for brightening, he continued, "I make you this promise, though, that I will keep nothing from you any longer. Whatever you wish to know I will tell, if it is in my power to do so."

"In your power," said Uleara, in a suspicious tone but brightening up as well. "That seems like a provision designed for you to escape your promise," said Uleara.

"I merely mean that I am not in possession of all the knowledge I would like to have. For all the wonders and secrets I have been allowed to know, I am denied some of the simplest memories, ones so common and elemental to almost all mankind that they are hardly regarded at all."

"Such as what?"

Kieran looked at Uleara. "My real name."

The abbot was speechless, but Kieran grinned.

"Don't look so, Uleara. I know my blessings as well, your friendship among them."

"I consider it an honor to call you friend," said Uleara, "though distance may separate us."

Their smiles both fell.

Kieran had tried to convince Uleara to remain with him as advisor to Aurelian, but the abbot, who had granted almost every other request Kieran had ever made of him, this time staunchly refused.

"You have already proven yourself such an asset to the new High Court," Kieran said, picking up in the midst of their last debate.

"In what fashion?"

"The calendar question," Kieran said, to which Uleara scoffed and recrossed his legs.

The question of religious reconciliation between pagans and Christians was at the forefront of many Britons' minds during the High King's first privy council. The priests of the many gods were accustomed to the numerous benefits of their current positions, and threatened to stir up sentiment among the staunchest believers if Aurelian did not make provisions for their "continued offices and tenures." Weeks of wrangling produced a resolution with no happy parties.

When it turned to the "calendar question," Aurelian had called on Abbot Uleara for the first time. "Tell me, abbot," Aurelian opened, "where do you stand?"

"You mean fixing the date of the Feast of the Resurrection?" Uleara had asked, previously hoping to avoid the very position in which he found himself yet again, the focus of everyone's attention, particularly the High King.

"I am anxious to hear your opinion," the king had said.

"It is a quite thorny problem, your highness…" Uleara began.

Aurelian cut in instantly.

"The worthless Bishop of Londinium appealed to the Holy See," the young High King had said, with annoyance yet exhuberance over a problem to solve, "and Rome insists we hold our spring festival to coincide with the Mass to commemorate Our Lord being taken into Heaven. I am told, however, by the ever-pious priests of the many gods that it is an affront to their deities to disregard the solstices and equinoxes, and all manner of disaster may ensue. None of these rituals are closer to their hearts (and wealth of the clerics, I will never fail to add) than the vernal celebration in honor of the fertility goddess Eoster. Their pull on the people is still strong and I fear disharmony if their wishes are not respected. This is a question I wish to resolve quickly."

The abbot had said, after a long internal deliberation, "Your highness, have you considered combining them?"

"What," Aurelian then replied, "hold remembrance of Christ's resurrection on Eoster's Day?"

"I myself hold celebrations on both the Roman and the pagan holidays, highness, and seek to combine them when I can. One may not change a person's beliefs by taking away his festivals."

"And do not you or your congregants consider this to be a sacrilege?"

"With respect, your lordship, I feel the Heavenly Father is pleased anytime his flock congregates to glorify his name and share the cup of brotherhood. Those who revere the gods of the earth can feel no offense, if we give thanks for to all those under God who have assisted in reaping it. A gathering in good will and celebration delights all deities."

"What did Rome have to say on the matter?" Aurelian then inquired.

Uleara had averted his eyes and gave a guilty smile. "We have held the position that the Holy See can administer only those things it can actually see."

"Do you remember what Aurelian said then?" Kieran asked, he and Uleara still chuckling over the memory of Uleara's first contribution to the life of the new united kingdom.

"He said he wanted me as his personal spiritual guide."

"And you declined," said Kieran. "Would you truly deprive this nascent kingdom of a strong creative and moral voice such as yours?"

"Now I know you are just attempting to flatter me into compliance," laughed Uleara. "No, I am afraid God is calling me in another direction from the one he has chosen for you. I received word this morning from Aelfarn. Yet another batch of the curious have stayed on as converts. That means in just a week after the coronation we have doubled the size of the flock."

323

"Congratulations, my friend."

"Ah, well, we will see if it is only a passing fancy. But I must return before winter sets in so that I may keep stoking the fires of these good people's faith."

"I see that you cannot be persuaded – but perhaps we might borrow you from time to time?"

"I hardly see how I can disobey a command from the chief advisor to the King of the Britons," said Uleara.

They turned as footsteps approached. A herald from Aurelian appeared in the doorway and saluted.

"My lord Kieran," said the guard. "The king awaits your counsel."

Uleara looked to Kieran. "This is just the beginning, you know."

"For both of us," said Kieran, as he and the abbot walked to the door and followed the herald down the hall. Each person they passed bowed as deeply as they could to the pair and scurried out of the way, which, though it had been occurring for a week, still left Uleara slightly unnerved.

"So you will tell me all I ask?" Uleara inquired of Kieran as they strolled the marble tile.

"Yes."

"Excellent. Let us start with where you are from. I mean, actually."

"I will indeed tell you," said Kieran, "though let us not start there. It is going to take a little while."

"How so?"

Kieran smiled a smile that spoke of deep mystery. "All in good time."

"Fine, then here is an easier one. What did you say to Aurelian on the way to the hilltop?"

"What did I say to Aurelian?"

"On the way up the hill, yes," said Uleara.

"I told him that I would help build his kingdom if he would promise me five things."

"Did he agree?"

"Naturally."

"What are they?"

"That he would accept my advice above all others in making his decisions, that he will form a code of justice even he cannot break, that he will seek peace and only war justly, and one other I cannot tell you yet."

"But you said you would tell me all!"

"Yes, dear friend, but I never specified when."

"This new Kieran is seeming quite like the old," grumbled Uleara. "All right then, what is the last one? You said there were five."

Kieran's expression changed, the joy bleeding away from it, and a fog passed over his eyes.

"That I can tell you," said Kieran, "but as a Christian you will not like it."
Kieran looked off into space. "I made Aurelian promise that when we fight and conquer the Saxons, and Ceradic's general Wulfric is defeated, they will do what they can to ensure he stays alive."

Uleara was agape. Kieran had only just told that part of his story. "Is that not the man who…?"

"He is no man," said Kieran. "But yes, it was he."

"Why, though, would you ask that they keep him alive?"

Kieran faced his friend and looked into his eyes. "Because," said Kieran, "I have to kill him."

PART III

Chapter Twenty-Two

For seven long seasons, Britain knew only war.

Battles raged all months, all over the island. Lines of control between native and colonizer swung by the week. A band of destruction nicknamed "The Burn," a hundred miles wide and thrice as tall, blazed down Britain's center, blackened by arson, rouged with blood. Not even Dumnonia escaped – Cunomor watched the harbor at Aberfal burn into the sea. Dubonnii, Deceanglii, Brigantes, Catuvellanii, they died by the thousands, and still the Anglo-Saxons came.

In the second year, the scales of victory shuddered, then tipped toward the Britons. More Celts in arms, more marvels turned out by Lord Maelgwyn, the High Protector, shoved the Germanics back. No longer were Jutes razing waterfronts, no longer Angles collecting severed heads from villages as if plucking berries from a thicket.

By the second summer, nearly three years after it began, the war was nearly won.

It was in that summer the Germanics, who preferred to fight in diffuse groups under their own thanes, consolidated their forces and drove deep into the Britonic heartland, a last-ditch offensive to turn the tide in their favor. It killed many Britons, but it failed. The push left their main body of fighters cut off from provisions and auxiliaries, surrounded. After a tenacious stand for survival, Ceradic effected an escape of his Saxon warriors, leaving the Angles to be slaughtered, and dug his army immovably into an abandoned Roman fortress that crowned Mons Badonicus, or Mount Badon.

The Britons were tired of war, and had learned patience in three years of it. So from the first frosts of autumn until the last ice melted, the Britonic legions besieged the Saxon fort at Badon.

Finally, they were drawn out.

Kieran scanned the field with his glass. The ranks of the Saxons had formed at first light, and arrayed themselves across the field where they would make their stand. Backs against the dawn, enveloped in a mist tinted red and orange by the rising sun, they were ferocious, a wall of enormous, inhuman silhouettes holding implements of war. The Saxon horde, which the Britons had not seen for a long half year of waiting and watching, looked more terrifying than many of them remembered. The natives were reminded why they had once regarded the Germanic invaders as nearly invincible.

However, as their veil of moisture burned off, a different picture was revealed. They looked eager for war, and were nearly two thousand strong, but it was clear the Saxons had felt the effects of being on the losing side. Their ill-fed six months left them in poor health, and defeat left them with battered equipment and dwindling prowess.

Kieran was positioned on a mound near the field, opposite the fortress, flanked by a dozen aides and the two tents where the particular equipment of Lord Maelgwyn was kept. He saw the sun coloring in the sky as a vivid blue, unbesmirched by clouds. The air was cool and smelled of blossoms. It was a beautiful background. Kieran hoped it would not be an ugly day.

Eye to his glass, he peered at the faces of the foe. Many were familiar from a time far in his past, a different lifetime, when he'd once shared their mead and greeted them as friends. When the war began and Kieran was seen by the Saxon ranks, the jeers were as loud as the battles that followed. Every time a thane or gesith cried "Ulstan, come fight like a Saxon – come join your wife in hell," it helped neither the morale of his men nor his standing among the leaders of the united army. Once they'd seen him directing the more advanced implements for which he was responsible, and cleared from the field the Germanic corpses they produced, the jeering stopped.

This isn't full fighting trim, thought Kieran. The faces of the Saxon warriors were sallow, gaunt, ratty compared with before. Some showed signs of fever, many of scurvy. Yet Kieran saw too in their faces that North Sea berserker spirit, that love of contest and conquest, that had already made all of Eastern Britain theirs, regardless of the war's outcome. The war's outcome might be beyond doubt, but Kieran read in the postures of the Saxons something dangerous for the Britons in the immediate fight before them.

Ceradic and Wulfric recognized triumph was impossible, but if they could break through the force of Britons and escape to their eastern strongholds, the Saxons could regroup and perpetuate the war for years, or force a permeable and temporary peace. The Britons were veteran warriors now, yes, but after months idle they were weakened and out of practice. A look around the sprawling camp revealed this fact in every quadrant. Kieran knew well that the Saxons had a lifetime of martial training and experience to keep their internal weapons of cunning, courage and discipline strong and well-honed during the respite. The Britons, for the most part, did not.

Kieran turned his glass, putting a pair of warriors on horseback in his sights. He could see the warrior chiefs, as well-fed as their men were malnourished, laughing to each other.

There they are themselves. Ceradic and Wulfric.

They had changed drastically little. Kieran watched them until the horns rang out, then put down his glass. Below him, twelve perfect squares of soldiery, a hundred men to a square, fell into formation at the foot of Kieran's hill. The men were mainly from the Dubonni tribe, with some Dumnonians eager to join the war among them, and were under Aurelian's direct command. They wore new armor, from a modified Roman model, and every piece, the helmet and chainmail each man wore, the embossed breastplate reserved for a captain and above, was brightly illumined where the rising sun hit it. The soldiers stood tall. These were the men of the Legio Nova Augusta, and they hadn't been beaten in many months.

The Brigantines, and those of the Catevullauni who had not gone home, commanded the right flank, while the Demetae along with other men of the west composed the left. The final division formed under a forest of banners, and the battle order was complete. Kieran looked to his aides.

"Get into position."

The opening scenes of the battle went as designed. The Saxons ran screaming at the Britons, shields pumping with their arms, filling the shallow valley with fury. The neat centuries of Britonic troops advance steadily, closing the distance from their side. Members of Kieran's elite unit, the Special Century, had already been in place for hours, waiting until the onrushing Saxons reached the appointed place. Two hundred, then one hundred, then fifty yards distant, the lines closed.

Just within missile range, Saxons streaked from their ranks, slim javelins readied. Kieran gave the signal.

The crackle that followed could barely be heard above the roaring marauders, but seven dozen of the Germanics' best and most admired warriors fell to the ground spurting blood, javelins useless at their sides, to be trampled by the stampede behind them. No arrow or spear had been loosed.

"Forward!" commanded Aurelian ahorse, and several thousand Britons charged toward the Saxon vanguard, led by a flying wedge of horsemen. The Saxons' confusion at their inexplicable casualties just moments before the two ranks of combatants collided, a mass assassination at the moment when they most needed war-strength, was an advantage the natives drove home. Germanic front lines were ripped apart by Britonic cavalry, Saxons falling like butchered kine, and the Celtic foot drove deep into the invaders' ranks.

The Germanics summoned their ancestral warrior rage, fighting to close the hole opened up by Aurelian's troops. Kieran watched a line of Saxon spearmen advance from the battle line and move into position at the Britonic rear. He gestured for one of his men and pointed.

"Target them."

The legionary ran to a wooden tower and relayed the order. Kieran watched through his glass as wounds sprouted on a score of Saxons a quarter mile away.

They're going to try again, thought Kieran, *but how many more times?*

Kieran heard the blare of calynxes, and looked to the extreme right of the line. The Brigantine forces were beginning their advance, five hundred troops and a fifth as many horse.

"No! It's too soon!" shouted Kieran.

The command signals were flying frantically to halt the Brigantine charge, but went unacknowledged. *King Catalacus – his pride is going to get them killed.* Kieran watched helplessly as the northerners met with the Germanic flank. Twenty-five yards out, the Saxons opened up with slings and javelins, raking the Britons and taking out a tenth of their number.

A shield wall locked into place before the Britons, and they sprinted forward to break it, their cavalry at the forefront. As the Brigantines were within stabbing distance, the Saxon line melted back, allowing them passage, and allowing them to be surrounded.

Concealed behind their shields the Saxons carried weighted throwing darts the Romans called *plumbata*, and they now hurled their darts by the hundreds. Horses screamed and men scrambled, seeking shelter from the razor-sharp iron rain. Kieran saw Catalacus slide from his mount, stuck with a half-dozen.

The Brigantine survivors either fled or joined the men of the Legio Augusta, and the Saxons, sensing possibility, redoubled their efforts. The Brigantines had been the reserve force, but now the Westermen filled the role, flinging their number into the fray.

A gruesome stalemate settled in, where the combatants looked to be in the jaws of a monstrous mouth, great rows of teeth grinding steel and bone against each other. The battle had only a vague logic, as predesigned movements gave way to chaotic scrimmages, and the Germanic tactic of targeting bannermen proved effective, as Britonic maneuvers were thwarted. Both sides were exhausted, and in their exhaustion the fighters reverted to the most rudimentary, most carnal of warfare, single combat rife with gouging, biting, head-slamming struggle.

A signal banner flew up from the high command tent: *Enemy on approach. East.*

Kieran whipped his glass to his face and found the bearing. A troop of riders was coming at a gallop, and Kieran saw one lone rider, and advance scout, rejoin them. His intelligence was good, and the riders instead of charging straight into the valley went around Badon Hill, emerging at the rear of the Britonic left flank.

Aurelian and those in the melee received the warning signal, but there was little they could do. The reinforcing Saxons slammed into the Britons, who were being pushed back toward the fortress. Kieran had to act.

"You there," he said to his nearest aide, "take all of the Special Century and get them down into that valley with all the equipment they know how to use."

"Yes, my lord!" he shouted, and the excitement was evident in his voice. Lord Maelgwyn had many wonders, but used them sparingly, secretively. The legionaries in his unit, armed with devices that shot fire and metal great distances, were getting their first taste of pitched battle.

A young, blood-soaked centurion came running at him, waving his arms. Kieran recognized Aelfarn, his one-time apprentice, who now of fighting age had insisted on joining a century of troops rather than remain with Uleara near Eilwath. They had seen each other frequently, but never acknowledged the connection – and never had Aelfarn forgotten to be formal with his old master. He was never "Kieran."

"Lord Maelgwyn! Please, Lord Maelgwyn, we need help!"

"What is it, Aelfarn?" said Kieran. "Is that your blood?"

"I, uh, not most of... No time! It's King Artros, my lord! He is in peril, and the entire right flank with him."

337

Aelfarn pointed, and Kieran raised his spyglass.

The carnage had not abated, despite hours of pitched battle, and it was hard to find any one person among the constant flashes of steel and sprays of blood, no matter where his banner flew, if it still did.

It was in the center of the slaughter, amid one of innumerable knots of combat, where Kieran spotted Aurelian and Dux Glawayn still on horseback, but supported by only a few dozen Britons, on foot. They were penned in by a wall of Saxons that grew thicker as more Saxons saw the position of Artros and his men. Chief among those hacking through Dubonni troops toward Aurelian was Wulfric and a cohort of his best fighters, getting ever nearer to delivering the final blow to the king's small band.

"Where are the horns? The signals?" shouted Kieran. He raced to the signal spot and waved the banner "Attention all" to coordinate a response from the kingly and ducal detachments, but only a few scattered replies came back from the bannermen on the field. To those three, he signaled "Rally Left" and did his best to indicate where Aurelian fought.

"What are we to do, my lord?" stammered Aelfarn.

Kieran turned to his remaining legionaries. "You mount the throwing machines. Release just before I am there." Kieran then swiveled to face Aelfarn. "You come with me."

"I, my lord? What do you want with me?"

"We are going to unleash The Dragon."

The young soldier"s face registered his abject awe when Kieran ripped down one of the field tents of the Special Century to reveal The Dragon. It was a large oblong vehicle of solid build, carved and painted to resemble the sort of serpent that men of all religions feared. From its snout projected two steel tubes.

"Help me," said Kieran, pushing a brazier full of glowing coals toward the contraption. He opened a panel and began to shovel in the coals, sending sparks and floating red embers toward the sky, the young man giving aid. When Kieran stopped, Aelfarn asked, "What now?"

"Now we're getting in."

Their heads banged against the wood as Kieran and the centurion rattled down the hill, crammed inside The Dragon. The young man was furiously working a crank at the back that in turn powered billows, while Kieran, looking out from narrow slats, did his best to steer through the battle.

"Faster!" shouted Kieran. Aelfarn looked at Kieran with desperation, but his cranking and their speed both increased.

The conflict raged to either side of the vehicle. All around were shouts and screams, the smell of blood and sweat and metal grease. Gore flew through the portholes periodically, and some soldiers fell beneath the wheels, causing The Dragon to careen as it crushed the life from the men's bodies. Kieran tried to maneuver through the skirmishes, around the heaps of corpses, and find a route toward Aurelian.

Thwack thwack thwack. Kieran felt the impacts against the side of the vehicle as he heard them, and shouted, "What was that?" to Aelfarn. The young man said, just as Kieran smelled smoke from a very close range, "Flaming arrows."

The heat inside The Dragon began climbing, and the steering mechanism started to jam.

Kieran was considering his options when he glimpsed Aurelian and his diminishing support troops through a break in a group of combatants.

"Brace!" said Kieran as he made a sharp left, narrowly avoiding three Britons who were finishing off a pair of giant Saxon warriors. He momentarily had a clear trajectory toward Aurelian, but a phalanx of Saxons appeared in front of him, pushing a cart to block his path. The collision was only seconds away when the cart was abruptly blasted harmlessly out of their way by a flying projectile. Dirt flew, and the Saxons converging to stop The Dragon died. Kieran's legionaries were hitting their marks.

Thanks, boys.

They were only a few dozen yards away, but the flames of the arrows were eating into the interior of The Dragon. Kieran looked at the centurion, who was still cranking and now had an expression of one who has accepted his death and is only trying to get from his last seconds of life all he can.

"Aelfarn," said Kieran. The young man looked up blankly.

"Kieran?" he said.

"You can stop cranking."

Kieran turned back to look through the front slat and saw another large group of Saxons forming between them and Aurelian. Kieran pulled a knob, and five seconds before reaching the

Germanics he pushed it back in. At once twin jets of flame shot out from The Dragon"s nozzles, obscuring Kieran"s vision behind a curtain of fire and consuming all other sounds with the roar they produced. Flames continued to spew forth until the fuel was spent, and then the view returned. It was one of anguish for the enemy.

Saxons, screaming, ran about attempting to douse themselves, while others were left as nothing but charred masses writhing in the grass. The Dragon came to a stop when enough blackened corpses had caught between the wheels.

Kieran burst out of the top and helped Aelfarn get free of the vehicle, which was now entirely covered in flames. Swords in hand, Kieran and his companion leapt from The Dragon and raced to where Aurelian was fighting. Just as they arrived, the king ran an opponent through, and turned.

"How was your journey?" Aurelian said. Kieran did not reply, but instead went to the king's side and, weapon readied to taste blood at last, surveyed the remaining Saxons. There were three for every Briton in range.

"This is it," said the king as the Germanics advanced. When the two sides raised their swords for the final clash, a tremendous sound froze all weapons and turned the attention of each man to it.

It was a great cheer, and it arose from the Britonic ranks. Far off Saxons could be seen to cease their fighting, and hundreds further away fell to their knees, hands outstretched before them. A ripple of celebration and supplication spread out from the epicenter of the cheers until it reached where the two exhausted commanders stood, just as the Saxons who moments before were delivering death to the Britons now bowed before them.

"What has happened?" Artros asked a soldier who had come racing from the direction of the noise.

"Highness, Ceradic has fled! The Saxon ranks are broken and in disarray. The day is ours!"

"What of Wulfric?" asked Kieran.

"See for yourself."

The soldier pointed to where a crowd was forming, partly made of Germanic prisoners held at

swordpoint, partly of the curious among the Britons, and the rest the commanders of the Britonic forces. Kieran saw Wulfric at the center of it, on his knees.

"At last! We got 'em at last!" whooped the soldier, racing off again. Kieran and Aurelian shared a wordless exchange, and they began striding toward the felled Germanic general.

Kieran called for an aide.

"Bring me the chest with the steel clasp."

The aide registered surprise, but did as he was bid, and hurried back with the small square box. The chest had been carried on every campaign of the war, but never before opened, and speculation among the Special Century about its contents abounded.

Kieran withdrew and adjusted a thick pair of gloves from the chest, and began on his way to where Wulfric lay. When he reached the fallen war chief and murderer, he saw the Britons had just barely fulfilled the order to leave him alive. Chunks of his skin had been cleaved off, as had his right leg below the knee. Most gruesome was the trench-like gash across his gut, which Wulfric fought to keep closed lest his intestines pour out. Yet for all of his injuries, when the Germanic marshal recognized Kieran he smiled.

"By Thor it is true," said Wulfric, his smile quavering into a sneer with the pulses of his pains. "I had our spies executed as double agents when they told us the Britons made you a dux." Wulfric laughed, causing his body to contort. "Only a native would think to make a peacemonger war chief and a schoolboy High King."

Kieran looked at Wulfric's savage face, a face he'd seen many times since Modranicht in nightmares and visions of revenge. He used all his strength to hold off the onslaught of emotion, and remained still.

"It is kind of you to provide my men a chance to see how a true Saxon champion dies," Wulfric said.

"They will not have that chance," said Kieran. "You are defeated, and must own it before your people."

"Who are you to speak of defeat or victory, you cur? You were never even a Saxon cherol, much less a noble! You prefer to work a plow like a slave woman rather than fight with men."

Wulfric managed to imprint a condescending look upon his waxy gray face, otherwise twisted in mortal agony, and addressed the now-gathered throng.

"Do they know, Maelgywn? Or should I say, Ulstan? ...Or should I say, Croepschen?" Wulfric laughed. "Do they know you were a slave? Do these dogs

343

of Britain know you, their hero, their brilliant savior, stood watching while I butchered your wife and children?" Wulfic savored the reaction from of those listening, including the many Britons who could understand some of the Ænglisch tongue. "That"s all you do is watch, slave. You watch other men make the sacrifices you can't. You watch other men fight and die for your cause as you stand safely by. You even watched as your bitch was run through by someone you can never be – a real man of Saxony."

The Saxon prisoners of war remained uncertain of the situation. One braved, "You show them, Wulfric!" and was immediately smacked into silence by the guards, but most simply listened. Few men, Briton or Germanic, knew anything of Lord Maelgwyn's past, and even Aurelian, who stood tensed with is hand ready around the hilt of his sword, was learning a new tale from Wulfric's words.

Kieran betrayed no feeling, and this calmness was more effective than anything he could have said to stifle the buzz of the crowd.

"Relent," said Kieran, looking only at Wulfric, "and let the last minute of your life make amends for every other minute before."

"Should I pray to Jesus?" said Wulfric. He appraised a pair of robed Britons who came forth and began dribbling liquid on him. "You're trying to baptize me!" howled Wulfric, sofrenzied with animus he seemed not to mind that each paroxysm of laughter caused wounds to gush blood anew. "Call off your Christian clerics. If the Eastern God wants me he may come to Valhalla – and kiss my ass!"

The Saxons now openly cheered and hooted, and some even ventured taunts at Kieran and Aurelian, though the culprits were roughly gagged seconds after.

Wulfric was drawing strength from the encouragement. A renewed light came to his face, and when the the robed men stepped away, Wulfric sniffed at the liquid. "Your sacramental spirits smell like horse piss," he said, and acknowledged the ensuing cheers from his men. Kieran remained impassive.

"Enough of this idle talk," said Wulfric. "Bring forth the man who will have the honor of slaying me, so dear Croepschen here may see how it is done."

None of the Britons moved. Their stillness at first made the Germanics cheer more loudly, but a hush took hold soon, and all became silent.

"I want you to know this," said Kieran, quietly enough that only Wulfric and those by his side could hear. "I spent more days than I could ever count wishing only for your death, praying to a multitude of gods that I could stand where I am, at this moment, with you before me thus. Your painful demise was sometimes all that kept me from taking my own life. I too can hate, because you taught me. I know the full measure of hatred I can hold in my heart."

"Ah, your plan is to talk me to death," said Wulfric. "Come, let your man get to business."

"That is not why I do this," Kieran pressed. "It is not a personal vendetta, but the requirement of justice. Your men must know how thoroughly you are defeated, in all that you are. You are anger and fear and greed and cruelty, and even as I triumph over you, Britain triumphs over what you are. For there to be lasting peace, they need to know that your brand of Saxondom dies with you."

Wulfric remained insolent, but his physical agony was returning with gusto. He winced when he said, "You won't do a thing to me. You don't have the stones."

345

Kieran stepped back, and spread his arms wide. The voice that emanated from him was hollow and profound, inhuman, and instantly recognized by those who had been present in the Council chamber at Glevuna three years before. Yet now it was in Ænglisch Lord Maelgwyn spoke.

"Dux Wulfric, you are no proud Saxon. You are a brigand and criminal, disgraced under the Saxon code, a repudiated war leader felled by the armies of great King Artros and brought here to kneel before justice. You are a debtor in arrears. You owe dearly, Wulfric: for the folly into which you have led your people, for the needless destruction of those you sought to subjugate, and for all the many innocents you have slain."

Wulfric was losing blood and self-assuredness in equal measure, and one could almost feel his men's bravado dissipate during Kieran's pronouncements, in such an otherworldly tenor. All defiance had disappeared. Every Saxon's terrified eyes were upon Kieran as he raised a clenched fist.

Kieran said, "Your debt shall be paid now, Wulfric. As High Protector of the Britons, Witan of the Saxon mot, husband of Freya Wearding and father of two children dead, I have come to collect."

At this, Kieran opened his hand and revealed a bright light that shone from within. The amazed spectators, Wulfric included, beheld a small luminescent object in Lord Maelgwyn's fingers, as if he had plucked a large star from the firmament. Kieran raised the fleck of pure brilliance until there wasn't an eye in the field whose pupil did not reflect its light, and with a tiny flick the morsel of luminosity sprang from his hand. For all watching it seemed to pause in its arc and hover in the air for a moment before drifting down to the soil a few feet in front of Wulfric. Amid the grass clods it looked like a tiny seed of fire, and indeed, once it touched the earth, it bloomed forth into a garden of flame. The

346

conflagration spread across everything touched by the liquid the robed men had poured over Wulfric, and the flames raced along the surface of the substance toward where Wulfric lay.

The Germanic general made a brief attempt to scramble from the fire's trajectory, but his lacerated arms and one remaining leg could not manage. Some of his entrails flopped out when he let go of his wound to cover his face just as the final moment came and flames erupted over his skin.

The air was rent by his screaming, an unbroken keening of agony. Wulfric at first frantically tried to roll and pat out the burning patches, but soon he seized up and shook all over as charring skin peeled back from his flesh, his cries continuing even as his lips melted.

Kieran waited until Wulfric's eyebrows caught fire and most of his movements were involuntary, then spoke in a voice flatter than a windless lake.

"Show him mercy," Kieran said.

An archer who had been standing by drew back an arrow and fired it into Wulfric's eye. The screaming stopped instantly, and the lifeless form of Wulfric slumped backward against the burning ground.

Kieran watched for a few seconds as the fire continued to consume the flesh of the man who murdered his family, emitting a crackling sound and an oily smoke that carried with it a roasted odor. He was suddenly untroubled by memories or emotions of any sort. He observed Wulfric's blackening form with dispassion and calm, then once more, and for the final time, addressed a Saxon assembly.

"Remember what you have seen here, and remember well my words: We will have peace in this land, or by Odin and the Hebrew God, each man among you will take his turn in the place of Dux Wulfric. Bring that promise back to your people."

At that Kieran left the sight of Wulfric's burning corpse, the silver wolf eyepatch of his foe melting to a pool in the hollow of a charred eye socket, and walked toward the cheering army of the Britons. The men raised their king and his councilor high on their shoulders, and left the field to hang up their swords at last.

Kieran awoke – was awakened – by a sentinel entering his chamber.

"My lord Maelgwyn?"

Kieran peeled his face from the desk and plucked a string of drool from his beard, taking a stray white hair with it.

"My lord Maelgwyn," said the sentinel. "Messenger for you, sir. Not the usual one though."

"Bid him come in," said Kieran. "I am in mind for the unusual today."

"He's a lad, my lord. Fionn's his name, he says. I get the idea he's quite a Lord Maelgwyn devotee."

"How nice."

The guard left, and Kieran reflected on his dream. The battle had been jumbled in his sleeping mind, but awake he rememberd it clear. Ten and seven years had passed since Badon, and still he was Lord Maelgwyn. Still he was in Britain.

It won't be long now though, thought Kieran.

Hieran heard the door open at the far end of his chamber. *Fionn, eh?*

Kieran composed himself. He slid a sparkling robe over his shoulders, ran a stiff hand over his face to collect any errant mucus, and picked up a book of Virgil.

Time for one last show.

Chapter Twenty-Three

Fionn's thoughts flew as fast through his mind as his feet did across the earthen path. Many questions arose as he dashed through the forest, the satchel beating against his back with the rhythm of his running, fairly radiating the importance of its mysterious contents.

He wondered firstly where he was going. There was nothing along the path to Cironium except the remnants of a small and long-abandoned Roman town, which he and his handful of friends dubbed "The City of Spirits." It provided endless opportunities to stage mock battles, but Fionn saw nothing to interest Lord Maelgwyn.

Second, Fionn wondered what it was he carried. The satchel did not feel heavy, but what matter would be an object's size in the hands of sorcery? He had no reason to disbelieve the rider who entrusted it to him, a man he'd watched tumble from his horse as the courier sped through the woods, and who bade Fionn make the urgent delivery his broken leg made it impossible for him to complete. But was there a catch? Was it possible Fionn had become the unwitting deliverer of something that could harm the High Protector? Then again, if that were the case, Fionn was sure Lord Maelgwyn would render it harmless himself.

Lastly, Fionn wondered if any of it were actually real.

Lord Maelgwyn. Those two words were the ones ever in his thoughts as he sprinted the path. It took some effort for Fionn to convince himself that, if the rider was to be trusted, he would soon be standing before the High Protector himself. Travelers stopping at his family's makeshift inn would often spin at least one tale of King Artros and his adventures, and there seemed no bottom to the well of yarns from which they could draw about the Ordo Equites, or Knightly Order, but it was Lord Maelgwyn who enthralled Fionn most.

The stories of Maelgwyn were the most unbelievable of all those told, and they were the ones Fionn most wanted to believe. Some said the High Protector was born at the end of his life and aged backward, while others were certain he was a thousand years old and could not be killed by mortal hands. There were odes claiming Lord Maelgwyn learned to control the elements from the spirits of the North woods, and changed the course of a river to drown a Saxon army.

It was also said he owned a copy of every manuscript ever written, and that was the magic that captivated Fionn. Ever since he first learned of the existence of writing, ever since one of the travelers had first let him look into the pages of a codex to see the nimble figures that covered the vellum leaves like tree branches or spindly flames, Fionn had wished for nothing more than to master the mysterious art. It was the one bit of necromancy he was certain he could learn.

Fionn, euphoric with the rush of physical exertion and the sudden splendor of life, came to the clearing that opened on the old Roman town, and stopped dead.

Where until two weeks before a forgotten field had lain, wild vegetation and crumbling structures sprouting from its fallow earth, a very different sight was to be beheld. Fionn's face stretched to twice its resting length.

Fionn said aloud, "It is a dream."

Instead of the ruins he'd known his whole life, there towered before him a massive fortress he had never seen. Palisades streaked a dozen meters high, and its perimeter stretched beyond Fionn's vision in both directions. He had never beheld a building so constructed, in scale or design. From the ramparts waved iterations of a banner that depicted a flaming sword, blade pointed earthward, against a field of pure white. It was a symbol of peace and order. It was the Emblem of Artros.

Fionn spent enough time marveling to regain his breath and remember his oath to the rider. Despite a feeling of dread, he sprang forth once more, into the field surrounding the fortress.

Fionn's look darted around as he hurried across the open, taking in the installation's odd design, such as cylindrical turrets built into the palisades, arrowhead-shaped earthworks projecting outward from the base of the walls, and unexpected zags in the perimeter of the fortifications. He had traversed the bulk of the clearing, zooming over the landscape, and was beginning to wonder just how he was planning to proceed when he heard a voice calling loudly, though indistinctly. As Fionn searched for the source of the yelling, his toe caught on a half-buried rock and stumbled forward, releasing a cry of surprise.

He looked up from the ground, heart throbbing, as suddenly a file of men emerged to fill the gaps in the parapet atop the fortress wall. Each held a bow, nocked with an arrow and drawn to anchor, and Fionn realized the archers were aiming at him. Only now did he understand what the calls were saying.

"Halt or die!"

The command was moot. Fionn had no intention of moving a muscle, though he was awkwardly crouched on all fours in the midst of the field. He was so choked by fear that he did not at first respond when he heard a command to get up.

"Approach!" called the voice, shouting from the turret. "Approach or we shall release!"

Fionn began moving against his volition, physically numb, peering ever upward to discern in more detail the men who held his fate in their hands. Calmly, precisely, the archers tracked his progress as he rose and walked forward, maintaining a slow march toward the gleaming points ready to be released into his small body at a word.

Fionn now stood beneath a turret, looking up to see who was calling at him. A perplexed face between two jingling flaps of chainmail leaned out of a portal and stared down at Fionn.

"What by St. Alban are you doing?"

"I have a delivery, sir," shouted Fionn skyward. "For Lord Maelgwyn," he added.

The man knit his brows and started to speak, but then ducked his head back inside, and Fionn heard whispering within. Seconds later the helmeted head again emerged and the man said, "Hold there and don't move!"

He disappeared once more, and Fionn stood as still as he could, though his nervousness caused him to fidget and cast looks over his shoulder, to see if anything else promising his imminent death approached.

Then something did. Fionn slowly pivoted when he caught sight of a pair of armored figures moving toward him at a rapid clip. He stayed where he was, but the more he saw of the men approaching the less he believed it wise to remain in place. One of them was lanky with a dull expression, but the other seemed more bull than man, and was staring Fionn down the way a fowler would a fox.

"Where do you think you're trying to get?" he snarled to Fionn when he and his companion were within a few steps. The boy did not know how to respond, except to keep quaking silently.

"Says he's got something for Lord Maelgwyn!" called the man in the turret from above, reemerging.

The soldier looked skyward in scorn and yelled, "We know that! I was asking him." He then turned to Fionn with an expression of intense pique and said, "Well?"

"I do, sir," the boy said. "I have a delivery for Lord Maelgwyn." Even facing such a fearsome man, Fionn's voice broadcast more pride than trepidation at being able to make the claim. However, the soldier and his companion were unimpressed.

"*You* have a delivery?" said the soldier, tromping closer. "Where is the messenger I've seen every week since I transferred into this unit?"

"His horse threw him near my family's stead, and he is laid up. There was no one else. He sent me."

The soldier looked to his partner, who shrugged.

"Alright then," said the scowling warrior. "Hand it over, and we'll make certain it's delivered."

Fionn's heart sank. He had the feeling of one who realizes he is waking from a wondrous dream, and clings to the last glimpses of his invented paradise. However, as his fingers tightened around the satchel strap, two considerations kept him from removing the bag. First, Fionn remembered the instruction the injured messenger had given him: "Put this in the hands of Lord Maelgwyn." It was a matter of honor for him to follow the rider's order to the syllable. There was, though, another reason Fionn clung immovably to the idea that he alone could make the delivery: He was determined to meet the High Protector, and that, he decided, was worth facing mortal peril.

Fionn released his fingers from the strap and bore himself up. "I am supposed to deliver it myself," he said, his voice far less sure than his posture.

"And so you have," returned the guard, coolly. "Hand it here."

The soldier reached to snatch the satchel from Fionn's shoulder. The boy stepped back, and said again, "It is for me to deliver alone, sir."

"You sow's runt, you will hand it over."

Fionn shook his head. The soldier made a move toward him, but his partner restrained him.

"It will not look well," the soldier's companion said.

The soldier ignored his partner and shot at Fionn, "How do I know you are not a Brigantine partisan? They are said to be throughout."

"If that is true, sir," said Fionn, "then how do I know you are not yourself one?"

The soldier's brows fell and his color rose. This time when he made to charge for Fionn, his fellow did not restrain him. The soldier raised the knot of his fist and readied to cuff Fionn upside the head when, from the gate, a booming voice ordered "Halt!"

All froze and turned.

"What is going on here, Vitrus?" demanded a squat man with an enormous belly who barreled toward them, head bent forward and massive balled hands pumping fast beside him. The waving crest of his helmet and impressive armor showed him to be the soldiers' superior, and it was clear his rank was achieved through combat rather than patronage. The soldiers stepped back a pace from Fionn, expressions falling fast as the stone of a man who was their commander rolled toward them.

"Why were you attacking this boy?" asked the superior officer.

The soldier, Vitrus, worked to order his thoughts, then poured forth: "This peasant's whelp came charging up without a word, breaching the perimeter, and gave me and Enys his cheek claiming he has something for the High Protector, but no one knows what." Vitrus glanced at Fionn when he said, "He's lucky he isn't a human quiver right now."

"Well, does he have such a package?" asked the superior.

"I do, sir," answered Fionn before Vitrus could. "I have an urgent delivery for Lord Maelgwyn."

The officer appraised Fionn with a pair of gray eyes. "How did you come by it?"

Fionn recounted the story, and when he finished, the officer took a few moments to think.

"Show it to me," he said.

Fionn did not pause this time. He unclasped the flap of the satchel and withdrew its contents: a rigid oilskin pouch. The officer took it from Fionn, squeezed the pouch to open its aperture, and tilting it vertically plucked from within a flat, folded material of slight ochre tint. With tremendous excitement Fionn realized it was a piece of writing vellum, sealed with green wax into which was pressed a shape like a horse's hoof. The officer looked at it, felt the wax, turned it over a few times and handed it back to Fionn, who received it with disbelief.

Still stern in his look, the officer said to Fionn, "You'll only get yourself shot charging at the perimeter of a war camp. Boys die for stupid reasons." He beetled his brow and gave a faint smile. "More caution in future, yes?"

Fionn nodded.

"And don't back talk guards of the High King either," he continued. "Even when they do have goose shit for brains."

Fionn, flanked by two uniformed escorts, entered a room at once large and cramped, its ample expanse saturated with clutter. They wended through a space so densely piled with crates, chests, trunks, and assorted captivating but unidentifiable items, that a woman of average height could not see across it. Nor, apparently, could a boy Fionn's height, though he tried, walking on his toes as well as he could without tipping into the artifacts around. The piles were stacked so precariously that Fionn had to closely mirror the movements of his guides to avoid disaster. These towers of bric-a-brac held objects so novel to Fionn that he did not even know how they were made, or from what, much less why. He fought between a desire to capture every strange sight, and an awareness of how perilous his situation was in every way.

The smells were as odd as the rest of the room, hitting Fionn's nose in various combinations that ranged from homey to enticing to acrid. Fionn picked up layers of scent, some well-known, others he could neither describe nor compare

357

to any other. Wafting through the air he saw strata of smoke, strands of blue-gray comingling with pervasive dust.

The trio came into the midst of a space entirely lacking in clutter. Fionn suddenly perceived how large the room truly was, and saw there was in fact an order to the stacks and shelves, albeit one that could only be discerned from where he stood.

"You may leave," came a soft voice, a rustle of dry leaves. Tiny hairs became rigid on Fionn's flesh, for he knew who was speaking. The soldiers looked at one another, unsure, while Fionn searched around for the source of the words.

 The soldiers looked at one another, unsure.

"Lord Maelgwyn, we do talk about this frequently," said the older of them. "It is our task to protect you from even the merest threat of harm."

"I am glad you are acquainted with your duties," the voice said. "You have your orders."

The men looked to one another once more, then brushed past Fionn on their way out. The boy crept forward, and in wavering firelight Fionn saw a man, and not simply a man. The person seated in the high-backed chair by a roaring brazier was the oldest person he had ever seen. Long, straight, ashen hair hooded his face, which was cragged and warped by age. His clothing, no more than a simple wool tunic of blue, hung like sheet on a hook over his gaunt frame. The man did not look up, but remained engrossed in examining the object he held in his gnarled, twig-like hands. It was a book.

"Lord Maelgwyn," gasped Fionn.

The High Protector responded to Fionn's presence. With tremulous hands the old man set the book atop a pile of other tomes near his knee, and turned his face toward Fionn. The boy thought his visage resembled more closely a cliff side than a human countenance, as acute furrows formed channels around a thin, wide mouth and long nose. His eyes were misted, but behind the clouds of age lay a gaze of such depth and complexity that Fionn was frightened into looking away from it.

The boy's eyes returned to Lord Maelgwyn, though, to confront nothing but mild amusement in the old man's face. Fionn felt small and bare beneath his scrutiny, though all in the High Protector's manner and mien suggested paternal warmth.

"Either you are Eidar and have shrunk considerably, or you are someone I do not know," said Lord Maelgwyn. His voice, heard from less remove, struck Fionn as very much like the forest in a windstorm, when the leaves tremble, the branches rattle and the trunks groan. It carried as much power and ancient mystery, and made Fionn feel just as overawed.

"I am Fionn, my lord," said the boy, with a slight stammer.

"The latter, then," said Maelgwyn. "Though I see you carry Eidar's satchel. What has become of him?"

"He is hurt, my lord. Thrown from his horse."

"Oh," said Lord Maelgwyn. "I see. Is he badly injured?"

Fionn gulped. "It seemed so, to me, my lord." He quickly added, "But I wanted to see about help. I insisted, but the rider, he wouldn't listen. He said I was to put this satchel in your hands." Fionn suddenly remembered the satchel, and

359

nearly choked himself in his haste to pull it off. He held it out before him, getting down on one knee and bowing. "Oh great High Protector Lord Maelgwyn, I, your unworthy servant, present this satchel to you, and… and I am your servant. At your service."

At Fionn's final words the boy heard a soft chuckle bounce in the old man's throat.

Maelgwyn took the satchel and withdrew the oilskin pouch from within. The High Protector's fingers found difficulty in closing around the message, and Fionn almost leapt forward to help him extract it from its envelope. Lord Maelgwyn succeeded in liberating the message, though, and with all his previous difficulties the old man surprised Fionn when he snapped the green seal along the fold of the letter with a strong, crisp motion that belied his apparent frailty.

While the High Protector examined the missive in his hand, Fionn examined him. The High Protector reminded Fionn of his Uncle Brycan, the sole person in Fionn's settlement who had witnessed the times and happenings described in the tales. He saw in his uncle, and now in the High Protector, a certain invisible mark that one only acquires through profound and terrible experience.

Each time he saw the look in his uncle's face when the wars were mentioned, Fionn sensed that the era to which Brycan bore witness was fuller, more vivid than the one in which Fionn lived. Despite the dangers, he knew there was also tremendous, constant excitement, and had lamented that such adventures now belonged only to the bardic tales. His cousin had teased Fionn for being so enraptured by the past, told him "there aren't any quests or secret missions anymore, and they wouldn't have you along if there were." Fionn had felt the words sting. He couldn't wait to return them, and then some, when he returned from a real adventure… if he did.

Lord Maelgwyn was growing frustrated. His eyes remained focused on the page before him but his look was increasingly one of displeasure. Finally he dropped the hand holding the sheet into his lap, disgusted, and said to himself, "It's no evening stroll, getting old." Lord Maelgwyn then took up a small object which first appeared to be just a loop of metal attached to a stick. Lord Maelgwyn moved it from left to right across the vellum, looking downward through the apparently empty circle, and relief came to his face, though only momentarily.

Fionn saw the object in the High Protector's hand flash in the lamplight. The boy intently stared at it, trying to learn the trick. At certain angles and in certain lights the air within the loop became shiny and translucent, and reflective. Writing leapt into the air when the metal ring passed over it, letters enlarging and shrinking as the device moved across the page.

Fionn realized it was glass, something spoken of as rarer and more valuable than gold.

The old man used the object to scan the message several times, and when he finished his last pass he laid both it and the vellum down. The old man sat staring blankly forward for a moment, hands on the rests of the chair, his visage betraying no thought yet clearly deep in contemplation.

"Tell me," said Lord Maelgwyn, "what do you know of Bishop Uleara?".

Fionn thought for a moment. The name seemed familiar, but for what reason he could not recall. Prudence compelled him to reply, "I think I know the name, my lord, but I cannot say I know the man."

Lord Maelgwyn nodded. "That is the way, I suppose."

Fionn asked, "He is a Christian then, my lord?" and immediately winced at how idiotic the question seemed. However, Fionn could see that Lord Maelgwyn had his mind half planted on another plane.

"Bishop Uleara, to my mind, is the embodiment of Christendom in Britain," said the High Protector. He then looked to Fionn, curious. "Does the Church interest you?"

Fionn's heart thrilled, and his face split into a giant smile. "Oh, very much, my lord," he said. "I long to be a Christian more than anything."

"Well then, why are you not?"

Fionn, ashamed, considered his answer before giving it. "My lord, I am from a poor village, only a mile or so from here, and we have never seen but one or two of them. Christians, that is, my lord. My clan does not know of my desires – they are good people, loyal in all other ways to the court of Artros, I swear. But they hold to the old traditions."

"And why do you want to be a Christian?"

Fionn vacillated between possible replies, partly convinced he had to choose one that flattered the man. Yet in that moment Fionn noted the piles of books and scrolls around, and saw the abaddonian well of wisdom in Lord Maelgwyn's eyes, and knew he would tell the old man the truth.

"I want to learn to read and write," said Fionn.

Maelgwyn said, after a beat, "You believe you must be a Christian to do this?"

"They are the only ones I know who have mastered the magic of figures."

Fionn found it hard to suppress the hope in his stomach. With a word the old man could change his existence, and Fionn was almost certain any alteration the High Protector made would be an improvement.

Lord Maelgwyn stared toward a shelf of vessels that bubbled and smoked, and said, "You are about a mile from here?"

"Yes, my lord."

"Tell me, do you know the old Angle fort on the river?"

"It is the furthest I have ever dared travel, but yes, I have seen it. There isn't much left nowadays." The Angle fort was bigger than the abandoned Roman town, but far further away.

"What do you know of the Angles?"

"I've been told a little, and know them from the poems." replied Fionn. "Many in my clan were killed in the wars or worked to death during the occupation."

"Then your family has been in this region for some time."

"Oh yes, my lord, six generations at least, but we like to say our ancestors were here so long ago they weren't buried in the mounds but had the hills form around their bones."

"Hmm…" said Lord Maelgwyn. He picked up a piece of fabric near him, green cloth under a pattern of thistles, and showed it to the boy.

"Have you ever seen this pattern before?" he asked.

A search of his memory returned nothing, and he shook his head. The old man sighed, but nodded his head and replaced the cloth, only to at once pick up a piece of parchment and draw a feather from a pot nearby. Then, he began to write. Fionn followed every dip of the quill and every line of ink it drew, witnessing the act of writing for the first time, until Lord Maelgwyn returned the feather to its stand and blew sand across the sheet. He folded the material and put it in the pouch from whence he'd drawn the original note.

"Is that the return message, my lord?" asked Fionn, who thought it a brilliant question of himself. He deflated at once when Lord Maelgwyn shook his head.

"No," said Lord Maelgwyn, "The reply I will deliver myself."

At this, the High Protector firmed his grip on a tall staff of polished wood beside him and, shaking with palsy, lifted himself from the chair. Fionn did not know whether to help or not, but decided that one had to be asked to touch such a man as Lord Maelgwyn. The old man got himself into standing position, and after a moment of leaning on his staff to recover, brought himself up to his full height. Fionn was astounded – the stooped old sorcerer in the chair was a strong-built man when standing, two feet taller than the boy and among the tallest adults he'd ever seen, with a physique that retained much of its former prowess.

Lord Maelgwyn looked down at Fionn, reached out the pouch and presented it to the boy. "This is for you."

Fionn forced himself to confirm the High Protector's words. "For me?" he asked.

"Present that to the Archbishop of Londoninium," said Lord Maelgwyn. "He will make certain you learn how to read. As for becoming a Christian, that you can decide for yourself, though I'm certain Bishop Restitutus will present a compelling case."

Fionn took the pouch in a daze, and not until he felt the soft oilskin on his fingertips did he allow himself to believe his fortune. Even this peak of amazement was surpassed only moments later, when a collection of gold coins slid from the knotty hand of Lord Maelgwyn into Fionn's smooth palm.

"That is so your labors will not be missed on your farm," said Lord Maelgwyn.

At these words anxiety and sadness intruded on Fionn's golden moment. He then knew what it was to face a choice one will always return to throughout life, and for the first time understood that adventure was predicated on uncertainty. He made his choice. Fionn's fingers closed around the coins.

"And now, young Fionn, we must both be going."

Fionn heard the door at the back of the room open, and spotted the helmets of soldiers trooping through the canyons of clutter. The men presented themselves before Fionn and Lord Maelgwyn.

"See that this boy gets back to his village safely," the High Protector commanded.

A wave of panic hit Fionn. He had felt as if he had been sleepwalking through the entire affair, and now, in its final seconds, he suddenly fought to remain.

"Is something wrong?" asked Lord Maelgwyn.

Fionn did not know what to say. Every raw thought in his head sounded mewling or impudent or ignorant to his internal ear, so what would they be to the High Protector of the United Kingdoms? At last he said, simply, "Nobody is going to believe me."

Lord Maelgwyn did not change his expression, but Fionn saw something shift behind his eyes.

"When you walk in truth, sometimes you walk alone," said Lord Maelgwyn.

Fionn knew his moment with Maelgwyn was over. He offered no resistance as the guards formed their ranks around him, and uttered not a syllable as he was led back through the tunnel and deposited outside the wall.

Fionn began to run.

He ran because the faster he ran, the sooner he would plumb the great mysteries, learn from the great minds. The faster he ran, the sooner he would be able to decipher and transcribe the potent symbols, draw out the figures and commit his words and thoughts to record for eternity. Fionn still regarded writing as wizardry. He was off to be a wizard.

Chapter Twenty-Four

Kieran paused to steady himself against his staff, letting his eyes adjust to the light and his lungs take in the air. The atmosphere was sweet with the smells drawn out by an overnight rain. He took it in as deeply as he could, though it made his chest rattle. His breathing had been troubled, concerningly so. It was all the more reason Kieran was glad to be forever rid of the smoky catacombs in which he'd been living. After that day he would be free of the camps, the tunnels, and most of the Lord Maelgwyn pretense entirely.

"It feels little like the end," he sighed to the birds rushing above.

It feels little like freedom.

He began his walk, nodding to the guards stationed outside the field tent that concealed the private entrance to his quarters below the earth, stabbing the packed soil with his staff as he trekked across the interior of the Fortress of Durlioponte, the newest and westernmost stronghold of the United Britonic Kingdoms. For years Kieran had portrayed Lord Maelgwyn as decrepit, in order to highlight his powers of mind, while the real man had remained virile beneath his formless robes.

Now, reality was coming to parallel illusion more closely than he cared to concede. The pangs and aches that intruded on his joints during any kind of exertion manifested themselves at the first of a morning, so he concentrated on controlling his facial muscles to maintain a look of equanimity. The one immutable rule of being Lord Maelgwyn was that no one could ever see him in pain.

However, the men among whom he walked paid little attention to his expression, puzzling instead at his clothes. After Fionn departed, Kieran had

367

taken off his elaborate garb, raiment crafted of fine fabrics and furs meant to dazzle the onlooker, in favor of a plain wool tunic of fading blue, a frayed cloak and boots that could have belonged to any lowly legionary. It was the first time most of the troops had seen him so ordinarily adorned, and Kieran was met with constant surprise along his path. The custom was for every man who saw him to kneel or bow, and since most didn't immediately recognize him due to his attire, dozens of warriors were taken by surprise, and some caused minor mishaps by their hasty genuflections in Kieran's wake.

 Kieran was still amazed by the awe he inspired. Most of those who were so quick to kneel before him had never witnessed any act of Kieran's to elicit such respect. Walking through the camp, Kieran mused that the battalions of soldiers who supplicated themselves before him as he passed provided proof of the power of a tale to outgrow reality. In his case, Kieran had cultivated that property and leveraged it to its maximum extent.

There were good reasons for Kieran to remember always his training from the Old Kind, the techniques to remove himself from his own thoughts, to concentrate wayward feelings into fuel for proper action. Looking around, Kieran saw thousands of such reasons: the loyal soldiers of King Artros and his dream of a people's salvation. The camp swarmed in the morning hours with drills, the building of fortifications and the support activities needed to sustain 20,000 fighting men. Though the main force would move on within a few days, the camp was, at that moment, the largest city in Britain.

The grid of muddy streets formed by rows of tents and hastily constructed sheds stretched for many acres, a martial metropolis. Along his way, Kieran passed a chow line a hundred men long, a massive tent devoted entirely to map storage and one which contained only shoes (which made Kieran think of Fionn and his bloodied, grime-black feet), a small market, and carts pulled by teams of eight oxen moving tons of timber into place along the perimeter, to be chopped into thick planks for the final section of the palisade. There were also a few of Kieran's more novel contributions, camped under heavy guard and concealment near the parade grounds.

Kieran passed these on his way to his destination, a stone reconnaissance tower set into the perimeter of the camp's walls. He turned his dimming eyes skyward when he was within the shadow of the great granite obelisk, and absorbed one of the more impressive examples of his handiwork. It reached over twenty yards into the heavens, and the artificial slope on which it was built added another ten yards of height, giving one who stood upon its topmost deck a peerless vantage of the network of valleys around.

"His highness is expecting you," said one of the guards at the entrance.

Kieran did not meet the man's eye, but instead looked above once more. *Impressive to behold,*

Kieran thought of the edifice blocking the sun, *and an ordeal to climb.*

It seemed his legendary inscrutability was declining along with the rest of him: Kieran caught a look of concern pass between the guards as he nodded his way inside. He wondered if his mood was palpable to everyone, or if he was becoming oversensitive with the progress of age. There were many things that had once been so clear to perceive, clearer to Kieran than others, easily organized and analyzed, easily understood. Now, the once natural distinctions diffused and ran together, so Kieran was often lost on once-familiar mental terrain. He was again glad to be shucking the shell of Lord Maelgwyn. *To Kieran, none of this makes much difference. Would it make a difference if I knew my birth name?*

369

An old man, not knowing what his mother called him. Kieran shook his head at the thought.

The guards knew to wait several minutes from the time the High Protector began working his way up the tower before admitting anyone else, even those authorized. It was a necessity Kieran tried not to loathe as much as he secretly did. He had to look to make certain each foot landed flush against the gray stone, that each effort to lift himself to the next step was sufficient to prevent him falling backward. He progressed in several bursts that were followed by long pauses to regain his strength, in the upper flights having to use both his arms and his staff in pulling himself up to the next step.

Kieran's climb finally came to an end, but it left him wheezing and doubled over. He spent a length of minutes in the darkness of the space recovering, becoming the High Protector again in all his mystery and might. When his heart was still and his breathing regular, he slid aside the oak slab that covered the hatch and climbed the last few steps into daylight.

It was ironic that of all the Britons, only one person still truly needed Kieran to be Lord Maelgwyn, and it was not Fionn. Kieran found him on top of the tower.

King Artros, still and always Aurelian when they were alone, stood at the eastern edge of the platform, peering through the eyepiece of an observation glass Kieran had fashioned for him. The king stood stock still, in survey of the sylvan landscape below, the only movement about him being his graying blond hair and the bristles of his sable cloak blowing in a steady breeze.

Kieran stepped forward, his staff clunking on the floorboards with each step. Aurelian could hear him approach, and called over his shoulder, "I think I might try my hand at falconry again today."

Kieran had not needed to hear the light confidence of Aurelian's tone to know the king's spirits were high. He had a certain way of posturing himself that spoke to a mood as elevated as the vantage, cocking his hip, holding his shoulders square but easy, setting his jaw forward and his head back, and gripping the purple sash that strained around the middle-aged paunch bulging against his gown of green. When manhood had come upon Artros Ambrosius Aurelianus, High King of the Britons, he'd found it to his liking.

The king did not stir when Kieran stepped to his side, but continued to peer through the glass.

The two men looked out at the land before them without words for a stretch of minutes. The day was one of greens and blues, and of a wind that transported the sun's warmth to the faces of the men atop the tower.

Had Aurelian looked to his right he would have thought the High Protector's face to be a portrait of contentment, never to guess that a sense of dissatisfaction ran deeply through his chief advisor. Instead, the king was scanning the forest through his glass, surveying the easternmost extent of his domain.

"It's beautiful, isn't it?"

"What, your highness?" asked Kieran.

"This. All of this. Being a bird."

"A bird?"

Aurelian grinned beneath his glass. "I am looking down now upon the imaginary line that separates us from the Angles, atop a stone aerie fit for the Roman eagle to perch, through a device that gives me the sight of a raptor. And later, I will try

371

my hand again at falconry, for it suits my mood. Yes, I think I should have been well-suited to an avian life."

"So it would seem."

"Congratulations are due you, Kieran. This fortress is the greatest work your engineers have yet managed, and I suspect it is your personal supervision of the project that made the difference." The king paused, with a meaningful look. "You took such a remarkable interest in its construction."

"It is the last stone in the edifice of peace."

"Is that what you have my heralds saying?" Aurelian laughed. "A pretty turn of phrase to summarize five years of war, two of treaty talks and another thirteen of completing the defensive line."

"And now it is complete," said Kieran. "The dream of peace is made real."

"Is it?"

"Is it not?" asked Kieran.

"With the Germanics perhaps. We shall see about peace when I receive the day's intelligence report."

"You still fear Morhegaine, then?"

"Oh, I do not fear," said Aurelian with a smirk. "I simply understand. She will not move openly against me, of course, but move she will."

"You speak with certainty."

"Never have I been so certain of anything. She claims relation to me yet cannot prove the link, and that means she has no choice but to utilize those malcontents who she calls her followers."

His grin faded. "That even desperate people can take her part over mine is baffling."

"There is still time to repeal the tax levy on the Brigantine tribes."

"It is not about that – it is that a scheming woman with appealing looks and enticing language can make corrupt old men and ignorant peasants do her bidding. It is about the ingratitude and short memories of petty people." Aurelian's look darkened as he followed a more shadowy trail of thought. "I am apprehensive that I shall someday have to deal with that son of hers. He has cold eyes, Kieran, cold and determined. I saw it when they were at court, and it gave me a chill such as I have rarely known… Yes, I believe it will come down to him or me."

"It is my experience, your highness," said Kieran, "that when two people set out to destroy each other, they often both succeed."

"I have built this kingdom defying what was declared to be unshakeable truth," said Aurelian. He smiled again, untensing, and put a hand on Kieran's shoulder. "Worry not, Lord High Protector. I will not allow Morhegaine's spawn or any other undo what good has been accomplished, I swear it."

The king trailed off, perhaps realizing his gaffe, perhaps not. The look on Aurelian's face in such a moment was what Kieran had climbed those many stairs to gauge. Was Aurelian all the king Kieran had foreseen?

He is wavering.

Perhaps sensing the altered atmosphere between them, Aurelian at last lowered his glass and turned to Kieran. The king's eyes widened when he saw Kieran's attire, and he exclaimed, "You are dressed like a peasant."

"It is a day for a change."

"Clearly. You have changed clothes with a beggar." The king adopted a tone of mock chiding. "Aren't you always reminding me of what we must project to the men? Pray, what does this…fashion project? Certainly not a wealthy court. Or must we now display piety over power?"

Aurelian kept grinning, expecting Kieran to return the japes. An unchanged look of seriousness on Kieran's face, though, was a weight to the king's countenance, and dragged the grin from it. "What is it?"

"We must discuss your plans."

"What plans?"

"For the end. For the unfulfilled promise."

Aurelian's eyes were troubled, and Kieran caught a flash of the young man he'd met so long ago. When the flash was gone, though, Aurelian seemed older than he had a few seconds before.

The hatch to the stairway banged aside, and they turned to see Hebros, chief of intelligence and Dux of the Shore Defense, burst through the entryway and present himself with a bow.

"Your highness, my lord High Protector," he addressed them, with a brief pause when he saw

Kieran's clothing, "I come to report."

Aurelian, who for the moment forgot about the grave conversation Kieran had begun, gave the High Protector a knowing look and said to his head spy, "Proceed, dux."

"Our agents in the north now agree that the splinter tribes will march on our strongholds in the Midlands by harvest-time. Those we have in hand among the Eirish claim the Scotii are planning an invasion of Cumbria." Dux Hebros bowed at the conclusion.

"And the two plots are in coordination?" the king asked.

"The timing would suggest it is not accidental," replied Hebros. "The hand of Morhegaine is suspected, but the evidence is lacking."

Aurelian thought for three seconds. "Alert King Cynfarch that his lands are under threat. And Dux Regiris is ordered to bolster our garrisons along the River Treynt. If his forces are lacking, he has leave to find local conscripts, by all prudent means."

"The messengers are already dispatched to Cumbria, at first light they rode," said Hebros. "Regiris is being alerted, highness, but I will immediately convey the conscript order. I hear nothing from him but complaints of how small his complement is."

"As do we all."

"Have you any news for me?" asked Kieran.

"I am afraid, my lord, that none of the reconnaissance parties have returned any recognition of the emblem you gave us," said the dux with a bow of failure.

"The radius was expanded?"

"Yes, Lord Maelgwyn," said Hebros, "but none of the local Britons recognize the pattern." The dux handed the scrap of fabric back to Kieran, who gazed at the purple flower stitched into the green cloth. He nodded, satisfied with the sufficiency of the report, though not its conclusion.

I will never find them. The Britonic family had saved his life, forty years before, and they would not even see so much as a square of cloth in reward.

"Hebros," said Kieran, "distribute a sum to all the households within the radius, from my personal exchequer."

"Yes, my lord. In what amount?"

"One in ten golden talents…"

"My lord, that is…"

"…shall remain to me. The rest give to them."

Nothing moved on Dux Hebros but his blinking eyes. At last he said, "It shall be done, High Protector."

Artros too was surprised, but clearly not much interested in his advisor's financial affairs.

"Return to me by evening with an update," Aurelian commanded Hebros, "even if the news is that nothing new has transpired."

Bowing almost to the floor, Hebros retreated below.

"Do you see?" said Aurelian.

"I do see," said Kieran. "Your mood of triumph owes less to the completion of the project of twenty years than the prospect of lending your legions to a new cause."

"Is it I who plans an Eirish invasion, or an uprising against my own rule?"

"I mean, your highness, that it is tempting but dangerous to conflate things that should remain separate. Uleara would tell you that one may win glory on the battlefield and remain in God's graces, but one can never attain favor with the Lord solely by waging war."

"You mistake glory for defense."

"If anyone does, your highness, it is not I."

Aurelian glowered. "I have kept my promise to wage more peace than war. I have kept all my promises. But now you want to talk to me about destroying my kingdom."

Kieran took a breath. There was tricky work before him

"It is a matter of preserving legacy, rather than undoing progress," said Kieran, easy and patient. "What you represent must live on, and your works, the structures seen and unseen you've built, must never become tools of corruption. Your legacy must be uncorrupted."

"And so it shall be," said Aurelian.

"Perhaps as long as you rule, but you can vouch for nothing past the time your crypt receives you."

"I will rule wisely, and I will choose a successor wisely, and he will rule wisely. I know this because you and I together are the wisest man in Britain, and you will not abandon me."

A tricky business indeed.

"A dynasty is not durable."

"But that is why we have our laws, our schools, courts, councils..."

"These are human institutions," said Kieran. "Like all things made by mortals, they someday must die."

"Bah! Not for centuries!" cried Aurelian.

"It is the idea and the hope that comes with it that counts."

"We can discuss this tomorrow," said Aurelian with a dismissive wave. "I promised myself hawking today."

Kieran paused. Softly, he said, "I will be gone tomorrow. I am leaving."

Aurelian's head spun toward Kieran.

"You are leaving? To where?"

"Eilwath. Uleara is ill. His latest letter leads me to think his health has deteriorated."

"Did he say so?"

"He hardly mentioned it, and that is what concerns me. He always complains least of what troubles him most."

"How long will you be gone?"

"It will be an extended leave."

"I see." Aurelian put his hand to his chin, massaging the grisled-gold beard. "Your path leads past Glevuna." He snapped his fingers. "I will journey with you. We will have a feast in your honor!"

"I thank you, but…"

"And along the way, we will discuss the final promise."

Kieran nodded in gratitude, and departed, but the interview left him uneasy.

He is wavering on something he cannot, said Kieran within. *It would be so simple if I could tell him directly.*

Kieran was tempted daily to divulge to the king that which he knew, but he never would. Nor would Kieran let the king know how long an absence he planned until the proper time. There would have to be some other way to convince Aurelian that the final promise to be honored. Kieran was leaving, and needed to be sure Aurelian followed through, and dismantled the empire they'd built together. Aurelian had to make sure the palace fell.

Because fall it would.

Chapter Twenty-Five

When Kieran looked upon the Old Kind, it was with eyes of hatred.

Sometimes he was catatonic. Sometimes he would weep and laugh at the same time, and sometimes he knew nothing but bloody-knuckled rage. Sometimes the bald, robe-draped men would open the outer door to his cell to find the wool and reed padding of the walls shredded, strewn around the small room, Kieran in a furor and only prevented from wringing their necks by the iron bars that remained in place. Sometimes they would discover him in a corner of the chamber, knees tucked tightly into his chest, gouge wounds covering his arms and a blank, impenetrable stare on his face.

They would not let him have his sword, that was all Kieran knew about them. Until they gave him the blade back, and he could decide whether to use it to end his own life immediately or after seeking out his enemies, the people who kept him from his fury would be his foes as much as the Saxons.

Kieran knew many of the druids were afraid of him, and he relished it. The novices especially entered his cell with trepidation, and though some showed disgust, all displayed caution. He heard the druids talking, and even if he did not understand their dialect he knew he detected their meaning. They wanted to throw him into the sea. Kieran often hoped one of them would have the courage to do it, perhaps after feeding him his supper. Then he would not have to stay awake a whole night, days at a stretch, ever again.

When he closed his eyes he saw his family being bled like carcasses, and when he fell asleep he was back in the storm that stranded him in Britain ten years before. Awake and open-eyed he disbelieved existence, and despised the lying druids who told him what he saw was real. He would ask them the year, and every answer provoked rage and a string of abuse in a language Kieran thought he had forgotten. Being awake was a torment, but it was better than being asleep. Sleep was when the dreams came.

One day, when the physical fight in him started to subside, Kieran was taken from his cell and led into a ceremonial circle of short grass and stone on the far end of the island. He was at first resistant, but as they neared the spot, Kieran's spirit heightened, for he believed he knew the purpose. *Finally*, he thought with joy, *they're going to kill me.*

Kieran was made to stand in the center of the field, while the druids formed a ring around him, linking arms. It was the first time Kieran saw them assembled. All were dressed in gowns of white, with garlands of flowers adorning them like embroidery.

Only one woman was present, and though the druids were arranged in a circle, she seemed somehow at the head of it, partly because of the unique indigo bands that broke up the white of her dress. She was middle aged and on the homely side of average, with rosacea skin and somewhat bulbous features, but everything about her suggested that physicality had little meaning to her or any of her followers. Looking at her, Kieran's rages were momentarily stilled.

"Do you know why you have been summoned, stranger?" said the woman, in Ænglisch.

"I am to be sacrificed," Kieran said with a grin of satisfaction. "And I am ready."

"You have already been sacrificed," she replied. "You came to us dead, slain, of lifeless heart and mind. Among us, you shall be restored to life."

381

Kieran's mood snapped back from joy to rage.

"I want to die! Give me my sword!"

"You shall have your sword returned to you when you are ready to yield it with correct action," said the woman with utmost serenity, a marked contrast with Kieran"s mounting rage.

"If you will not kill me then return me to my cell!" Kieran hollered.

"But then the dreams will never stop."

Kieran had been quaking with emotion, but upon hearing her words he was paralyzed.

Each night he dreamed of the storm, and each night awoke screaming. The dream was a memory, on this

Kieran was as clear as on anything, but it was an impossible memory, and never remember clear in daylight.

"You can reach into my mind and strangle my nightmares?" scoffed Kieran. "You lie."

"I never lie," said the woman. "Neither do you, while you sleep."

Kieran looked around the circle, and beyond it. He could hear the collision of water against stone, far below, just over the lip of the plateau on which they stood.

"I can jump. Right over there, I can go make a little splash in a big sea. That will stop the dreams too."

"It will not help you understand them."

Kieran was crazed, but he was also listening. He waited for the woman to go on.

"We know why you have come among us. We know why you are here. We want you to know."

Without a second's warning, Kieran's eyes filled with water. His lip quivered like a child's. "No you don't."

The woman slowly stepped toward him, a not-quite-smile on her lips, arms minutely outstretched, in a posture of welcome, of peace.

"Yes, we do, and we will show you. Right now you are broken, and broken you are useless. We will help you mend, become useful again."

She was directly in front of his face. She smelled of things beyond time.

"We will put you to the greatest use you could ever know."

Kieran was jostled awake as the carriage wheel dipped into a hole. He jerked his head from the window against which it had lain, and found a clump of foam at the side of his mouth, which he wiped away with his tunic. For a few moments he looked around perplexed as to where the Night Druid had gone. The memory retreated from his comprehension and his eyes focused to see Aurelian looking at him.

The king's immediate expression was one of amusement at the old man's state, but the corners of his azure eyes told of the concern and tension he felt.

"I was asking you," Aurelian said.

"Asking me what?"

Kieran looked out the window. The carriage and its four fine horses were racing along the road, a blur to anyone watching from the woods. The trees rushed by, stretches of forest upon which Kieran would never again gaze. He readjusted himself against the cushions on the carriage bench, rubbing his eyes. "What did you want to know?"

"If we should switch over," said the king. "We are probably deep enough into the woods."

"Right. Quite right," said Kieran. He reached for his staff and thumped the ceiling of the carriage, signaling the coachman above. There was a clank, a metal squeal, and suddenly the ride became far smoother. The sound of the hooves dropped considerably, but the carriage maintained its speed, and if anything accelerated.

"Better," said Aurelian. "By God, I do so love your way with mechanics."

"Yes," returned Kieran. "Brecca will be glad for the rest."

Aurelian tried to hide the look that at once came to him, but when Kieran caught it he realized what he had just said. Brecca had died five years before. Such slips of memory were as yet only just noticeable to Aurelian, but they were worsening. Recollections were not only getting lost but becoming jumbled, memories from different eras of his life melding together in odd and disorienting ways. Kieran could take any number of aches and stiff joints, while maladies of the mind were a different, more terrifying matter.

"You cannot have simply decided to leave today," said Aurelian, letting Kieran's slip go by. "I was thinking about it. Nothing you do is the result of a mere day's preparations, so nothing from Uleara that just reached your eyes could have spurred your decision to travel." Aurelian looked at Kieran. "What are your true reasons? And how long will you be away?"

A smart king is a double-edged dagger, one that demands careful handling.

"The greater part of my leaving is due to you, your highness."

"Me? Have I done you some offense?"

"It is just the opposite. I have little in the way to offer you anymore."

"Nonsense. If I say it is not so, it is not. Come now, you are a legion unto yourself, and a general to lead it. I will not tolerate such a loss."

"The season is changing. We all must do what nature demands to prepare for the next. For me that means a journey, for you it means fulfilling a promise."

Aurelian jerked in exasperation.

"I made the promise in order to learn the secret of that sword."

"And you will keep your promise because I was correct to let you have it."

Aurelian tossed his gaze out the window and stayed silent, avoiding the High Protector's look. Kieran leaned forward across the coach toward the king.

"It is not an easy thing for any man, less a great one, to undo all the works he has toiled to build, to erase the traces of his life, particularly when the reasons require a better part faith than thought. It is a difficult thing. However, it is

385

because I knew from the first that you are a man who succeeds at difficult things when others would not dare attempt them that I helped you gain and keep your crown."

Aurelian rolled his eyes to meet Kieran's, then he leaned back and went limp against his seat, staring into nothingness, his paunch bulging and contracting with his breath. He remained so for over a minute, until a wan, rueful smile formed at Aurelian's lips, which burst into a laugh.

"Life is going to be far less interesting without you at court."

Glevuna, all its sumptuous splendor on display, did its best to lift Kieran from his consternation. The city was never so bright, so well adorned, so orderly yet full of activity as when its people turned out to greet the king, as if every day Artros was home was that coronation day of a generation before. No personal gloom, however pervasive, was a match for Glevuna festooned in purple, green, white and gold, its banners aflutter and signs fresh-painted, and all its citizens of a mind to rejoice.

The crowds, drawn from miles around by news of both the king"s return and a rare gathering of the full Ordo Equester, clogged the East Gate Road into the city, making progress difficult for the coach. Flurries of flower petals and blossoms filled the air, lobbed by the throng alongside cheers and laudatory calls.

Kieran leaned out the window and extended his hands, catching rose blooms, peering into every upturned face, but not letting his fingers graze the outstretched arms or objects held forth by the people for him to bless. He did not any longer think about it, maintaining Lord Maelgwyn's mystique now second nature, though Kieran was not altogether certain what constituted his primary nature anymore.

They passed under an archway into the city and came to a near-standstill. The streets shimmered with the massed citizens, and Kieran felt the old rush of euphoria mingled with fear that used to accompany the sight of thousands flocking around him. At a centipede's pace the carriage crept toward the center square, well-wishers impeding their progress to such an extent that the driver began to curse at them and threaten the biting end of his whip to those who would not step aside. The smells of a hundred cooking hearths around the city mingled with the odor of new paint and sawdust, but the strongest scent was the floral aroma that rose up from petals crushed beneath the feet of the citizenry, filling the spaces between the stones with trickles of fresh perfume.

On they continued into the square, where their progress halted entirely. Kieran watched as the already saturated square attempted to absorb another mass of people pressing in at them from the west, a thousand or more converging on the city center like reinforcements entering a battle.

Kieran saw the oncoming throng had, at its nucleus, a number of finely-clad figures riding finely-clad horses to match. This clutch of cavalry pushed the pedestrians onward and pulled hundreds in its wake, so that it seemed the group was a comet composed of humanity, blazing not through the heavens but along the West Gate Road.

"It is them," said Aurelian with a broad beam. He came to Kieran's side of the coach, and together they watched the men of the Ordo Equester greet the clamoring crowds of Glevuna.

The renaissance of the Ordo Equester was Aurelian's idea, and its genesis was one of the proudest moments in Kieran's career as his instructor and aide. Though for several reasons

Kieran realized he should have been the one to originate the idea, the fact that the king created it of his own initiative gave Kieran more proof that the man was worth his legend, and worth the assistance Kieran had provided him.

In the early days of the Roman Republic, the army had required skilled horsemen in their wars against neighboring cities and tribes, and formed the Ordo Equester to meet the demand. At first only the patricians, hereditary elites, could field cavalry troops, but politics and an ever-growing need for fighting men opened the ranks to qualified commoners with noble ambitions.

Throughout the centuries, as Rome rose to dominate the Mediterranean world and the Republic became the Empire, the Ordo Equester expanded and transformed as well. The *equites,* knights of the Order, adopted new and diverse roles, becoming the bankers and administrators of the Empire as well as its defenders. Deployed to rid the Peloponese of pirates, an eques might transfer to become inventory overseer of a trade colony in Nubia, only to be brought back to Rome to sit as a supreme court justice.

The men who rode toward the carriage surrounded by admirers and attenders did credit to the thousand-year-old society. Kieran noticed that not all of the equites were in the approaching group – it was absent those newer members who had taken the place of the retired or departed from life. Only the five besides Aurelian who were still active among the original members now came to greet them.

All who came forth were legends in their own light. Whatever toll the passing of time had taken from them, more than enough remained of the knights who saved the Britons from the Anglo-Saxons and then themselves that the people of Glevuna saw little difference. Kieran remarked the progress of the decades against what he knew of these men before, but as he watched their high-stepping mounts press forward through the square, they were colored with a shade of the old days, the days of splendor, the first days of the Ordo Equester.

Caius was the most battle-proven of the Order. While Aurelian, his distant cousin, never lost a certain boyishness, Caius seemed to have never been but a man. His teeth formed a near-perfect smile which he displayed to the throng through a full, groomed beard, gray mixing with flaxen hair in a way that only enhanced his virility. The still-steely muscles that bulged through his gown and chain mail did the same.

In his wake rode the Brothers of the Bay, Cardeag and Meirion, alike in their receding hairlines and opposite in demeanor. Meirion was a solitary man who commanded the naval defenses, Cardeag an intense and ambitious cavalry master, with designs to consolidate a great kingdom from the tribal lands of the western shore.

Porys was next, scholar among the equites, who fathered an entire congregation of God-fearing children and sent them about the known world to spread the word of Christ. He rode at an easy, thoughtful gait, the vestal hood of his strict Christian order hiding his cunning face and the pox scars upon it.

Cynfarch of the North, a lean man as cold as his realm and utterly devoid of humor, had not been seen by the Order since taking up a kingdom between the Angles and Picts, but now he rode back to Glevuna in the company of his son Uriel, a strapping teen being groomed for equites.

Charging up from behind came Rhighan, earning his moniker Fireball as the blazing red hair he inherited from his father flew behind him with the frightening pace of his approach. Laughing with the thrill of his ride and the happy chaos it caused, Rhighan joined his fellows just as they all came to a halt, assembling before the carriage that bore their king.

Aurelian gave a wide grin to Kieran, then reached out the window to the top of the coach and pulled himself up to its roof. Kieran heard his boots against the wood above, and the thousands in the square erupted in wild cheers. Kieran shook his head, smiling, and clambered out of the coach – using the door – to join the High King in accepting their welcome.

The knights of the Order dismounted, and as Kieran embraced each of equites who had been there from the first, his spirits lifted further. All around, Kieran saw the faces of the Britons, many of which had been hastily washed and thus showed their normal state of griminess all the more starkly at their edges, beamed in pride and acknowledgement of their luck in seeing King Artros, Lord Maelgwyn and the rest of the Order with their own eyes. The older of the peasants especially showed one emotion on their faces more than any other: gratitude.

When all had exchanged their greetings, the equites formed a rank. Caius, as their senior, stepped to the fore.

"Fair Artros, King of the Britons, and Lord Maelgwyn, High Protector of the Realms, hail."

"Hail!" shouted the knights.

"As in war they returned to this great city victorious, our High King and our High Protector have come back to Glevuna victorious in peace. Let us rejoice in their success, in success for all true men of Britain!"

The throng roared again and petals showered down afresh. Kieran and Aurelian accepted their praise, the king effusively, Kieran stoic. When the din subsided, Aurelian spread his arms as if drawing the entire city into his embrace, and proclaimed, "With a heart lightened by your greeting, I thank you for your welcome. The love I feel for this realm and its people cannot compare to any treasure upon this earth. People of Glevuna: I am home. And it is good to be home!"

When the wave of cheers passed, Aurelian turned to the knights and said, "Glevuna welcomes the return of its finest, the defenders of Britain and conquerors of the Germanic menace. Hail, Order of the Noble Cavalry!" Each knight then took his turn to be cheered by the peasants, after which Aurelian raised his arms again.

"Equites de Ordo Equestrum," called Aurelian, "mount once more and ride with me to commune in council. Master of spirits, bring forth the casks! Master of revels, bring forth the dance! Ignite the braziers and set the pots to stirring! Today the fair people of Britain will taste the delights of peace and drink the wine of glory!"

The thousands assembled cried with joy and began filling clay cups with the liquor that poured from three enormous containers brought forth by a team of ten oxen. Sharing kind words with the peasantry the entire way there, the knights, their king and Kieran rode toward the hall atop the Glevuna Hills to dine together again.

A gentle pandemonium pervaded the Great Hall. Hours of food, beor and hedromel, hours of toasting, laughter, lechery and two fistfights, left all who remained both sufficiently intoxicated where sleep or calamity could befall them at any instant, and craving more of the feast's everything. Though night had fallen many drinks before, the festivities continued without abating, and though none of the older equites were able to remain standing upright indefinitely, they seemed fine sitting down.

A tumult erupted a few seats down from Kieran when a large horn of mead tipped and its contents spread across those nearby. Kieran saw the gaunt, heavy-lidded lad Cadog, pious son of great Glawayn, beneath whose shield he sat, looking about desperately for an avenue of escape. Rhighain's lap had become the repository of most of the horn's contents, and the flame-headed man jumped up in a rage.

He made as if to cuff Cadog, but paused.

It was not the melancholy face the young man turned to Rhighain, but the visage of Glawayn, commemorated on the shield behind him, that compelled Rhighain to refrain. Glawayn, pirate lord of the Silures, had turned Christian out of convenience first, but was converted in earnest by Uleara. Glawayn became a proselytizer and monastery founder with the same zeal he once conducted mercenary raids. Rhighain was too superstitious to hit the deceased knight's son in front of his memorial shield.

"Watch it, you clumsy corpse!" said Rhighain, and stormed off, wiping mead from his crotch.

Rhighain was seated next to Maelgwyn the Lesser, named in Kieran's honor by his father, Cadwallon, the Deceangli chief who ruled the newly-formed kingdom of Gwenedotia in the North. The lanky lad, like his famous sire, was never without a pair of enormous hunting dogs by his side, and the hounds now took the opportunity of Rhighain's absence to raid the food he left on the table, competing for the biggest share of a mutton joint. Laughter and applause rang through the hall as Rhighain, slipping on the spilled drink and grease on the floor, gave chase and attempted to retrieve his pilfered meat.

The atmosphere was as jovial and relaxed as Kieran could have hoped, and the hedromel was pleasant as it suffused through Kieran's chest and brain, attempting to drown his ebullient unease.

I so rarely indulge these days, and I must take from it all the indulgence I can.

Enjoyable as the evening was, Kieran remained in a mood of rumination, and could not commit himself to the festivities as he had hoped he could, for just once in his career as Lord Maelgwyn.

Half of the flames in the hall were devoted to illuminating the twelve circular shields that hung along the periphery, which told the Order's story in the pictures painted upon them and the battle damage hacked into their wood. Each had been used by one of the first twelve knights of the Order who fought alongside Artros in the War of Liberation, and hung above the chair where he who had owned it once or still sat. Lamps illuminated the artwork upon each one, which depicted its hero's greatest moment of glory.

Caius fared best of all, little change discernable between his portrait and his current appearance. Kieran caught his eye and the knight raised a horn to him with a nod. They had been on amicable terms for over a decade, but before that

393

he had become the only person to ever provoke open anger from Lord Maelgwyn. The silent toast they shared was a toast to the accumulation of common experience.

Placing the knights as they'd become, aging men of failing flesh and dulling minds, directly under the portraits of themselves in their prime only highlighted the difference. No one needed to say that feasts like this were the denouement to the glorious life, for a look around the table at the shields and the men who once carried them table made it as clear as could be.

I helped create this, all that this has become. And yet it must be swept away…

"…And then she said 'His ways may be mysterious, but yours are just wrong.'"

The girlish voice that spoke these words broke into laughter, followed by the laughter of another: Aurelian. Kieran spotted the man with whom he'd built a kingdom, as the king barely managed to maintain his royal self propped against a wall. A beaming grin lit his face, in conversation with a golden-haired girl in a long green dress. Aurelian saw Kieran and gestured for him to come over.

"I have a young lady who was hoping to be introduced."

She was not above seventeen, but the attributes that would hold the attention of the High King were evident. Hers was a lithe but feminine physique, slim waist above and slender legs stemming from mature hips. Her bust would never be notable, but her breasts complemented the rest of her, and between them hung a large, ornate cross. She was crowned with silken blonde hair that swept over her oval face and partially veiled her soft green eyes, which widened when she turned to greet Kieran.

"It is a true, deep honor to make your acquaintance, Lord High Protector," she said with a deep courtesy and a blush.

"This is Gwynnefir."

Kieran smiled.

"The pleasure is mine, Lady Gwynnefir."

"She was recounting what brings her to Glevuna, for her first time. She is building a church in Britonia," said Aurelian, referring to the Britonic colonies on the large peninsula that stuck out from what used to be western Gaul.

"I am not building it," she said, with a smile to Aurelian. "My family is sponsoring it. I am traveling there to see my brother, who will be minding the workers."

"They do need minding."

Aurelian was bright with beor, his leer unconcealed. He looked steadily at Gwynnefir, who was terrible at ignoring his interest and just as bad at suppressing the smile it brought to her face.

"We must send for more libation," said Aurelian. "What is my lady's preference? I have a commendable selection."

"Thank you, your highness. Water will serve."

"It is a celebration tonight, and wine is the friend of revelry."

"Water is a better friend to continence," said Gwynnefir.

Aurelian smirked. "I hope I understand your meaning," he said, pointing out the pun.

The girl thought for a second, then burst out laughing.

"I didn't think of that. Of course I mean chastity. Oh your highness…" she said, resting a hand on his arm, before remembering the personage that arm belonged to and withdrawing it with a bashful look.

Kieran asked her, "Where in Britonia will you establish your church?"

"We shall present ourselves to Albinus of Tintillac for guidance on that matter, and visit with your highness's namesake, Abbot Paul Aurelian."

"You know him," said the king. "Porys's son."

"Indeed," said Kieran. The abbot had helped Cunomor some years back to get a church up at Land's End in Cornovii territory, on a budget. "You will do well to consult with him."

"I will make certain he receives a letter of introduction from me," said Aurelian, to her amazement. "That should speed things along."

"Thank you, your majesty," she said. "It would mean… it would mean everything!"

Aurelian nodded slowly in acceptance of her thanks, with a penetrating gaze.

A change happened in the room. Old and young, veteran and novice, the equites of the Ordo Equester knew among themselves when it was time for the bard to mount the table and the musicians to take their marks. Aurelian, stepping forth imprecisely with the weight of mead and growing girth, called for the songmaster.

The bard, a slight man with a pointed beard and delicate, expressive hands, stood before them for an hour and kept them enthralled as he rendered two tales in manly tenor, accompanied by string and drum. Though fine were his words and moving his voice, there was a stir when the bard, his second song barely ended, began to sing a ballad of longing and voyages far from home. It was a beautiful air, but not the song the assembly wanted to hear.

The equites began to bang their beverages against the table. Bedwyr, one of the first to join the Order and he who would rule if Artros were slain or captured, rose to address the bard.

"I ask now, why do you not let us hear what you know our hearts crave? We implore you, songmaster: Let us hear the tale of the age."

The bard looked uneasy.

"Most honored lords," said the man, "I must ask you for your guidance. Two songs of Mons Badonicus and its battle I know – that which I carry with me to the towns and hamlets of Britain, and the other."

"Which is the other?" asked Aurelian.

The bard hesitated. "It is called the Lord on High version, beg pardon, your highness."

"And how is that?" asked the king.

"It is the tale as seen by the Almighty, who knew of the dishonor that was shown Britain by

Britons, the war within our ranks that raged even as we fought to repel the invading hordes," said the bard. The equites looked one to another, then to the High King.

"Let us please the Lord," said Artros, with a short laugh. "Tell us how we remember, not as we might care to."

The strings were plucked anew and the thumping of drums recommenced, a military march with a melancholy accompaniment. The bard sang the first lines, and the veterans, knights, Aurelian and Kieran, settled back in their seats, retreating into their memories, letting the songmaster's words coax forth recollections never fully absent from their minds.

Strong Artros and court knew two fronts of war

One against Germanics, gardeners of gore

One against each other, discord rot at their core

Disunion of Britons gave Ceradic to smile

Squabbling enemies gave ease to his trial

Each contest close fought, each leaving its dead

War the husbrandy by which corpses bred

By the priest of the blade, each man to death wed...

Each man and woman there in the court of High King Artros became lost in revery, finding memories in their minds to match the music. Kieran was no different. His thoughts wandered far away from the feasting hall, far from the field at Badon, far from this end of Britain, far from the life he knew.

Chapter Twenty-Six

Kieran had lived on the island for over two years, and in that time he'd only set eyes upon the Sun Druid thrice.

He had joined the others in their routines and rituals, their training and their study. He built up his body strength, hauling rock, grinding grain, until he could hazard a swim along the shore on a calm day, when the breakers were not guaranteed to be deadly. He learned their prayers, and under the tutelage of the woman he met in the circle, the one called the Night Druid, Kieran began to employ their wondrous techniques, physical and mental. Each day he gained more mastery of their learning, poring over their writings, partaking in their dance-like exercises, sharpening his perceptions inside and out. He absorbed the Night Druid's lessons, and both peace and understanding began to grow in his breast again. By his second anniversary on the Island of the Old Kind, he could comprehend their pictograms, pull a full-laden cart, and control his heart rate at will. He could go a day without thinking of Freya.

And, like all on the island save the Night Druid, he was forbidden even to set foot upon the stairway that climbed the spine of the island up to the Temple, a terraced redoubt built into the rock of a cliff high above the clashing waves. The walls of the Temple were ornately carved inside and out, and though at the distance to which Kieran was relegated none of the carvings were discernable, the whole mass of them made the rocky surface seem more like skin than stone.

There, within the titanic Temple, the Sun Druid dwelt all his days. He was the nominal spiritual and intellectual compass of the Old Kind, pointing the way forward for the clutch of people who inhabited the Island, the dwindling remnants of a civilization that had once held dominion over all of Britain and far beyond. While his counterpart, the Night Druid, performed most of the daily and seasonal rituals and guided the people with an active hand, her opposite emerged from the sanctum sanctorum but rarely and only ever briefly. He spoke on exactly one day per year, on a date of his choosing, to as many or few as he wished. That was the custom of the Old Kind.

Kieran first saw him several months after the boatman brought him across from the mainland. The Sun Druid, long beard braided and robe gleaming white, face and hands tattooed in a design of barbs and curls, showed himself for only a moment, standing on one of the levels of the Temple and peering down with keen, clear eyes. Kieran had the oddest feeling that the old man was deliberately staring at him.

Kieran first heard the Sun Druid's voice far later, when the training had taken a firm hold on Kieran's soul. One early morning the Night Druid found Kieran in his hut while he slept and bade him rise.

At her command, Kieran left his sodden home to trek into the night, holding a poor torch to guide him up the treacherous heights, mounting narrow, crumbling steps set into the wall of rock above the sea. When he approached the gaping edifice, his torchlight caught in the carvings, and their meaning was revealed. They were pictograms, and they told the history of the world. Each loop and spiral, vine and bloom, animal and woman and god etched into the rock related a piece of the vast story only the Old Kind knew completely. Kieran explored the surface of the rock for many minutes, then stepped through the black portal to find the Sun Druid alone within his lair, seated without a cushion on the floor.

"What do you know of us?" asked the priest without preface.

When you speak in righteousness, fear not your words. "I have learned much," said Kieran, "though mostly I have learned how little I understand. Your knowing is astounding, your philosophy and cosmology is profound. Taking two lifetimes together I could not plumb a tenth of it."

"And yet, it will all be gone, too soon, too late."

He looked over at Kieran, who had never seen such stillness in a person.

"We have existed on these islands for hundreds of generations. We came before any others, and we watched the foreigners arrive. They came from the same direction with the same purpose, the only differences garment and tongue. In ignorance they were all the same to us.

"At any time we could have repelled the newcomers, such was our knowing, such our strength. We did not. When the first new people came, they lived alongside us. We shared our lands and discoveries, but sharing would not suffice for the strangers. They grew jealous of our knowing, and impatient with the centuries needed to build for themselves what we had constructed. They accused us of demoncraft, of cursing the land with hexes and aligning with dark spirits. When war came, we withdrew. Our meaning of worth cannot be assessed in yards.

"We came to call ourselves the Albann," he said. "It is how the island was called by outsiders: Alban, Albion, Albianus. It meant white – the white of the sea cliffs, the white of the many clouds reflected in many waters, the white of fire pure. Alban is the light of the solstice sun and the spinning stars, from which we draw insight into the scapes of creation.

"Soon, the strangers' ways brought them low. Folly led them to ruin. Fathers, who like poor herdsmen had driven away as pests a flock worth a fortune to them, sent their sons like lambs to ask for our forgiveness and aid.

Our ancestors were begged to return, as guides and seers, and we once again spread through the land. In time, we sent some of our learned in amongst them, who were hailed as great teachers and judges. We who knew better chose to remain hidden."

"Dwell in the shadow to walk in the light," quoted Kieran.

"Even so. Most chose to maintain the purity of our ways and wisdom, not treat with the strangers who swarmed our shores. While some of the Albann became the priests of the Brythonii, we learned to keep our world distinct from theirs. Peace reigned so long as they lusted for our learning and the harmony it brought, more so than they lusted for our women and gold.

"When the next storm of strangers battered our shores, bringing those who were as much metal as man, the old perils returned once again."

"You speak of the Romans?" asked Kieran.

"They were the most curious of the strangers we've seen," said the Sun Druid. "They possessed learning of some things that surpassed our own, while of others they remained entirely ignorant. They built everything and nothing together. And in the end, they were the same"

"Master," Kieran interrupted, hesitantly, "there are new strangers, and these are the most dangerous."

"Dangerous is a word oft dangerous to use," said the druid. "All is dangerous, and nothing is, by whose eyes you see a thing. What the people of the dragon boats do is no different from what this land has seen before."

"It is different. I have seen."

The Sun Druid looked closely at Kieran.

"I knew it was still there."

"What?"

"Your hatred. Progress is not completion, which it seems some of my acolytes have yet to learn," said the priest. He raised two fingers to still Kieran before he spoke, and continued, "You have done well – excelled in your learning, and many layers of your soul have been stilled and repaired. It is now on the deepest layers, of both learning and yourself, where you must put your focus."

"It is hard, master," said Kieran, taken aback that a man he'd never met should be so intimately aware of his inner life. "Every time I think I have expelled all of my hatred I find the well has filled up anew. I try not to live for revenge, but nothing else is so compelling a quest. My feelings are too many to be banished at once. I still remember what I try to eliminate, and no matter what techniques I try, and still nothing I do brings back the memories I seek."

The priest drew nearer and peered more closely into Kieran"s eyes. He held out his ink-inlaid hand, fingers gnarled as roots and dry as straw.

"Feel my hand," said the old priest. Kieran did as he was told, and found it vibrating rapidly.

"What do you notice?"

"You seem to have a tremor," Kieran said, adding, "a slight tremor."

"True," said the Sun Druid. "It has been there for hours."

"Do you know its cause?" asked Kieran.

"It is from my boundless joy, that I may speak to another human being today, to touch his hand.

It is the day I anticipate every year with extreme enthusiasm."

Kieran now peered back into the old man's face as closely as the priest peered at him. He saw the Sun Druid was not making a joke – his eyes were full of joy and shiny with tears. Their hands closed around each other's.

"You cannot banish your emotions. You must instead become master of them, as I have, and use them to help the channels of the All Spirit."

"How do you do that?"

"By accepting them. The power of emotions cannot be denied, for they come from a place beyond our logic, beyond our learning. Emotions are a language we have spoken since well before the advent of words. As such power can overwhelm easily, so can it overcome anything, even itself."

Kieran had been cheered and comforted by the Sun Druid's lesson, but now his mood turned.

Ordinary sorrows may be overcome perhaps, he thought, *but a hurt as deep as mine seems mortal to my soul. I doubt this man, though wise, has tasted this kind of pain and come out so calm and accepting. He has never had a Freya.*

The Sun Druid laughed, startling Kieran out of his thoughts.

"You will not always be trapped within yourself," he said, still chuckling. "Soon you will see that to assume you know another person's life is both perfectly correct and incorrect. None entirely escape the trap of thinking that only what they understand what is real or important. But you must."

"How did you know I was thinking about that?"

"You are good at looking within yourself, and good at looking within others."

"Not as good as you, it seems."

"Correct. That is because you do not yet realize they are the same."

"And what must I do, master?" asked Kieran. "Why have you summoned me, and me alone, on this day?"

The Sun Druid smiled, a smile untroubled by the cares of passion or time, the smile of one who knew the value of both.

"You desire to know who you were, before you came to Britain," said the druid. "It is time you do."

Chapter Twenty-Seven

The song was concluded, but it was a minute before Kieran realized. The High Protector relocated himself within the feasting chamber and reattuned himself to Aurelian's court, shaking away the grogginess that traveling nearly three decades backward left him with. Kieran looked around the hall.

Though the music had stopped, the tears had not. The equites, the councilors from the old days, they did not weep from the sadness or joy of the battle at Badon itself, not from any particular memory, but simply from the energy of remembrances long absent given new power, the force of confronting what was gone and irreplaceable. Whether a good end to the feast or not, it was fitting.

One by one, the members of the Order departed, wishing Kieran farewell, some maudlin, some somber, some telling ribald tales to the last. Other guests in the hall filed out too, saying their goodbyes. The last to whom the king and High Protector spoke was the girl in green.

"It seems I will now leave you, my sirs," said Gwynnefir with a courtsey.

"Sleep well, Lady Gwynnefir," said Kieran.

"Thank you, my lord, and you."

Aurelian came forth and extended his hand, and the girl took it, tenderly.

"It was a dream come true, your highness," she said.

"A rare pleasure," returned Aurelian, as they shared a frozen instant. With reluctance the king and the lady broke their stare.

"Until tomorrow," said Gwynnefir. She dashed for the door, and just before she was through it she cast a look back – not at Aurelian, Kieran noted, but at himself. For the split second he saw her expression, it was a study in dissimilarity from her earlier countenance. In a wink, though, both her expression and she were gone. Aurelian was smiling after her.

"Tomorrow?" said Kieran, as he and the king strolled to the villa.

"Yes, I have news," said Aurelian, the smitten grin still there, bringing out the Golden Prince he would always partly remain. "We will have company on the way to Eilwath."

A rare arch came to Kieran's eyebrow. Aurelian laughed.

"I am coming with you. I long to greet some true country Britons, see what has become of Cunomor's lands now that they honor the cross, and of course, see Uleara."

"And to keep company with Gwynnefir."

"Pure coincidence. It is a happy accident, our travel routes converging." said Aurelian. He added, "She is refreshing."

"A lively girl, to be sure."

"Her father is King Vortiporis, of the Demetae. You do not know him well. He never sat the Oak Table himself and has no sons to send. They come from Eire originally and keep up those unaccountable church services they practice, but they are sincere in their Christ worship. Fervent would be a politic way to describe their faith. The Demetae do not view the term 'warrior for Christ' as symbolic."

Kieran cleared his throat, and said, "You will still have time for our discussion, won't you?"

"Perhaps."

"We must speak about this. I must hear your plans for disassembly."

"Your highness."

Aurelian's voice was hollow, and his face was livid when Kieran looked at him, pupils mere dots, cheeks ablaze with crimson outrage. Kieran began to speak, but Aurelian cut him off with a raised hand. "I am king. I am High King, and I should not be as used to hearing 'You must,' 'you should,' 'you will' from you. Perhaps it is good you are taking an absence." Aurelian cooled. "I will continue our discussion of this matter, but it will be fully at my pleasure. I do not want to hear you mention it again."

Kieran stood for a few moments, then said, "Good night, your highness. Until tomorrow."

"The bard's tale at the feast amazed me, more than I believed it would," Gwynnefir continued.

She'd spoken without pause these last several minutes, emboldened by her king's encouragement. Aurelian had listened enraptured, and Kieran had been paying close attention too, for an entirely different reason.

"I can't stop the song from playing through my head," she gushed. "I'd heard others tell of Mount Badon, like everyone has, but the way the bard spun the poem – sometimes it actually scared me, as if I were in the heat of it, and worried for the lives of Britons I knew survived! I have such endless gratitude for all those who held the line against Germanic aggression." She beamed. "Most of all my escorts."

"Thank you, dear Gwynnefir, for that kindness," said Kieran.

"It is no kindness, but only your due!" she said. "It takes a powerful bard sometimes to make one realize how close we have oft come to oblivion, and the bravery that kept us from the brink."

"You are a burgeoning poetess yourself," said Aurelian, causing the girl to blush and turn her face.

"I meant," she said, "it is an epic, a chapter of scripture, the end to that war. I only wonder the Anglo-Saxon horde any use in coming out to fight at all. Certainly they knew they were broken after that day."

"If only it were that simple," scoffed Aurelian. "It was another two years of skirmishes and more of negotiations before we won a lasting peace."

"That was to be expected of Germanic pride and foolishness," said Gwynnefir harshly. "The heathen masses know nothing but war and conquest."

Aurelian was taken off guard by her sudden vehemence, Kieran less so. *Perhaps not so feeble as I thought*, Kieran remarked of himself. He thought back to what he'd seen the night before, or thought he'd seen, less sure of his faculties than he would desire.

"They're as vicious foes at the bargaining table as on the battlefield," said Aurelian. "How long did we wrangle over the Angle frontier?"

Kieran humphed. "Months, highness."

Aurelian turned again to Gwynnefir. "Your father was a strong ally in that fight."

"My father is ever ready to serve you, your highness. He sees in you a champion of Christ, and you have only won greater respect from all the Demetae with your campaigns to secure the domains of the Britons and increase the dominion of Lord Jesus at once."

She spoke with the zealotry of youth, the true and pure faith of one first beginning to take ownership of her beliefs. Aurelian was impressed with her fire, Kieran with her earnest speech.

It is all the more impressive if she is more than she seems.

The larger question unanswerable at present, Kieran saw an opportunity to satisfy a smaller curiosity of his.

"You admit then of no redeeming value in Germanic society?" Kieran asked.

"Should I?" she shot back, entirely forgetting her modest posture. "All my life I've heard only of their depravity, brutality, treachery and pagan ways, and at the feast I heard nothing different."

"You see, Kieran, how I warned you of the efficacy of your messages to the people regarding the Germanic threat?" teased Aurelian. "You were the Pandora of these prejudices," he laughed.

Gwynnefir's adopted a puzzled frown. "I do not understand, my lords," she said. "Am I somehow deceived? Are these hellish men not every bit as wicked as portrayed?"

"More so," said Aurelian, with a charming smile.

Gwynnefir returned his smile, but said with seriousness, "Am I to believe that you, Lord Maelgwyn, who have more reason to hate the Anglo-Saxons than any man alive and are the chief architect of their ruin, would now take their part?"

"Your facts are correct, but your perspective is flawed," said Kieran.

"Forgive me, Lord, but my perspective is based on my knowledge," she said, pink-faced, flustered, "and that leads me to say that there is something in the very nature of their people that demands domination, and will never allow them to enjoy the warming glow of Christ. This cannot be denied."

"But Lady Gwynnefir," said Kieran, "are there not still pagans among the Britons? The resistance to conversion has been at times fierce. And we, no less than the Saxons, prize fertile lands."

"Please pardon my impudence, High Protector, and know that of course my respect for you is endless," answered Gwynnefir, with a hint that this was an exaggeration. "But is there not a question of right? By all true values, surely you assert virtue's right to triumph over evil?"

"Of course such values exist," said Kieran, "and in this battle ours were superior."

"It was providence," said Gwynnefir, making what she thought an unassailable point, which in turn made Kieran want to chuckle.

"Be that as it may," said Kieran, "perhaps the next time that shall not be the case, as perhaps it was not the case before."

"Next time?" asked Gwynnefir. "What do you mean?"

Aurelian, himself uncomfortable at the implication, looked to the girl and said, "Fear not, this is one of his explorations of imagination. He does this often. It is baseless."

"It is not," said Kieran, with a sudden gravity that turned the other two's heads. "It is the immutable flow of events, and I tell you this, the wheel turns slowly but unstoppably."

It was Aurelian's turn to question. "What say you, that our purpose was without purpose? I am just as confused as our young guest to hear our Lord Maelgwyn predicting defeat and conquest, and act as if it is nothing of consequence."

"Consequence exists in all," said Kieran. "But do not believe that delineations between the just and corrupt exist so starkly in every conflict, or even in every conflict with the Germanics. It is foolish to mistake your enemy for being as inhuman as rhetoric paints him. All peoples have something that will enhance those with which they come into contact."

"I cannot possibly see what those barbarians have to offer us," said Gwynnefir with a slight scoff.

"You do not believe they could invent such a fair law code as we have, or run the affairs of their villages with the same respect for all voices?" asked the High Protector.

"I find the suggestion somewhat comical," said Gwynnefir, smirking.

"Many of our reforms, especially those respecting the rights of women and peasants, were direct transplants from the Saxon Code."

Gwynnefir was quite still at that, eyes wide, lips pursed.

"I did not know," she said.

"And why should you?" said Kieran. "It is right and good that people should believe themselves right and good, so long as they are. Only when virtue demands a villain, when goodness is by necessity derived of its reflection in evil, does it become oppressive, and the opposite of itself."

"But does that mean," asked Aurelian, "that if God and the sweep of history ordained that the Germanics overran our defenses, you would accept it as inevitable and not a defeat of virtue?"

"Though your armies have guaranteed that will not happen in our lifetimes," said Kieran, "I tell you this truly: The Angles and Saxons may yet rule this land, and it will not be the end of the civilization of the Britons, no more so than Roman rule was. Both of you are proof of that. The conquerors of one generation see their progeny conquered in the next, by the very people they presumed to master. These Germanics are only the latest in a long line of invaders who came to these shores, who found people living in Britain and displaced or disposed of them for their own ends. They, the Romans, and even the Celts, who slaughtered the Old Kind and drove them into the woods, came here for conquest, and let bards drape their deeds in the cloak of righteousness."

"But..."

"This is how civilizations rise and grow stronger. It has been since mankind's beginning and will continue until mankind disappears. Take heart, though,"

Kieran said. "I have lived among the Germanics, and if the day comes when the Britons and Anglo-Saxons are fused as one people, the resulting nation shall be a powerful one indeed."

That night, Kieran confirmed his suspicions with the help of the High King's guard. Kieran gathered all the information he could, then ordered Aurelian awakened. The ruler, dazed and angry, charged from his tent. He stopped short when he saw Gwynnefir kneeling on the dirt, hands tied behind her.

"Gwynnefir... Kieran, explain this."

"Perhaps she can explain better, your highness."

The girl's face was a mess of sweat and saline from crying nonstop on a balmy night. Her green eyes looked unearthly with the red surrounding them.

"I am so sorry, your highness. I..." She broke down again, bending double and mashing her face against the ground.

"Someone explain what is happening, instantly."

One of the king's guard approached in three quick steps.

"My king, this girl is a spy and a traitor. We caught her giving communiques regarding your royal person to her lover, under cover of night."

"No!" wailed Gwynnefir. "He isn't... I didn't..."

Aurelian's face was unreadable beyond disquietude.

"Gwynnefir," said Aurelian, standing over her, "what did you do?"

"It was my father. He told me to. He said it was my duty."

"To do what?" Aurelian snapped.

"He trusts you," she said. "But the pagans you keep around you. Especially…" Her eyes flicked toward Kieran. "He wanted me to find out, to persuade you to purge the heretics. He wanted me to…" She looked imploringly into Aurelian's eyes. "He said it would be no sin to lie with you, in service to Christ."

"Where is her lover?" Aurelian asked a guard. "Have they begun interrogating him?"

"He is not my lover! I am untouched!" she wept. "He's my cousin. My father sent him a day's ride behind me." She looked desperately between the High Protector and the High King. "I try to be an obedient daughter, a faithful Christian. I am so confused, though. Please don't hurt my cousin, we're just doing what we've been commanded." She turned to Kieran, and getting hold of herself, said, "My father is wrong about you. I see that. I just… I don't know what to believe."

Aurelian turned to Kieran.

"What is your advice?"

Fall it will, one way or another.

"Marry her."

Kieran's words forced all present into silence. He repeated himself: "Marry her."

"You're joking."

416

"No, your highness," said Kieran. "I am advising. Vortiporis is clearly a liability, so remove him as such. There is no better way to ensure his loyalty than by taking his daughter to wife. The dowry alone should do some to support our legions, and his connections give you influence beyond the Channel."

The group shared unbelieving looks, a few of which passed between Aurelian and Gwynnefir. Soldiers, the prisoner, and the king digested his words.

"And, of some importance at least," said Kieran, "this girl has an effect on you I have not before seen, whatever mistakes she made from perceived virtue. She is young, but she is your match. She is clearly loyal to those she loves, and daring in their service. You have fought your opponents for two decades, achieving total victory. Perhaps it is time you wed, and gain a worthy adversary."

Aurelian puzzled and pondered. An assortment of moods passed over his fair visage, until a decisive set appeared to his face. He withdrew his short sword and advanced on Gwynnefir. She watched him come nearer, but did not stir, even as he held the blade aloft, even as he swung it down.

The cleft rope dropped to the ground. Aurelian reached out his hand, and helped the Lady Gwynnefir to her feet. A sigh escaped from several pairs of lips.

"What say you, my lady?" asked Aurelian of the trembling girl. "Do you wish me for a husband?"

Tears of a very different nature ran down Gwynnefir's unblemished cheeks.

"I do," she said. "I most fervently wish it."

They would make no announcement yet, so Britons went about the following day unaware their king was betrothed. Kieran watched the couple with pride as they rode side-by-side all morning, as happy as he'd hoped, until a messenger came for Aurelian.

"It seems peace remains ever elusive," he said, riding back from his rendezvous. "The Scotii have already begun the invasion of Cumbria. Do my instincts fail, Lord Maelgwyn?"

"Never in war, your highness," said Kieran.

Aurelian swiveled his mount toward Gwynnefir. "May we have a few moments, my dear?"

She rode off with a nod, and the two most powerful men in Britain rode alone together at a casual walk.

"I must head north immediately," said Aurelian. "It is my wish that Gwynnefir continue on her original course and travel to the Continent. She will be assigned an escort, of course."

"I am sure she will be well protected."

"Yes, and I will be better informed."

Aurelian had nothing of the puppy about him then.

"I feel you have nothing to suspect from her any longer."

"Of course not, or I would not be marrying her," said Aurelian. "But engaged or no, I am High King, and will not have vassals taking their own part at my

418

expense. At the expense of Britain." Aurelian did not speak again for a quarter mile, until he said, "I will do it."

A thrill ran through Kieran. *Could this be it?*

"The promise, you mean."

"Yes. The final promise, the last stipulation. I will fulfill it. The empire will be dismantled. The United Britonic Kingdoms will be dissolved. I will take it down."

Kieran looked at Aurelian, studied him, and the king did not turn to meet his stare. It did not matter. Kieran knew it was true. Kieran was finally free.

"I have kept something from you, Aurelian, and you must know it now."

"I am certain you have kept many things from me."

"I am leaving."

"Yes, I know," said Aurelian. He paused after seeing Kieran's expression. "Oh. You are leaving."

"The last promise will be fulfilled. It is time."

Even then, Kieran wanted to tell him why the promise had been requested, why it needed to be honored.

The kingdom will disappear from history, from all but myth. If you do not dismantle it yourself, my Golden Prince, it guarantees someone else will, and I have never been willing to risk finding out how they would go about it.

"Those powers of the Old Kind must be terrible to bear sometimes," said Aurelian, as if from telepathy. "I could not so readily submit to the whisperings of spirits, were I able to hear them."

"Spirits are not my tormentors."

"Knowledge?"

Kieran paused. "It is as I have said, your highness, a great destiny is the thief of peace. You and I are brothers in knowing that."

"Aye," said Aurelian, a small smile breaking through his gloom. "Brothers we are." He put light into his tone when he followed, "I'd imagine you have grown tired of always leaving places."

"Yes, Aurelian," said Kieran. "But then how else would I continue arriving at new ones?" He smiled at the king. "The greatest lesson the Old Kind taught me was the hardest to learn. It is to be present, to live with active awareness of the moment. To dwell in the past is to be paralyzed; to live for the future is to build a tower upon air. We may only validate the struggles we have overcome, and construct the successes we will enjoy, if we are true to our immediate existence and honor each day's opportunities to experience creation."

"It is a way of looking at the world that, for its appeal, lies outside my grasp," Aurelian said.

"I once thought so as well," replied Kieran, "but life is long, and ever surprising."

Kieran saw Gwynnefir avert her gaze when he caught her staring. It was the fourth such occasion, and finally the old man asked, "What is on your mind?"

Gwynnefir looked away hurriedly again, embarrassed to be found out.

"I have such questions."

"Such questions as?"

"Well…" she said, thinking. "About the Old Kind."

Kieran let out his breath slowly. He had been asked about the Old Kind as often as anything except the sword, and had remained reticent on both topics, divulging nothing about them except what the Britons needed to hear. Some things he would keep for himself forever, out of necessity, but some he'd always wished to share. *And I can now, as it will all soon be ended,* he thought, yet even as he did, from habit he scrutinized the guards riding several lengths before and behind them, looking for signs of eavesdropping.

Kieran said, "What would you like to hear?"

"I am curious about their faith. They do not seem so unlike the Christian priests I know, though they are heathens still. What do they worship?"

"Creation," said Kieran. "They believe nothing is created or destroyed, only changed. Their faith teaches that everything that has happened will happen again, forever, but that everything still moves forward, forever."

"Do they not have a heaven, or a hell? It sounds as if they do not even have gods."

"Where you have the Holy Trinity, they recognize only one aspect: the All Spirit, that which infuses and connects every single thing, the river formed of many drops. One can never be separate from the Spirit, only blind to it. Perfect sight of the Spirit, perfect action within it, are the desires of any soul wanting to be part of the progress of Creation, and not trapped in its pools and eddies."

Kieran turned onto his side to ease his breathing, and the new comfort brought a fresh pulse of sleepiness. He yawned and let his eyes remain closed.

"I don't know if I understand," said Gwynnefir, "It seems complicated."

"It is complicated to understand," Kieran said, yawning again. "Once you do, though, living the Druid faith is simplicity itself."

"You speak of them with love."

"They were the midwives at my rebirth," said Kieran.

"Do you ever think you will return to their land?"

Kieran was silent for a span of moments until he finally said, shortly, "No."

Chapter Twenty-Eight

The Sun Druid's chanting never modulated as Kieran lay on the stone slab, cold
and nervous. The potion, the perfumes, the drone of the druid's voice were
taking effect. Kieran closed his eyes, opened them, closed them again. He
wondered when it would finally seize him. He wondered if -

*His life is classrooms, classrooms and hallways, classrooms, commutes and
hallways, until he feels boarded up by the billboards and corkboards and
whiteboards everywhere he looks. Today it doesn't faze him, though. Today it
would be turned on. Today was full power.*

*He feels like running there, though he is early. He sees people he knows and
they walk together, enter the building together, gather togther in the room.
There is a buzz of excitement. Through the window they see what they have seen
every day, a device of mind-rending size, and the part they view through the
rectangular portal is like sets of steel windmill blades, fastened together and
vined with metal strands.*

*He feels he is where he must be. There is a countdown. There is a deep hum
above the laughter and talk, and it is growing louder. Something is about to
happen, and that is why they are happy. That is why Kieran is happy, even
though he has an inkling that something...*

"...the readings should be truly..."

"...two on the same day. It might not register at all, or..."

"...because we just don't know what is going to..."

The hum is all there is, the hum and the vibration, and it begins. The people are excited, he is excited. He is looking at the screen, at the windmill blades and the arcing blue and orange sparks, the haze of indigo at their edges. The voices around him are still excited, but no longer happy. He looks to the panel himself. He sees the inevitable. The instant before full power he says, "So beautiful."

He thinks about gravity when the faces around him start to bend. Slow lightning creeps along warping walls. A tempest rushes through the room, and parts of everything are in the air. Zephyrs of cosmic strength pull the world all apart.

Something is happening to him. His spine is a harp string, his heart a rattle. His breath is sucked away. Every particle of him is oscillating, his body becoming its constituent organs, then their elements. He is only held together by consciousness.

A flash of perfect blue, and then a nothingness. He is frozen. He has no form, his existence is a conception. Nothing is happening, and nothing will ever happen again. For eternity he will exist and that is all, never moving or changing, being and never again becoming, imprisoned in a hell of pure existence. His energy is as close as it can come to disappearing. He has fallen between cracks in creation. Then, he hits the river.

Water rushes all around, pushes stinging into his nose, balls him up and hurtles him forward, a plaything for the current…

Kieran was shaking, and the druid's arms were wrapped around him. The old man was saying his name. Kieran looked around. He was back in the Temple, back in…

"MY GOD," he said. Kieran threw the Sun Druid off and darted confusedly about the chamber. "I'm not, I'm not, this is... AHHHH! I'm not supposed to be here!!!!"

Such panic Kieran had never known. *Kieran, there is no Kieran. This is a nightmare, a nightmare...*

"Kieran."

No Kieran, no Kieran, Kieran is here, in this now. Not me. Only me. I am me, just me, and I – do – not – belong –here.

"Kieran."

He looked again at the Sun Druid, at his impossibly placid face.

"Kieran, please sit."

It was not for an hour, or more, that Kieran could have the conversation the Sun Druid wished. Calm took hold though, eventually. Most of his memories from before the storm were still obscure, and those afterward all too vivid. There was a reality, and Kieran eventually convinced himself he was in it. He had many questions, but the Sun Druid promised to answer the "why." So Kieran listened.

"You are not from here, and we are from nowhere else," said the Sun Druid. "That is why it is most fitting that you be the last of us to return."

"Return? To my own... my own time?"

"No. We do not know how you came, nor how you can leave. You must return to the Great Island, to Britain."

425

Kieran slumped. "Now that I know, I wish to stay here."

"You cannot stay," he said in his broad, flat way of speech. "Do you believe we have trained you for two years only to keep you here? That we have revealed your past to allow you no future? You were always meant to return, to do what we cannot. We are no longer of the world in which we found you. Though you did not start there, you are now intertwined in its workings. The newcomers believe us long dead and passed from this plane, and let them so continue to believe. It will likely be true soon enough. But through you we will ensure that our kind never entirely disappear, and that our past becomes part of the future of Albion."

"How?"

The Sun Druid banged a steel plate that gonged throughout the stone halls. At once three acolytes appeared with a hot brewed beverage in a steaming decanter and plates of cooked tubers and sliced fish. The servants kept coming, bringing more to eat.

"I will not compose a poem to tell you it is raining," said the Sun Druid later, using an expression common to the Albann. "Our kind is dying. A generation ago we saw the end of this era, the turning of the wheel to a new alignment, and we have no place in the new order. When our souls regenerate, it will not be in Albann form. You see few women because we sent them where we knew they could be safe, to try to reenter the world, along with any others who wanted to go. Among those who remained, no new generation has been propagated, nor shall be."

"I see young people here, though," said Kieran.

"Foundlings and travelers on destiny's roadways," said the old priest, "just like yourself."

"Why do they not sit where I do, then, at your feet?"

"They do not have your terrible and ecstatic burden. None of them can be the bridge that stretches as far as the one you span. Only you have already traversed far enough reaches to cross this chasm."

"So you are sending me away."

"It must be so," said the Sun Druid. "But not for another year, and by the time the first wheel has turned fully you will be more than prepared. You will be eager for the undertaking."

"Which entails what?" asked Kieran, showing for the first time exasperation. And The Sun Druid, for the first time, smiled.

"That is the amazing thing, Kieran," said the priest. "None of us yet know." He patted Kieran's hand. "But know it you will, when it comes. You are the only one who will know."

"What do I even watch for? What is my mission?"

"Your mission," said the druid, seizing a pickle, "is to be the instrument and the hand that wields it. It is to serve Creation. Your most important mission is to find your mission."

Kieran sighed. "That strikes me as... unhelpful."

"On the contrary, it is all the guidance you need. I will elaborate, though, so you may rest easy while you train hard. If you believe you have found the object of your preparation, and it does not seem like a pursuit the Universe would send a person across more than a millennium to accomplish, you must keep looking."

Kieran smiled. That did make sense.

"Now," said the Sun Druid, "take some of these peas. They are always tasty, and I am usually the only one who eats them."

"I''m sorry, my lord, but I cannot accommodate that wish any longer," said Gwynnefir with the peculiar maternalism shown by a youth speaking toward one several decades her senior.

"My lady Gwynnefir," said Kieran, "I thank you, but I am perfectly capable of riding a horse, as I have successfully done for…"

Gwynnefir did not wait for him to make his point, but instead moved her steed so it blocked the narrow road entirely, and gave a level look to Kieran, daring him to challenge her. It was a side to her Aurelian had perceived instantly, while only now did Kieran realize it was there.

"I won't have you breaking your neck while I am along."

And she not even queen yet.

Though loath to admit it, Kieran, as Gwynnefir said, had been falling asleep on horseback while their small entourage approached Eilwath. In the first instance, when Gwynnefir noticed him slumped over in his saddle, Kieran pretended his snoring had only been a spell of stuffiness, and his head bowed simply to shield his eyes from the sun. The second time his mount had tracked onto a diverging path, and only an observant soldier in the escort prevented Kieran and the horse from becoming lost in the woods. Kieran deflated with the recognition of defeat.

"Quite right," he sighed.

She allowed him to continue on his horse until they stopped for rest and water. They were in a hilly land, near the vast moors of Dumnonia, and Kieran heard the shush of a stream flowing through a series of hollows. The mounds were not all natural – many were barrows, relics of a very old and long-dead civilization, and these had lain untended for at least a few years. They were not long abandoned relative to their ages, and still recognizable at their stony entrances and in their human geometry, but the site contained signs of the mounds being tended carefully, and then not at all.

The copse of trees toward which they rode was not a copse, but rather one enormous oak. It was a magnificent sight, even though it was evident it was slowly dying. Where other trees were laden with leaves, each the intense green of ripest summer, this oak was nearly bare and it leaves somehow pale. The vines that were sucking the life from the wooden goliath were perversely vibrant compared to the paltry offerings from the branches of the tree. However, one of the branches had a very rare offering – there was something hanging from it, something big. He rode his mount around the tree, into a stone circle as old as the barrows, and was awestruck by what he saw.

It was a skull of fantastic proportions, once belonging to what some would know as an elk and others simply as the largest species of deer to ever live.

Torcs like those he'd seen in Saxon hoards jangled on the antler prongs of the deceased beast. Kieran suddenly realized it was the Godskull of the Cornovii. This place, then, was the Spirit Hollow.

The skull was impressive – easy to see how it could inspire such a devoted religion, a fierce identity. Kieran had not seen it before when he lived near Eilwath, staying on the other side of its sheltering hills whenever he walked up to the site of his ritual, never closer than within earshot of the ceremonies that took place within. Now, though, King Cunomor was King Marcus, and his Cornovii had been Christianized along with his name. And here was the Godskull, with no place in the new Dumnonia.

Vines were crawling through it, peeking out of the eye sockets, weaving between the prongs of its antlers. Part of the outer bone had come off on the snout, exposing the creature's spongy sinuses. The leaves of parasites tickled at the relic in a mild breeze, but none of the oak's sparse leaves disturbed it. It would not be many seasons before the oak shed its leaves for the last, and not long until the new growth overtaking the oak would also break the skull apart.

Time is relative, thought Kieran, *but it is also undeniable.*

After their respite, Gwynnefir ordered the troops to fix up a bed for Kieran in the back of one of the small supply carts, and though it embarrassed him to be helped into what far too much like a crib full of swaddling cloth, he also saw how much more comfortable it would make the trip. His joints became so inflamed during long rides that he was barely able to get to sleep when they stopped, and Kieran wanted to be rested to greet Uleara when they arrived. The bed was perhaps infantilizing, but it was very soft.

Kieran awoke several hours later.

"Where is Lady Gwynnefir?" Kieran asked immediately. "Where are we?"

"The lady had gone on ahead into Eilwath, Lord Maelgwyn. She is organizing your welcome."

"Are we close, then?" Kieran asked, suddenly alert and working to prop himself upright on his bedding. Two of the soldiers came forward to help him.

"We are not close, my lord," one said. "We have arrived. Look for yourself."

Kieran assisted in turning himself around, and his heart leapt when he saw the sight – Lihane's mill. It was no longer Lihane's mill, Kieran knew, for Lihane had passed from life three years before, after living for five years as the wife of he who had long sought her favor: Uleara.

Kieran did not know who ran the mill now, but he saw it was turning smoothly, swiftly and silently, and steady billows of grain dust rose from a vent in the roof – a new innovation, not one of his.

Even Eilwath is not immune to time, Kieran thought.

As the cart moved toward the village gate, he was gratified to see how much was still as it had been when he first saw the village, three decades before. At that time he'd spoken little Britonic, had almost no possessions and knew not a soul. Kieran was different now, old, having attained as much fame and accomplishment as any could hope to garner. He had lived under several guises, different lifetimes, changed in every dimension. Yet the granary silo still stuck like a spindly digit from the soil, as it had when he left Eilwath for Glevuna, and the moss-encrusted earthen wall looked as undisturbed as it had when he had first passed through it.

Entering the village, though, Kieran was perplexed. The streets were entirely devoid of people.

The sun was shining, and no black banners hung to indicate the presence of plague. And they had known of his coming.

431

A rider galloped toward him. At ten yards distance he recognized Gwynnefir, sweat beaded on her brow and tears spilling from her eyes.

"Lord Maelgwyn…" she began. Her lip quivered violently.

"What has upset you, Lady Gwynnefir?" he asked, though as Kieran spoke the words he knew.

"Lord Maelgwyn," she said, fighting sobs. "Bishop Uleara is dead."

Chapter Twenty-Nine

The line of mourners extended all the way down the hill to the crossroads, near Kieran's former house. Eilwath in its entirety and all the inhabitants of the settlements beyond its walls who could walk had joined the queue waiting to pay their respects to the abbey community at the top of Cairn Mountain. Gwynnefir offered consoling words to him on their way toward the summit, but Kieran had heard few of them. None of his senses offered much input in the aftermath of the news.

At first Kieran, wrapped in his grief, barely noticed any of the Britons he nudged past on the narrow road, many of whom clutched offerings to be burnt in Uleara's memory, still unsure of the difference between the Eucharist of the pagan faith and the Christian. Kieran's progress up the path was unsteady, but he refused a horse or any assistance, preferring no comfort on the climb. He was recognized by several of the mourners, who passed the information up the line far faster than Kieran could travel. The further he went, the earlier the peasants began to bow or kneel in anticipation.

Word of his impending arrival reached the abbey itself, for when he entered the courtyard of the compound he was immediately greeted by a number of men in clerical robes who stood at the ready to receive him. Though nothing could overcome their sadness at losing a man who had in many ways been as a father, the clerics also showed joy at Lord Maelgwyn's arrival, knowing only but little that it was Kieran's return.

One of the churchmen, his black-banded purple sash indicating a bishop-designate, Uleara's acting replacement, seemed particularly overcome. Stepping closer, Kieran saw why, and forgot his sadness for a moment.

433

"Aelfarn," Kieran said.

 "My lord." His face fell. "Kieran."

Aelfarn rushed to embrace Kieran as the tears began to spill from his eyes. Looking into his face, Kieran could see no change since the man in front of him was the boy he had known on the battlefield of Mount Badon.

Aelfarn led him through the abbey, which donations of gold and vast labor had transformed from the rude one-room edifice of yesteryear into a structure befitting the favorite bishopric of King Artros. Aelfarn and Kieran walked wordlessly down vaulted passages banked by the quarters of clerics and acolytes, the scope impressive even to the High Protector.

Aelfarn was embarrassed when he helped Kieran down a flight of stone steps into the storage cellar, at both acknoweldging his former mentor's advanced age, and regarding what he was about to show. As they passed barrels and stacks of provisions, the new bishop explained, "The heat of the day made it impossible for us to keep his remains elsewhere."

Kieran gave a laugh he could not stifle. "It is of course where he would have chosen to lie: among the food and liquor."

Aelfarn was forced to smile, the first time he had done so since seeing Kieran, but it disappeared as swiftly as their breath in the chilled space. "He is this way, my lord," he said.

The rector held the candelabra before him, pressing deeper into the labyrinth, until they heard the sploshing of water and faint mumbling. In an annex around a corner, noticeably cooler than the rest of the cellar, Kieran came upon the corpse of Bishop Uleara.

Soft white light suffused the bier on which he lay, lit by rings of candles set around it. Kieran saw that the source of the sploshing was a young acolyte in a white tunic, who knelt by the body dipping a sponge into a pail set by his knees and applying it to Uleara''s cold form, nude but for a cloth above his genitals. Another man, face obscured behind the hood of his black robe, sat near Uleara's head and recited from an open hymnal codex, bobbing his head and rocking his body with the rhythm of the prayers.

"I am sorry you have to see him thus," said Aelfarn.

Kieran did not reply, but instead stepped forward, to look directly over Uleara.

My God, he thought, *he is so thin.*

They had known for some months that a series of tumors were eating his body from within, and likely had been for years. However, Kieran had not lain eyes on his friend for some time, since well before the sickness that killed him. The tumors had done their work well.

Uleara's skin hung lose where once fat had been, used up in the futile fight to keep him alive, and his face bore angles and proportions Kieran had never in twenty-eight years of friendship seen. The novelty made it easier for Kieran – he was able to sufficiently repress the sorrow threatening to spill forth from him at any instant by convincing himself, if but briefly, that it was an impostor the young deacon was cleaning, an instance of mistaken identity, and that Uleara was somewhere else, alive.

Kieran said nothing for the minutes of his vigil, listening only to the recitations of the priest and the splishing of water droplets, smelling incense from a censer and the rose-scented water in the basin.

"Now you know more than I," said Kieran at last to the body of Uleara, putting his fingers to the back of Uleara's frigid hand, taking a last moment with his friend's earthly form.

Aelfarn went over the order of the funeral once they returned above, assuring Kieran that the liturgy was being followed to the letter. Kieran let him talk, knowing that Uleara's death had affected no one so much as he who would soon be bishop, successor to a man in all ways larger than life.

"The interment would take place at sunset, with the Mass to follow. Then, I suspect, there will be a celebration in the village," said Aelfarn, with a sigh. "It seems the only time the Dumnonii allow themselves to enjoy their lives is when someone else has just died."

When Kieran emerged from the abbey, the townsfolk were still gathered, but now it was not to say farewell to Uleara but to greet Kieran. They pressed in around the courtyard, each of them fighting the opposing impulses to rush up out of gladness and keep a distance out of respect.

Kieran moved through the crowd as one by one the people of Eilwath welcomed him back. There was none of the hesitancy or suspicion that had characterized the farewells from the village.

Each time someone called him Lord Maelgwyn, he corrected them and instructed them to refer to him as Kieran, but none listened. That man, Kieran, belonged to a distant and forgotten past, even to those who had known him longest by the name. In their minds and memories, he had always been Lord Maelgwyn; if asked, they had known from the first he was a great leader, never doubting the rightness of his presence.

"Lord Maelgwyn, do you remember me?" asked one of the tanner's boys, now the proud patriarch of a brood that clung by their father, wide-eyed and silently staring up at Kieran. Kieran assured him he did.

"Greetings, Lord Maelgwyn – guess who it is," said another man. Kieran could not recall the face, until the man standing next to him piped up and said, "Of course he won't remember you. But you remember me, don't you, your lordship?"

Kieran smiled when it came to him.

"Eion and Bannan," he said. The brothers returned the smile and came forward to clasp Kierans arm, jostling each other to be first. "Still haven't settled your differences, eh?"

"Oh, certainly we have," said Eion, the elder.

"Yes, Lord Maelgwyn, we have agreed that we will never like each other."

They laughed again, but then Bannan said, "It is not right for us to be joking, on this day."

Kieran put a hand to his shoulder. "Tears are not the only way to honor the dead."

The throng pushed in around him, and Kieran spoke to as many of them as he could. Some had never known him, but told of the ways their lives had intersected his. Some people were drawn from miles beyond Eilwath by the mourning bells, and some had been his neighbors, but all pressed his hands and gave him gifts of prayer and offering.

Kieran noticed one woman, pretty and youthful, standing back from the others, never faltering in her gaze at him, but never approaching. She held an infant in her arms, and her eyes gave him the strangest notion that it had something to do with him. Finally, Kieran went to her.

"Do I know you? Have we met?" Kieran asked.

The woman smiled, broadly, warmly, but shook her head.

"Not met. We crossed paths, once, the night before you left for Glevuna."

The night before…

He had performed the Rite of Being and Becoming that night. It was when he had the vision. Yes, he did know this person. She'd been a slip of a girl passing by in a blink on the night road. *The only one who ever saw me.*

"What is your name?" he asked.

"Elyn, my lord," she said with sparkling eyes. "But I am consuming your time, and there is another with whom you should speak – my husband."

She surprised Kieran by taking his hand and leading him through the crowd to its edge, and beyond. There, a solitary figure stood down the hillside, only his lean frame and mop of dark brown hair visible.

"Honey! Love! Over here!" she called. The man turned around, and Kieran's breath caught in his throat. He felt weak and tingly, and thought he was getting his realities confused again.

When the man faced him, Kieran saw himself, forty years younger.

"Daweth, come here," said Elyn, and the man approached. The closer he got, the less Kieran could believe what he was seeing. There were differences – Daweth had Boudicca"s beautiful blue-green eyes – but the young man was by most measures a replica of his father. He looked like Kieran.

Daweth and Kieran stood facing each other without speaking, father and son alike in the blankness of their faces. Though the entire mourning party was now spectating from the hillside, for their purposes Kieran and Daweth were alone.

"I was sorry to hear of your mother's passing – sorry I could not return."

"She knew you could not," said Daweth. "She died content."

"She didn't tell me," began Kieran. "Boudicca. She told me I wasn't... that you..."

"I know," said Daweth. In his look there was none of the recrimination, none of the angst that

Kieran had expected to see. The young man seemed to have no interest in punishing Kieran for his lifetime of absence.

"How long have you known?" asked Kieran.

"The resemblance was there from an early time. By my fourteenth summer it was undeniable.

Thankfully my father died before then." Daweth and Kieran both registered how he had used the word.

"He was a good man – a good father," Kieran said. "I wish I..."

A cough from behind him alerted Kieran to the rows of observers watching the scene.

"We will have time later," said Daweth, putting an arm around Elyn.

Kieran said to his daughter in law, "A pleasure, a true pleasure to meet you my lady – properly that is."

Kieran touched the head of the baby Elyn held out to him. "And to meet… is it him or her?"

"Her. We don't have a name yet," said Elyn. "Would you like to do the honor?"

Kieran looked down at the new life, his grandchild, a new generation for a new Britain. It would only be accomplished with work, and understanding. And love.

"Freya," said Kieran. "Call her Freya."

"It is a strange name," said Daweth.

"But beautiful," said Elyn.

"It is a Germanic name, but it is the name of someone who should be remembered."

"Freya." said Elyn. She tickled the newborn under the chin, saying, "Hello, Freya, hello," and the tiny girl in her arms gurgled and pumped the pink egg of her fist in the air. The adults laughed. "It's settled then."

"Settled," said Kieran, with a sigh.

The old man clambered back up the hill to the abbey, to help Eilwath say goodbye to the most renowned of its own. Kieran asked Aelfarn to lead him to Uleara's study and leave him amid the mess of the bishop"s effects. Kieran eased himself into Uleara"s seat at a table covered in piles of dried candle drippings, across which multitudes of scrolls, codices and chalk tablets were strewn. The mass of documents Kieran surveyed showed the reach and complexity of a bishopric see that once boasted of only nine congregants and eight believers. At his death, Uleara, the unassuming, unambitious outcast who had extended the hand of generosity to Kieran all those years before, was responsible for the salvation of over a thousand souls, scattered over more than a dozen villages and towns. Accounts, provision lists, disciplinary reports, endless transactions and a plethora of edicts to be issued or reviewed now formed on his desk a wordy obituary in praise of Uleara's leadership and administration.

A wave of regret and loss swept Kieran, and for a few moments he let the thought that his friend was gone overwhelm him.

You are dead, and will be reborn in another form, thought Kieran, *while I will be born again in this one, fifteen hundred years from now, and for eternity.* Kieran had traveled a millennium and a half to befriend Uleara, but a span of a hundred miles prevented him from saying goodbye. He wept.

After some minutes Kieran's eyes began to range over the dead abbot's papers. One of the piles was reserved for correspondences, and Kieran delicately leafed through it. Some messages hailed from as far as Alexandria, from no less personages than King Clovis himself. He picked up a paper at random and began to read, but set it down when he noticed an oddly positioned vellum that had been folded and placed under Uleara"s wax seal. Kieran liberated and straightened the document, which was written in a shaky but recognizable version of Uleara's hand. From its position on the pile it seemed to be the last letter he had meant to send. After a few seconds of reading it over, Kieran stopped and put it aside, gathering the strength to continue. It was written to him.

I am sorry, my friend, I have not been forthright with you regarding my condition. I have kept the advanced state of my illness even from Aelfarn, though I know he suspects it. I can no longer deny there are few grains left to drop in my glass of my life.

Part of me hopes you have somehow guessed my state and are even now on your way to

Eilwath, despite the degree to which the Themesa Ford undertaking has you consumed. I wish to share once more with my old friend the wonders of each day. No one who is aware of how amazing a thing it is to exist ever exhausts reasons to do so.

It seemed Uleara had penned the letter over the course of several sittings, for the handwriting differed almost by the line, becoming fainter and more imprecise as it progressed. Kieran in part wanted to pause in his reading, to prolong the last communication he would have with his friend (*until we go around again*), but he persisted in order not to prolong the pain.

*I am writing you this missive in case you arrive after I have
gone. I do not want to pass into the embrace of the Lord
without letting you know that I am prepared for eternity. Most
of my hours have been spent in solitary prayer, and each time
I bow my head in supplication to God I lift it again with spirits
replenished. Each man"s faith is tested by his mortality, and
secretly I have feared throughout that in this trial I would be
found wanting. It relieves and somewhat flatters me to
discover that my faith has never been more ironclad than upon
the precipice of my death.*

*It is amazing, the difference between the strength of my spirit
right now and the weakness of my body. It is further reminder
that all flesh passes away while our souls endure, and with
your help, Kieran, I have no fear that my soul is strong
enough to pass through the gates of Heaven.*

There were a few lines more, but Kieran never reached them. He began to notice
the ink exploding into blotches here and there on the parchment, and it occurred
to him that the cause was his tears before he even realized he was crying. They
fell soft when they began, but soon gushed forth so forcefully Kieran had to
push back from the table to prevent ruining other of Uleara's papers. He pressed
his hands to his face and the tears leaked through his fingers.

Kieran was not quite sobbing, for it was not quite sadness that forged the tracks streaming from his eyes. It was recognition, seeing the wheel forever turning, seeing the web that connects all to all. It was beauty. It was creation.

Kieran was ready. He knew what he wanted to say to Daweth, what he had to say on the occasion of both he and Uleara's permanent departures by different means. He had in his mind the words he had to deliver at the evening Mass.

"Thank you," said Kieran to Uleara's spirit. Then he picked up the stack of letters he had written to Uleara over the course of their lives, the collected thoughts and emotions of the two men across two decades, and tossed them into the hearth. Twenty years of friendship was enough to feed the fire beyond the time Kieran walked out.

Chapter Thirty

Only a fraction of the procession returning from the burial mound could fit within the church, so Aelfarn, in consultation with Lord Maelgwyn, made the decision to hold the second funeral Mass outside, in the courtyard, the villagers to stand or choose a seat on the rocky slopes per their wont.

Aelfarn made the offering of the Holy Sacrament, and led the converted in a recitation of The Lord's Prayer. He next opened Uleara's copy of the Book of Psalms, and read the bishop's favorite, beginning, "The Lord is my light and my salvation. Whom shall I fear?"

The fading light made Kieran's eyes even less keen, but Kieran could still discern those assembled: Eion and Bannan, Elyn, Deargh and the family he'd raised in Kiearn's old house, the tin smithing clan and the paupers' broods, the farmers' families. He even saw Grundfyrdd, who sat miserably in a place of honor. A wasting of the throat had taken his ability to speak, and only grunts and taps with his cane served as means of communication. When he saw Kieran, he nodded his head in a show of respect.

Kieran's time came, and he rose to address the mourners of Eilwath, though there was only one to whom most of his eulogy was addressed: Daweth. He stood in a back row next to his wife and daughter, his face pacific. Kieran finally understood the complaints lodged against him about emotionlessness. He now saw in Daweth's face the reflection of his own cryptic, opaque mien, as his son"s stoic expression obscured the signs of emotion Kieran hoped to discern.

"You all know me," Kieran said. "You know my tales. You know of the great deeds done by the court of Artros." Many nodded their heads.

"Know this: None of you know who I am, and none of you know what greatness is. The man who was lain on the altar this day, the bishop now eternally asleep, was the best of us. His definition of glory was the only one that is true. He knew me as he knew all people – flawed creatures of God, each needing guidance, each deserving of love.

"I stand before you the High Protector of the Britons, the architect of our salvation. Not one of you would refuse me if I asked for your help. But who among you would take in a vagabond, a stranger with no wealth, and way of speech sounding like that of an enemy? Uleara did this, for I was that vagabond. It was here, where we are gathered, half a lifetime ago, that I stood before only him, adorned not by power, gold or fame, simply a man. That day Uleara demonstrated a greatness that none of my deeds have ever matched. When Britain thought it needed enchantments and shows of power, Uleara"s simple goodness showed that our salvation lay in what we already had – our humanity. That is glory.

"Cathedrals are not built with stones, but with faith. Empires are united more wholly by belief than by arms. Though not all of you be Christians, and though I be of the Old Kind's faith and could never count myself among Uleara's flock, none can deny the great gifts Uleara gave the world while he lived, and what he has left us after his death. What he represented need not be given a name or paired with a particular people to be recognized as the truth. In the darkness, Uleara kept the light aflame, and in a time of savagery he kept open the doors to the temple of humanity.

"It may be that Uleara's name is forgotten in the annals, when the history of our time is recorded for the ages. Ones such as Uleara oft make way for bloodier men of less noble deeds in the songs. Let us then make a vow this day, that Uleara's memory will not die so long as we draw breath. We are indebted to

Bishop Uleara, and it is a debt of goodness we can only repay in kind, to all. We must hand down to generations not yet born the essential truth that we are all brothers and sisters, the central truth of the holy life. We must keep the flame alive.

"Uleara tried for almost thirty years to bring me into the fellowship of Christ, and for just as long, I refused, preferring different rites. However, today I will pray to Jesus, and ask for his help to keep his faithful servant, Bishop Uleara, eternally in our hearts and minds. I will pray, too, for Uleara to enter heaven, though it cannot be necessary. If Heaven did not exist before, God would have to create it, that a soul as perfect as Uleara's might find a place of eternal purchase."

Kieran looked to Aelfarn, indicating his eulogy was given. The bishop-delegate nodded. "Let us pray."

When the bowed heads were raised again, Kieran's gaze immediately found Daweth. Kieran uneasily walked through the crowd, which parted for him, to where Daweth stood. Before all assembled, Lord Maelgwyn, High Protector of the Britons, gripped his son by the shoulders and drew him into a deep embrace. Taking his arm, Daweth led Kieran onto a winding, deserted path down the mountainside. None followed after them.

Daweth took with good nature the barrage of questions Kieran asked of him. The young man was the physician for the area, the result of a curiosity his mother said he was born with, along with years of instruction from Uleara and Aelfarn. He knew his figures, Latin and Greek, and the entirety of the Holy Scriptures – "though I have questions never satisfactorily answered," he said to Kieran, who nodded deeply.

447

As a boy, Daweth had suspected there was something different about him compared to his siblings, but never knew what it was until the first time someone called him a "bastard." Still, Boudicca denied his parentage until the man he had known as his father died, and the customary mourning period passed.

"It must have been hard," said Kieran, a phrase he had repeated innumerable times during their conversation.

"I was upset for a time," said Daweth, "but I came to understand. My emotions gave way to my reason, and I saw each choice you and Mother made for what it was, when it was made. I did not see what I would have done differently. While some of the past has been hard to feel good about, it is impossible to feel resentment for any of it."

Kieran was more pained by the methodical and dispassionate way Daweth laid out the history of his upbringing than if his speech had been filled with scorn.

Sensing this, Daweth said, "I was angry, father, very much so. I raged at my mother, at the bishop. I visited the low parts of seaside towns, and once even went to the gates of Glevuna with no plan but to confront you. I stayed two days before returning home."

"It is understandable."

"Yes, but it did not last. I came to see it from my mother"s view."

"Your mother knew me quite well," said Kieran. "She was a remarkable woman."

"She was," said Daweth. "She was in love with you until the day she died. I only saw it after she was gone, but it is undeniable."

Kieran could tell what question was on Daweth's mind. It was uncanny how well he and Daweth understood one another with only a few hours' acquaintance.

"I was different after Wulfric did his work," Kieran said. "After the Old Kind had resurrected me. There was less humanity than purpose, sometimes."

"She knew that," said Daweth, "but enough humanity still to earn her love."

"I knew I would leave when the time came, and so did she. She deserved much better, but there was nothing to be done about it. We loved as well as we could for as long as we had. It's all anybody can do."

Kieran and his son looked upon Eilwath, watching the lights of the party.

"Where will you leave to now?" Daweth asked.

"I don't know," said Kieran. "Perhaps I will finally travel to the East, attempt to track down some possessions I let go years back. I may go to the Frankish court, or Rome. Or perhaps I will travel back across the sea, to find my native soil, where my bones can lie in wait to be joined by my ancestors, when time comes around again."

"This is the land you spoke of to the bishop?" Daweth asked. "The one in which you lived, before you crossed the bridge of time?"

Kieran did not know how to react. Daweth explained. "Bishop Uleara showed me your missives, once I reached my maturity. It kept me from doing some foolish things, to make me understand who you and I both are." Daweth put a hand on Kieran's knee, a reassuring look on his face. "I understand, father."

Kieran felt the tears come once more to his eyes. He placed his hand atop his son's. Never was he so happy to have kept a promise, never so happy to have made one, as the oath he swore to Uleara that he would share with the priest all he knew. The letters had been encoded, and come only by the most circuitous methods, and then only in the last years when Kieran understood better the nature of time and the risks one takes within it, but Kieran did tell his story. It had enabled him, in a way, to be a father to his boy. Now they were burned with the rest of the papers.

"There must be so many questions that yet linger for you," said Kieran. "Ask, and I will tell you whatever you wish to know."

Daweth though for a few moments.

"Well," he said, "I have always wondered about the substance on the sword. What was it? It was not in Uleara's papers."

Kieran smiled. "Uleara did not persist in asking after its identity. My other explanations, about where I had come from, and how, the subjects of my studies in my former realm, and so forth, dampened his curiosity about more arcane topics."

Daweth returned the smile. "I know. Those were the ones for which I most hungered. My mother never tired of telling me how much of you I possessed, and when she died, Bishop Uleara took up her chorus."

Kieran smiled, unable to ignore how strikingly similar they looked. *I got my mirror back after all*, he thought, but said, "If I tell you about the substance, you

450

can tell no one, even Elyn, even your children. This is a knowledge that will be interred with your body, never to be exhumed," he told his son. "Do you make this vow?"

"I swear it."

"Good," said Kieran. "It is a pure type of the most basic of substances – elements, they are called in my age – but one that does not congregate easily. Though this element exists all throughout you, composes what you are made of, aids in determining the form of all life, its secret will not be found for many centuries to come."

"What is it called, father?"

Kieran looked at Daweth, whose face was now illuminated more so than at any other time, blazing with intense interest. Kieran smiled. The best part of him would remain in Britain after he left.

"Phosphorus," Kieran said. "It is called phosphorus. One of the most common materials on earth, but as yet unknow to the world."

"Even though it changed its course forever."

"What could have been if I remained," said Kieran, smiling into Daweth's face. A look of consternation fell across the young man's features.

As he and his son had spoken, Kieran was obliged to continually dismiss a stream of temptations to delay his departure for a day, or a week, or a year. He had to let go of these thoughts as soon as they were conjured, for he was aware that if permitted to take root they might not be able to be plucked out.

"I understand," said Daweth, with a truth that fractured Kieran's heart. "It is good, though, that you will at last be able to depart this land, which you tried so long to leave."

The one accomplishment that had eluded him throughout the years was now within Kieran's grasp. He had never truly stopped wishing to see shores beyond those of Britain. He had spoken of it with Freya, with Boudicca, with Uleara, with Aurelian. He had spoken, and never had his words done a thing to move him from where he was. Words carried too little wind to power sails, lips too little motion to push a row of oars through the water.

Now Kieran saw so clearly, felt so warmly how it could be if he remained: he and Daweth, he and Eilwath, he and Britain, surrounded by comfort and acceptance as he completed his slow fade from life.

Kieran knew it could not be. He had no more allowances left for himself. The fact of a day with his child was more than enough, a reward more splendid than any for which he'd hoped since being slain and reborn in the Yuletide snows. Having already broken the proscription of the Old Kind against leaving anything of himself behind, by leaving the most essential part of himself in Daweth"s existence, he could not tempt fate, so suddenly and unexpectedly kind, by compounding his transgressions. Since returning from the island of the Old Kind, he knew how his tale would end.

"Is there nothing else you would like to know?" Kieran asked. Daweth made to speak, but Kieran saw him pause in his mind. The question that came next was the most important to answer, and though Kieran could not, for the sake of his son the old man tried.

452

"What was all of this?" asked Daweth, intense. Kieran knew why his son"s eyes flashed, his voice quavered when he asked the question. "Did you know what would happen? What would become of it all?"

"I did not know, but I had an idea."

"Because these deeds and places, these women and men, these times of ours were remembered in the age of your birth?"

"Not remembered, but spoken of." Kieran added, "More than that. Believed in."

"I do not know much of the faith of the Old Kind, but for what Uleara told me. He said your most ancient tenet is that the soul is reborn again and again, knowing life that begins in the dust between the stars and ends in the firmament again, when perfect enough to gain purchase in the heavens."

Kieran said, "It is spoken beautifully. That is true, but to look only at one soul is to miss the point. The Old Kind believe that a soul finds meaning in the channels of the Spirit, which guides and enhances all things that possess a drop of it."

"To what end though, father? That a man like you should be taken to an island of time apart from his own, made to find his way without guidance, only to discover madness and the burden of becoming a myth?"

Daweth paused, staring down. Kieran let him think.

"Father, there must be a reason," he said. "The universe bent to bring you here, and myth was made by your coming. And here I stand, a man of flesh, no faerie story for people centuries from being born, and am the product of the bridge that brought you here as much as I am the product of your seed. Here we stand, in a

453

stone-and-flesh kingdom that sprang from your own head, forged by your personal grief. Do you not know why?"

Why? It was a question Kieran had screamed at the precipice of insanity, and whispered as a prayer in triumphant moments.

Unbidden, an old memory emerged, and Kieran was thrown back in time momentarily, to his last conversation with the Sun Druid.

"You cannot return to our refuge," the Sun Druid had told him, "and you cannot remain in Albion once you are no longer needed. You have been brought here as an implement, and an implement that is not useful ceases to be one. You must leave nothing of yourself behind."

"Can I choose not to be an implement?" Kieran had asked. "Cannot I be a man?"

"If you will be a man," the Sun Druid had told him, "you will fail, and your soul will suffer. You were put on your path to meet the universe's ends, and it was not a route chosen at random. You will be tested," said the Sun Druid. "You will never cease being tested. And as a man you will fail. But as an instrument, you will serve fate, and your will always prevail, for you will act with true purpose."

"But there is choice?"

"There is always choice, even where fate is master."

Kieran came back to the present, or what was the present to him, just then. He knew, sitting with Daweth, that he had done what the Old Kind thought impossible. He had been the implement, both the tool and the hand to wield it, but something else besides. He had done his duty, and yet remained a man.

Kieran told his son, "We choose our purpose, even when it chooses us. We choose to follow through. We choose to answer the 'why' for ourselves."

Daweth asked his father: "Which purpose did you choose?"

Kieran had never been asked such a question. It surprised him how ready the answer was.

"To carry the light," said Kieran. "In every one of my designs I was acting to perpetuate the spark that can ignite the flame of humanity and civilization when all else is dark. Now, sitting with you, I do the same, fulfilling no mission but my own, yet still carrying, and spreading, the light. This place, this era, will enter the realm of legend, and serve as a beacon for all to follow, but the epoch is only the people who live in it. We in our finite lives must prepare our age to exist forever."

"And that is why it happened, then. Why I happened." Daweth stared off. "I will help the real become myth, and the myth real. I will help carry the light." Father and son shared a smile of knowing that could not be replicated by any others on earth, and Kieran put an arm around Daweth"s shoulder.

"Come," said Kieran. "Let us join the festivities, while we still may."

"Lead the way, father."

Chapter Thirty-One

Daweth carefully picked his way down the rocky edge at the coastline, in time to see the white-robed man disappear around a bluff to his left. He proceeded with care across the large blocks of stone, slick with slime and seawater, around which the waves sloshed and sprayed. It was slow going and dangerous, his footing under constant threat, and sometimes he was forced to jump over wide gaps to get from one monolith to the next.

Despite the perils, Daweth could not help making observations of the sealife around him. Even while he worked to keep from falling into crashing surf, he took note of the algae blooms that clung to the rocks, undulating with the rhythm of the sea – silken, verdant beards worn by ancient stones. They differed from the river algae in key ways, Daweth could tell, and he remarked inwardly that he needed to return to the seaside more often, to continue building on his investigations and collecting examples.

The Sabrina Sea was only a few hours' ride from Eilwath, and Daweth began the trek before dawn. He had been unable to find sleep during the night, as he continually thought on the reunion of a few hours earlier. He had spent most of his lifetime trying to prepare himself for it, but no matter how often he'd played out the possible scenarios over the years, nothing was adequate to ready him for the reality. The talk with his father had given him much more than he could have known, but left him without the twin compass needles of reason and righteousness, as neither were proper tools for the situation.

It was in the first hint of dawn's light that Daweth saw the robed figure of his father mounting a sturdy horse and setting off through the morning mist. Daweth did not spend too much time in deliberation before he mounted his horse too and followed the road he'd seen the old man take.

The damp dirt of a dewy morning made tracking Lord Maelgwyn easy, and allowed Daweth to keep his distance. He knew his father wanted to depart in solitude, whatever that departure entailed, but Daweth had only been a true son to someone for a few hours, and would not let his last chance to glimpse his father pass by.

That brought him to the rocky coast he was trying to navigate. Daweth continued along the stones until he rounded a curve and saw Lord Maelgwyn a few yards distant, expectantly staring at the sea. Daweth retreated back up to higher ground, and settled in to observe from the stone lip of the cliff above.

As he waited with his father, Daweth thought about what it must have been like for Lord Maelgwyn all these years. He was not just a stranger to the land, but to the time. He was never fated to have a true place where the strange magic of creation had put him. Everything he had built was only fated to be destroyed, everything he loved to be taken, and yet he persisted through it all, coming back from every calamity even stronger. Daweth at once hoped he would never be so tested, yet envied his father in a way: He was one man at least who got to find out what he really held within him.

Daweth knew the worry of responsibility, of having a knowledge no others possessed. As a doctor, he was more familiar with sleepless nights than those of undisturbed slumber.

Yet he was caretaker to no more than a few hundred, and they were people who knew him, trusted him. His father had been charged with the fate of the entire land, and often been reviled in the process. Daweth remembered well the feelings of being an outcast, his anger toward Lord Maelgwyn for his abandonment, at his mother for her lies, at Uleara for abetting it all. It was inconceivable to him the loneliness and sorrow that must have been his father's to wrestle with through the decades, and never to have a partner to take some of the pain. Daweth had always had Elyn, ever since that night, when the veil was thin.

He'd put it to Elyn the night before, obliquely enough to keep his father's confidence, but concretely enough to have meaning. Elyn had a mind to rival anyone Daweth knew, and often when he explained a concept to her she would explain it back more clearly, and elaborated. Regarding the puzzle of Lord Maelgwyn, though, she was stumped.

"It's hard for me to keep in my mind," she'd said. "No wonder Lord Maelgwyn looks so old."

"I didn't say his name."

Elyn rolled her eyes. "Daweth, please. But what I keep thinking is, to travel between times, at some point you have to be outside of time. If you cross from one side of the River Fawey to the other, when you are on that bridge, you're not on either side."

Daweth nodded.

"Well, only gods can exist outside of time. And Daweth, your father is a great man, but he isn't a god."

A broad streak of white appeared at the horizon, coasting along the blue stretch of sea, until it became a beautiful, sleek ship to Daweth's eyes, long and elegant. Lord Maelgwyn, gray hair waving in the breeze, sleeves and hem of his robe flapping, lifted his arms to hail the arriving vessel.

"Hail, High Protector!" called a woman"s voice from the stern. Her figure was silhouetted through the sails before she emerged on the bow. She was a beautiful woman, Daweth"s age, with a small, sharp nose and tight curls of dark hair tied at the back with a strip of sail cloth.

"Who is that?" said Lord Maelgwyn.

"I know you don't remember me, but I remember you," she said, the ship maneuvering into port. "You know my father. The last time we met I was a young child, in the Silurian ghetto of Glevuna."

"Why – is that Laghal's little girl?"

"Gwenna," she said, proud to be remembered.

"Ah, Gwenna! How is your father?"

"Still alive, still thinking of money all hours of the day," she said, "though your help has certainly made them happier hours for him."

"He is a good man – and provides a fine ship," said Lord Maelgwyn.

"Along with the finest crew, at your disposal," said Gwenna.

Daweth did not notice one of the rocks begin to give beneath his palm. It skittered down the cliff side and drew Lord Maelgwyn"s notice. Daweth did not duck when his father turned to see him.

The two of them stared at one another for a moment, exchanging silent feeling. Finally, the old man raised his hand in farewell, and Daweth raised his.

What needed to be passed from father to son, did.

"Well my lord, we have a fair wind and an eager crew that's tired of looking at these shores. But we do need a commander."

Lord Maelgwyn let the moment linger between Daweth and himself a few seconds longer, then turned to Gwenna.

"Quite right, captain," he said, accepting the help of another member of the crew to step aboard.

The men of the crew now used the poles they had utilized in docking to push off, and oared out of the harbor until the gusts could fill the sails.

"What is our bearing, my lord?" Daweth heard Gwenna say.

"It is a clear day and a calm sea," said Kieran. "Let us give the helm to the wind until a better idea occurs."

"Aye, my lord," said Gwenna. "I believe I will quite enjoy being under your command."

"It will never be dull, captain," said Lord Maelgwyn. "For good or for ill, it will never be dull."

Daweth caught his father's look several times more as he watched the sails finally start to collect the wind, then snap taut and billow forward, pulling the vessel out to sea. He believed he felt his father's eyes even when he could no longer discern them, and hoped his father could feel his.

Many thoughts occurred to Daweth during the hour he sat there, looking out on the water even after there was nothing more to see – thoughts about himself, his family, the Britons, the Saxons, God and the world. He contemplated loss and history, knowledge and angst, time and splendor and the feel of sea spray on the hairs of his neck.

A thought struck Daweth as he watched Lord Maelgwyn, the High Protector, the man who had changed everything, blink out of sight for the last time. It was a thought to live with, to accompany all the unfading images when the last day came in Daweth's life. It was purpose.

They may grow in their telling, thought Daweth, *but all legends begin as truth.*

ACKNOWLEDGEMENTS

When a book takes five years to finish, a lot of people accrue who deserve gratitude.

First, I am thankful for my family, especially my mother and my sister Emily, for their support and encouragement over the years. This would not have happened without you.

Caryn Mickle deserves her own line, for a plethora of reasons, mostly to do with turtles.

Then there are those without whom this book would still be a series of files on my laptop. The generous support of my friend Will Silke made this book's publication possible, and he has my undying praise and best wishes. The team at The Editorial Department, particularly my editor Shannon Roberts, and my spirit guide Jane Ryder, helped transform this book into something people will actually want to read. Ben Exler's exceptional cover design made it a book people will want to display. Thank you.

So much of Alban Fire is due to the research of historians, archaeologists, novelists, and Dark Ages enthusiasts too numerous to name. They all have my respect and gratitude.

I owe a deep debt to those who helped me get over the finish line, in one way or another (usually, in a great many ways): Jon Kovel, as true a friend as ever was; Oz Blaker, Matt Broad, and Rob Rabiee, the Sharp Dogs; Erin McConnell; Kate Hubbard; Jeff Errico; Amanda Crawford, especially for the use of her Celtic library and spare bed; Pamela Grant, my wonderful godmother; Victoria "V" Chenoweth and the Fancy Shack denizens; Katie Costigan; Alex Brant-Zawadzki; Ruben Gallego, Lauren Harmon, Chris DeRose, Alejandro Chavez, Josh Kilroy, Danny Mazza,Jeremy Duda and other Blue Cometeers; Alicia, Bruce and Kay Dukov; Profs. Stacy Pies and Antonio Rutigliano, for their generous brilliance; Drake Booth; Greg Bloom; Bailey Hollingsworth; Chris Zemba; all other friends I leave unnamed; and the many café friends, from NoHo Coffee Bean to Old Saybrook Starbucks, Tim Guartha particularly.

Finally, thanks to my father, whose philosophy and teachings, and examples through life, reside at the core of all that is best about Alban Fire. You will never be forgotten.

www.ingramcontent.com/pod-product-compliance
Lightning Source LLC
Chambersburg PA
CBHW071341020726
47502CB00001B/193